Also by Jennifer Hartmann

Adult Romance from Bloom

Still Beating

Lotus

June First

Young Adult Romance from Bloom

Catch the Sun

THE
WRONG
HEART

JENNIFER HARTMANN

Bloom books

Published by Bloom Books, an imprint of Sourcebooks
P.O. Box 4410, Naperville, Illinois 60567-4410
(630) 961-3900
sourcebooks.com

Cataloging-in-Publication data is on file with the Library of Congress.

Originally self-published in 2021 by Jennifer Hartmann.

Printed and bound in the United States of America.
SB 10 9 8 7 6 5 4 3 2 1

To the fractured and broken:
You are worth fixing.

Prologue

from: Magnolia <greenmagnolia@gmail.com>
to: Zephyr79@gmail.com
date: Jul 7, 2020, 12:09 AM
subject: Widowed & Wilting

You don't know me, but you have my husband's heart.

I shouldn't be doing this. I shouldn't be contacting you. It's wrong and foolish, and probably illegal, considering I received your email address through confidential medical records.

You have every right to turn me in.

Hell, maybe there's a part of me that wants you to. I don't know how to live in this world without him, anyway. Prison could be a welcome distraction to the knee-buckling pain I'm faced with day after day.

But there's also a part of me that hopes you won't—a desperate, twisted part that is begging for you to find sympathy in that heart I've come to know so well.

A part that will wait for you to write me back.

No names. No personal details.

Just a conversation.
The only thing I have left of him is inside you.

Magnolia

1

MELODY

I'VE ALWAYS HAD A WEAK STOMACH.

Skinned knees, roadkill, slasher films—even a rare steak makes me woozy. So when I slice my finger on the serrated knife and blood pools to the surface, I go ashen.

Charlie leans across the table, snatching up my hand and examining the wound. "Nice one, Mel." He shoots me a sympathetic smile, then wraps my finger in the dinner napkin from his lap. "You okay?"

"I'm only panicking on the inside," I croak, reining in my nausea.

The handsome face shining back at me settles my swelling anxiety as I blow out a breath. Amber-infused eyes dance across my features, assessing fondly, bathing me in a warm familiarity. Like peach pie.

I compared Charlie to peach pie on the night we met. I was deliriously drunk on Schnapps—peach flavored, coincidentally—and thought he had the sweetest, warmest eyes I'd ever seen. Just like peach pie. Charlie was somehow swept off his feet by my intoxicated babbling, slurred words, and strange comparison to dessert, and even though I ended that night by puking on his Skechers, he asked for my hand in marriage one year later.

That was seven years ago, and today we're celebrating our five-year wedding anniversary.

With peach pie, of course.

I heave in a rattled sigh, unwrapping my finger and zoning in on the tiny cut as I pucker my lips. "It's fatal," I decide.

"Clearly. The infection is spreading already."

"Only a kiss can save me from a slow, painful death."

Charlie tsks me with his tongue. "You've been watching too many Disney movies," he chides. "You can only be saved by a highly skilled sex machine, willing to ravish you with his ultra-healing *weapon*."

My husband's ensuing eyebrow waggle has me holding back an unladylike snort. I gasp at his audacity. "Where on earth will I find such a noble savior in a place like this?" Glancing around the restaurant for effect, I eyeball our waiter. "Geoffrey. He was very efficient in providing us with sustenance. He *must* be skilled in other areas."

"False. I caught Geoffrey flirting with the busboy—he's not the one," Charlie assesses, then sighs overly dramatically. "However…"

I straighten in my seat, intrigued. "Yes?"

"There *is* someone willing to perform this harrowing task. He's ridiculously good-looking."

"Go on."

"He *always* remembers to put the toilet seat down."

I place both hands over my heart. "Impossible."

"He doesn't snore. He never steals the covers. He cooks a mean goulash, enjoys doing the dishes, and has quite an impressive…weapon."

A wink follows, and I swoon. "I love goulash."

"We must act now. Time is running out."

"But…" My bottom lip juts out, pouty and adorable. "Peach pie."

We both glance down at the half-eaten confection adorning my plate, gooey and glazed, topped with a heaping dollop of whipped cream. As much as I love Charlie's "ultra-healing weapon," there's no way I'm leaving until I finish this pie.

"Fine." Charlie relents, leaning against his seat until the chair tips back on two legs. I always scold him for it, but he does it anyway. One of these days he'll fall, and I will laugh. "I suppose it's hard to compete with that. At least you'll die happy."

A smile breaks out across my face as I dig the tines of my fork into the warm dessert, my gaze still fixed on the man across the table. His bangs fall over his forehead in a swirl of chocolate and caramel, a boyish charm that adds to his youthful appearance. His dimpled grin is the icing on the cake.

Or…the whipped cream on the pie.

My tongue licks at the sweet cream coating my fork, and I watch my husband's amber eyes heat with bronzed flames.

I'm an evil tease.

He captures his lip between his teeth. "On second thought…"

Five minutes later, the bill has been paid, Geoffrey has been generously tipped, and all thoughts of pie scatter from my mind as we skip out of the bar and into the gray mist.

The southern Wisconsin air feels fresh and musky, a prelude to springtime and new beginnings. The faint scent of impending rainfall fractures the heady Saturday night aroma of downtown pizza joints, mingling with engine fumes from the stream of traffic beside us.

I swing our interlaced hands back and forth as we glide down the sidewalk, my smile bright and beaming like the string lights connecting one lamppost to the next. Passersby return the sentiment with their own cordial waves, head bobs, and smiles to rival mine.

"I'll never understand it," Charlie murmurs, his feet trying to keep up with my swiftly moving legs as I pull him forward, reveling in the way the breeze dances across my skin.

"Understand what?"

"How you suck everybody in like that. You're like a happy vacuum."

My giggles have me doubling over, so I squeeze his palm to keep me upright. "God, Charlie. You can't be slinging those sexy nicknames at me in public." His rumble of laughter floats up to me, and I shoot him a nose crinkle over my shoulder. "And I can't take all the credit. It's Saturday night. People are always happier on Saturday nights."

He gives me a tug until I'm falling back against his chest, two arms encircling my waist in a protective grip. "No, Mel. It's all you."

People dodge us when we come to a complete stop in the middle of the sidewalk, but we're uncaring, totally oblivious to the world around us. It's just Charlie and Melody standing beneath quiet rain clouds, a new chapter blooming like the magnolia trees budding in our backyard. My eyes close through a sigh of contentment.

Charlie's chin rests atop my shoulder, his warm breath kissing the curve of my neck. "Do you think it worked?"

A grin curls my lips. I twist around in his embrace, catching the quick flash of nerves in his eyes. "You make it sound so technical."

"Well, it sort of is. It's science."

"You're really bringing your sexy *A* game tonight. You *do* want to get laid, right?"

Charlie presses his forehead to mine, tawny bangs tickling my hairline. And then his hand crawls up the back of my thigh, landing on my backside and cupping gently, our groins melding together. "What do you think?"

The jitters in his gold-dusted irises flutter away, manifesting into a colony of butterflies in my belly. "I think—"

A tipsy brunette bumps into us, laughing her apology as she stumbles by, and we're reminded of our audience. We take our two-person rendezvous to the far-right corner of the sidewalk until Charlie's back is level with the brick building. I dip two fingers into his front pocket, while my purse dangles beside me in my opposite hand. "Is this normal?"

His warm gaze flits across my face. "Grinding on each other in front of Benny's Diner?"

"The fact that we still *want* to grind on each other in front of Benny's Diner after seven years together. When does the light dim? When does the spark fade?"

"Never." Charlie traces his fingertips along my parted lips, that familiar knowing smile etched into his. "You're the sun, Melody March. The sun only knows how to shine."

Lord help me. Only this man could be equally proficient in computer analytics *and* spouting off glorious words like poetry. "I'm the sun, and you're the sky."

I try to hide my adoring smile in the buttons of his dress shirt, but he tips my chin up with two long fingers. "Do you think it worked?" he repeats, soft and subdued, eyes twinkling when they meet with mine.

"Yes." It's a cautious, hopeful whisper. I lean up on my tiptoes, my five-foot-two frame hardly able to reach his lips. He bends down, and I seal my declaration with a kiss. "Do you?"

Charlie grins as he sweeps his nose against mine. "I hope not. I really enjoy practicing."

"God, you are—"

I intend to swat him with my purse, but I'm almost knocked off my feet when that purse is ripped from my hand in a sudden flash, and I stumble, momentarily stunned and confused, my next breath sticking to the back of my throat as I try to process what the hell just happened.

But I don't have time to process it because Charlie takes off, leaving me in a stupefied haze on the sidewalk, knees struggling to keep me upright.

My purse was stolen.

And my husband is chasing the thief through the crowded downtown, dress coat billowing behind him as he bumps into slack-jawed bystanders and hollers at the stranger to *stop* and *get the fuck back here.*

The fog lifts, enabling me to follow. "Charlie!"

My sky-high wedges are hardly effective running shoes, and my ankles keep twisting, my miniskirt hindering my speed.

Is this real life?

I still can't process the fact that I've been robbed, and Charlie is chasing him down, and I'm chasing Charlie, and not a single goddamn person is trying to help. They just stand there gawking, watching the scene unfold through their cell phone screens.

"Charlie!" I call again, begging him to stop, to *let it go.* This is madness. The offender makes a sharp left into the middle of the street, Charlie right on his tail. "Charlie, please!"

He keeps going, keeps gaining speed, lessening the gap between them.

The moment he reaches for the man's arm, tearing the purse from his grip, a scream erupts from the bowels of my very essence. A Category 5 hurricane. It shreds my insides, liquifies me, whittles me down to dust and debris.

"Charlie!"

A pickup truck blows the red light and slams into my husband.

Tires screeching, glass shattering, metal breaking bone.

Screams, sobs, gasps.

Charlie is struck hard, bouncing off the windshield, tumbling over the hood, and rolling off the vehicle, landing in a heap on the pavement.

The thief climbs to his feet and hops into the passenger's seat of the pickup, then the truck takes off.

It just bolts.

It leaves the scene of the crime in a flash of burnt orange, rusted hubcaps, and a plume of exhaust—a cloud of carnage.

And then I'm running.

I think I'm running, but it's all in slow motion, and I'm not sure what happened to my shoes, and people are gathering, shrieking, bellowing for help, but I must be dreaming, and it will all be over soon. We'll wake up in our king-size bed, rested and satiated, snuggled up in the brand-new bedspread I just purchased that smells like Charlie's favorite fabric softener, birch water and botanicals. I'll prepare breakfast, blueberry pancakes and turkey bacon, while Charlie does the dishes because he enjoys doing the dishes. He's weird like that.

I'll turn on some music, probably a mix of CCR and Taylor Swift and Jimmy Eat World.

Because *I'm* weird like that.

Charlie will tease me for singing off-key, and then we'll dance, stepping on each other's toes, and I'll giggle when he dips me too low, falling to the tile floor, collapsing into a pile of laughter and limbs. We'll make love right there in the farmhouse kitchen, and it will be the perfect beginning to our fifth year of wedded bliss.

Yes.

I'm definitely dreaming.

But the gravel digging into my heels as I race to the love of my life feels painfully real, and the tears are warm and wet as they spill down my cheeks. My ears are ringing, echoing with a wretched, vile sound that appears to be light-years away. Something chilling and bloodcurdling.

It's a scream.

It's *my* scream.

A hollow, broken wail pulled from someplace dark and untapped.

I don't recognize it, but how could I? I've never made this sound before. I've never experienced this unique kind of heartache—the kind that steals away your senses.

Vision blurred, body numb, taste thwarted by ashes and soot.

I can hear, though.

I hear that scream reverberating through me, that heartbreaking scream, and I'll hear it over and over and *over* again for the rest of my life.

It's an overture to dissolution.

My kneecaps find the pavement as I collapse beside him, my hands reaching for every piece of him I can grasp. He's still warm, still alive, still mine to hold. "Charlie…oh my God. Oh my *God*. Baby, talk to me."

Charlie groans, his dark brown lashes fluttering as he tries to roll toward me. "Mel," he croaks, voice scraped and splintered, matching the fresh wounds that mar his beautiful face. When he locates my eyes, amber locking on emerald, a smile stretches as he chokes out more words. "I got your purse."

Tears blind me as I glance over at his hand, his bloody, bruised knuckles, and note that the leather strap of my handbag is still twined between his fingers. Another sob leaves me shaking, hands trembling as they clutch the front of his shirt. "So stupid. So, so stupid," I wheeze.

"It was epic, though, right? You were totally impressed?"

Charlie's smile lingers, a tiny sunbeam poking through dark gray storm clouds. I sniffle as my head swings side to side. "It was just a purse."

"It was your purse."

His response is organic, quick and easy.

Like there is no other response.

Sirens howl in the distance, and people gather closer, whispers and noise shredding our intimate moment. I cradle his face between my palms and lift his head, inserting my legs underneath him until he's draped across my lap. "You're going to be okay," I murmur through tearstained lips, brushing his bangs away from his forehead. "You're going to be fine."

Charlie grits his teeth together, trying to hide his pain from me. "Only a kiss can save me from a slow, painful death."

He's trying to lighten the moment, bring teasing to the turmoil.

So authentically Charlie.

I lean down to kiss him, a new wave of anguish spilling from me as our mouths collide. "I love you. Stay with me, okay?" I kiss him again and again, repeating those words, carving them into his bones, so he can't forget. "I love you so much."

"Don't cry, Mel." Charlie raises one unsteady hand to my cheek, thumb dusting over the tears, a gentle caress. "The sun doesn't cry."

We say it at the same time: "The sun only knows how to shine."

But I'm the sun, and he's the sky, and I don't know how to exist without him.

What happens to the sun when the sky falls?

No, no, no.

Stop it, Melody.

He's going to be *fine.*

Charlie starts coughing then, sputtering in my lap, blood misting my face like a grisly rainfall. "Charlie, Charlie…oh God, *Charlie.*" I shake his shoulders and squeeze him to me, holding tight to keep him warm…because that's what I do.

I'm the sun, after all—a beacon of warmth.

His throat bobs as he swallows, one lone tear collecting at the corner of his eye and gliding down his temple. Blood tinges the droplet as it makes a slow descent and lands near his ear. It just sits there, like it's trying to hang on for dear life.

Charlie inhales a jagged breath. "You smell like peaches, Mrs. March."

He's still smiling. He's still *smiling*, despite his broken body and bloodstained skin. "Your eyes remind me of peach pie," I rasp, trying to stay strong. Trying to stay *so* strong.

Just like him.

"It's meant to be."

That singular tear finally falls, collapsing onto the cement, and then the ambulance and police cruisers pull up while people scatter like the clouds above us. As the medics approach, the sky explodes with thunderous lightning, a piercing crack that rattles my bones.

Freezes my bones.

And when the rain pours down like grief, drenching me in its sorrow, I shiver and shake, teeth chattering, warmth eclipsed.

I cradle Charlie in my arms, rocking us back and forth, side to side, drowning in rainwater and blood and bitter tears.

He is cold now, and so am I.

Today was supposed to be beautiful—a new beginning, a new chapter, a new year of dreams and possibilities.

Our wedding anniversary.

But now it's just the day the sun died.

2

PARKER

WHEN I OPEN MY EYES, I'M FUCKING PISSED.

All I wanted was peace.

I wanted to fade away and drown myself in darkness, but instead, this brassy, artificial light is scorching my goddamn eyeballs. I blink back the hospital fluorescents, mentally cursing my insufferable luck, while strangers who are getting paid to give a shit about me wheel me down the long corridor.

This is her fault.

She put me here. She spit me out, branded me with all these scars and ugly stains, then left me here to rot with a stubborn death wish that won't abate and won't come true.

A growl erupts from my chest, an angry, embittered roar, and a baby-faced man in scrubs leans over to quiet me as we roll down the bright hallway.

Why is it so fucking bright?

"You're okay, sir. Try to stay calm."

Calm.

I try to remember the last time I felt calm, and I'm momentarily whisked away to one of my very first memories, shoulder blades pressed to the bark of a cherry tree as a young border collie licked the sticky fruit juice off my chin. The sky danced with pillowy, white shapes, and I laughed when the grass tickled my bare toes.

I'll never forget that the midsummer breeze smelled like daylilies.

I only knew that because my father loved lining the front of our porch with daylilies, and he'd sit outside and watch them, eager to catch the first sign of life. They only stayed in bloom for one day—*one day*—before the yellow and orange petals closed up and went to sleep for another year.

It confused me.

Out of all the flowers in the world, why did he love daylilies so much? Their beauty was so short-lived.

I asked him once—why he loved them, why he enjoyed temporary things.

His reply has always stayed with me: "Fleeting beauty is the most precious kind. You appreciate it more."

It's one of my few good memories, and I wish it were strong enough to replace all the others.

I'm ripped from the reverie by a needle jabbing into the underside of my elbow, a lifeline of sorts, to keep me bound and tethered to this mortal hell. My fingers curl around the cords in an attempt to pull it out, but I'm hindered by hands and arms and words of protest, words to sedate me while they poison my veins.

While they try to *calm* me.

I want to laugh, a crazed, maniacal laugh, but I can't recall the last time such a sound escaped my throat, and I wouldn't even know how.

So I just lie there instead, as apathetic as ever.

Just fucking *over it.*

And that's when I hear it. That's when something other than my own dispassion, my own resignation, burrows inside and invades me.

An intrusion.

It crawls along my skin like decay. Something visceral, raw, unhinged.

It's a woman's scream.

She's mourning, howling with an anguish that some fucked-up part of me wishes I could relate to.

It's a ballad for the dying.

I don't know why I let it in, why I let it cling to me like a dark passenger, but I feel compelled to carry it with me.

It's comforting somehow. I'm not alone in my misery.

As I continue to lie there, the doctors and nurses transform into a blur of flashes and movement, their voices fading, words incoherent.

Maybe it's the shit they fed me through the IV, polluting my veins.

Or maybe it's my new companion.

Whatever it is, I'm grateful for it because I realize that, for the first time in decades, I am calm.

3

MELODY

I'LL NEVER FORGET THE LOOK ON HER FACE WHEN SHE WALKS INTO THE SMALL, delicately furnished room, her eyes like acorns, hair dark and curly—a mess of chaos, like my petrified heart.

Her name tag tells me she is Dr. Whitley, but I think it's a lie.

Her expression tells me she's the Grim Reaper.

My legs are physically trembling as I stand from the chair, hand planting against the wall for support, while the other grips my chest. I still feel him in there, settled beneath my ribs, beating and warm. The vibrations tickle my fingertips, a soothing lullaby to outplay the dirge.

"Mrs. March…I'm very, *very* sorry."

Her voice is sweet, so gentle and kind.

A sympathetic whisper.

It's the antipode to the hideous moan that erupts from my core, like I'm a weeping volcano, exploding with denial, disbelief, and hot-lava tears.

She catches me before I hit the ground, but it's not enough. Her arms weren't built to hold the weight of my grief, so I fall—I fall so hard, I know there's no crawling out of this black abyss, this endless hole of despair. The sun has permanently set inside me, hijacked by a cruel winter.

Dr. Whitley wraps her arms around my shaking shoulders as I wail and sob, begging for it to not be true, cursing and blaming and self-destructing in her embrace. She's trying, I know she's trying, but her efforts are futile—she did not prepare for this winter, and neither did I.

I'm not sure how long we stand like that, crumpled in the middle of the bereavement room, but I don't think it's very long. Dr. Whitley has more patients to care for, more lives to save.

More seasons to change.

Life goes on around me as I numbly follow behind Dr. Whitley, and I don't think I've ever borne witness to something so honest when I pass the waiting room.

So stripped down and painfully raw.

Conversations. Sitcoms on the television. The rattling of a vending machine while children purchase snacks. Telephones ringing.

Laughter.

Someone is laughing while my husband lies dead in a hospital bed.

It's then that I grasp the fact that I have my own conversations to have, my own phone calls to make—I need to talk to the detectives who are waiting for me. I need to inform my family.

I need to inform *his* family.

Oh *God*.

His mother. His poor mother.

My grief washes over me like a tsunami as I make my way through the hospital hallways to say my final goodbye to Charlie.

But my knees buckle, my ankles giving out, and I collapse before I make it very far.

My purse falls beside me on the tiles, spilling its contents everywhere. Lip balm, loose change, random receipts, an assortment of junk and knick-knacks.

All of it stares back at me, a scattered mess of drivel, and I realize—I realize with a sickening cry of horror—

This is what he died for.

TWO WEEKS LATER

The shower jets are hot, pelting me with liquid fire—a feeble attempt to cauterize these open wounds.

With my palms pressed against the fiberglass walls, fingers splayed, I bow my head when I feel an added warmth trickle down my inner thighs.

My throat tightens.

The lump swells as my stomach churns, causing my legs to quake.

No.

Please, no.

I watch in horror, mute and numb, as the water runs red, and my only remaining glimmer of hope disappears down the shower drain.

My period.

It didn't work.

Two hours later, I'm curled into the fetal position on the bathtub floor. The water is now ice cold, raining down frost and hailstones.

Winter is here, and I think it's here to stay.

4

MELODY

ONE YEAR LATER

"Y OU SHOULD EAT SOMETHING."

I spare West a quick glance before returning my attention to the assortment of baking ingredients strewn about my kitchen countertop. "I will. After the batch of red velvet."

"I'm not a cupcake expert, but that looks like vanilla."

"It's cookies and cream." Swiping my hands along my apron, I avoid eye contact and reach for the hand mixer. "Red velvet is three batches from now."

"Melody."

West murmurs my name like an affectionate warning—in that way he always has but more so lately. He's my big brother, after all, so I suppose he's entitled. "West."

"You're too old to spoon-feed."

I blink. "I'm glad we're on the same page."

"But I will if I have to."

A sigh escapes me, pausing my feet as I lean forward on the heels of my hands. "Tell Mom she doesn't have to worry. I'm twenty-eight years old. I'll eat when I'm hungry."

He puckers his lips, mimicking my stance on the opposite side of the island. "You look thinner."

My eyes flick up to my brother, catching his concerned expression. He looks exactly like our father when he assesses me this way, his eyes all sapphire and sensitive, forehead creased with worry lines. When his dirty-blond hair catches the overhead light, the faintest flecks of silver dance beneath it. He's six years older than me, but our age difference has never impeded our bond. "West, I'm fine. I promise. I have a crap ton of orders to get through, so I'm just focused, okay?" I smile for added effect and because it's something I've always been good at—even when it's not entirely genuine.

My brother scrubs a palm down his face, his shoulders deflating with an air of submission. But his eyes don't leave mine, and I know it's his way of trying to get the last word in.

I can't fault West for always checking in on me, just like I can't fault Mom for calling a hundred times a day, or Dad for showing up and doing random house projects, or Leah for blowing up my Facebook Messenger with GIFs and funny memes to keep me smiling.

I can't fault them for caring, just like I can't fault Charlie's mother, Eleanor March, for abandoning me when I needed her most.

She was my final tie to Charlie.

Charlie was her final tie to me.

It took a long time for me to realize that those ties were not the same.

And when ties that bind turn to cinders in your hand, you learn to make new ties. New tethers. So I started an in-home confectionery business in Charlie's honor, because of his peach-pie eyes and marmalade kisses. He'll always remind me of sweet things, even on the sourest of days.

The last few weeks have been a blur of Easter baskets and springtime treats, and now Mother's Day is right around the corner.

West watches me mix the batter, gaze drifting from my face to the ceramic bowl, then back up again. He scratches at the nape of his neck. "You're going to burn yourself out, Mel. You have plenty of money from the life insurance policy and your savings to keep you comfortable for a long time."

My grip tightens on the bowl. "It keeps me busy. Distracted."

"There are other ways to stay distracted," he counters. "Why don't you come out for a beer with me and the guys tonight? Bring Leah."

"Leah doesn't like you."

"Leah likes me. She just doesn't like that she likes me."

West shoots me a wink, pulling a reluctant smile from my lips.

"Besides," he presses. "A break will do you good. You're always cooped up here in this…house."

There's an emphasis on the word *house*—a weighty timbre that makes my skin feel itchy. It's my house with Charlie, yes, but it feels like *his* house, and no one understands why I chose to stay here instead of move, why I wanted to strangle myself in these dying roots when I could plant new ones.

It's for the same reason I didn't wash the bedsheets for months, and why I showered with his Irish Spring soap, and why I didn't have the heart to throw away the mail that had his name on it.

It's why I'll never get rid of my purse—*the* purse.

I'm connected to him here.

I still *feel* him here.

And when I finally washed those sheets, when the soap ran out, and when the stacks of envelopes grew too high…I still had this house. His scent lingers on the drapes whenever a tepid breeze blows through. His fingerprints are on these walls, and his custom-built shed sits out back, filled with his tools and hardware. Our prized magnolia tree is blooming to life, bursting with pastel petals, a deceiving contrast to the ghosts that haunt me here.

I love this house.

It's my favorite place to be, ghosts and all.

"I'll think about it," I respond, my tone flat. I'm not doing my believability any favors. "Thanks for stopping by."

West's defeated sigh is a prelude to the look of disappointment that I'm certain adorns his face, but I wouldn't know because I don't look up from the cookies-and-cream cupcake batter. I keep stirring and stirring, mixing and folding, even when I sense him rummaging around the kitchen, sifting through the refrigerator, and poking inside cabinets.

A few minutes later, I hear him retreat with a hollow goodbye. "I'll call you later."

"Okay. See you."

When the front door closes and my brother is gone, I finally release the mixer and lift my eyes from my task. I swallow down a lump when I spot the peanut butter and banana sandwich sitting atop a paper plate, cut diagonally just how I like it, paired with a glass of cold milk.

"Thank you," I whisper to the empty kitchen before picking the mixer back up and drowning myself in cupcake orders.

I keep working.

I keep going.

I keep myself busy to the point of exhaustion, because if I don't burn out… I'll burn away.

And that seems infinitely worse.

———————

I'm just as surprised as West and his friends when I stroll into the brewery that night with Leah's arm linked through mine. It was a last-minute decision after a black cloud decided to infiltrate me, all sharp teeth and long talons, and even reruns of *Veronica Mars* couldn't pull me out of the funk.

I definitely look the most homeless out of everyone in the bar, with my petite frame swallowed up by one of Charlie's old hoodies and faded leggings hanging loose off my too-thin legs. I brushed my teeth, but I didn't brush my hair, and lip gloss is the only makeup that found its way to my face.

But I'm here.

And I'm smiling.

"Ladies, grab some chairs," one of West's buddies hollers over to us as we saunter up to the round table featuring my brother and his two longtime friends, Alex and Shane.

West leans back in his seat, knees spread, beer dangling between them. The smile he sends me is laced with tenderness before it transforms into something more guileful as he sets his sights on Leah. "Hey, tiger."

"Hey, *Westley*."

My best friend gives my upper arm a light pinch, then releases me to drag a chair over to the table, situating herself beside my brother.

West purses his lips at the sound of his full name as his gaze floats back to me. "I thought I told you not to bring her," he teases.

"Yeah, that's totally what you said." I watch as Leah flips her shiny, black hair over one shoulder and props her high heels up on West's thigh. These two have been ready to ignite since Leah and I were in high school. I have no idea why it hasn't happened yet. Pulling my own chair up to the table, I return the welcoming head nods given by Alex and Shane and take a seat. "Long time, no see. How are you guys?"

Their responses disintegrate into background noise and static almost instantly. Their words are secondary to the sound of my blood pumping through sullied veins, a cruel and constant reminder of the fact that he is gone and I'm still here. Charlie should be next to me, his arm draped protectively around my waist as he talks sports with West and sips on a craft beer. He'd be deep in conversation right now, fully engaged, and yet his true focus would somehow still be on me.

Fingers dancing along my hipbone. Ankle crisscrossing with mine beneath the table. An unspoken *I love you* filtering into my mind, the affection palpable.

I realize I'm smiling and bobbing my head at Alex, watching his lips move, his hands waving animatedly. To him, I'm fully engaged.

But I haven't heard a word he's said—*my true focus is elsewhere.*

"Anyway, you look great, Melody. It's nice to see you out."

Alex's words finally break through my barrier, causing me to blink. I clear my throat. "Thank you. I've been so busy lately with the business, it's hard to find time to socialize."

"I feel you. Dad life is a bit of a fun sucker."

So is grief.

Shane cuts in, his blue-gray eyes pinned on me. "You do look good."

For some reason, I glance at Leah, as if he's speaking to the wrong person.

Leah's smile is more genuine, her laugh a little louder, her clothes fashionable and flattering, showcasing her ample curves. She's a vision, and I'm a blur. I never used to fade into the background, but my extroverted personality has dwindled over the last year. It's been chipped away by scalpels and spears, leaving me feeling small.

But the smaller I get, the easier it is for me to hide, so I'm content with that for now.

Leah wiggles her eyebrows at me, almost like permission. Permission to accept this compliment. I duck my head, shifting my attention back to Shane. "Thanks."

God, who am I?

Where did I go?

I used to be funny. Witty. Chatty.

Now I'm just a shell of my former self, spewing out lackluster words and robotic replies.

My fingers curl around the beer that's been placed in front of me, gripping hard, and I know exactly where I am.

I'm still doubled over in the middle of that downtown street, sobbing beneath rain clouds and a sunless sky, my arms full and heavy, my heart wilting.

The bitter taste of beer coats my tongue as my gaze flicks back to Shane. He's still staring at me, and he's staring in a way that's unfamiliar. West's friends have always looked at me the same way for as long as I've known them.

As Charlie's wife.

But Shane's eyes tell a different story now, and I suppose that's because my own story has changed. There's been a plot twist.

I'm suddenly feeling self-conscious, drab, and unkempt, so I skim unpainted fingernails through my white-blond hair that hangs around my shoulders in long, knotted strands.

Why isn't he staring at Leah?

She's gorgeous with mocha skin and eyes spun with copper and gold. She giggles at something my brother says, and her laughter sounds like music. A symphony or an orchestra.

I am nothing but bagpipes and sad violins.

It takes a moment for me to realize she's speaking to me, and when I do, those striking copper eyes soften with worry.

"You okay, babe?" Leah removes her feet from West's lap and twists around in her chair to fully face me. "Bathroom break?"

"Sure."

Shane pulls his attention off me as Alex goes on a tangent about co-sleeping. West looks as if he's about to stand to join us, to make sure I'm really okay, but I shake my head with a tight-lipped smile, assuring him I'm fine.

I'm fine.

Such simple yet destructive words.

Leah drags me through the bar by my wrist, and we don't even make it to the bathroom before she stops, turning around to study me. People bump into us as we come to a screeching halt in the middle of a high-traffic area, but Leah doesn't care. She reaches out to tuck a loose strand of messy hair behind my ear, her expression full of love. "Don't think you need to prove anything to anyone—even *you*. There's no time limit on healing," she whispers with delicate care. "I'm not going anywhere, West isn't going anywhere, bars and fun and social gatherings aren't going anywhere. No one gets to decide when you're ready, except for that beautiful heart of yours."

Tears prickle my eyes, loud and defiant. I try to hold them back with a sharp inhale. "You remind me of him sometimes." I'm not sure where the words come from, but I know it's from someplace raw and real, so I continue, my breaths ragged, my chest tight. "You always know exactly what to say… just like Charlie."

Leah crinkles her nose as her hand runs up and down my bicep, squeezing affectionately. "The right words are easy when they come from an unselfish place. Don't listen to anyone who doesn't have your best interest in mind, baby girl."

I nod with my lip caught between my teeth, eyes averting to the now-tattered ballet flats Charlie purchased for me when we first started dating.

This place feels so foreign despite the fact that it was our favorite hangout. Our most-frequented establishment to grab a drink with friends or just relax and talk about our day over beer nuggets.

Our.

It's foreign because I'm a foreigner in my own life. A stranger. I've lost my way, and I'm not sure how to get back to the girl I used to be.

Before him.

Before tragedy *infected* me.

With a sigh, I raise my chin and offer Leah a remorseful smile. "I think I'm going to go."

"I know." Leah smooths my hair down, her catlike eyes flickering over my face. "And wipe that apology off your lips. You have nothing to be sorry for."

A chuckle slips out. "Except for these shoes I'm still wearing from 2012."

"You can only see the holes if you look *really* close."

We laugh together, and it's a liberating sound, an eager ray of sunshine poking through my stone cracks. But the feeling is fleeting, and the clouds soon roll in because I can't help but think…

I wish I could say the same thing about me.

On the drive home, I remember that I'm out of butter, so I make a quick stop at the grocery store to prepare for another day of baking. A yawn escapes me as I stand in the checkout line, drained from the mental exertion of socializing and faking my way through conversations and pleasantries. I shuffle forward, distracted by my own hollow thoughts, when chitchat behind me catches my attention. My eyes remain fixed ahead, but my ears soak up every word.

"Did you hear about that hit-and-run in Lake Geneva yesterday?"

"Oh my God, yes. Terrible. I heard the child survived, but the mother is critical."

"My worst nightmare…"

My stomach coils as the voices fade out, and I become drenched in my own horrible memories. There were two men involved in Charlie's murder, but only one was caught. A bystander grabbed the license plate number off the truck that hit my husband, and Alfred "Alfie" Kent was quickly arrested, then eventually sentenced. He refused to give up his accomplice.

An elderly gentleman begins ringing up my items, puncturing my bleak fog.

"Yer eyes are too pretty to look so sad," the man mutters, slipping the sticks of butter into a paper bag. "That'll be seven twenty-one."

I stiffen as I swipe my debit card.

He hands me the purchase, along with my receipt, when the transaction goes through. "Have a nice night, Peaches."

Something inside me freezes—a snap, a trigger. An ice-cold draft rolling in like a winter stormfront.

"You smell like peaches, Mrs. March."

The old man flashes me a toothless smile, reminding me that I should return the gesture.

I'm good at smiling. I'm good at sucking people in like a happy vacuum.

They have no idea my real smile was sucked away almost one year ago today—that it's now permanently shrouded in gray clouds and should-have-beens.

But I do force a smile as I tuck the paper bag underneath my arm, and it's wide and bright, eerily authentic. "Goodbye."

I tell him goodbye, not good night, because when I arrive home ten minutes later, I wander aimlessly into the kitchen to discard the butter and my purse, then pluck a paring knife out of the silverware drawer.

Swallowing, I carry the knife into the living room and collapse to the floor, my back pressed up against the front of the couch with my legs sprawled out in front of me, my heart thumping. I decide to remove my hoodie because I don't want to get blood on it. It was Charlie's favorite, and I can't bear the thought of being responsible for any more stains.

The knife feels weightless in my fist, and I'm grateful that I sharpened it not too long ago. The blade is smooth and cunning. It shouldn't hurt too much.

Not that I'd really notice.

I inhale an abrupt breath, rolling up the thin fabric of my long-sleeved blouse until the underside of my wrist comes into view. Blue veins stare back at me, swimming with winter and twilight, so striking against my milky skin.

A hollow calm sweeps through me, a foggy disconnect. It's almost as if I'm out of my own body, observing from afar, as the knife lifts and the pointy tip digs into the soft flesh. It doesn't take much pressure for it to pierce through, to puncture my skin, and I watch, almost catatonic, as the blood pools to the surface. I dig a little deeper, dragging the serrated edge downward and releasing a sharp hiss when the pain hits.

The sight of the blood has my stomach twisting into knots as a wave of dizziness claims me. My eyes flutter, and I start to sway.

I've always had a weak stomach.

I just never knew I had a weak heart.

As the blood begins to spurt, a notification pings from my cell phone beside me. I squeeze my eyes shut, hardly hearing it at first.

Leave me alone. I'm busy.

I'm too preoccupied with dying.

But something niggles at me, pokes and prods. It buzzes in my ear until reality comes crashing down around me, detonating at my feet and stealing my breath, ripping a battle cry straight from my throat. There are explosions behind my eyes and ashes in my lungs.

On instinct, I reach behind me for the blanket sprawled over the armrest of the couch and wrap it tightly around my pulse point, trying to halt the blood.

What am I doing?

My God, what am I doing?

Panic sinks its teeth into me, and my breaths come in quick bursts of chaos as I near a hyperventilative state. I sift through the pocket of Charlie's hoodie and locate my phone, consumed by violent tremors, my blood-tinged fingers swiping to unlock the screen so I can dial 9-1-1.

I'm not ready.

I'm not ready yet.

But I pause when the notification catches my eye. The notification that interrupted my suicide attempt.

I pause because it's an email.

It's an email from…*him.*

I quickly open it, trying to make out the words through a wall of tears.

from: Zephyr <Zephyr79@gmail.com>
to: greenmagnolia@gmail.com

date: Apr 12, 2021, 9:22 PM
subject: Re: Widowed & Wilting

Hey.

I'll be honest, I had no intention of writing you back. Hence the nine-month delay. A better person might apologize for that, but I'm not that person.

    I'm not exactly a wordsmith either, and I'm certainly no expert on grief.

    But I do know a thing about wilting.

    I feel like it might be a fate worse than death, you know? It's a slow, soul-sucking process, where you're stuck in this limbo between fading away for good and making a comeback, but you can't quite obtain either. So you just wilt.

    I've been wilting for a long time, and it fucking sucks.

    Anyway, I hope you found some sunlight and have been watered properly.

Zephyr

My eyes scan over the email a dozen times, soaking up the words, feeling my heart sputter and short-circuit as trails of blood trickle down my arm and saturate the rug beneath me.

A ghastly reminder of my near-fatal choice.

I try to process it, I try to process the letters and sentences and what it all means, but I'm fading, captured by a sky full of stars in the veil of night.

Before I'm fully possessed by darkness, I find the strength to dial those three numbers to call for help, to save myself from…*myself.*

And when I finally come to, I'm lying in a new bed in a strange place, blinded by the bright lights overhead.

They singe my eyes.

Harsh and artificial.

But I find myself smiling as I drift away once more, and this time it's a real smile, a sincere smile, because the ceiling lights manifest into something else, and all I feel is warmth dancing across my face as the clouds scatter.

The sun is looking for me.

5

PARKER

THE SOLE OF MY SHOE TAPS THE LINOLEUM IN PERFECT TIME WITH
Ms. Katherine's ballpoint pen.

Ms. Katherine.

Like we're fucking kindergarteners gathered around the area rug for a riveting rendition of *Goodnight Moon*.

I wish I could say good night.

Good night, room. Good night to the old lady who smells like mothballs.

Unfortunately, I'm stuck here because the only person in the world I give a shit about wants me to get better.

Yeah. *Better.*

As if I have an affliction I can cure in a matter of a few months by attending kumbaya classes with a merry band of idiots. Classes that reek of drivel and falsities, packaged neatly in a big ass box of bullshit, tied with glitter-infused ribbon.

As if I'll suddenly care enough to…*care.*

The old bat blinks through a thin smile that appears drawn on with a plum-colored pencil. Her pen continues to drum against a leather-bound journal, spurring my feet to tap faster to drown it out.

Tap, tap, tap.

It grates me. My jaw tenses, teeth gnashing together until the enamel nearly chips. Eyes narrowed, focused and razor sharp, I almost miss the sound of my name penetrating the vanilla-scented air.

Vanilla and honeysuckle, to be exact. I saw the empty package of wax melts in the garbage can when I was grabbing a cup of stale, shitty coffee, and I had to scoff.

The fragrance is designed to be calming. Soft and sweet.

Feminine.

Bullshit. The association is equally laughable and infuriating.

"Mr. Denison."

My scowl is enough to have the portly woman teetering back on her chair legs. Other than the menace in my eyes piercing through the layers of cakey foundation settled between her wrinkles, my face remains expressionless.

This lack of reaction seems to fluster her further. "Mr. Denison," she repeats, clearing a hitch in her throat that resembles pure terror. "Why don't you start us off today?"

I try to keep my face stone-cold and stoic, but my left eyebrow arches automatically.

Rebel son of a bitch.

"I can start, Ms. Katherine."

The timid voice of some emo chick beside me steals my rebuttal. Her hair is black, like a starless sky at midnight. Like mine. Only, mine doesn't have the ridiculous violet streaks and goofy headband.

Emo Chick scratches at the back of her hand, knuckles red and raw, pinholes of blood dotting the chalky skin around the bones. She is also tapping her feet.

Tap, tap, tap.

"My hamster, Nutmeg."

Her words are whispered so delicately, I can't help but fracture them with a mocking huff. I feel the gaze of a dozen horrified eyes on me as I lean against the seat back, arms folded.

A gasp carries over to me. "Parker."

I'm being scolded by the shrew.

At the beginning of these gag-inducing meetings, we're supposed to go around the room and list off something that matters to us. It's called a "starting point."

It's a reason. A reason to keep us alive another day.

Starting points are intended to be small—trivial, even.

The smell of freshly mowed grass, extra syrup on our pancakes, that first sip of coffee in the morning, our favorite song—things we'd miss if we chose to jump off that building or shove a pistol down our throat.

But a fucking hamster? Hamsters have a three-year lifespan, and they eat their offspring.

This girl is a goner.

See you on the flip side, Emo Chick.

"She's a good friend," the raven-haired waif continues, earlobes stretched to a frightening level and decorated with silver skulls. "She makes me happy."

The shrew returns her attention to my right, her pinched features relaxing as she responds to Emo Chick. "That's wonderful, Amelia. Animals and pets make great starting points."

My eye roll is monumental.

But it's interrupted when the double doors plow open, revealing a disheveled sprite of a woman whose beltless belt loop gets snagged on the door handle, causing her to be yanked backward, purse falling and dispensing lipstick, coins, and tampons everywhere, while her skinny latte from Starbucks slips from her grip as she tries to catch the fallen purse.

The scene would be amusing if I gave a flying fuck.

Chair legs screech against tile as members rise and jump into action, eager to help the inept stranger. I remain seated, bored but mostly irritated that I haven't figured out a way to fast-forward time yet.

I curse my dreadful sister as I wait for the chaos to simmer. She's my foster sister, technically, but I've never been big on titles, and I've certainly never put much weight into blood.

Bree is an anomaly. A *woman*. But it's different with her—I've never really noticed her gender. I only see her heart.

I pull my chin from my chest when I catch a whiff of something girly and citrus. Something like sunshine. The new girl stumbles past me, cheeks stained pink and hair so light it resembles cotton fields. She's careful not to trip over my outstretched legs as she finds a seat on the opposite side of Emo Chick, then slinks back like she's hoping it'll swallow her up.

Looks like we've got one thing in common.

Ms. Katherine settles back into her own chair, while the rest of the circus quiets down and we resume circle time. "Let's welcome our newest survivor," she says, fisting her journal between knobby fingers. "This is Miss March."

"Melody," the woman corrects, voice cracking slightly. "Just Melody."

Melody.

Yeah right—a melody she is not.

She is noise, discord.

A sour note.

They all are.

Everyone welcomes her with a warm hello, except for me, and somehow, my silence must be the loudest of all because she turns to me then, seeing me for the first time.

She's all big green eyes and pale skin. Emerald and ivory. Her frame is petite and willowy, a sundress hanging loose off her modest curves, while a bandage adorns her wrist like a dismal focal point. My gaze shifts from the bandage to her bony collarbone, then skims back up.

She has that kind of face.

Like maybe she was happy once.

I pull away with a crude exhale, tipping my head against the seat back and closing my eyes, zoning out of this embarrassing spectacle. Bree means well, I know that, but I'm only here because she asked me to be here. I know these meetings won't do jack shit—I'm confident I'll walk out this door the exact same man I was when I walked in.

But she asked me.

She begged and pleaded with tears streaming down her freckled cheekbones: *"Please, Parker. If not for you, then do it for me. I can't lose you."*

So I did.

I'll do anything she asks me to because she's the only person who's ever had my back. She was the only one to give a shit about me, to pull me out of that black hole, and there's no favor in the world that can compensate for one small act of compassion in the midst of brutality.

The starting points have transformed into sob stories now, and I heave out another jaded sigh when Robert starts rambling on about his shitty day at the car dealership and how a customer was going to buy a car but didn't, and now he feels worthless.

Go play in traffic, Robert.

Just when I don't think it can get any worse, the woman to his right speaks up with her own tale of distress.

"He won't talk to me." She sniffles, nose red and blotchy, her fist coiled around a well-used tissue. "I just don't understand why he won't talk to me. He sees me so upset, so hurt by his avoidance, and I don't know what to do. I'm not sure what else to say to get him to hear me, to look at me, to *see* me, and it's just so painful that we can't have a normal conversation because he won't even talk to me—"

"Maybe because he can't get a word in."

I'm still slouched down in my chair, head tilted back with my eyes shut. The words just slipped through without warning, as they often do, because it's easy to have no filter when you don't give a shit. The silence is deafening, but that's not what has me twisting in my seat, eyelids popping open.

It's a laugh.

It's a quick, genuine burst of laughter that seems to have been expelled as unintentionally as my own outburst.

The new girl.

She glances at me briefly before clearing her throat, then inching back into her seat, head ducking downward. She's a contradictory mix of sunshine and sadness as she becomes engrossed with the dirty linoleum beneath her shoes.

I keep my eyes on her another minute, more curious than interested, before Ms. Katherine breaks the awkward lull with a light humming sound.

"Melody, why don't you share a little about yourself? What brings you to Loving Lifelines?"

I hold the groan in the back of my throat. Stupid fucking name.

My eyes narrow as I watch the new girl fidget in place, toes tapping in opposite time, hands gripping the handbag in her lap. She sweeps trembling fingers through her hair, still looking down.

"I, um, lost someone," she replies, her voice no more than a shaky whisper. "And then I lost myself."

Ms. Katherine bobs her head slowly, brimming with artificial sympathies. "What brought you back from the point of no return?"

"Hope." Her response is swift and pointed. "I had a glimpse of hope in that dark moment."

"It's a lie, you know."

There I go again, running my mouth. I feel their offended stares on me, but I pay them no mind. Arms still folded across my chest, legs sprawled out in front of me, I keep my gaze on little miss sunshine as she turns to look at me with a slow, languid crane of her neck.

Wide, searching eyes meet my cool indifference as I continue. "Hope is a toxic, false sense of optimism created to keep us going, but all it does is prolong the inevitable," I say, unblinking and unemotional. "Hope is for the weak."

I'm ambushed by a collective round of murmurs and gasps, but I don't flinch as my sights stay fixed on the frail woman two seats over, frail in both body and spirit. She looks breakable in every possible way—the counter to my stone walls and steel truths.

"Parker, I know this is an open forum, and we encourage healthy discussion," the shrew cuts in, stealing away whatever objection may have escaped the new girl's lips. "But let's try to keep things positive."

I sniff, shrugging my shoulders and pulling myself to my feet.

Works for me.

Without another word, I see myself out, feeling the heat of her stare burning into my back like fiery rays of sunshine as I walk out the door.

The gravel crunches beneath rubber tires as I pull into the driveway, scanning all the unfinished projects that litter my front yard.

I'm busy as hell this season, my job being a one-man contractor specializing in building renovations and home improvements. I was employed with a larger construction company for most of my career but found that I don't work very well with others.

Not exactly a revelation.

Bree suggested I start my own business, which sounded awful at first because self-employment involves shining customer service and fake-ass smiles, but when she volunteered to take the reins in the people department, I was sold.

I'm not sure how she does it. She works ridiculously long hours as it is, lots of overnight shifts, yet still finds time to keep my business up and running, securing new jobs and handling the customers. She even stops over to let my dog out for bathroom breaks as often as she can, occasionally leaving home-cooked meals or freshly baked desserts on my counter with a cutesy note.

Today is no different when I walk into the modest house I built from the ground up in my early twenties. I'm thirty-two now, so I've had this place for nearly ten years. It sits in a secluded, heavily wooded area on the outskirts of Delavan, suiting me just fine. I hate a lot of things, but neighbors are at the top of that list, right along with football and hipsters.

Walden lifts himself on unsteady legs as I push through the front door and toss my keys on the side table with a jarring clatter. He's a border collie mix, older than dirt, and I get the feeling that the mutt enjoys life just as much as I do—which is not in the least. His black-and-white tufts of fur have been falling out since the day I found him wandering on the side of the road a mile from my house, feeble and malnourished. I don't think I've ever seen him wag his tail.

But every time I walk through the door, he stands and hobbles over to me. He doesn't beg for attention or bark or lick my hand. He just kind of lurks a few feet away until I notice him, and then he shuffles back over to his dog bed with a sigh.

I blow out my own sigh, scratching my head and tousling my mop of hair as I venture into the cramped kitchen. A plate of lemon pound cake rests on the portable island, covered in plastic wrap with a note taped to it:

> *Eat up, little brother. Lemon cake is the happiest dessert, and*
> *if anyone needs a bit of sunshine in their life, it's you.*
> *And your dog.*

Please give that dog some damn lemon cake.

—Bree

I would smile if I did that sort of thing.

Instead, I peel back the plastic and pluck a yellow, miniature loaf from the platter, eating half of it in one bite. I turn around, glancing at my dog from across the room as I chew, his melancholy eyes staring back at me while his chin rests between two paws. Swallowing down the cake, I reach for a red ball sitting atop the adjacent counter and toss it up and down with one hand, my attention still on Walden.

I approach him, crossing into the living room, then crouch down and throw him the ball.

He just stares at it, unmoving.

I try again with the same result.

Nothing.

Totally unimpressed.

The ball rolls right up to his wet nose, but Walden ignores it, his only reaction being a long, heavy sigh. Annoyance, maybe. He probably thinks I'm a fucking idiot, tossing him this pathetic toy like it's supposed to be exciting or something.

My dog looks at the red ball like I look at life.

My chest hums with resignation, and I abandon the ball and straighten my stance. I debate whether I want to finish the custom dining table I have partially assembled under the carport while there's still daylight, considering it's due to be delivered to a client in less than a week, but I'm honestly not feeling it right now. I kind of just want to go to bed.

It's my favorite part of the day.

As I make up my mind and choose the latter, I can't help but glance over at my open laptop before I disappear down the hallway. I have a new email notification, and I already know who it's from.

Magnolia.

The wilting widow who I found myself responding to one night when sleep wouldn't come, my demons were aggressive, and an anonymous outlet sounded strangely appealing.

After years and years of unsuccessful therapy, a slew of doctors who considered me a lost cause, and no one, literally *no one* aside from Bree, to care whether or not I took my next breath, this nameless, faceless stranger called to me somehow.

While I couldn't relate to her grief, I could relate to her loneliness, so I finally wrote her back. And I actually slept that night.

I pause my steps, hesitating between the edge of the living room and the hallway, palm massaging the nape of my neck.

Fuck it.

A moment later, I'm seated in my computer chair, opening up the email, my eyes scanning over the stranger's words.

> *from: Magnolia <greenmagnolia@gmail.com>*
> *to: Zephyr79@gmail.com*
> *date: Apr 18, 2021, 2:33 PM*
> *subject: Serendipity*
>
> *Zephyr,*
>
> *Do you believe in perfect timing? Fate? Aligned stars, serendipity, meant to be?*
> *I didn't think I'd ever hear from you, and here you are.*
> *Right at the perfect time.*
> *So now I have to wonder. I have to consider the possibility that maybe we are not alone in this. Maybe there's something else out there calling the shots, like some kind of mystical mediator.*
> *Silly, right?*
> *Probably.*
> *But it gave me a real smile, and that's something I haven't done in a while.*
> *Thank you.*
>
> *Magnolia*

Sighing, I send my reply.

from: Zephyr <Zephyr79@gmail.com>
to: greenmagnolia@gmail.com
date: Apr 18, 2021, 6:45 PM
subject: Re: Serendipity

Magnolia,

I hate to burst your bubble, but there's no such thing as perfect timing.
Perfection is an illusion, as is time.
Man-made. A synthetic coping mechanism.
I don't like to bet on fate or circumstance. I bet on experience. Reality. Things that are tangible and proven.
That's probably why I'm forever wilting.
You say I wrote you back at the perfect time, but maybe you were just searching for something to cling to in that moment—a reason to make a comeback.
That's not fate or aligning stars. That's all you.
Give yourself some credit.

Zephyr

I click send, then shut down my computer and head to bed.

6

MELODY

I FIDDLE WITH THE BANDAGE ENCASING MY WRIST, PICKING AT THE STICKY adhesive. It's been two weeks since my brush with rock bottom, and while the wound has been healing appropriately, the evidence of my crime is still glaring.

A grisly, jagged branding of my pain. My ghosts are now corporeal, carved into my flesh, visible to the naked eye. I can't hide them anymore.

And I don't have to hide them here, in this white room, with faces that are unfamiliar yet so kindred. Fellow companions in pain. My eyes float around the circle, making up stories for each troubled soul. Loss, breakups, mental ailments, death. Their sagas are written all over their faces, scribbled into their fine lines and shadows. Glowing in their hollow eyes.

The eyes are always the mecca for grief.

Except…it's different with him—the dark stranger with hidden tales I can't seem to read. He's illegible. He doesn't wear his pain like the others, and that fascinates me somehow. I want to learn how he did it, where he studied, what tools he used to perfect such a thing.

Parker. I think that was his name.

I can't help but glance over at him, surprised to see him in the same seat, one chair over, after his dramatic exit the week before. He clearly finds no healing between these four walls, so what keeps him coming back?

Raindrops cling to inky hair, one going rogue and gliding down the side of his neck—a testament to the storm raging outside the tall window, rainfall pelting the roof above our heads. I zone in on that lone droplet as it makes a languid journey to his shirt collar, collapsing into nothing, like it never even existed.

Poof.

While I'm spaced out, envious of a raindrop, the mysterious man looks up, feeling my attention pinned on him. Jade eyes, almost violent in their scrutiny, assess me in a slow pull, from my scuffed ballet flats to my curious stare.

If he's undressing me, it's not my clothes he's peeling off. It's everything else.

A hard lump catches my throat, and I jerk away until my gaze is focused on the sterile wall across from me. A safer canvas. A reprieve.

But I still sense his perusal prickling my skin, making me feel itchy and unnerved. He's digging and digging, hollowing me out, pulling all my buried pieces to the surface. He's a human excavator.

Biting my lower lip, I can't help but glance over at him again, an invisible force drawing our eyes back together. He's still staring. Still poking around my burial grounds.

Still digging.

He doesn't blink or smile. His eyes are beryl and brimstone, unwavering, his jaw shadowed in stubble, cheekbones high, eyebrows dark like his hair. Like his clothes.

Like his stare.

Part of me wants to storm over to him and demand he back off, quit exhuming me. I feel vulnerable and exposed, laid out, shaking and bare. The *nerve.* The nerve of this man—this intruder. And yet, I can't seem to do anything but stare right back at him.

Our hold is eclipsed when a voice startles me, causing me to blink and cower against the plastic seat back, a feeble attempt to hide. A tension releases inside me, and I think that means he finally tore his eyes away.

"I'm Amelia."

There's a young woman standing in front of me, and I recognize her from the prior week. She sat between me and the dark stranger, quiet and timid, nearly blending into the background. She looks young, possibly still a teenager, and her hair is jet-black with purple highlights. Her porcelain skin is studded with piercings and silver hoops, and her lipstick is black, matching her hair. A soft smile upstages her harsh exterior.

"Hi. I'm Melody," I respond, forcing my own smile to the surface. The smile that has always sucked people in.

It must still hold some power because Amelia's shoulders relax as she approaches, taking the seat to my left. Her softness lingers. "You don't look like you belong here."

"I don't?"

"No. You remind me of sunshine. It's too cold for you here."

My body stiffens at the analogy, the one I used to adore. The one that would spill from Charlie's lips like a summer breeze, the perfect complement to the sun.

Parker's eyes find me again. I can see his head turn toward me, just a blur in my peripheral, but I keep my attention on Amelia. "Appearances can be deceiving," I reply gently, then decide to change the subject. "Have you been coming here long?"

Amelia twists her thin, stringy hair over one shoulder, her knees knocking together beneath a black shirtdress. "This is my fifth week. My parents enrolled me after I tried to hang myself inside my mother's greenhouse. She always seemed to like it more than me, so it felt poetic somehow."

My mouth goes dry at her blunt confession. "I'm sorry to hear that. How old are you?"

"I'm almost twenty."

Twenty. At twenty years old, I was falling in love with Charlie, making plans, envisioning a bright and fruitful future.

She's so young. *Too* young.

But I suppose grief doesn't take age into consideration—it just takes what it wants when it wants it. Grief is the most selfish thing in this world.

"I'm glad you're okay," I tell her through the lump in my throat. "I'm glad you changed your mind."

Amelia shrugs. "I didn't. My dad and his mistress came barging in to screw or something. She started screaming her head off when she saw what I was trying to do."

Her honesty startles me, stealing a response from my lips. I have no idea what to say as I watch Amelia nibble on her chewed-up fingernails, her demeanor casual, as if we were discussing something insignificant like the weather.

"Who would like to start us off today?"

Ms. Katherine's kind voice slices through my somber haze, and I straighten in my seat with a choppy exhale.

Amelia responds first. "My hamster, Nutmeg."

Starting points. Little things we would miss about the world if we chose to leave it. It's a powerful concept, something I couldn't stop thinking about all week. Everyone has something big, something important they would leave behind, but what about those little treasures we walk past every day, such as anthills in the sidewalk cracks, or butterflies with tangerine wings, or the way water laps at a sandy shoreline?

What about the smell of deep-fried delicacies at a street festival or buttered popcorn when you walk into a movie theater?

Ms. Katherine's eyes drift to me, so I speak next. "The sound of violins."

I'm not sure why I look at him after the words escape me, but I do, and I'm not surprised to find him watching me.

"Such a sad instrument," Ms. Katherine replies, her tone tender. "But so very beautiful."

"They make me feel," I continue. "Whenever I hear the sound of violin strings, I always get this emotion in my chest and tears in my eyes, ever since I was a little girl."

"That's fitting," Amelia cuts in, her umber irises appearing a shade lighter. "Since your name is Melody."

I can't help but chuckle. "Unfortunately, I'm musically challenged. I'm pretty sure my parents started regretting the name choice the first time I attempted karaoke."

Everyone laughs except for him.

The meeting continues, and we are given a "homework" assignment of creating a vision board, consisting of dreams and goals we aspire to reach one day. It's supposed to keep us focused on a positive future.

Halfway through the meeting, we are allowed to mingle and stretch our legs for fifteen minutes. It's an intermission—an emotional recharge. I watch as fellow members engage in conversation and check their cell phones, collective sighs and laughter breaking the silence.

Parker stands, and my eyes trail him as he saunters over to the little snack table, stocked with a Keurig, along with packaged crackers and cookies. He flips through the coffee flavors while I make a quick decision to join him. I'm not sure why. He's not at all approachable—in fact, he hasn't said a word this entire meeting. Parker doesn't participate in any discussions or offer his starting points. He never smiles.

I'm pretty sure I even caught him sleeping.

But something pulls me to my feet and guides me over to him, an invisible force, an insatiable curiosity. I'm desperate to learn how he's tempered his pain.

Parker is fiddling with the Keurig machine when I come up beside him, lacing my fingers together in front of me and gnawing at my lip. I clear the hitch in my throat. "Hey."

He ignores my greeting, pressing an assortment of buttons until the coffee maker roars to life. His hair is a mess of unruly waves and curls, longer up top and short in the back. It's a dark, dark brown, almost black, which makes his light green eyes all the more striking.

Those eyes flicker over to me, skimming down my body, then back up in a quick sweep until he returns his attention to the table.

"You were watching me," I say, my voice surprisingly steady as I take in the way he sifts through the basket of assorted crackers.

"Was I?"

He doesn't spare me a glance as he replies, his focus pinned on the little bag of Wheat Thins. Parker pulls it open, eyeing the contents, and I drum my fingers along the floral tablecloth. His dark denim looks worn, his T-shirt faded. He's put no effort into his outward appearance, and yet he still commands attention somehow. I swallow. "Yes."

Shaking the bag around, he takes a cracker out between two fingers and pops it into his mouth. Then, he finally turns to look at me, slipping his unoccupied hand into the pocket of his jeans while he chews. "And you want to know why?"

"No. I want to know what you saw."

Parker hesitates mid-chew, his jaw ticking, almost as if I've taken him off guard by my answer. But he recovers quickly, his expression turning stoic. "I saw what I always see when I look at your kind."

My kind?

The broken? The grieving?

I'm about to ask him to clarify, but the car salesman, Robert, pushes his way between us to sort through the snack basket, and the connection is severed. Parker doesn't elaborate and, instead, pushes off the table and makes his way back to his chair, leaving me frowning and confused.

And oddly, more intrigued.

————————

When I'm stressed, I bake.

When I'm restless, I bake.

When I'm on the verge of an emotional breakdown…I bake.

Some people exercise or read or take hot baths with scented candles and mood music. I knead batter, weigh flour, and play with fondant like I'm a toddler with Play-Doh. It sedates my inner demons in a way nothing else can, and I think it's because I feel close to him when I'm in the kitchen, mixing and blending and measuring.

It's my vice. My escape.

My cell phone pings from the kitchen table, so I swipe both of my white-dusted palms along my apron and fetch it, letting a smile lift when I see Leah's name light up the screen.

Leah: LOVE YOU SO MUCH. Miss your face. And that cute ass of yours. Has anyone told you what a nice butt you have? Seriously. It's fantastic. I'm sure you already know. Am I making this weird? Fuck. I always do this. It's totally weird now. But you still love me, right? Muahhh.

God, I adore her.

I shoot her a quick text back, taking a seat.

Me: It's always weird. That's why I love us. Coffee talk on Saturday?

While I await her response, I scroll through my unopened texts and nibble my lip when I notice a missed message from my mother.

Mom: Give me a call when you can, sweetie. Dad threw out his back and won't be able to finish the remodel on your bathroom. He's okay, don't worry. I will try to see if Al is able to give you a good price.

A knot forms in the back of my throat as I attempt to call her back, but it goes straight to voicemail, which means she's probably in bed already.

The bathroom.

It was one of the last things Charlie and I discussed before…

Before winter rolled in.

We bought this house together three years ago, and it was a fixer-upper to say the least. Drab carpeting, funky wallpaper, a mauve master bathroom. *Mauve.* It was a running joke between us for years, but it was always pushed to the bottom of the to-do list, trumped by other projects and financial commitments. But Charlie had received quite a large pay raise at the beginning of the year, giving us the opportunity to finally tackle the bathroom.

It was one of many things left undone, and one I finally decided to pull the trigger on after an entire year of crying myself to sleep on those mulberry tiles, begging the floral wallpaper to bring him back to me.

I send my mother a reply, licking a dab of lemon batter from my index finger.

Me: Give Dad a big hug for me. Don't worry about the bathroom. I'll stop by for dinner this week. xoxo

There's a heavy weight in the pit of my stomach when I set my phone down. A tumor. And it's the malignant kind, that I know, invasive and deadly, spreading rapidly and infecting all the parts of me I try to keep from its reach—from its stems and hungry roots.

But I'm stronger than my sickness.

I have to be.

Heaving in a calming breath, I pluck my phone from the tabletop and open up my email app. An unsent draft stares back at me, riddled with clumsy words and ill-defined thoughts.

What does one say to the man who holds her husband's beloved heart in his chest?

What am I supposed to say to this person, this faceless man, who is by all accounts a complete stranger but who feels closer to me than anyone else in this world?

He has what I want. He has what I *crave.*

He has a piece of *my* heart inside of him.

I enlarge the little window that hosts my response, worrying my lip between my teeth as my brain scrambles to assemble words and coherent thoughts. And then my thumbs start swiping at the digital keypad, transmitting a frenzy of feelings.

> *from: Magnolia <greenmagnolia@gmail.com>*
> *to: Zephyr79@gmail.com*
> *date: Apr 25, 2021, 10:33 PM*
> *subject: Unperfect*
>
> *Zephyr,*
>
> *I'm sorry it took me so long to reply. I was trying to find the perfect words, until I realized…you're right. There's no such thing as perfect. There are only words and what we take from them. So here are the unperfect words I have for you today.*
> *Grief is a mechanical bull.*
> *You can hold on as tight as you can with white-knuckled fists, clenched teeth, and tears biting at your eyes, but you're destined to lose your grip. You're going to get thrown.*

And when you hit the ground, it's going to hurt like hell.

People will try to help you up, tell you it's okay, encourage you to hop back on and try again.

So you'll try again, expecting a different result or, at the very least, hoping that you can hold on a little tighter this time—stay on a little longer.

But you'll still get thrown. And it will still hurt.

I think the key to healing is accepting that your grief isn't going anywhere, then getting back on the bull anyway. One day, you'll start to enjoy the ride more than you'll fear the anticipation of the inevitable fall.

I can't wait for that day.

Magnolia

I hold my breath, squeezing the phone in my hand as I click send.

And then my heart starts to thump erratically when I notice the little dot by his name turn green, alerting me that he's online. He's probably reading my email right now.

Something about that feels so…intimate.

My feet tap the wood planks beneath my kitchen table as I wait for him to respond, my palms sweaty, my chest rattling with suspense. I wait a few minutes, then a few more, almost ready to turn off my phone and call it a night, when a little message box pops up, and my breath catches.

Zephyr: I think you meant "imperfect."

I blink at the response, frozen. Mentally tongue-tied. Those five words hang between us, nearly palpable, something I can almost reach out and touch. With the email correspondence, there was a bit of a disconnect—room to pretend.

The imaginary Zephyr and his make-believe heart.

But *this*, this instant messaging, this live conversation…it all feels too *real*.

There's a bitter sting in the back of my throat, and I notice that my hands are trembling as I hold the phone a few inches from my face.

Think, think, think.

Words.

I need words.

I swallow back the sting and the residue it leaves behind, then type out a rambling reply.

Me: I didn't. Unperfect and imperfect are both accurate and carry the same meaning, but unperfect is less recognized. It's overshadowed by its prettier, shinier counterpart, and I can't help but relate to that. Everything deserves a chance to make a comeback, you know?

A heartbeat skips by before his response comes through.

Zephyr: Touché.

It only takes one more heartbeat for me to realize that I'm smiling.

7

PARKER

D ANCING IN THE LAKE."

I find myself watching her again, elbow to knee, my chin propped up by the heel of my hand. Her heartbreak is tangible, engraved into her voice, carved into her skin, and coiled around every piece of her like barbed wire.

But something about her looks different today, and it pisses me off that I even notice.

It pisses me off because that means I've been paying attention to something other than my own hollow misery. Something other than my cemetery of scars.

Her spine is straighter, her eyes brighter. There's color in her cheeks.

It's almost as if she's getting something out of this charade.

Ms. Katherine offers a simulated smile, head bobbing slowly. "That sounds wonderful, Melody."

Melody.

Honestly, her name irritates the fuck out of me. No woman should have a name like music and a face like poetry. She's a walking contradiction.

I pull my eyes off her when it registers that I just compared her face to poetry.

What the fuck?

Leaning back in the chair, my teeth grind together so hard, I'm pretty sure I might pop my carotid artery. But I can't stop my gaze from trailing back to the curious blond when she continues to speak.

"My father used to take me down to Delavan Lake when I was little. The water would frighten me, and I wasn't a very strong swimmer. I would just kind of tread along the shallow end, wishing I were brave enough to join my brother and his friends," Melody explains, the hint of a smile tugging on her lips. She pauses for a moment, lost in some kind of idyllic reverie. "One day, I had this mini meltdown in the sand, frustrated, angry at myself for being too scared to swim. So my father told me to dance instead. He said there was nothing scary about dancing."

My eyes flick over her face, my jaw still rigid, molars aching. She fists the hem of her tunic between tight fingers, a conflicting mix of liberated and timid, as the members of the circle watch with interested stares. Some even have tears in their eyes.

Dumb.

"Did you dance?" the shrew probes.

Melody finishes with a soft nod, clearing her throat. "I danced. I danced for a long time, until the sun started to set over the lake and the water turned orange. I danced until I could swim."

"I think that's a pretty incredible metaphor for life, don't you think?" Ms. Katherine offers with a soothing lull to her tone. "I really love that, Melody."

Gag me.

I'm inclined to say something, to poke holes in that foolish metaphor, but the words are cut short when Melody twists her head to the left and our eyes meet.

And then she fucking smiles at me.

The gesture procures a frown between my eyebrows. I'm confused as to why she's smiling at me, confused as to why she's smiling *at all*. But even my scowl doesn't hamper the way her lips curl up, the way her nose crinkles slightly, or the way the green flecks in her eyes spark to life with something akin to benevolence.

It's not pity. Pity I'm used to—pity I can do. It's not any kind of come-hither advance either.

I can easily transform those things into more bitterness and hostility.

I'm accustomed to vapid, brainless women trying to stick their claws in me, trying to lure me with their coy words and flirtation, just because my physical appearance exceeds social standards. They have no idea the ugliness that dwells inside or what lurks within the shadows.

I look down at the floor, breaking contact and running my tongue along my top teeth as I mentally retreat from the unfamiliar exchange. Refusing to humor her with any more attention, I remain zoned out and focused on the wall in front of me for the remainder of the meeting.

"I want to remind you of the importance of Lifelines," Ms. Katherine announces before wrapping up this ridiculous waste of time. "If you haven't connected with anyone yet, I encourage you to take the opportunity to get to know your fellow survivors. It's advised that you seek out a same-gender Lifeline. Build that connection, create that link. You never know when you might need it."

Ah, yes. *Lifelines.* It's similar to having a sponsor, like in AA, only no one is more progressed or further along in the healing process than the other. It's an arranged, mutual commitment between two complete strangers, where they are expected to reach out to one another if any suicidal tendencies emerge. If the desire to die becomes too tempting.

It's utter bullshit.

If you can't decide for yourself that you want to wake up the next morning, Robert at the car dealership sure as fuck isn't going to convince you to step away from the edge of the tall cliff.

People begin to disperse, and I bestow a quick glance to my right and catch Emo Chick conversing with the new girl, discussing Lifelines and hamsters and a bunch of shit that is of zero interest to me. Taking that as my cue, I raise from my seat and stalk toward the exit, eager to get the fuck out of this special level of hell.

"Parker."

A soft voice meets my back, giving me pause, causing my legs to still before I reach the double doors. I'm not used to hearing the sound of my own name, mostly because no one is ever around to say it.

Just Bree.

I don't turn around right away, but I feel her body heat closing in. Radiating into me like fucking sunshine.

I hate sunshine.

"Sorry," she says, coming up beside me until I finally pivot toward her and we're face-to-face. "I brought you something."

The fuck?

That frown is back, that frosty scowl that would send most people running in the other direction but doesn't seem to have the same effect on her. "What?" I say the word like I didn't hear her. Maybe I didn't.

"I brought you something," she repeats, blinking as she looks up at me, her petite frame hardly coming up to my chest. Melody falters briefly, almost as if her eyes are stuck to me, then clears her throat and glances down at a little gift bag in her hand. "Here."

The offering is just a blur in my peripheral as she holds it up. I don't look at it. I don't say anything either, which always makes things nice and awkward.

Melody gnaws on the underside of her bottom lip as the silence envelops us, and the gesture captures my attention for a moment before my eyes slide back up in haste as if they were scolded.

"Here, take it," she insists, shoving the bag at me.

I release a stoical sigh and snap my wrist up, curling my fingers around the drawstrings. A cupcake sits inside the decorative sack, encased within a plastic container. "What's this?"

"A cupcake." Her subsequent frown replies with *Duh, you moron.*

"A cupcake," I parrot.

"Yes, a cupcake. It's lemon-flavored cake with meringue filling and raspberry cream frosting."

Shit. That sounds kind of fucking delicious.

Luckily, I've perfected the art of indifference, so I just stare at her, the little bag dangling from one finger. "Have I mistakenly given you the impression that I like handouts? Or people?"

Melody flinches ever so slightly. "I mean, I brought one for Amelia too, so you don't need to feel special or anything. I'm a baker. It's what I do."

"A baker? You do this for a living?"

"Yes." She dips her eyes to my chest, scanning the lettering across my T-shirt, the one I didn't have time to change out of before coming to this shit show. "Are you in construction?"

"Yeah, why?"

"Um…" Melody squints her eyes, still focused on the *Denison Demos & Designs* logo across my dirt-smudged shirt. "I need some work done, actually. My dad was renovating our bathr—" Something steals her words, and she drops her chin to her chest. "*My* bathroom. I need someone to finish it."

It takes a moment for her eyes to trail back up to me, and when they do, there's a shift. The light dims and the green dulls. "You're looking to hire me?"

"I think so. Sure. If you're available."

"You're not going to pay me in cupcakes, are you?" It wasn't meant to be funny. I'm not a funny person. But Melody fucking smiles again, causing my glower to reappear, an overcast sky to her sunshine, and I shuffle backward, gaze lowering to my sawdust-speckled work boots. "Fine, okay. I'm pretty busy right now, but I'll take a look at the schedule."

And then I turn and walk away, not giving her a chance to respond, although I think I hear a faint "thank you" filter out the door, and it follows me to my truck.

I feel on edge as I settle into the driver's side. The gift bag is still laced through my fingers, so I toss it onto the passenger's seat to join my hoodie and stray tools. That's where I plan to leave it as I rev the engine, but I falter, glancing to my right and eyeing the treat.

Damn it.

Two seconds later, I'm digging into the bag and pulling out the cupcake, finishing it in just two bites.

And it's really fucking good.

I'm up early the next morning, chugging down a cup of black coffee and pouring kibble into a metal dog bowl. Walden totters over to the corner of the kitchen, his cloudy eyes shifting between me and his breakfast. The red ball sits dormant in the middle of the floor after another failed attempt at fetch, and I eye it with disdain.

"Eat up," I tell the dog, but he only stands there and stares at me, causing me to wonder for the millionth time if he's going deaf or if he's just real stubborn. "Or don't. I don't like being told what to do either."

Filling my cheeks with air and blowing out a hard breath, I snag a granola bar for the road and make my way out of the house for a job. The sky is blooming with bright oranges and fuchsias, lighting up the treetops, sunbeams on evergreen. It's not something I usually notice, but it gives me pause today as I hesitate beside my truck, squinting up at the first blush of dawn. A peculiar feeling sweeps through me, a quick shot of warmth to my veins, and I find myself thinking about my father and his daylilies.

Fleeting beauty.

My brows knit together as I shake my head, pulling my gaze from the painted sky, and it's then that familiar tires roll into my driveway, gravel and stones crunching beneath the wheels.

Bree parks diagonally, jumping out of the SUV in her scrubs and wild hair, her door hanging open as she jogs over to me. "I'm glad I caught you." She beams, her voice an octave higher than usual as it penetrates the music blasting from her Bluetooth. Kelly Perry or something. "Off to the Jameson's? The third floor reno, right?"

"Yeah." I sniff, tossing my keys into the air. "That for me?"

Bree holds up a plastic grocery bag. "Yup. Lemon poppyseed muffins, your favorite. Plus, dental sticks for Walden because his breath is bordering on toxic and a new tool belt I got on sale. Yours is looking rough."

I glance down at my belt, thinking it looks just fine. "I like this belt."

"So did I. Twelve years ago." Bree steps forward, handing me the bag. She wavers when she catches me momentarily spaced out, my gaze pointed over her shoulder, then she follows my line of sight. "Pretty sunrise today, huh?"

I blink away the colors. "Not really."

"You're such a Scrooge. You'd have the women lining up at your door if your face didn't permanently look like you scheduled a root canal, colonoscopy, and vasectomy all on the same day."

"You know I don't like women."

Bree scoffs at that. "I know you like to tell yourself that. Breaking news: I'm a woman, and you love the crap out of me."

"You're an alien," I say, dismissing the idea and folding my arms over my chest, the bag of goodies dangling from my grip. "Possibly a robot. Did you seriously come all the way out here at six a.m. to drop off stocking stuffers?"

"My shift starts in an hour. You're basically on the way."

"Bullshit. I'm eleven miles in the opposite direction."

"Yeah, well, I guess I just love the crap out of you too."

A sigh filters out, and I wish I could return the sentiment match the tenderness of her words and the humanity warming her brown eyes, but that's not me. I'm not wired that way, and she knows that, so she just gives me a light punch to the shoulder and trudges backward.

"Keep me updated on materials," Bree says. "I can order more boxes of the walnut flooring on my lunch break."

"Yeah, okay," I shoot back. Before she disappears into her car, I call out, "Hey, can you text me another copy of my jobs lined up for next week? I need to squeeze in a bathroom remodel."

"Talking directly to the customers? Shit, little brother. There's hope for you yet." She grins, then adds, "But don't overdo it—the last thing we need is another hospital stay. You're busier than usual this year."

"Tell me about it. I've been pissing sawdust since March."

Bree's laughter rings loud over the music as she hops into her SUV and backs out of the driveway, a happy little wave sending me off before she vanishes down the dirt road.

There's hope for you yet.

A grating huff passes through my lips as I spare the rising sun a final glance and climb into my pickup truck.

I'm on my knees pulling up carpeting, staples popping up from the subfloor, thinking this is the worst fucking part of the job, when my phone vibrates in my rear pocket.

Leaning back on my haunches, I swipe the back of my wrist over my sweat-lined brow because it's hot as shit up here on the third floor, then reach behind me to fetch my phone.

A familiar name stares back at me.

Magnolia: I'm not sure where you live, but I'll assume you're relatively local to me given our circumstances. If that's the case, I have to know... did you see the sunrise this morning?

I purse my lips together, rereading the message, then I slip my phone away and smooth the dark tufts of hair back from my forehead. Adjusting my tool belt, I shuffle out of the room to find a bathroom. Activity buzzes two floors below me, some prim housewife making plans for a lavish tea party or something. Pretentious bullshit.

Eyes casing my surroundings, I see what looks to be a washroom down the hallway to the left, so I head toward it. But when I peek through the crack in the entryway, I'm startled to find a little boy sitting at the foot of his bed, knees drawn up, face buried between them.

He's rocking back and forth, muttering something into the valley of his kneecaps.

The image sucker punches me. I'm thrown back in time, locked in that dark closet, huddled up and petrified in the exact same position.

"Zephyr. Zephyr. Zephyr."

My throat tightens up like I've coiled a noose around my neck, and my lungs burn, crying out for air. The little boy looks up then, sensing my presence, hearing the pained gasp that must have escaped me, and our eyes lock from a few feet away. Tearstains track down his chubby cheeks, winding through the assortment of freckles like connect-the-dots. There's a frightening familiarity shining back at me, almost like I'm looking into a mirror, a time machine, and it makes my stomach stagger with unease.

"I'm sorry," he croaks out, an apology for something.

Always an apology.

"You're good. I was just looking for the bathroom."

He sniffles, squeezing his little legs to his chest as he blinks back tears. "There's one on the second floor. It smells like old lady perfume."

"Old lady perfume?"

"Yeah, like my grams."

My lips twitch. "What's your name?"

"Owen." The boy relaxes a bit, his knees straightening until his legs dangle off the edge of the bed. He looks young, maybe seven or eight. But his eyes tell me he's seen more than the average kid his age. "What's your name?"

Hesitation grips me. I don't like sharing things about myself—even my name. "Parker."

"Hi, Parker." A little smile forms on his mouth, something innocent. Something that hasn't been stolen from him yet. "Will you be back?"

I nod. "Yeah. I'll be back."

We share a final exchange before I dip out the doorway and traipse back down the hall to the staircase. I hesitate on the landing, my jaw taut, my teeth clenched together, then fish through my pocket for my phone.

Opening Magnolia's message, I finally send a reply.

Me: I did see the sunrise. But I don't think I saw what you saw.

8

MELODY

Me: QOTD: Pineapple on pizza? This could potentially be the turning point for us, so choose wisely.

Zephyr: It's trash. That isn't a matter of choice—only fact. But pickles are a different story.

Me: You passed. I'm just going to sit back and relish in your answer.

Zephyr: Punny.

Me: I think you meant cheesy. 🍕

Zephyr: Also punny.

Me: The best puns come in pears.

A SMILE STRETCHES AS I CURL INTO THE CORNER OF THE COUCH, PULLING my ankles up beside me. I nibble my lip, sending him one more message.

Me: Did you see the sunrise this morning?

Zephyr: I did. But I don't think I saw what you saw.

A sadness sweeps through me, as it always does at his reply. I've asked him that question every day for the last ten days, and his response hasn't changed.

I flinch when Leah slides down the couch and peers over my shoulder, trying to sneak a peek at my messages. "Girl, you have that look on your face. Who are you talking to?"

"What look?" I wonder absently, closing out my email chat.

"That look I haven't seen in a long time."

This catches my attention, and I'm certain "the look" promptly fades. A sudden surge of guilt permeates me, as if I were just caught doing something wrong.

Was I?

Is it wrong to smile again, to feel a small weight lift with each passing day, to watch the sunrise every morning with hopeful eyes instead of an insatiable yearning for sunset?

Is it wrong to communicate daily with the man who has Charlie's heart?

Is there something wrong with *my* heart for wanting to move forward and live a life without him in it?

Leah gives a pinch to my thigh, her gilded eyes twinkling when our gazes meet. "That's not a bad thing, honey. That's not a bad thing at all."

"It feels like I'm cheating on his memory, on what we had together." My confession is heavy, enveloping us both in a dense cloud. "It feels like a betrayal."

"What does?"

I swallow. "Living."

Leah runs her palm up and down my jean-clad thigh, her softness the antidote to my thorns. "Mellie, listen to me. *Living* is the greatest honor you can give his memory. Do you really think Charlie would want you to walk around like a zombie every day, with that smile he loved so much snuffed out?"

My eyes water.

"I know it sounds cliché, but he would want you to be happy. Truly *happy*. And I think, deep down, you know that too," she finishes.

The back of my throat feels tight and prickly, like I swallowed a mouthful of needles. "I told you Charlie was an organ donor…" I begin, eyes slipping down to the little pink polka dots on my ankle socks. "I, um, located the recipient of his heart, and we've been…talking."

Leah blinks, eyebrows dipping. "What?"

"It's all anonymous. I promised him I wouldn't invade his privacy or ask personal questions. I honestly didn't think he'd ever contact me back, but…he did. And it's been helping me with the healing process."

"Babe."

Her tone is a little bit of love and a whole lot of warning. I continue to stare at my socks. "It's nothing, really."

Leah lets out a hard exhale, her lips puckering as she falls back against the couch cushions. "Your therapist and support group are there to help you heal, Mellie. This sounds…messy."

"It's totally innocent," I counter.

She spears me with a pointed look. "The fact that you need to tell me it's innocent makes me wonder."

I clench my jaw, trying not to let her words sour the little bit of joy I've managed to pull from the rubble. My correspondence with Zephyr has heightened over the past week and a half, and while our conversations are vague and casual, there is still something earnest, something deeper, hovering beneath the repartee and easy exchanges. There's good advice. There's heart.

There's hope.

And I think there's something else—a blossoming connection.

Something kindred.

Something potentially *messy*.

Zephyr strikes me as a broken soul, much like myself, only he's broken in a different way. Longer, maybe. His pieces are scattered in the wind, some long gone.

But broken is broken, and we cut ourselves the same.

Leah nudges me with her toes when she catches me zoned out, picking at my fingernails. "You know I'll never judge you, right? I'm not trying to hinder any progress you've made. Shit, girl, nothing compares to seeing you smile again." We share a tender look. "Just be careful. And don't tell West—you know he'll get all weird about it."

Speaking of West, his timing is impeccable.

The front door busts open and my brother saunters through, a little grin unfolding when he spots Leah beside me on the couch. "Morning," he mutters, kicking the door closed with his heel.

"What are you doing here?" I inquire, but it's a pointless question. West always drops by unannounced.

"Dad said to take a look at your bathroom, and I finally have some free time. The master, right?"

I frown. "I'm good, West. I hired someone already. He should actually be here within the hour."

West slips out of his shoes anyway, eyes locked on Leah. "Sweet. I'm off the hook."

"How is Dad? I need to stop by for dinner. I've been so busy."

"He's good. Still overfeeding the dog. Still pissing off Mom."

I let out a chuckle, despite the pit that forms in my chest when I think about visiting Mom and Dad. I love my parents, I love them so much, but they remind me of him. They remind me of the life I no longer have. When I look at them, I see dinner dates with Charlie, I see bonfires in their backyard, I see my wedding day, my father walking me down the aisle and my mother weeping in the front row.

I see their horrified faces when I finally woke up in that hospital bed, teetering the line between fading away forever and making a comeback.

I know I can't stay away forever, but I still need more time.

The sound of my name has me jerking my head up, pulling me from my idle thoughts and wicked memories. West eyes me from the opposite love seat, a cup of drive-thru coffee twirling between his fingers. I blink. "Huh?"

"I asked if you were coming out with us tonight. To the brewery."

"Oh."

Maybe. Maybe I can do that.

I do feel better. More composed. More...*me*.

I'm about to respond when a knock at the front door has me jumping to my feet and instinctively smoothing down my hair and adjusting my blouse. Leah sends me a curious look as I shuffle to the front entryway, clear my throat, and pull the door open.

Miserable.

He looks absolutely miserable.

I've determined this is just his face, so I hide my wince and smile at him. "Hey. Thanks for coming."

Parker's eyes hold mine, and I can't tell if they are ice cold or blazing fire. Either way, I feel a temperature shift as he stares at me. His work T-shirt is scuffed and faded, his jeans worn and hanging low on his hips, weighed down by a tool belt. Dark hair curls along his forehead, a little shaggy and mussed, giving his hard exterior a flare of boyish charm. But the rough stubble shadowing his jaw and the muscles that flex beneath the thin layer of cotton when he steps forward tell me he's all man.

"That's the arrangement."

I chew on my inner cheek when he pushes through the threshold with his toolbox and his clean, woodsy scent. "I know. But I'm sure you're busy, so I appreciate you squeezing me in."

He makes some kind of humming sound, or maybe it's a grunt, giving me a quick once-over before shifting his attention to the right. Parker's eyes drift between West and Leah as he stands there, rigid, sporting his trademark scowl, looking as if he was trying to find a church but walked into a brothel instead. He's clearly not a people person.

"Hey, man." West holds up his coffee cup in greeting. "How's it going?"

Leah sends him a little wave, her cat eyes assessing him like she's on the prowl.

Shameless.

"This is Parker. I met him through…" I trail off, remembering that I met him through a suicide prevention group, and that's probably the most awkward introduction ever. Regrouping, I clear my throat and finish, "A networking thing."

Leah mouths to me, *Sign me up.*

I feel my cheeks heat as I shift back to Parker, who towers over me like a giant shadow, dark and mysterious.

Parker blinks back at me, expression unchanging. "Bathroom?"

"Yes. Right. Follow me."

My eyes pop open over my shoulder as I issue Leah a glare of admonishment, but she only waggles her eyebrows in return. West shakes his head, bringing his coffee to his lips.

Leading Parker up the staircase to the second floor, I glance back at him with a floaty chuckle. "Sorry. That was my brother and best friend."

I'm met with another grunt-huff.

Cranky.

When we reach the top of the stairs, Parker drifts to the left, so I instinctually reach out and curl my fingers around his upper arm, guiding him to the right. His bicep ticks beneath my touch, his gaze zoning in on the contact, then flicking back up to my face before he pulls his arm free and moves around me, trudging toward the master bedroom. The pads of my fingertips tingle with warmth, so I swipe them along my thigh as I trail him.

I gave Parker the basic rundown of my renovation needs at our last group meeting, saving his number into my phone and texting him a few pictures of the unfinished job. Most of the hideous pink wall tiling has already been removed by my father, the new boxes of subway tile stacked along the wall, ready to go. White, clean, a little sterile.

Nothing that will remind me of Charlie and his bright personality or the way we would take bubble baths together in the soaking tub and make love beneath the shower jets.

Slipping my hands into my pockets, I linger in front of the bathroom, watching Parker assess the workload. "Do you think it'll look good?"

His eyes skim the space before he pins them on me. "Can't go wrong with subway tile."

"I agree. I wanted something simple…understated."

A few beats pass between us, gazes still locked, and I wonder how he always manages to say so much without saying anything at all. While I can't decipher what he's trying to tell me, I feel the vibrations of his unsaid words beneath my ribs, in my throat, and low, low in my belly.

Fidgeting under his jade stare, I'm unsure of what to say, so I just smile, bright and happy. I get the feeling that people don't smile at him often. Or at all.

Parker's jaw clenches at the sentiment. "You do that a lot."

"What?" I slink back, a little self-conscious. "Smile?"

"Yeah." His eyes narrow with a semblance of scrutiny, brows furrowing. "People smile too much. I never understood it. Smiles should be saved for things that bring us real joy, and we give them away so easily, so carelessly. To strangers on the street, to people we don't even like."

I'm not certain if I'm more taken aback by the fact that he just strung together more than three words or by the words themselves.

Or…that he's noticed me. My smile.

Parker seems to share in my surprise and quickly averts his eyes, scratching at his hair. He looks frustrated with himself—with his brief burst of vulnerability.

I blink myself from the stupor. "I don't see it like that at all. I think—"

"I'm going to get started. I'll have it done in a couple of days."

Parker disappears into the bathroom without another word, successfully shutting me down. I suck my bottom lip between my teeth, making a hissing sound, observing the way he gets right to work, kneeling down with his T-shirt riding up his back to reveal a small stretch of bronzed skin. Shaking my head, I shuffle backward until I'm moving out of the bedroom, and I can't help but wonder what his story is. What broke him. I wonder if his pieces are scattered like Zephyr's—how far they've traveled, how long he's been walking around with cracks and missing parts.

But what I've learned about broken things is that they can always be put back together. It's just a matter of how much time you're willing to put into making the pieces fit. How much patience. How much diligence.

I finally head back down the stairs, unsurprised to find Leah sprawled across my brother's lap, head perched on the decorative pillow atop his thighs.

She shoots upright when she spots me. "Girl."

Here we go.

I fiddle with the long sleeve of my flowy, white tunic. "There's no point, Leah."

"You don't think he'd be into me?"

"I don't think he's into…anyone. Or anything."

"Okay, okay," Leah breezes, nodding with consideration. "The tortured silent type. I can work with that."

West scoffs. "That was your takeaway?"

"Yes, *Westley*, that was my takeaway. Not everyone can pull off the 'drooling and desperate' angle like you can."

He tosses the pillow at her.

My eye roll is automatic as I saunter over to the couch, plopping down beside my friend. "I didn't want to say it in front of him, but I met him at Loving Lifelines. He doesn't talk to anyone. He doesn't share. I think something bad happened to him."

"Shit." Leah's eyes soften as she turns to look at me. "Maybe he needs a friend. You should invite him out for a beer with us tonight. Sometimes people just need that little push, you know? To feel included. Noticed."

"I don't think he wants to be noticed."

My response spills out unsought and candid, and it's a sad declaration.

Sad and relatable.

And then I think…

Some people don't want to be noticed, but maybe that's exactly what they need.

———————

Charlie thought I looked sexy in red.

"It's a striking contrast to your skin, like holly berries sprinkled into a winter snowfall," he told me once, always the poet. Always the romantic.

I'd wear red as often as possible because it made him happy. Cocktail dresses, high heels, barrettes, lipstick. Crimson, scarlet, roses, and wine.

The tube of lipstick slides along my lower lip, butter soft, complementing my matching maxi dress. I press my lips together, then pucker my mouth, noting how my fingers are trembling as I pop the cap back on. The reflection staring back at me is one I haven't witnessed in well over a year—face decorated in makeup, lightly curled hair, a pretty dress.

Effort.

With a quick smile at myself in the mirror, I reach for a small bag resting on the counter and make my way out of the hall bathroom. The trek toward my bedroom feels longer than usual as the sound of a power drill welcomes me like a musical score for my grand entrance. I clench the little paper bag between nervous fingers, shuffling my bare feet when Parker comes into view on the floor, installing the new bathtub.

"Hi." He doesn't hear me over the shrieking drill, so I clear my throat. "Hi," I say louder, until he lifts up on his knees and twists to face me, silencing the drill. There's a smear of pewter paint along the side of his jawline and a sheen of sweat glistening on his forehead.

Parker frowns slightly, eyeing me from toes to top. "Did you need something?"

The bag crinkles as I grip it tighter. "I, um…well, I just wanted to see if you…" I trail off, biting on my lip. Parker's eyes narrow as my thoughts race, almost like he's trying to read them before I can spit them out. "I was wondering if you wanted to go—"

"Don't. You're just going to embarrass yourself."

His unexpected words cut me off, rendering me silent, save for the tiny gasp that escapes and joins the heaviness now hovering between us. I'm certain my cheeks are flushed as red as my dress. "Excuse me?"

"If you're about to ask me out, I'm saving you the trouble. Just don't. I'm not interested."

"I wasn't…" I'm stunned, my legs starting to quiver, my tongue tying into knots. Is he for real? What an *asshole*. "I wasn't coming on to you."

"No?" Parker stands slowly, flicking wood shavings from his work pants. He sighs, a little exasperated, his eyes skipping around the bathroom before they finally land on me. "You're standing in front of me all made up, wearing some kind of fuck-me dress, looking nervous as shit. I'm not an idiot, and I'm not interested."

I feel myself shutting down, inundated by the cruelty of his words and the acidity in his tone. Bitter and venomous. His light green eyes are swimming with something…*repugnant*. An eerie juxtaposition to the beauty of them.

A *fuck-me* dress? What the hell?

I'm torn between being outraged and throwing this bag at his face, and bursting into tears. "That's bold of you to assume. You must have a very high opinion of yourself."

"Not really."

"So you just enjoy being mean, then? Tearing people down when they're trying to be nice?"

Parker hesitates before glancing my way. "Just people like you."

"People like me," I echo softly.

I can't help but study him through brimming tears, desperate to expose what lies beneath the anger and the rough foundation. I've never responded well to negative people—I gravitate toward kindness, smiles, positive lights. People like Charlie.

And when my own light dimmed and my smile waned, it only intensified my increasing feelings of despair. My grief was turning me into something I loathed.

I was that negative person. *I* was the thing people like me avoided.

My eyes dip down to the carpet when his sharp stare becomes too overbearing, and I determine his walls are far too hardened for me to poke through. "I wasn't making a pass at you," I mutter gently, swallowing down my own anger. "I assure you I wouldn't be trying to seduce a man I just met in the bedroom I shared with my deceased husband."

Parker's silence has me glancing up, catching the wrinkle that creases his brows, the tiniest indication that he's listening. He's waiting for more words.

"I was inviting you out to the brewery tonight," I continue, the paper bag now clutched between two hands, crumpled tight. "There's a group of us going. Nobody you would know, of course, but I wanted to extend the offer. I thought maybe…maybe you could use a friend."

His frown deepens, his grip on the drill tightening. Tension rolls off him in waves. "I don't need any friends. I like being alone."

"Do you? Or are you just more comfortable with it?"

"What does that matter?"

I force a smile, the smile that seems to irritate him somehow. The smile I offer so easily—so carelessly. Then I step forward, pushing through the bathroom threshold and setting the little bag beside him on the sink. "People like me might not be so different from people like you."

Something flashes in his eyes, something fleeting, and he stiffens, his gaze drifting to the bag, then back to my face. We're only inches apart now, and I feel his warmth, I feel his heat. He's not as cold as he appears to be.

Parker remains silent.

Unmoving.

He's watching me—waiting for what I'll say next, what I'll do.

So I do what I do best.

I leave him with another smile and exit the bedroom.

9

PARKER

NINE YEARS OLD

I DON'T LIKE IT HERE.

I think I'm supposed to. I think I'm supposed to feel grateful and happy that they rescued me from her. That they found me curled up in that closet one day, so thirsty and weak, and saved me from my brush with death.

But...have I really been saved?

Is being transferred from one horrible place to another actually being saved, or is it just a different kind of pain?

I don't get burned anymore, so that's good. I'm happy for that. I don't have to worry about the cherries of a cigarette scalding my belly and chest, making me squirm and scream until I almost faint.

My mother would always laugh at me. She'd say I sounded like a squealing pig, and then she'd hit me to shut me up when I wouldn't stop crying.

The memories are still fresh, still vivid in my mind.

I sit on my creaky mattress on the floor with only a thin blanket to keep me warm. It's itchy, and I wonder if there are bedbugs crawling all over it. Dipping dirty fingers underneath my T-shirt and lifting it up, I inspect the marred flesh that lies beneath. Some of my burns are still fresh, still red and swollen. Some are faded scars, only a memory.

I remember every one of them.

"Ewww! You look gross!"

A young girl named Gwen pokes her head into the room and points at me. I drop my shirt quickly, embarrassed that she saw my wounds. My horrible truth.

"You look like a gargoyle," she snickers, covering her mouth with her hand to hold back more giggles. "You should never take your shirt off."

Tears prickle my eyes as I watch her skip away.

There's so much noise on the other side of that cracked door. So many kids chasing each other through long hallways, tattling and bickering. Laughter and friendships. I can't relate to any of it. I have seven foster siblings, and no one really talks to me. No one notices me. I arrived at this house over a week ago, and not one person cares about me—not even my foster mother.

Her name is Wendy, and she reminds me of my own mother. Her hair is a reddish color, cut short and cropped, her gangly frame somehow powerful and intimidating. I don't think she drinks a lot of vodka like my mother did, but she's still cruel. She banished me to this room all by myself, saying I was trouble.

All I did was try to eat a cookie. I was hungry. My mother hardly fed me anything.

Anger boils inside me when I think about the woman who birthed me, who gained custody of me when my father passed away four years ago.

I was only five years old when my life turned into a terrible nightmare.

The only time I'm at peace is when I'm sleeping. I dream about him sometimes—my father. He was a good man, a wise man, and he taught me a lot of things before he died. He loved history and Greek mythology. My favorite memories are listening to his stories on the front porch and watching the daylilies bloom while the breeze rolled through, as our pup, Roscoe, chased his tail in the center of the lawn.

I wish he didn't die. I wish he didn't die and leave me with her.

A trail of tears inches down my cheeks, a feeling I'm used to. I cried a lot, especially when she locked me in that dark closet without food or water for hours, sometimes days. She forgot about me all the time. Mostly when she drank the vodka.

Everyone here forgot about me too.

I guess I'm just forgettable.

Swiping at the tearstains, I sniffle and lift my chin when there's a soft knock at the big wood door. I blink, wondering if it's Gwen playing a prank on me. She's so nasty, always making fun of me and calling me names.

But the person doesn't come inside, so I wait another minute before standing up on skinny legs and trekking over to the door. I'm cautious as I pull it open, afraid Wendy might see me and punish me with whips or burns.

I don't see anyone at first. And when I dip my eyes down to the floor, there's a special treat waiting for me. A cookie.

A cookie!

There, on a white paper plate, rests a yummy chocolate chip cookie.

I bend over to snatch it up, my mouth already watering. I haven't eaten since breakfast yesterday, so my belly is singing extra loud.

But…who was here? Who left the cookie?

It certainly couldn't have been Wendy. And it definitely wasn't Gwen. As for all the others, I don't think they even know I exist.

Wondering if I'll ever know, I stand up straight, backing into the room with the cookie clutched to my chest. Before I shut the door, my sights land on a figure at the opposite end of the hallway, poking her head around the corner. My eyes pop.

It's a girl. She looks a little older than me, maybe eleven or twelve. Her hair is a mess of crazy brown curls, and she offers me a little wave as I watch in curious wonder.

My entire body warms in response. My heart skips a beat. I'm not sure how to react to this, how to thank this mysterious girl for her kindness.

But she doesn't wait for an offering of gratitude. She doesn't expect anything in return.

She just smiles at me.

She *smiles*.

And I think it fills me up more than the cookie ever could.

The girl disappears then, moving out of sight behind the wall, and I stand there frozen for a moment, wondering if I'll make a friend in this scary place after all.

The thought is a comfort to me as I traipse back to the mattress and sit down, taking hungry bites out of the sweet treat, still warm from the oven.

It's so good!

I can't help but let my own smile slip out, and I don't even remember the last time I did that. Maybe with my father. Maybe it was when Roscoe was licking cherry juice off my chin as we toppled over beside the fruit tree in the backyard, then joined my father on the porch to watch the rising sun.

I used to love the sunrise. It made me feel fuzzy inside, like something magical was about to happen.

I have that same feeling right now, only it's not the sunrise. It's not even the cookie.

It's the girl. It's the girl with curly hair and a crooked smile who did a nice thing for me when nobody else cared.

Swallowing down the last bite of cookie and savoring the chocolatey taste, I let out a thankful sigh and lie down, pulling the itchy blanket up to my chin.

She can see me.

NOW

"People like me might not be so different from people like you."

I feel my limbs stiffen at her words and proximity. She sets a paper bag next to me on the new marble sink, and I spare it a glance before returning my attention to her.

Her fluffed hair and painted lips. Her citrus scent made of lemons and sunshine. Her dress that would have most men itching to know what's underneath it.

But I'm not most men, so my attention settles on her eyes.

Not the interesting shape, of course, or the deep-emerald color or the way her long lashes flutter with a conflicting mix of timidity and surety.

I'm struck by the vulnerability. The softness in her gaze.

It baffles me because I just insulted her, speared her with my hate and pent-up bitterness, leveled her with my scorn against the female species…and yet, she's standing in front of me, only inches away, all sweetness and light. Any other woman would have likely fired me on the spot, told me to get lost—possibly slapped me. I would have deserved it all, but I wouldn't have given two shits about it. I have enough jobs to keep food on my table for a long time.

Fuck, I was goddamn *sure* she was coming on to me. The amount of pathetic housewives who have hit on me during a job, gawked at me with their googly eyes, and thrown themselves at me with no shame because their corporate pieces-of-shit husbands don't know how to get them off is astounding.

What would make Melody any different?

She sends me another smile, prompting my fingers to curl into fists at my sides because I'm really goddamn irritated that she keeps doing that. I want her to leave me alone with her soft edges and sunshine smiles. I never asked for any of that shit.

I'm irritated because, for the first fucking time in my life, I almost feel a little bit…*guilty*.

Like she didn't deserve that.

Melody turns to leave, her scent a cruel reminder of her existence, and my body finally relaxes when she's out of sight. I close my eyes, trying to regain my wits, trying to calm the pressure in my chest. But I'm not calm, I'm never *calm*, and when I glance back at the little paper bag with a girly heart sticker fixed to the front that says, "Thank You," that tension instantly reappears.

I already know what it is.

Snatching the bag and blowing out a hard breath, I unravel the rumpled top and peek inside. Another cupcake stares back at me, looking just as appealing as the last one.

This one has a cherry on top.

And motherfucking sprinkles.

I toss it back onto the countertop, knowing damn well I'm going to eat the hell out of it later, and collapse onto the toilet seat, ruffling my hair with one hand.

My tools lie strewn about the new tile flooring, beckoning me to get back to work, but all I can think about is sitting all alone in that foster house, rooted to a flimsy mattress that reeked of mildew. I didn't even have a pillow. All I had were my dark thoughts and a hell of a lot of scars.

I swallow, thinking back to my years in that house.

There was so much noise, so much chaos, so many kids running round, screaming and laughing.

Nobody ever noticed I was there.

Nobody except for Bree.

As I lose myself in old memories and bleak thoughts, my eyes land on the cupcake bag again, and I grit my teeth, knowing exactly what it means.

She can see me.

10

MELODY

THE SONG 'UNCHAINED MELODY.'"

I fist the hem of my blush-colored blouse between my fingers, sinking into sweet memories. I love discussing starting points. I love acknowledging the power of simple things—things we don't even realize are important to us.

Ms. Katherine offers her kind smile, clutching the leather-bound journal to her chest. I'm not sure if she's ever even used it, but she brings it to every meeting. "The Righteous Brothers. One of my favorites."

"It's kind of old-school, I know, but my parents named me after that song. It was *their* song."

"And now it's your song," she concludes, her grin broadening.

"Yes. I guess so." A warmth sweeps through me as I recall standing on my father's loafers and slow dancing to the classic ballad in our living room while Mom made dinner in the kitchen. The savory scents of garlic, butter, and sautéed onions would always beckon us to the table before the song was over, but Dad would wave his silverware in the air, mimicking the epic crescendo at the end, and I would laugh while Mom would just shake her head at him.

I decide in that moment that I'll go visit them tonight after the meeting.

"I don't think I know that song," Amelia adds, leaning back in her chair with crossed legs. She's wearing all black like she always does, and her eyeliner is winged and purple, matching the streaks in her hair. "I'll have to listen to it."

I turn to my left, gifting her a smile. It's impossible not to notice Parker on the other side of her, bent over with his elbows to his knees, watching me. He always watches me when I give my starting points, almost as if he's soaking up every word. It's confusing.

He doesn't watch anyone else.

"You should," I tell Amelia. "It's a little dated for your generation, but it's really beautiful."

She nods, lowering her eyes and picking at her fingernails.

Amelia and I became Lifelines at a recent meeting, exchanging phone numbers and addresses. While I can't imagine ever feeling the way I did on that dark, dark night, knife in my hand, heart in my throat, I feel safer with Amelia's number saved in my phone. Desperation seeps in unplanned, blackening our veins until all we feel is…*done.*

I never want to feel done.

I'm not ready.

I know I'm not ready yet.

We take our fifteen-minute break, and Amelia leans over to me, holding out the underside of her arm. "Do you ever compare scars?" she wonders aloud, her arm twisting side to side, a smattering of scars illuminated by the recessed lighting.

Amelia's arms are usually covered by black sleeves, so I've never noticed the puckered marks underneath, alarmingly striking against her porcelain skin. I pull my lips between my teeth and shake my head. "No. That's like comparing tragedies. Pain is pain."

She smiles softly. "Can I see yours?"

"Oh, um…" Tinkering with my sleeve, I fidget in place, gripped by a wave of insecurity. I'm not proud of my scar. It's not a noble battle wound or honorable trophy. It's evidence of my weakness, my lowest point. But I nod anyway, lifting the fabric until my own scar is revealed, a jagged, ugly blemish carved into my skin by my own design. I gulp, looking away. "I'm embarrassed by it."

"You are? I think it's beautiful."

My head jerks toward her, my brows knitting together. "It's horrifying. It's…sad."

"Sad things can be beautiful," she counters. Amelia's eyes case the ghastly scar that travels midway up my arm. "Scars tell a story. We're storytellers, you and me."

The lump in my throat swells. "You did that to yourself?"

"Yeah, I'm a cutter. Most cutters try to hide their scars, but not me. Every one of these little scars tells a story," Amelia explains, her smile still etched upon her amethyst-tinged lips. "They're kind of like tattoos, you know? Only, I'm the artist. And no one really knows what they mean except for me." Her grin broadens, almost eerily. "I'm decorated in beautiful secrets."

Out of the corner of my eye, Parker shakes his head with a miserable groan that he can't quite hide. He's slouched down in his seat, legs sprawled out in front of him like usual, matching his *I don't give a crap* attitude. His eyes are closed now, but his ears are clearly taking in our conversation.

Amelia notices, asking, "You don't agree, Parker?"

One eye opens, then the other, and he stares straight ahead and sighs. "I think anyone who finds pleasure in carving themselves up needs therapy far more advanced than this three-ring circus that has nearly enticed me to jump off the nearest bridge a lot more frequently than my own misery, which is literally the opposite of its purpose."

If she's offended by his tirade, it doesn't show. "Maybe cutting *is* my therapy," Amelia tells him, her inflection still soft and amiable. "Not everyone heals in the same way."

"That's not healing," he mumbles. "That's an excuse. That's a justification to remain stunted and stagnant because you're too lazy to put in the actual work to get better."

Amelia finally flinches, as if his words physically slapped her.

Parker rises from the chair, his gaze flicking to me, then back to Amelia. "There's nothing beautiful about pain and suffering. Anyone who thinks otherwise never truly experienced it."

My chest constricts with labored breaths, my throat tightening at his words. Amelia remains silent, scuffing her knee-high boots against the linoleum and avoiding my stare. "I'll be right back," I croak out, instinctually standing from my own seat and following Parker over to the snack table, where he's aimlessly spinning the little carousel of coffee selections.

"That wasn't helpful," I say, my words sharp, but my tone gentle.

"No?" Parker uses one finger to sort through the different flavors, not bothering to look over. "I disagree."

"It was harsh."

His eyes finally fall on me. "Harsh or honest?"

The question gives me pause.

Maybe he's right. Maybe some people need the kind of honesty that sucker punches you in the gut and steals your breath. The kind that enrages you. Offends you, even.

Until you put aside your ego and truly *listen*.

I nibble my lip, arms folding across my chest, our gazes locked for another beat before he pulls away and chooses a coffee flavor. "I was thinking about what you said the other day. About smiling."

Parker wavers, then pops open the top of the Keurig. "Yeah? I bet you were thinking about how right I was."

I'm almost certain there is a trace of levity in his tone. Something sort of... *playful*. But the thought alone seems preposterous, so I convince myself it was only wishful thinking. "The opposite, actually. I was coming up with a thousand different reasons to counter your theory."

"A thousand," he quips. "I'll wait."

"But I only need one."

Parker gives me his half-hearted attention, only a side-eye, but I know he's all ears. He leans forward on his palms, waiting for the coffee to dispense.

Waiting for my reason.

"You noticed it," I finally say.

Parker's shoulders tense, his head bowing briefly as his jaw clenches, then he lifts his gaze back to mine. I have his full attention now. "What does that mean?"

"You noticed my smile," I explain. "And you don't notice much of anything. You said I smiled too much—you twisted it into something negative, but you only did that because you didn't *like* that you noticed it. It made you uncomfortable. You hated the way it pierced through your heavy armor and warmed you up inside." My words and thoughts spill out completely unrestrained, and I only stop to take a quick breath. "It means I'll give away all the smiles. I'll smile at strangers on the street, at people I don't even like. I'll smile all damn day, even if only one person notices, because maybe it's all they need to feel better that day. Maybe it's what they secretly crave. Maybe it will give *them* a reason to smile...and I think that's pretty powerful."

My cheeks heat as my unfiltered truth bomb detonates between us, and Parker only stares at me—he just stares in that way that he does, where I feel utterly naked and exposed, my skeletons on full display.

But then his lips twitch, and he says, "I think that was more than one reason."

I'm not expecting that response or for that almost-playful tone to reappear, so I stand there frozen for one long moment before I manage a head shake. "It wasn't."

"It was a lot of words."

Well, crap. Now I'm pretty positive he's teasing.

And I have no clue how to handle it.

I don't know what to say. I'm all out of words.

So...I smile.

Because that's what I do best.

Parker's eyes dip to my mouth, and his gaze lingers there for a beat longer than expected. When he finds my eyes again, all remnants of humor disintegrate. "Stop doing that."

I smile bigger. "Nope."

"It's obnoxious."

"It's contagious."

"Hardly." I nudge him in the ribs with my elbow, causing him to reel back with a frown. "Ow."

"Smile."

"What? No."

"You know you want to."

"Actually...no."

My smile blooms even brighter. "Please?"

"No."

When I go to bop him with my elbow again, I'm startled when Parker reaches out and grabs me by the shoulders. His hands slide lower, fingers curling around my upper arms—not too hard but enough to cause my lungs to expel a stunned breath, my lips parting with a tiny gasp.

Parker's eyes go straight to my lips as he whispers, "Stop."

He feels so close, closer than he actually is, and I'm suffocating on his scent. Clean and crisp. My skin warms beneath his fingers, the heat traveling up my chest, my neck, and settling in the apples of my cheeks.

And then I feel it.

Something familiar yet obsolete.

A tingle.

Coiling deep down, sparking to life, and rising from the dead.

There's a séance going on inside of me.

And I think it should be a good thing, this feeling.

But I'm a little bit horrified, mostly confused, and I'm wondering why the hell he's still so focused on my mouth when my smile is long gone.

Parker blinks, his eyes skimming back up my face, eyebrows furrowing into his usual scowl, the lines in his face hardening. He releases me like I just burned him.

But I'm honestly not sure who burned who.

His Adam's apple bobs as he steps away, far away, a vein in his neck bulging. "You're like the goddamn sun," he spits out.

The analogy all but stops my heart.

"You're the sun, Melody March."

My blood freezes, a winter draft whispering along my skin and burrowing into my bones.

It's strange. It's strange how something so precious, so romantic coming from Charlie, can sound so hostile on Parker's tongue.

It's an insult.

Gathering my wits, I inhale a rickety breath and wrap my arms around myself in an attempt to subdue the chill. "Bright? Happy?" I offer, knowing full well that's not what he means.

Parker squints his eyes, taking one more step back. "Intrusive."

He levels me with a final glare, then spins around and walks out of the meeting, abandoning his coffee. Abandoning whatever the hell just happened.

I let out the breath I was holding and turn to face the center of the room, where the meeting is about to resume.

But my feet halt before they can move because I notice…all eyes are on me. Watching. Observing.

With flushed cheeks and my eyes to the floor, I slink back over to my chair and sit down. I send a quick glance over to Parker's empty seat, and I wonder.

I can't help but wonder…

What did they see?

11

MELODY

Later that night, I'm lying on my parent's rose-patterned sofa, my belly full and my thoughts scattered.

I love this couch. It's the most hideous thing I've ever seen, but I love it anyway. It reminds me of tickle fights and drippy popsicles and sick days from school, where I'd spend the whole day lounging and watching Nickelodeon.

"I'm so glad you came by," Mom says, hovering at the edge of the living room as I smile over at her. She dries her hands on a dish towel, returning the sentiment. "We haven't seen you in weeks."

My heart aches. "I'm sorry."

My mother, Claire Dahlberg, is short and stout, the laugh lines and wrinkles around her mouth a testament to her perky disposition and a clear indicator that I'm her daughter. I look just like her, with our matching smiles, green eyes, and light, light hair, our skin pearly and sallow. West looks more like our father, Lucas, his Swedish descent evident in his crystal-blue eyes and tall stature. Dad had to work late tonight and won't be home until close to midnight, so I make a mental note to swing by for another dinner date this week.

Mom props her shoulder against the wall, studying me with motherly worry. "West says you've been doing better."

My hands are perched beneath my cheek as I rest atop a decorative pillow. Our dog, Marley, an old dachshund, lies curled up at my feet. "I am doing better."

I'm not *great*. I'm not *thriving*.

But I'm better.

And better is better.

"How are the therapy meetings going?" she wonders after a thoughtful sigh.

My cheeks grow hot when the first thing that pops into my mind is Parker and our strange altercation this evening. I should be thinking about the starting points, or Ms. Katherine's kind smile, or Amelia's sad stories, or Robert's brush with death when someone lost control of a Civic and almost flattened him.

But all I see are Parker's flaming green eyes and the feel of his fingers curled around my biceps. All I smell is his earthy shampoo and body soap. All I hear are the thunderous heartbeats in my chest when I felt it.

The tingle.

Swallowing, I shift on the sofa and avert my gaze. I can't tell my mother any of that. I don't even understand it myself.

Parker is a jerk. A closed-off, emotionally stunted jerk who probably spits on my cupcakes before tossing them to the ground and smashing them beneath his dirty boot.

It was just a fluke.

"They're going good."

So lame but so safe.

Mom sighs again, then shuffles back into the kitchen with a nod. Restlessness claims me within moments, and I pull out my cell phone. I'm prepared to Facebook scroll when I notice the little green dot by Zephyr's name as I do a quick check of my email.

He's active.

I'll take that as a sign.

Me: What are you doing tonight? Nothing too specific, obviously, but I need to know you're out there killing it—unlike me, who is wallowing on her parents' ultra-90s couch with food regret, mismatched socks, and an overwhelming desire to watch "Are You Afraid of the Dark?" reruns.

Not thinking he's going to reply right away, I set my phone down on the little side table next to the couch—the same old oak table I remember my parents picking up at a garage sale when I was seven or eight.

There are rooster drawer handles.

Smiling to myself, I ponder whether or not Zephyr will even know what television show I'm talking about. I've been trying to figure out what the seventy-nine in his email address alludes to, and birth year is statistically the most probable. That would make him…forty-two.

I'm startled when my phone instantly vibrates, and I snatch it up, my eyes scanning the reply.

Zephyr: I'll sound a lot cooler if I lie to you.

A grin pulls at my lips.

Me: Fair enough. I'm expecting gold now, though…no pressure.
Zephyr: I'm fantastic under pressure. Picture this: Gloucestershire, England, UK.
Me: Fancy.
Zephyr: I know. But it gets better…there's cheese.
Me: Cheese?
Zephyr: Yeah. A nine-pound wheel of double Gloucester cheese.
Me: The mental image is a bit unclear and also bizarre. Go on.
Zephyr: It's a race down Cooper's Hill. There's danger, intrigue, steep hills, stones, and sharp objects. The speed of the cheese is harrowing at best.
Me: The speed of the cheese? I thought you were eating the cheese.
Zephyr: No. I'm rolling the cheese. It's a cheese-rolling race, and it's highly competitive.

A laughter-infused snort escapes my lips, and it takes a moment to gather my bearings.

Me: I'm dying over here.

Zephyr: I hope not. Who will celebrate my victory when I become the cheese champion?

Me: Stoppp. I can't stop laughing. What do you even win?

Zephyr: I'm not sure. Google hasn't told me that yet. But I really hope it's cheese because I'm suddenly hungry.

My smile is so wide, my cheeks ache.

Me: That was great. I feel better about my inadequate life now.

Zephyr: I'm here to help.

Chewing my cheek, I debate my next reply. While I enjoy our light and witty conversations, part of me is craving more. I promised I wouldn't ask him anything personal, but…

Me: Hey. Can I ask you something?

There's a brief pause that has me fidgeting beneath Nana's lime-green quilt.

Zephyr: I never understood that question. Can you? Obviously. Will I answer to your heart's desire? Inconclusive.

Me: Fine…I'll ask, but no pressure to answer. I just wanted to know… how is your new heart? What's it like?

I wait.

I wait some more.

Anxiety surges inside me, and I wonder if he'll ever respond.

Shit.

Maybe I crossed a line.

"Did you want dessert?"

Shutting off my phone, I sit upright on the couch, watching Mom approach from the kitchen. "Oh, no thanks. I was actually going to head out. I'm drowning in my own desserts at home."

That's code for: *It's hard to be here. Conversations are difficult. Sitting in this living room without him makes me want to jump off the roof.*

But I can't tell her any of that, so I just smile my farewell.

I'm good at that.

I'm sitting with my car in park, waiting for a freight train to pass through, when I notice my phone light up from the passenger's seat. Thinking it might be Zephyr, a little zing of anticipation shoots through me and I snatch it up, checking my notifications.

Only, it's not Zephyr.

My stomach drops when the name stares back at me: *Eleanor March.*

Charlie's mother.

I haven't spoken to Charlie's mother since the funeral. Her heartbreaking wails still rattle my eardrums whenever it's too quiet. I still see her swollen, lifeless eyes whenever I close mine. Sometimes I feel her stiff embrace as I collapsed into her arms in front of his casket, ambushing her with my grief and despair, soaking her dress with a cataclysm of tears.

And I still feel the way my skin prickled with goose bumps and dissolution when she let me go.

She *let me go.*

I needed her then; I needed her more than I needed air. Eleanor March was my final link to the biggest piece of my heart, and I think that's why I never made any progress in my healing. Losing her was like losing Charlie all over again.

Every day that she shut me out was just another day he died.

My hands begin to quake as a torrent of rainfall blurs my windshield, the wipers hardly able to keep up. I open her text message, my throat burning, my ribs aching with the weight of my heart.

Eleanor: You're a wicked girl

I blink, and then I blink again. I'm having trouble processing the four words glaring back at me. I don't understand what they mean. Did she text the wrong person?

No.

No, these words are meant for me.

She hates me.

She hates me.

A sob pours out of me, and I don't even notice the train has passed, even when cars begin to honk from behind me, demanding I move. But they don't know that I'm frozen, suspended in disbelief, so I just reread her message over and over again, crying harder, sinking further into darkness and self-loathing.

I'm a wicked girl.

Horns blare, people yell through their windows, cars swerve around me, but the only thing that registers is my cell phone vibrating in my grip when her name lights up the screen.

She's calling me.

And I know I'm in no state to answer. I'm parked in the middle of a rainy highway at nine p.m. with vomit in my throat and ice in my lungs, but I answer anyway because emotion is always mightier than logic.

"H-Hello?"

My voice is a pathetic quiver, and Eleanor's is slurred and spiteful. Her hate rings out through my Bluetooth and buries me alive. "I wish it were you," she rasps.

I clasp a hand over my mouth to keep the sobs from pouring out, but all they do is erupt inside me, turning everything to ash. "Me too," I croak.

Me too.

She's drunk—I think she's drunk, but I'm not sure if she's intoxicated from alcohol or grief. Eleanor lets out a painful moan, then goes quiet for a beat before repeating, "Oh, how I wish it were you."

Her confession blankets me in heartache, so I curl into myself. "Why are you saying this? What did I do?"

"You stole from me, Melody, and I hate you for it."

I sniffle and hiccup, trying to understand, trying to comprehend why she feels this way.

My relationship with Charlie's mother was always strong—or so I thought. She made me feel warm and welcome, just like her son had. But something changed that day, the day the sun died, and everything shifted. I felt her animosity toward me. I felt her blame like I felt his loss.

It was all-consuming.

I just never understood *why*. It wasn't my fault. It was a horrible, unfair accident that debilitated me just as much as it destroyed her, but it wasn't *my fault*, and I would take Charlie's place in a heartbeat if I could.

God, I wish I could.

I'm about to counter her words, tell her that makes no sense, insist that I did nothing wrong…but all I can do is mutter a weak, "I'm sorry."

There's a prolonged pause, riddled with so much left unsaid. So much baggage and loss and irreparable damage. So many things I *wish* she would say. But she only whispers, "So am I."

And then the line goes dead.

I sit there for a moment, staring out through the rain-laden window, listening to the wiper blades squeak against the glass. My throat feels raw, my skin crawling with penitence.

Am I responsible?

Am I to blame for Charlie's death?

I chose the restaurant that night. I chose the time. I chose to stay for dessert, even though Charlie was eager to get home and celebrate in the privacy of our own bedroom.

I didn't run fast enough. I didn't scream loud enough.

Maybe I didn't give him enough reason to hold on.

I decide to mull over my impossible regret at a local dive bar a mile up the road, sucking down shots of tequila as if they might fill the empty holes inside of me. They don't, of course, but they do numb the pain, and that's a start.

Hobbling off the barstool over an hour later, I teeter on both feet, slinging my purse strap across my shoulder.

The bartender eyes me warily, swiping up the cash I left for her. "You have a ride, right?"

I blink, her question registering like slush.

She leans forward on her arms. "Do you have a ride home, honey? Want me to call an Uber?"

"I, um…" I shake my head, and the action prompts little stars to dance behind my eyes. "I have a ride. Thanks."

Not waiting for her reply, I traipse out of the bar, swaying as I push through the doors and head out into the rain. I slip into the driver's seat of my Camry, trying to find the keyhole and missing multiple times. My brain is foggy, my movements sluggish.

This is stupid. Call an Uber.

Hesitation seizes me, and I close my eyes.

Stupid or not, I do it anyway, because the alcohol and anguish are screaming at me to drive, telling me that nothing fucking matters.

Nothing. Fucking. Matters.

I step on the gas and peel out of the parking lot, tires and heart screeching in my ears. My vision is blurred by the downpour and pool of tears coating my eyes, headlights resembling little lightsabers as they zoom past me. Grasping for a semblance of reason, I jerk the steering wheel onto a desolate dirt road and take the long way home in an effort to stay away from other vehicles. It's just me and my sadness now, fighting off rain clouds and regret.

As I speed down the deserted road, gravel kicks up, clanking against steel, and a tall tree comes into a view a quarter mile up. It's big and solid. The impact would be devastating.

It probably wouldn't even hurt.

My shoe pushes on the gas pedal, the engine revving and the car careening toward the tree.

You're a wicked girl.

I hate you.

I wish it were you.

Her cruel words push me forward, and I scream, loud, hysterical, desperate, gaining speed, getting closer…

And then I feel a shift. My thoughts mutate into something else.

I can almost make out an orchestra of violins playing in the distance.

I feel water lap at my skin as I dance in the murky lake.

I hear my father's laughter rumble through me as "Unchained Melody" sings through the record player.

Squeezing my eyes shut, I slam on the brakes so hard, the car spins out, tires squealing out of control, until I come to an abrupt stop, half-stuck in a muddy ditch.

I'm not ready.

I'm not ready.

I'm not ready.

My frantic breaths mingle with the sound of rain against glass, and I feel a breakdown crawling up my throat, ready to combust.

So I do what I've been trained to do.

I call Amelia. I reach out to my Lifeline.

My fingers are violently shaking as I scroll through my contacts, eyes stinging with hot tears. I'm weeping, wilting, as I call her number over and over again.

Straight to voicemail.

No.

An ugly cry tears through me, frustration mixing with fiery rage, and I think about contacting my parents.

West. Leah.

Zephyr.

But…*God*, I can't. I can't let them know how broken I still am. I can't let them see me like this, so pathetic and lost, so stripped down to almost nothing.

Just cowardice and bare bones.

Heaving in another rattled breath, I keep scrolling through my contacts until I settle on his name. My thumb hovers over the six letters that are bleeding together through my tequila haze and near-death adrenaline spike. But it's the combination of those things that has me doing the unthinkable. I click his name.

It rings. And rings. And rings.

And then…

"Hello?"

There's a familiar annoyance in his tone, gruff and gritty, and it quiets me somehow. My angry tears fade into whimpers, my breath hitching as I try to catch it.

"Melody?"

It occurs to me that he's never said my name before. He's never properly addressed me, and I'm not sure what that means or why it even matters. I swallow down a dry lump and force out, "Amelia didn't answer."

A few silent beats go by, and I wonder what he's thinking, what he's piecing together from my elusive response. I'm about to explain, to let him know I'm reaching out, to tell him how pathetic and wilting I truly am, but his long sigh filters through the Bluetooth.

He understands.

He knows.

"Text me your location."

12

PARKER

I TRUDGE THROUGH HEAVY SHEETS OF RAIN, MY SHOES SINKING INTO THE MUD like quicksand.

Motherfuck.

Why am I here? Why the hell did I even answer my phone?

Melody's number was saved into my contacts from our string of messages about her bathroom reno that I completed. When her name flashed across my screen as I was finally responding to Magnolia after hours of stalling—because fuck talking about my damn heart—something in me felt compelled to pick up.

"Amelia didn't answer."

Jesus Christ.

I'm pretty sure rage is what's dragging me toward her stalled car in the middle of this fucking monsoon, soaking wet and ready to blow a fuse. Her silhouette is visible through the drenched glass, her fingers curled around the steering wheel, head bowed.

I pound my fist against the window when I approach, causing her to nearly hit the ceiling. Melody clasps both hands over her heart, scared shitless, then finally pushes the door open.

"Get out of the fucking car," I order, watching her red, puffy eyes slowly roll up to me. "Now."

Her gulp is almost audible as her throat bobs and two shaky legs step out. "I'm sorry."

I don't want her apology. I just want her to move faster.

Snatching her wrist, I pull her to her feet and yank her away from the car. She squeaks, then stumbles toward me…and it's then that I smell it.

She reeks of fucking liquor.

I drop her arm. "Are you *drunk?*"

Melody refuses to make eye contact with me and, instead, dips her chin and wraps her arms around herself like a security blanket, shivering as the rain floods her. "This is a mess." She looks up at the sky, letting the rain douse her face as she releases a pained breath. "I'm a mess."

She wobbles and sways, talking to me but looking to the stars for answers. I grit my teeth. "You're an idiot."

This gets her attention. Melody whips her head toward me, eyes narrowing with disdain. "Excuse me?"

"You heard me."

"You're an asshole," she spits out, all venom and vitriol.

"Maybe. But I'd rather be an asshole than an idiot."

Two shaky hands plant against my chest, and she shoves me backward, her cheeks flushed. "Go home, Parker. I can't believe I called you."

She storms away, feet splashing in mud puddles as she heads toward the hood of the car. I follow, still instigating. Still poking. "Yeah, not too smart of you. Then again, I don't expect much from someone who gets behind the wheel shit-faced."

"Please leave."

"I'm already here," I say, trailing her. "Trust me, the last thing I wanted to do tonight was play therapist to little miss sunshine. Poor you, right? Poor you with all of your support and fucking cheerleaders—friends, family, strangers, all flocking to the sun. It must be such a burden."

"I'm not the sun. I'm just a shadow," she grits out over her shoulder. "You don't know a thing about me."

"So enlighten me. I can't wait to hear this. I'm shaking in my sopping fucking boots."

"Stop!" Melody spins in place, visibly shaking, wet clothes clinging to her. "This is the last thing I need right now."

"Is it?"

"Yes!" she shrieks, swiping a soaked piece of hair from her forehead. "Just get the hell away from me, Parker."

I move in closer. "No."

"You're a bully."

"Keep going," I press.

Melody raises her hands to shove me away from her again, but I catch her by the wrists. She growls in protest, trying to wriggle free. "You're the opposite of me," she continues, her anger spewing out in waves. "You're cruel and hateful. Cold. You don't smile. You don't laugh."

"Keep going."

She squirms against me, still trying to free her wrists. "You disgust me."

"Keep going, Melody. Get mad. Let it out."

"I—" Her words break off, and she goes still, relaxing in my grip, and I'm pretty sure she's crying, but her face is streaked in raindrops, so it's hard to say for sure. "I...I'm not okay."

I stare at her. I stare at the way little water droplets stall on her upper lip and just dangle there, almost floating, before her tongue slips out to lick them away. My eyes lift to hers, green on green, and I can see a shift—the anger morphs into something softer. Acceptance, maybe. Possibly a revelation. "Keep going."

Fuck, I hate the way my voice cracks. And I really hate the way my fingers feel curled around her, my large palms swallowing up her tiny wrists. Delicate and breakable. She doesn't stand a chance against my iron and steel.

I let her go, my feet stepping back, but my gaze still hard and leveled with hers.

Melody's arms fall to her sides, a sound escaping her, piercing through the heavy rainfall. A laugh, a cry, a penance—its origin is unknown. "I'm not okay," she repeats, and a roll of thunder follows. "I'm still there."

"Where?" I make her say it. I make her talk.

"On that street."

"What street?"

Her gaze cuts away, landing just above my shoulder as her thoughts drift. "With Charlie."

Charlie. Her husband.

Magnolia also lost her husband, and I wonder if they grieve the same. I'm not familiar with that kind of grief, so I'm not sure if there are different types, different levels. All I know is that I'm envious of *both* of them in this moment. I'm goddamn jealous of their loss.

To lose is to have loved.

It's when we have nothing left to lose that we truly know suffering.

Melody runs both hands through her hair, smoothing back the wet strands. She's illuminated by the headlights of her car and the partial glow of the moon, shadows carved into all of her curves and crevices. Laying claim to her darker parts. "He fucking left me here alone to sift through the debris of everything we had together. And I'm not okay with that. I'm not okay with his mother calling me wicked and blaming me for his death when I was a victim too. I'm not okay with the color of the living room because *he* picked it out, and every time I stare at those rust-colored walls, I cry. I'm not okay with sleeping alone or mowing the lawn or peach pie. I'm not okay with that look my mother gets when I zone out of a conversation because I thought I heard his laugh."

She's shrinking in front of me, her weights lifting. She looks lighter somehow.

I'm no expert on living, and I sure as fuck don't have any advice for her, so I just listen.

And I think that's all she needs right now.

"I'm not okay." She keeps repeating it, making that sound again, and I think it's a laugh this time—a delirious laugh. A bolt of lightning brightens the sky just as Melody begins to climb on top of the hood of her car, shouting, "I'm not okay!"

Pacing closer, all I can do is watch while she pulls herself up straight, legs unstable, everything about her unstable, and throws her head back with another roar.

"I'm not okay!"

Melody laughs again, releasing all these feelings I don't understand. She spins around in clunky circles, arms spread wide.

I'm standing right in front of her now, nearly grazing the front end of the car. Watching. Still watching. I've been watching her since that very first day, and I haven't figured out why.

Her laughter quiets down, her arms dropping, and she whispers to the stars one more time, "I'm not okay." Then she slides down to her butt, her shoes squeaking against the hood, and leans forward until we're only a few inches apart. Words of resolution follow as she stares right at me. "But I will be. I'm not ready yet."

Despite the ice-cold rain, I feel a current of heat travel up my neck. My eyes slide down her face and land on her drenched blouse, stuck to her skin, accentuating the swell of her breasts sheathed in a black bra. They heave with every drawn-out breath.

And then I feel some kind of ancient stirring from down below.

What the actual fuck?

I don't notice shit like nice tits, or a woman's smile, or the way she smells like fucking lemonade. My biological attraction to women has always been trumped by my emotional resentment toward them. Sex isn't a part of my life—I haven't been with a woman in well over a decade, and even then, I never truly enjoyed it. It almost felt like something I *had* to do—a societal coercion.

I don't do intimacy, and sex is a breeding ground for intimacy. I much prefer my own hand whenever the itch arises, which isn't very fucking often. I just don't really care.

But I feel the itch right now, standing beneath the dark sky, breathing in her rain-soaked skin, and staring at her tits like a fucking asshole while she's in the midst of a mental breakdown. I gnash my teeth together and back the hell up, returning my attention to her face.

Her eyes glaze over when they meet with mine, maybe from the booze or maybe because she noticed my brush with madness. Maybe she noticed me noticing *her*, and that makes it all the more irrefutable.

Fuck.

There must be something in the rain tonight.

"Parker." Melody pierces through my miserable thoughts, her voice rough like sandpaper, raw from her screams. "Why did you come?"

I swallow, my jaw stiff. Everything stiff.

Damn it.

Dodging the question because I don't fucking know, I counter with, "Why did you call me?"

Her legs dangle over the edge of the hood, swinging in opposite time, occasionally grazing my wet pant legs. She gnaws at her bottom lip, glancing away. "Amelia didn't answer."

"That's not what I asked."

The rain slows as we face each other through the drizzle and humidity, soaking wet, beaten down, and watching each other with matching eyes, green and tired. Melody doesn't respond to the question, just as I didn't, but her expression shifts slightly. Her eyebrows wrinkle with an air of scrutiny, like she's trying to read me somehow, trying to piece together a puzzle. Unravel my mysteries.

It's almost as if her demons are interrogating mine and comparing notes.

The look in her eyes, the probing, invasive look, causes my defenses to flare, and a surge of anger pumps through my veins. Cocking my head to the side, I say bitterly, "Don't. Don't look at me like that."

Her brows dip farther, confusion marring them. "Like what?"

"Like I'm something you can fix."

Melody hesitates, my response soaking in like the late-spring rainfall. She worries her lip again before sliding off the hood and landing on her feet, until we're nearly toe-to-toe. Her body sways and teeters, still unbalanced from the alcohol she poisoned herself with, and she tilts her head up to meet my steely gaze.

And then she fucking smiles...because of course she does.

"All broken things can be fixed. The hard part is deciding that they're worth fixing."

She makes a little sound after the words spill out, almost as if she surprised herself by them, caught herself off guard. Maybe she never thought to apply them to her own dents and cracks. Melody stares off over my shoulder, the ghost of her smile still lingering.

But the moment is shattered when a car engine roars up, lights flashing at us, and a juiced-up Land Rover slows to a stop a few feet away. Melody jumps back, moving out of my bubble that she had no business invading in the first place, and her whole body tenses when she spots the vehicle.

She runs her fingers through her mess of matted hair. "Great," she murmurs.

The driver hops out, looking ready to kill something. "What the fuck, Melody?"

I recognize him then as the headlights brighten his silhouette against the dark night. It's her brother. He's got fury in his gait and murder in his eyes. His sandy hair flies in a thousand different directions as he stalks over to us, and I inch backward with my hands in my pockets, kind of wishing the storm would start up again, so maybe I could fall into that super low statistic of people who get struck by lightning.

"What are you doing here, West?" Melody almost tips over when her left foot sinks into the spongy mud.

"Tammy from O'Toole's called me and said you walked out of the bar plastered. Then she saw your car speed out of the parking lot. What the hell?" West suddenly seems to notice my existence and pulls his eyes from his sister, pinning them on me. A frown follows. "Aren't you the contractor?"

Awesome. I'm fucking soaked and miserable, my dick is acting up, and now we're having conversations. I blink at him, hoping my face portrays the fact that I'd rather be eaten alive by ancient scarab beetles than be standing here right now. "Yeah."

West narrows his eyes at me like he's trying to force pieces together that don't fucking fit.

"I called him," Melody says, intervening, taking her brother by the arm and trying to guide him back to his car. "It had to do with Loving Lifelines. It's a thing."

He pulls his arm free. "Why didn't you call me? Or Mom and Dad? Or Leah?"

"Can we talk at home? I'm emotionally exhausted right now."

"Do you not trust us? Are you embarrassed that you're still hurting? Jesus, Mel, we all love you. You don't need to hide from us."

Melody seems to wither, like she *is* trying to hide from him, and glances my way before reaching for her brother's arm again. "Just take me home. I'll get my car in the morning."

Pinching the bridge of his nose, West reluctantly follows her lead with a harrowing sigh. They both climb into the vehicle while I watch from the ditch, up to my ass in muddy water. The engine rumbles to life as Melody fastens her seat belt and wrings out her hair, her image hindered slightly by the rainy window. But she turns her head to look at me when the vehicle begins to pull away, tires tossing up mud and gravel, the stereo sounding through the glass with some kind of alternative rock bullshit.

I stare right back at her, our unanswered questions still hovering between us. Still lurking.

"Why did you come?"

"Why did you call me?"

I'll reckon she called and I came for the same reason our eyes always seem to find one another's, even when there's a dozen other people in the room—but I don't have a reason for that right now, so I bury those questions away with the rest of my ghosts and old bones.

And as the car peels off onto the dirt road, I catch the little smile on her face as our eyes hold tight and she mouths, *Thank you.*

Walden gets up when I trudge through my front door at nearly midnight looking like a drowned rat. The dog appears confused as hell as he stands a few feet away from me, eyes bugged out and probably judging me. The red ball hasn't moved from its place beside the couch, and his food bowl remains untouched, leading me to believe he enjoyed his night just as much as I did.

My car keys clank against the little glass table as I pull off my soggy T-shirt and toss it into the heap of other stray shirts I still need to wash. Walden stares at me, unmoving, as I saunter into the living room, bare chested and bad-tempered, but his eyes never stray from my face. They never dip any lower, and I appreciate that.

He doesn't notice my scars.

Then I scold myself because he's just a dumb dog that doesn't know what scars are, and also, he's probably going blind, so my thought process is being really fucking stupid.

Shaking my head, I reach for a random banana sitting on the ottoman and peel it, debating whether I want to head straight to bed or go jerk off in the shower because my dick is still restless and pissing me off. But I think *handling* that situation will piss me off even more since I know exactly what triggered it.

And *fuck that.*

Fuck giving any more ammo to that absurdity.

That *fluke.*

I eat the banana in three bites and glance at my laptop before heading down the hallway. My unfinished response to Magnolia glares back at me, and I hesitate, finally sighing as I make a pit stop at the rolling chair and gather my thoughts.

Words appear in the little Hangouts message box as my fingers type away, but I backspace and delete them at least five times before settling on something. As I'm reading over my reply, Walden lies down beside me with a little grumble, making his presence known, and I have to do a because he always wanders back to his dog bed after greeting me. He rests his chin between his paws and looks up at me with only his eyes.

I don't smile, even though the thought crosses my mind, but I do soften my gaze.

I see you, old mutt.

Then I click send.

Me: You asked about my heart, so here's my answer...this heart is a burden. It's a fraud. Most days I resent it and wish it had been given to a better man. A worthier man. And I know that sounds shitty because your husband is gone, and here I am complaining about my healthy, beating heart. Doesn't seem fair. But it's the truth, and I won't ever lie to you.

Before I rise from the chair and head to the bathroom, because I think I'm going to take that shower after all, I add one more thing:

Me: Unless it's about cheese rolling. That never happened.

13

PARKER

A UGUST."

Melody sweeps her hair over to one side, crossing her legs at the knee. Her voice doesn't crack or waver in detailing her starting point, and her eyes even sort of twinkle as I study her from one seat over.

Wait...*twinkle?*

No. Fuck no.

I don't notice shit like eye twinkles. I don't even fucking remember my own eye color half the time.

"Growing up, all of my friends hated August—it's hot, school was about to start, and summer was coming to an end. But I always felt like it was a new beginning," Melody explains as the rest of the group listens fondly. "Fall has always been my favorite season, and August is kind of like a prelude to colorful leaves, apple cider, and bonfires. Plus, my birthday is in August...which also happens to be National Rum Day, so it all makes sense."

People laugh. I groan.

August is the worst month. The sun is way too bright, fuck rum, mosquitoes are literally plotting their apocalyptic reign over humanity, and it's hotter than Satan's ball sack.

August can suck it.

Melody spares me the tiniest glance, lips curled up, cheeks pink, probably checking to see if I'm one of the people laughing.

I make sure my face looks extra insufferable.

When the meeting wraps up, I fucking book it, and my chair nearly tips backward as I jump to my feet and make a hurried escape out the double doors. I don't want to deal with her today. I don't want to deal with her sunny smile, citrus shampoo, and goddamn eye twinkles.

Sifting through my pockets for my keys, I half jog to my truck, eager to get the hell out of here before anyone tries to talk to me—before *she* tries to talk to me. I don't have many hobbies or interests, but if I had to put something at the top of that list, it would be avoiding people.

As I squint my eyes against the setting sun, I tug open the door to my pickup truck and attempt to dive in, but something stops me.

There's a container of a dozen cupcakes sitting on the driver's seat with a cheery little note on pink paper attached.

Of course there is.

I'm not sure what it says because I don't really bother to read it.

Instead, I turn toward the front of the building just as Melody saunters out through the main entrance, her yellow sundress billowing as a quick breeze tries to lift the skirt. She fluffs it back down and pauses her steps, her chin tipping up to meet my stare from across the parking lot. It's a brief pause, a fleeting moment of eye contact, before she resumes her pace and moves toward her Camry a few spots over—almost as if she didn't just catch me discovering her futile gift.

I follow her.

"Hey," I call out, gaining her attention before she slips inside the car. "What the hell?"

Melody falters, her hand curling around the doorframe. She watches as I storm over to her, a frown unfurling, then tucks her windswept hair behind her ear. "What's wrong?"

"Why are there a dozen fucking cupcakes in my truck?"

Her frown deepens. "You don't like them?"

"They look fantastic, but that's not the point. Why are they there?" I stop right in front of her, maybe a few feet away, but it's close enough to smell her shampoo when that breeze blows through again.

"Did you read the note?"

"No."

Melody's lips part to speak, but only a little burst of laughter spills out. "I just wanted to thank you for…last week." Her smile brightens with genuine gratitude as she glances at me. "And thank you for driving my car home that night. It was unexpected."

My fists clench at my sides, my teeth grinding together. "Yeah, well, you left the keys in the ignition. I didn't have much of a choice."

Her face falls, her smile fading, but I refuse to feel bad about it. This is better—this is so much better, this anger and resentment. It's better than whatever the hell else has been simmering beneath the surface, trying to crawl its way inside, unwanted and unwelcome.

Trespassing.

"Well, I do appreciate it."

No, Melody, get mad. It's easier that way.

"I don't need your appreciation. Or your cupcakes. Or your damn love notes," I bark back, inching closer, so she can *feel* my anger. She can soak it up and throw it back at me, just like she did last week, beneath dark clouds and furious rainfall.

I want her to throw punches, hurl her bitter words at me, *get fucking mad.*

And she does raise her hand to me, she does, but it's not a strike. There's nothing violent in the way her hand elevates and her fingers reach out, applying a soft pressure to my forearm. A gentle caress. Careful and delicate.

I rip my arm away. "Don't do that."

"I'm just—"

"I don't like to be touched."

She swallows, her eyelashes fanning across her cheekbones as she blinks up at me. "You don't like it, or you're not used to it?"

How about this: the one person in the world who was supposed to care for me, love me, protect me…abused the fuck out of me. Instead of hugs, I got hot cigarette butts to my skin, covering me in hideous scars. Instead of cuddles, I got a leather belt across my face. Instead of kisses, I got broken bones. And when I wasn't being beaten down until I went numb, I was neglected. Locked inside a dark closet with only my imaginary friend to keep me company.

I *feared* touch.

But all I say is "Both."

Melody reaches out again, to prove some kind of moot point, so I snatch her wrist before she makes contact. Her breath catches, her fingers relaxing in my grip.

"Stop," I tell her, my tone low and bordering on threatening. "You're like a lost puppy, looking for a bone. But you're barking up the wrong tree, sunshine, because I'm not your friend, and I'm sure as hell not your next fuck. So whatever hand you're trying to play, I suggest you fold now. You're in the wrong game."

She's quiet for a while, making me all too aware of the way her wrist feels tucked inside my palm. *Again.* She's always trying to touch me somehow—playful, hostile, kind. She's trying to get close and eradicate my walls. But I've been building these walls for a long, long time, and they were built to last.

Maybe that's why I'm so good at my job—at building things. I've had a lot of fucking practice.

Melody doesn't pull away from me or fire back like I want her to. I'm begging for her wrath, but she only gives me warmth. "You said I look at you like I'm trying to fix you," she says softly, her eyes scanning my face, searching for a crack. A hole. *A way in.* "You look at me like you're trying to break me."

My scowl meets her soft gaze as I release her arm, but she doesn't step back, and neither do I. It's like we're both standing at the brink of a battlefront, but I'm the only one ready to fight.

"I'm done breaking, Parker," she finishes, letting out a breath that sounds like surrender. "It's time to rebuild."

A grumble escapes me. "You can't build something from nothing."

"No one has nothing."

"That's a bullshit, privileged answer."

She surprises me by reaching for my own wrist and tugging it to her chest, and I'm too startled by her boldness to pull away at first.

Then I'm too curious.

Her heartbeat thumps beneath my palm as she presses it to her breastbone, making her point. It feels warm, like her skin. Like the color of her eyes.

Like the way the sunlight plays with her hair in a way that is gravely captivating.

It's evident insanity has possessed me once again because I make zero fucking effort to move away or tell her to back the hell off. I just stand there like a fool, my hand a centimeter away from groping her tit, while we stare at each other in the suicide support group parking lot.

Why am I not moving?

Why is her heart rate quickening?

Why is my dick getting hard?

Fucking hell.

I think the only thing that pisses me off more right now is the fact that *she* pulls back first. A look comes over her, something almost panicked, and she flees, fumbling for her car door and leaving me rattled.

"I hope you like the cupcakes," she mutters, her voice unsteady, her eyes avoiding mine. "They're chocolate cake with peanut butter frosting and a caramel drizzle."

Pretty sure my dick gets harder.

Melody spares me a final glance, her cheeks flushed pink, then escapes into her Camry. "See you next week."

The slam of her car door makes me flinch, but I still just stand there as she reverses and pulls out of the parking lot with squealing tires. I don't even have time to process that fuckery when a familiar voice has me spinning around in place.

"You like her."

Amelia hovers beside her own car, all creepy-like, probably getting ready to go haunt something, and I hold back an eye roll. "I like her as much as I like Ms. Katherine's hairy forehead mole that resembles the state of Rhode Island."

"It does, doesn't it?" She snickers, her teeth almost looking yellow against her snow-white skin. Then she sighs, leaning back against the trunk. "You must really like that mole."

"Don't you have something better to do? Occult rituals? Blood sacrifices?"

"Way to stereotype. I actually enjoy crocheting and listening to Fleetwood Mac."

"Cool. Go do that. Send my love to Pumpkin Spice."

"Nutmeg," she corrects.

I raise my hand in a "fuck off" kind of a wave and whirl around, heading toward my truck.

"You know, Parker…you don't have to be here."

My eyes roll up again when her voice meets my back. "There's someone who wants me to be here."

"Yeah," Amelia replies softly. "But I don't think that someone is who you think it is."

Her response has me turning around, my eyebrows raised in question.

She finishes with "Hint: it's the same person who is keeping you from jumping off that bridge or swallowing a whole bottle of Valium. Think about it." Amelia sends me her own wave—one far more amiable—and disappears into her car.

It doesn't take long for me to think about it, and while all I want to do is contest that theory because I like to believe that I don't give a fuck about anything, she kind of has a point.

Well played, Emo Chick.

Owen.

I'm working on the third floor reno at the Jameson property the next day, covered head to toe in sweat and sawdust, when I hear a little voice from behind me.

"Hey, Parker."

I twist around from my place on the newly installed Brazilian walnut flooring and see Owen shuffling in the doorway, his hands tucked into denim shorts. "Hey."

"You've been here a lot this week."

"I have a lot of work to do."

The little boy with auburn bangs inches forward, making footprints in the sawdust. "The floor looks nice."

Falling back on my haunches, I shrug. "It's okay. Not really my style."

"Yeah. These are the kind of floors I'll get yelled at for scratching with my race cars. I build them, you know."

"You do?"

"Yeah, want to see?"

Normally, I'd say no. Normally, I wouldn't give a crap about model cars or random kids I meet at jobs…but I'm compelled to say yes, so I do. "Sure."

Owen leads me to his bedroom, the same room I discovered him crying in my first day here. The bed is made up, decorated in a red-and-blue race-car pattern, and the border along his navy walls matches the theme. I try to think back to my own childhood room, my *real* childhood room, before she stole everything away from me, but the images are so hazy now. All I remember is a sports lamp beside my bed. It had a baseball, bat, football, and a soccer ball attached to a green base, and sometimes my father would switch the light bulb out to make it shine different colors. It would be orange during October and green in December.

Pushing aside the vague memories, I follow Owen across the room and pause beside his desk, bestrewn with all kinds of wooden creations on wheels.

It's actually really…impressive.

I clear my throat, crossing my arms. "You made all these?"

"Yep. Do you like them?" His face lights up as he reaches for a car painted red with yellow lightning bolts. "This is the Kamikaze. He's the fastest."

Owen makes a few zoomy sounds through his teeth, and I feel myself relaxing. Softening. "I do like them. You're talented."

A smile washes over his innocent face, his cheeks round and pink, his nose spattered in freckles. "Thanks. My neighbor thinks they're dumb."

"Your neighbor?"

"Yeah…Brody. He thinks I should be playing video games like the other kids, but I'm not any good at that."

"I don't care much for those either."

I've never really liked video games or watching television because my mind always wanders. Mindless activities are a cesspool for unwanted flashbacks and overthinking. That's why I work with my hands—I need to keep busy, focused on a task.

Owen's smile broadens. "You're really cool, Parker. I bet you have a lot of friends."

My body tenses, wondering how he came to that conclusion. It couldn't possibly be my dazzling smile or charming personality. "I don't."

"You don't have friends?"

"No."

"Not one?"

"Not one."

Bree doesn't count. She's just stuck with me.

Owen considers this, worrying his brows together, his tongue poking out to wet his lips. "I don't either. Maybe…maybe we can be friends?"

This fucking kid might actually raise my cold, decrepit heart from the dead. I swallow, shifting from one foot to the other. "Yeah, okay. You can be my very first friend."

Jesus, who am I?

It must be the cupcakes. She laced them with her happy sunshine juice.

"Cool." Owen beams, setting down his car with an extra bounce in his step. "I think my mom wants to be your friend too. She was watching you paint the other day."

Yikes.

"Was she?"

"Yeah, and I heard her talking about you to her lady friend. She said she wanted to take out a second mortgage on the house just to hire you as a live-in contractor. Then she did that weird giggle she does sometimes."

I almost laugh. "You remember all that? Those are big words."

"Yep. I like to listen."

Nodding, I take a quick step back and click my tongue against the roof of my mouth. "Hey, wait here. I have something for you."

"You do?"

"Yeah, I'll be right back."

A few minutes later, I traipse back up the staircase with the container of cupcakes from Melody—minus one. I devoured it in my truck the second I hopped in, and goddamn, I have no fucking regrets.

Owen is sitting on the edge of his bedspread when I return, kicking his legs forward and back. His big chocolate eyes light up, only he hasn't even noticed the cupcakes yet. He's just smiling up at me, overjoyed. "You came back."

"Of course I did. You thought I wouldn't?"

He shrugs, and it's a little dagger to my chest. I wonder what this kid has been through.

"What are those?" he wonders, his attention finally landing on the treats. His irises sparkle with excitement when he makes the discovery. "Are those for me?"

"Sure."

"Wow...thanks, Parker!"

Owen jumps off the bed and reaches for the confections, and when he takes them from me, I feel something shift. A little weight lifting. It makes me uncomfortable, unsettled even, but it also prompts me to snatch the sticky note off the top of the plastic container and stuff it into my pocket before I trudge out of the room. "I need to finish up, but I'll see you around, okay?"

He bobs his head, his lips already dusted in peanut butter frosting. "Okay!"

Once I'm alone again, about to finish up my paint job, I reach into my back pocket and uncrumple the pink paper square, then scan the girly handwriting staring up at me:

Parker—

I have my starting points.
Now, I have my turning point.
I think you saved my life that night.

Melody

14

MELODY

THIS CANNOT BE HAPPENING.

I'm standing in my kitchen, ankle deep in water and drywall, with a caved-in ceiling and a screaming Leah.

Actually, she's kind of squawking. Her arms are flapping, and she's hopping up and down, shaking insulation out of her hair while her voice shrieks in a way that does not sound human. "Oh my God! Oh my God!"

I just stand there numbly, staring up at the giant hole that used to be a ceiling, wondering if this is some kind of twisted metaphor for my life.

Twenty minutes later, West is beside me whistling his condolences as Leah recovers on my living room couch with an oversized blanket and leftover cupcakes.

"Leaky pipe," my brother says, shaking his head. "Not good."

"Not good?"

"No. Not at all."

"Thanks, West. A startling revelation."

He fills his cheeks with air and blows out a hard breath, planting his hands on his hips and gazing up. "My buddy Shane is a plumber. The best. I can probably get him out here by tomorrow."

"Does he fix ceilings too?"

"Doubt it, but I'll check. You might have to call your guy for that."

I blink. "My guy?"

"Yeah, the douchey one."

Oh. Parker.

Fidgeting, I cross my arms and pick remnants of my ceiling off my shirt-sleeve. "Maybe."

West throws me a probing glance before wading through the two inches of water in my kitchen and bending down to the lower cabinets for pots. Then he asks casually, "You sleeping with him?"

"What?" My head jerks up, my cheeks instantly flaring red. "No!"

"So, what you mean is...not yet."

Leah pipes up from the couch. "Don't be a dickhole, Westley."

"I can't believe you asked me that," I snap.

"Why? You guys looked like...I don't know, like there was something."

"Something?"

"Yeah, *something.* Don't know, Mel—that's why I asked."

My arms tighten defiantly across my chest. "Loathing and disgust are probably what you saw."

West straightens, seemingly considering my response, then quips, "Nope. Wasn't that."

"It was called: none of your business," Leah adds, gliding off the couch and strolling over to us, licking peanut butter frosting off her fingertips and making little popping noises.

"Put the claws away, Tiger." West gives her a blatant once-over, then shoots her a wink. "For the time being, anyway."

"Gross."

"Can we stop with the sexual innuendos while we're standing in my flooded kitchen?"

West demonstrates his maturity by stepping into the living room with a sly grin. "I'm just saying, if you're looking to start dating again, you should let Shane take you out. He's divorced, stable, pays his taxes. No felonies at the moment."

"I'm not looking to date."

It's the truth—*I'm not.* The thought of dinner dates, holding hands, inside jokes, all with someone who isn't Charlie, makes my insides twist with dread. It makes me *ache*.

I have no idea what my brother thinks he saw with Parker. The man is an emotionally stunted bully, void of feelings, lacking in empathy, zero sense of humor.

He's nothing like Charlie.

And I think that's why I feel so disgusted with the way my body has been reacting to him lately—all tingly and starved, like it's craving something only he can give. The way he looks at me sometimes, dark and heated, *penetrative*, sends my heart into a tailspin and my lungs into overdrive.

It's confusing. Maddening.

Parker is the opposite of me in every way, the antithesis to my very soul, and yet I'm drawn to him somehow. There's a darkness inside of him that speaks to my light. He was right when he said I wanted to fix him because I *do*. My nurturing heart wants to glue his pieces back together until he's whole again. I'm yearning to see him smile. Laugh.

To let go and feel free, even for just a moment.

And then there's a part of me that wonders if I'm just lonely, and I'm latching on to the first attractive man who walks into my life because I miss having a warm body wrapped around me. I miss strong arms holding me tight, keeping me safe and protected.

I miss intimacy.

I miss bear hugs and grand kisses.

I miss sex.

Charlie is the only man I've ever been with. I gave him my virginity and my heart beneath a starless August sky, and I never looked back.

But now I'm forced to look forward without him, and it's daunting. *Terrifying*. I don't know which way to turn because every direction feels like it drags me farther and farther away from *him*.

I'm jolted out of my musings when Leah leans in and throws an arm around me, tugging me to her. "Don't listen to him, baby girl. He's still single for a reason."

"I'm holding out for *you*, Leah."

My sigh is heavy with annoyance. "West, I don't want to date anyone. I'm not ready for that yet. Parker is just…a friend. Sort of."

Parker's words echo in my mind, harsh and haunting: *I'm not your friend, and I'm sure as hell not your next fuck.*

His words hurt, I'll give him that, but I refused to give him a reaction. I refused to give *myself* a reaction. I'm done being angry.

"Whatever you say, Mel," West says, wringing out water from the saturated towels into metal pots. "I'll call Shane and send him over to look at the pipes. If you can't get ahold of your 'sort of friend,' I'll see if Dad has some referrals to get your ceiling fixed."

I swallow. "Thanks."

West takes off an hour later after helping us unflood the kitchen, only getting into two water fights with Leah, and Leah stays behind to help me finish up. I'm shoveling drywall and insulation into garbage bags when my backside vibrates from a cell phone notification.

I can't help the organic smile from blooming on my lips when his message pops up.

Zephyr.

Zephyr: Did you know the hashtag symbol is actually called an "octothorpe"? It means "eight mystery." I feel like this needs to catch on. Regardless, it would make a pretty epic band name. This concludes my random fact of the day.

Oh, Zephyr.
My faceless friend. My anonymous confidant.
The final link to the man I love.
I whip out a quick response.

Me: Are you saying we should start a band? I'm so in. With that name, I feel like we would need eight members.
Zephyr: Agreed. And our music would need to be super mysterious. I call drums because they're loud and obnoxious.

Me: I'll take violin.

There's a pause before his reply comes through.

Zephyr: Popular instrument these days.
Me: It's so underrated. Like nitrogen.
Zephyr: Nitrogen? Explain.
Me: Oxygen gets all the cred. Nitrogen takes up three-quarters of our atmosphere, but when do you ever hear, "Nice job today, nitrogen. Well done"? Never. #teamnitrogen
Zephyr: To be fair, I've literally never heard anyone say, "Nice job today, oxygen. Well done," either. People just don't talk like that. Nice use of an octothorpe, by the way.

Leah suddenly appears over my shoulder, and I nearly hit the ceiling. Or…what's left of my ceiling.

"Is that the heart guy?"

I quickly close out the app and stuff my phone back into my pocket. "Yes. His name is Zephyr."

"Like, that's his given name?"

"No, obviously. We don't know anything about each other."

"Bummer. Sexy name." Leah leans back against my kitchen island, her fingers curling around the edge of the countertop. She tilts her head in the way that she does when she's trying to get a read on me. "What do you think it means?"

"Zephyr?"

"Yeah."

Pursing my lips, I twist my hair over my left shoulder, fiddling with the split ends I need to trim. "Do you think it's an acronym for something?"

"Ooh." Her golden eyes glow brighter, widening as her mind tries to conjure up something amazing. "Zombies Eating People's Hearts Year-Round. He's a zombie."

"That took a very dark turn."

Leah waggles her perfectly shaped eyebrows at me. "Maybe he just likes Madonna."

"Or maybe it's a code word."

"Or a *safe* word, during sex. Maybe he's a kinky son of a bitch."

We both laugh, but my laughter ebbs the moment Parker's face flashes through my mind. Because I was thinking about sex.

Damn it.

While Leah starts wiping down the countertops, I pluck my phone back out and scroll through my contacts until I find his name. I shoot him a quick message.

Me: Are you busy? My ceiling tried to kill me.

———————

"I really, *really* appreciate you coming out."

Parker plods through my doorway, stomping his work boots against my entry mat. His dark hair is a chaotic mess of overgrown waves, and his skin is scuffed with dirt and paint smudges. He eyes me with that same penetrative stare that rattles my insides, like he's trying to see beyond the words. "Yeah. Not a problem."

His gaze skims over me, and I kind of wish I'd changed out of my comfy clothes. All I'm wearing is a pair of cotton shorts and an old college T-shirt with my hair thrown up in a messy bun. But then I scold myself for wishing that—it doesn't matter. I'm not trying to impress him. "Did you just come from a job?"

"I did."

"You seem to have a good business going. I'm happy for you."

Parker's eyebrows dip as he registers my response. He does that sometimes—frowns at compliments and my smiles. Acts of kindness. At first I thought he was just an asshole, but now I'm wondering if he's genuinely not accustomed to those things.

"I like staying busy."

I flash him my teeth. "I get that. That's why I went a little overboard with my baking business. It keeps me focused. Distracted."

"They were good."

His reply takes me off guard, and my smile wanes. Did he just say something...*nice*? To me? "Oh...the cupcakes?"

"Yeah." Parker clears his throat, dipping his head toward the kitchen. "This way?"

I blindly nod, watching as he moves around me and shuffles toward the scene of the crime with his toolbox. Wringing my hands together, I follow, wondering if I should incite more conversation. More nice words. "So, um, do you live around here?"

Absolutely gripping, Melody. Great job.

"Ten minutes, give or take," he says, peering up at the gaping hole when we enter the kitchen area. "Jesus."

I wince as I follow his gaze. "I wish I had a cool story—a meteor shower, maybe a mysterious transient living in my ceilings. But my brother says it's just a leaky pipe."

Parker spares me a curious glance. "Leaky pipe sounds less life-threatening."

"Not a cool story, though," I say breezily, flicking my finger at him.

He presses his lips together, and I choose to believe he's holding back a smile.

"I'll go grab the ladder from my truck," he murmurs, his toolbox clanking against the countertop. "I can measure and shit today, then I'll be back tomorrow to finish. I have another job during the day, so it'll probably be early evening."

"That sounds great. Thank you."

Parker gives me a little nod, averting his eyes and moving around me to head out to his truck. His arm grazes mine as he passes, and I'm zapped with a shot of warmth that turns my skin flush. The fleeting over-the-shoulder look he sends me has me wondering if he felt it too.

I wrap my arms around myself, trying to scrub the goose bumps away. They are physical evidence of this *feeling*—this nagging curiosity that is quickly blossoming into something else. And maybe I should be happy about it. Relieved. It's proof that I'm still alive, that I'm capable of feeling something other than overwhelming numbness.

But truthfully, it angers me.

How dare my body react in this way? How dare it *feel?*

How dare it feel roused by a man who isn't Charlie?

My eyes trail to our wedding photo, hanging on the far wall, the one I've debated taking down at least fifty thousand times. It hurts to look at it. It hurts to see his smile, so blissful, so in love—so unaware of how swiftly our love story would be snuffed out, ending in bitter tragedy.

Tears burn my eyes, my throat stinging, so I distract myself in the kitchen and begin to bake. I try my best to ignore Parker's presence as he sets up the ladder, carrying tools and measuring equipment between his teeth. I try to ignore the way the muscles in his back pull and stretch against the fabric of his light gray T-shirt and the way a faint whiff of his shampoo or deodorant mingles with the brownie batter—something clean and outdoorsy. Organic, like the way a gentle breeze might smell way up in the mountains.

A smile pulls at my lips—*a zephyr.*

"Fucking hell."

I snap my head up from the bowl of batter, watching as Parker grumbles through the tape measure in his mouth and examines his finger. My face goes ashen when I spot the blood. "Oh my God…you're bleeding."

"I'll live." He climbs back down one-handed, holding his injured finger up to keep the blood from dripping. Plucking the tape measure from his mouth, he tosses it to the counter and moves around to the sink, mumbling, "Got a Band-Aid?"

Swallowing down the queasy feeling roiling in my chest, I meet him at the sink and snatch his hand before he dips it under the running water. "Parker, this looks terrible."

He tries to pull away. "I got it. It's not a big deal."

"Let me help, will you?" Reaching for a clean dish towel, I wrap it around his index finger and hold tight in an attempt to control the bleeding.

"I told you I don't like to be touched."

Our eyes meet, my breath sounding choppy when I inhale. "And I've been known to faint at the sight of blood."

"Sounds like you should go back to being Betty Crocker while I deal with this." His Adam's apple bobs, his entire body tensing at my nearness. "Both problems solved."

"Or you can let me help, and we'll face our fears together." I force a megawatt grin despite my nervous belly and wobbly knees, causing his gaze to dip down to my mouth with that trademark glower. When his eyes lift back up, they look darker somehow. More ablaze.

"You and your smiles…" he says in a low voice.

He's trying to project his annoyance, but I don't buy it. Applying deeper pressure to the towel, I tease, "I know they're growing on you."

"Like fungus, maybe."

"But the good kind of fungus."

"No, like ringworm."

My smile lingers as I unravel the towel to inspect his wound, noting the cloth is saturated in blood. "What the heck did you do? Does my ceiling have teeth? Maybe I'll have a cool story, after all."

"Got myself on a nail. Amateur move." Parker finally tugs his hand free of my grip and spins around to the faucet. "I'll take a bandage if you have one."

"Are you sure you don't want a ride to the hospital?"

"I'm really fucking sure."

Stubborn.

After sifting through my linen closet for bandages, I find a first-aid kit with antiseptic and gauze and carry it back to the kitchen. Parker is applying pressure with a new towel, looking massively ticked off. I hesitate for a moment before approaching, swallowing my pride and closing in on him. "Let me see."

"Will you stop?" he barks, trying to dodge me as I reach for his hand.

"I used to be a nurse."

"Really?"

Holding him steady in my left hand, I rummage through the kit for the antiseptic with my right. "No. But I've seen three or four episodes of *Grey's Anatomy.*"

My eyes flick up, and I swear to God I think I see a smile begin to surface. But he squashes any trace of it and grunts his irritation instead. "So damn intrusive."

"Like the sun, right?"

My tone is gentle and unoffended as Parker's jaw tightens, and he whispers back, "That's right."

I nod slowly, watching as the blood flow finally ebbs, and I dab the antibiotic cream onto the wound with a fresh gauze. Parker hisses through his teeth, trying to pull back, but I hold firm, knowing he could push me away if he *really* wanted to.

I don't think he wants to.

"My husband used to compare me to the sun," I tell him softly, still working, still fixing him. "It was kind of our thing. I was the sun, and he was the sky, and for the longest time, I didn't know how to survive without him. When you build your entire life around another person and that person just disappears… what's left?" I don't dare glance up at him as I peel open a bandage, too afraid his deep stare will eclipse the rest of my words. "I've spent over a year trying to figure how to build a new life around *me*. But as you probably know, given your line of work, with building comes the occasional collapse. The inevitable downfall. Pieces don't always fit the way you want them to, and then…starting over again sounds so *overwhelming*. I've had my share of downfalls, and I'm sorry you had to witness one of them."

Parker is still and silent, his breath beating down on me, tickling my baby hairs. He hardly flinches when I wrap the gauze around his finger, securing it with a bandage.

"Anyway, I'm not the sun," I finish, tracing my finger along his dressing, caught somewhere between this moment and a past life. "The sun only knows how to shine, and I've seen too much darkness."

A beat passes, a quiet, poignant beat, and Parker asks, "What happened to him?"

Part of me wants to hide from those words because reliving the worst moment of my life is really, really *hard*. But the other part of me recognizes the beauty of his question.

He cared enough to ask it.

My grip on Parker's hand clenches out of instinct, the memories brutal and unforgiving. "It was our wedding anniversary. We had just left a restaurant and were walking home, discussing life. The future." I inhale a frazzled breath, forcing myself to continue. "We were happy. Kissing, smiling, laughing. We were so, so happy, and then it's almost like time froze, and evil seeped inside of our little bubble, and everything changed. A stranger came out of nowhere and stole my purse while we were talking about becoming *parents*, and Charlie chased him, because that's what Charlie did. He was my protector. He chased him into the busy downtown street and was hit by a truck."

I finally lift my eyes, my blurry, watery eyes, and discover Parker staring down at me with an expression I've never seen before. Confusion, maybe, mixed with…a shred of emotional turmoil. It's like he has no idea what to do or say, but my words are affecting him, and that's new. That's something startlingly unfamiliar.

He doesn't say he's sorry or offer his sympathies, and I'm okay with that. I'm tired of people being sorry. I'm sick of hearing it.

Parker's response to me is in everything he *doesn't* say or do.

He doesn't pull away. His hand remains enclosed in mine while he allows me to graze the tip of my finger up and down his bandage, and I feel like this is his *own* way of opening up and sharing a part of himself. Not with words— not with words that can feel hollow and superficial, but with vulnerability. By breaking down a wall he's probably spent a hell of a long time building and letting me in.

And I think we both realize this at the same time. We both notice the shift, the power of this moment, the undeniable energy swirling between us—we notice it at the exact same time, and that makes it all the more potent.

My finger goes rogue and travels along his palm, tracing all the little lines and divots, a maze of untold stories. His skin is warm, so warm and inviting, despite his chilly façade. I feel him tense against my touch, his body's way of trying to resist me, but he still doesn't pull away.

Parker lets me touch him, really *touch* him, and I have no idea what it means. It's beautiful, and it's intimidating, but I'm not sure I understand it quite yet as we stand here in my kitchen beneath a busted ceiling, while my body starts to lean into him like he's some sort of magnetic forcefield. Like I'm drugged and loopy, unable to hold myself upright, desperate to steal more of his warmth for myself.

I look up at him then, swaying and delirious on whatever this is, and goddammit, I can't help but smile. It's instinctual, involuntary—just like Parker's reaction to it.

He heaves in a jerky breath, his whole body stiffening. I can feel him harden, his muscles clenching, because I'm *that* close to him. And then he finally pulls his hand away, tearing his eyes from mine and looking down.

The connection snaps, and it's for the best, it really is. I take a step back and bite down on my lip, smoothing out my hair and sucking in my own deep breath.

"I'm going to head out," Parker says, breaking through the thick silence. His voice is raspy, a little rattled. "I'll see you tomorrow."

He gathers up his tools, and I just stand there, watching him, my skin buzzing and my cheeks hot. "Don't worry about it. You're injured, Parker. I'll find someone else to take care of the ceiling."

Parker folds his ladder and tucks it underneath his arm, reaching for the toolbox with his opposite hand, careful not to make contact with his wound. He pauses in front of me before he leaves, his eyes pinning sharply on mine. "I'll see you tomorrow."

A heartbeat goes by before he sweeps past me and out the door, and I finally let out that breath.

15

MELODY

I T'S ANOTHER MONSOON.

Is there a monsoon season in Wisconsin?

If there's not, there should be. The weather has been bizarre this year with frequent storms, high winds, an abnormal amount of rainfall, and now there's talk of tornados this evening. As I stare out the rain-streaked glass, I'm grateful that my water issues were only a leaky pipe and not a leaky roof, or I'd be in a bathing suit right now, swimming to the liquor cabinet.

"Mel, check it out," West hollers at me from the kitchen, where he's helping Shane with the pipe situation. Helping, as in, watching from the sidelines as he sucks down beers and makes useless commentary.

Wandering over to the two men, I fold my arms and glance up, having no idea what I'm checking out. "Looks great," I try, hoping that it really does look great. To me, it's still just a giant hole in my ceiling—a hole I worry won't be going away anytime soon, thanks to the inclement weather.

"Right? Shane's the man." West grins, tipping his beer at his friend.

Phew.

Shane gives me a quick sweep, his dusky eyes rolling over me, and I'm reminded of the way he looked at me that night at the brewery. That *new* look.

The look that screams, *I'm newly single, and you're newly single, so what should we do about it?*

I clear my throat. "Thank you so much. I really appreciate you squeezing me into your busy schedule."

"It's no problem at all. I'm glad I could help." Shane reaches for the fresh beer my brother holds out to him. "That's a nice dress, by the way. Pretty color on you."

Oh.

Interesting subject change.

Folding my arms tighter, I glance down at said dress. It's a casual dress, periwinkle blue, and it cuts off at the knees, featuring short sleeves and a V-neck. I spin the skirt, fidgeting through my reply. "Thank you. You're sweet."

Is this what the dating world is like?

Or am I just a special brand of awkward?

I comb my fingers through my hair, smiling.

Awkwardly, of course.

Shane continues to stare at me with interest, nodding his head. "I can be."

Oh boy.

"Well, I'm going to head out. I have that pool tournament tonight as long as the weather doesn't get all *Wizard of Oz* on us," West cuts in, glancing my way. "You and Leah coming out?"

"Oh, no, I don't think so. Parker said he was going to try and stop by to fix the ceiling."

"Douchey contractor guy?"

I groan. "Yes, West, douchey contractor guy."

The ensuing knock at my front door has my belly flip-flopping, my hands smoothing out the nonexistent wrinkles in my dress, and my eyes dodging my brother's questioning gaze.

"I-I'll be right back," I mutter, spinning in place and heading to the front of the house with reddening cheeks, my heart rate quickening.

I'm being stupid. It's just Parker.

Well, it could also be that random betta fish tank that doubles as a plant holder I bought on Amazon at three a.m. during a bout of sleep deprivation… but it's probably Parker.

And just because we shared some kind of moment twenty-four hours ago, it doesn't mean anything. It doesn't justify these butterflies and clammy palms, because at the end of the day, he's still a closed-off brute, and I'm still a grieving widow.

With a calming breath, I pull the door open and promptly get blasted by a gust of rain-infused wind, nearly tipping me backward. Parker stands there on my porch with his ladder and tools, drenched from head to toe, his magnetic green eyes enough to pull me upright. Collecting myself and shaking out the water droplets from my hair, I step aside to let him in. "You came."

"I said I was going to," he says softly, his tone missing its usual bitter edge. Parker shuffles through the entryway, smelling like a rainy Colorado mountainside, and leans the ladder against my rust-colored wall. "You have company?"

"My brother and the plumber." I chew the inside of my lip and observe the way he tousles his wet hair back from his forehead. Little drops of water trail down his arms as he slips out of his boots, causing my eyes to follow. His skin is bronzed from the sun, his tan lines evident when his sleeves lift, revealing strong biceps. Parker isn't overly bulky, but he's lean and fit, perfectly in shape, a testament to how hard he works. "If you can't finish everything today, it's no big deal. I know the weather is going to get worse."

"I heard there could be tornados and shit," he confirms, rising back up and towering over me by a solid foot. "Hopefully, you have a basement." His irises flicker like emerald lightning when we lock eyes, a complement to the booming thunder outside, and then he moves around me, toward the kitchen.

My own heartbeats sound thunderous, rattling my chest, as I think about hunkering down in the basement with Parker.

I gulp.

As I follow behind him, my brother straightens from his perch against the island, his focus drifting between us. "Hey, man."

Parker nods his greeting, resting his toolbox on the counter, remaining silent.

I feel an overwhelming duty to fill that silence, so I chime in, "Parker, this is my brother, West."

"We've met," Parker deadpans, sifting through his supplies.

"Right. Um…and this is Shane, my brother's friend."

Shane sidles up beside me, tossing a beer bottle into the recycling bin, then brazenly drapes his arm over my shoulders—some kind of unprecedented, territorial move. "I'm your friend too," he notes, the flirtation heavy.

My body stiffens, my gaze instantly floating to Parker. I watch the way his eyes lift, zeroing in on the brawny arm wrapped around me, his jaw ticking. He forces his attention back to his tools as I unravel myself from Shane's embrace with an uncomfortable chuckle. "That you are. Are you about finished with the pipes?"

"Yeah, just give me a few minutes to gather my stuff and I'll get out of your hair."

West saunters over to me, ruffling that hair with his meaty palm. "I'm taking off too. Stay safe with the weather warnings."

"Ugh." I shove him away, irritated, fixing my newly disheveled locks. "Thanks. Be careful driving."

When my brother ventures out of the kitchen and the front door claps shut, Shane begins to gather his own supplies, while Parker fetches the ladder and sets it up below the ceiling hole. I catch the two men eyeing each other every now and then, so I resort to what I always do when I need a distraction: bake. As I'm pulling out baking sheets and mixing bowls, Shane makes his way back over to me with his hands in his pockets.

I swallow as I blink up at him. "All set?"

"Yep. Should we go over payment?"

"Oh, right, of course." Swiping my palms along the skirt of my dress, I reach for my purse behind me on the back counter. "Is a personal check okay?"

Shane scratches his head, approaching me with a sluggish gait, a coy smile tipping his lips. He curls his fingers around my wrist and begins to tug me away from the kitchen.

I can't help but glance at Parker's perch from atop the ladder, noting how his eyes keep cutting over to us, dark and stormy, his stance rigid. Biting into my lip, I lace my fingers together in front of me and trail Shane until we're just out of Parker's line of sight. "You don't take checks?"

"I do." Shane laughs, still messing with his hair, then massages the nape of his neck as his blue-gray eyes rake over me. "But I was thinking something a little more unconventional. Let me take you out."

"Take me out?"

"Yeah, like a date. Dinner."

"Dinner," I parrot.

He chuckles again, bobbing his head. "Look, I know you've had a really hard year, so I'm not trying to rush you into anything. But if you're ready… well, I'm interested."

My cheeks heat at his proposal, and I resist the urge to repeat his words in an attempt to delay my floundering response. I've never been asked out before. Charlie and I just *happened*, all fireworks and fairy tales, and there was never any need for this…formality.

And while I'm flattered, certainly, I don't feel any sort of attraction to Shane.

I don't think—I guess I haven't given him much of a chance yet.

Scuffing my bare toes against the carpeting, I smile. "I'm not really sure what to say. I think I'd feel more comfortable paying you for your time."

"You'd rather pay me than go out with me?"

"Well, I'd feel better if we kept this a business arrangement, you know? I'm not saying we can't go out sometime…in the future."

Shane narrows his eyes, registering my words as he runs his tongue along his upper teeth. "Are you seeing someone?"

"No, I just—"

A familiar presence closes in on me from behind, radiating warmth and command, inciting goose bumps to dance across my skin and light me up like a heat wave.

Parker stalls his feet right beside me, propping a power drill against his shoulder, and my insides buzz with anticipation as I wait for him to say something.

He doesn't.

He just stands there, looming over us with silent intensity, with some kind of control I don't understand, glaring daggers at Shane.

Shane raises an eyebrow at him. "Can I help you?"

"No."

I hold back an abrupt laugh, tucking my hair behind both ears.

Both ears that are currently burning fire-engine red as Parker's arm tickles mine while we stand there, side by side.

Curse my Swedish genes.

Shane's gaze travels between us until he slowly nods his head, then scrubs at his nose. "Got it," he mutters, but he never indicates what he "got." "Check is fine. Just give it to West, and I'll grab it from him this weekend."

"Oh, I can do it now. It's n—"

"Take care, Melody." Shane bumps shoulders with Parker as he stalks through the living room to the front door, slamming it shut.

I brave a peek up at Parker, trying to read him, trying to make sense of what that was, but he just lets out a sigh, his eyes closed, then traipses back into the kitchen.

Giving chase, I call out, "What was that?"

"What was what?"

"You know exactly what I'm talking about," I reply to his flexing shoulder blades, his wet shirt molded to them. "Why were you just standing there smoldering?"

Parker finally pauses his escape attempt and turns toward me, the power drill tapping against his thigh. His eyebrows arch with bemusement. "I don't smolder."

"You absolutely smolder."

I swear his cheeks twitch with the hint of a smile. "I was telling your douche-canoe of a friend to back the fuck down," Parker replies. He presses the finger trigger on the drill, and it buzzes to life. "Points for subtlety?"

My mouth goes dry, like I swallowed sand, but I try to downplay the dust storm funneling inside of me. "That wasn't subtle, Parker. Zero points...actually, *negative* points."

"Then why did you ask me if you already knew?"

"I..." Shock, disbelief, denial. Swallowing down more grit, I reply in a whispered breath, "I thought you hated me."

Parker frowns slightly, glancing away before meeting my confused stare. "Who says I hate you?"

"I got the impression you hated everyone."

His eyes flick over me like jade flames, drinking me in from toes to top as his jaw clenches, the tendons in his neck straining when he makes his way back up to my face. "Not you."

And then he spins back around and trudges toward the ladder, leaving me dazed and dumbstruck as I watch him retreat.

"I'm pretty sure a cow just flew past my window."

There's a resounding chill dwelling inside my bones as I watch the storm die out through the pane of glass, replaced by an eerie sky, painted dark and green. Only the howl of the wind can be heard while everything else seems to go still. A shiver sweeps through me.

The calm before the storm.

Parker plods back down the ladder, the soles of his feet against the metal rungs causing me to blink myself back to reality. I glance at him over my shoulder, his hair dusted with specks of white drywall.

"If you need to get home, you should probably leave now," I encourage him, hugging myself to repel the chill. "It looks like Judgment Day out there."

"And leave you here alone to be all scared and shit?" He musses his hair, the Sheetrock scattering. "Kind of a dick move."

I look back out the window. "I've been through worse." When I feel him approaching me, I twist in place, facing him, noting the way he fidgets with the bandage on his index finger. "How's your finger?"

"Still attached."

"You should change the dressing," I tell him, pacing forward. I reach for his hand, not asking for permission, but he dodges me. "Let me see."

"It's fine, Melody."

The sound of my name on his tongue sends a blast of heat through me, settling deep. I've only heard him say my name twice, which makes it feel so… *intimate.* "Can I see?" My request is gentle, laced with sweetness and delicacy, as I slowly extend my arm toward him and brush my fingertips against his hand.

But the moment I make contact, the sirens go off.

Loud, shrieking tornado sirens.

Oh no.

We glance at each other as my heart picks up speed, and I lower my arm, spinning back around and rushing to the window.

"Jesus, you're not supposed to stand in front of a window," Parker scolds me, and before I know it, he's taking me by the wrist and dragging me away. "Basement?"

Sirens, wind, black skies, and *him*.

I'm incapacitated by equal parts terror and thrill.

"Y-Yes…that's the door." I point, my finger trembling. "Hold on, let me grab my phone from the kitchen."

I pull free from his grip and race to the kitchen island, quickly pulling up my Hangouts app.

Me: The tornado sirens are going off. Are you safe?

He answers right away, and I let out a relieved breath.

Zephyr: I'm safe. Are you?
Me: Yes.
Zephyr: Are you alone?
Me: No…I'm not alone.
Zephyr: Good. Check back in soon.

As I shoot off a group text to my parents, West, and Leah, letting them know I'm taking cover, I join Parker by the basement door just as he's slipping his phone into his back pocket. When our eyes meet, something passes between us, something akin to allegiance—like we're heading into war together, not knowing if we'll make it out alive.

Which is silly, honestly. We've had tornado scares before; it's the Midwest. It will probably pass by us, and everything will be fine.

But maybe it's not about *if* we'll make it out but about *how* we'll make it out.

Somehow, I feel like everything is about to change.

Taking the lead, I pull open the door to the finished basement and head down the stairsteps with Parker on my heels. While the primary space has narrow windows along the far wall, there's a little, windowless den we can hole up in until the threat passes. "Follow me," I say over my shoulder. "We can hang out in here."

Whistles and howls sound on the other side of the basement wall, making me tremble, and just as we reach the old wooden door to the den, the lights flicker out.

Shit.

Out of instinct, I reach for Parker, pulling him into the now pitch-black room and latching the door behind me. When I turn around, he's *right there*— flush against me, my nose grazing the front of his chest, inhaling his earthy scent. I swear I feel him shudder as I let out an unsteady breath, clenching my fingers into fists at my sides in an attempt to keep them from reaching for him. From holding on to him for dear life. "We lost power. That can't be good," I say, murmuring against his T-shirt, all breathy and weak.

I hear him swallow as he stands there motionless, and the only soundtrack to our heavy breathing and rapidly beating hearts is the sirens sounding in the distance, mingling with the angry wind. Parker hesitates before he grits out, "You all right?"

God, his question does something to me. There's a cyclone headed our way, but it's my insides that are all twisted up and pinwheeling.

Feeling nearly dizzy from his proximity, I lean in closer, just an inch, until my forehead presses against the hard planes of his chest and my hands lift of their own accord, despite my resistance, despite my fear. They raise up and rest along his hips, dipping just beneath the hem of his T-shirt and grazing the leather belt that encircles his waist. One of my fingers slides through the belt loop as I let out another drawn-out breath and hold him to me. "I'm okay. Are you?"

Parker remains rigid, but I feel his breathing quicken. I hear his heartbeat pulsing in my ears, louder than the warning sirens.

He doesn't respond right away, so I inquire more specifically, "Are you scared?"

His answer comes quick. "Yeah."

"Of the storm?" I probe, my forehead pivoting against his torso until my temple is level with his heart.

"No."

He's scared of *me*, of whatever the hell is happening between us. I know this, I know exactly what he's implying because I feel the same way, but I still ask. "What are you afraid of, Parker?"

A deep sigh hits the top of my head, shaky and agitated. Parker's arms still hang loose at his sides, refusing to hold me back, refusing to give in. "Don't make me answer that."

I cling tighter, and he doesn't pull away.

He doesn't pull away, and I *know* that means something.

I drop the question because he's not ready, and truthfully, I'm not ready either. Instead, I close my eyes, squeezing them shut, as the screeching wind echoes through the darkness, causing a fearful gasp to escape my lips. The house rattles around us, my skin vibrates, my throat burns, so I just keep holding him, tighter and tighter, until my arms are fully wrapped around his waist. "Tell me a story," I say, needing a distraction, needing to hear his voice. It's so dark in here—I have to know that I'm not alone.

Parker falters for a moment, heaving in a breath and letting it out into my hair. "What kind of story?"

The wind roars, the windows clamor, the shutters clap, and the sirens sing loud, all trying to outplay the racket of our frazzled hearts and cluttered minds.

I never much cared for the dark, but right now, it feels like a friend.

Nuzzling in closer, I whisper into his T-shirt, "Tell me *your* story."

16

PARKER

"Tell me *your* story."

She's wrapped around me like I'm her favorite fucking blanket, and it's the only thing keeping me from spiraling back in time and returning to that closet. To that *prison*.

It sounds like there's a freight train on the other side of the door, but she is louder—her presence, her breaths beating against my chest in sporadic bursts, her pulse vibrating beneath my skin, the goddamn feel of her arms clutching my waist, so delicate and fragile yet so, so *loud*.

She's louder than the voice inside my head screaming at me to resist, to push her away and get the fuck out of here, tornado be damned.

She's even louder than my inherent fear of dark, enclosed spaces.

Yeah, Melody is louder…and I'm paralyzed by every decibel, by every deafening note.

Inhaling sharply, I reply, "You don't want to hear my story. It's not a nice story."

"That doesn't mean it doesn't deserve to be told," she whispers back.

My eyes squeeze shut, as if that will somehow make her disappear.

This is just pretend.

This is just the darkness fucking with my head like it always has.

I hate the dark, I really do, and I know that sounds weak and pathetic, considering I'm a grown-ass man. But this kind of darkness, the kind where you can't even see your own hand in front of your face, takes me right back to that closet when I was five years old, all alone and scared shitless.

All I had were ghosts to keep me company.

All I had was Zephyr.

And now I have her.

Tipping my head back, I blow out a hard breath, then inhale deeply through my nose. I do it again and again, closing my eyes and trying to center myself before I unravel.

Melody must notice my tension, my mounting panic, because her hands unlink from behind me and glide up my chest, gripping the material of my T-shirt between two fists. "Are you okay?"

"Fine," I force out, shoving her hands away and sliding them back down to my hips.

I don't want her touching me *there.*

Melody fiddles with the belt loops as she drops her head, forehead pressed to my front. "Talk to me."

"No."

"You're shaking."

Shit, am I?

Stupid, traitorous body. My hands ball into fists on either side of me as my teeth gnash together, and I grit out, "I don't like the dark."

I wait for her reaction, her imminent pity. Laughter, maybe. I don't really know what to expect because I've never shared that with anyone before, but I can't imagine anything but ridicule.

She surprises me, though. She's always surprising me.

"I don't like it either," Melody responds softly, her index finger tracing the waist of my pants. "But it's not so bad with you here."

The whooshing sound grows closer, and the house rattles around us, causing me to stumble, my balance off-kilter due to the surmounting anxiety. My back hits the wall beside us, and I take her with me, instinctually wrapping my arms around her and tugging her farther against my chest.

Melody lets out some kind of breathy moan, maybe a gasp, but I'm not sure if it's out of fear or because we're fully entangled with one another now, and my fingers have somehow crawled their way up to her hair, weaving through the strands and fisting gently.

My panic seems to ebb the moment she's in my arms—the moment I give in and hold her back. She's chipping away at my brick walls, and her sunny rays of light are seeping through the cracks, trying to bring me warmth.

Fucking hell, what is she doing to me?

I slide down the wall, my back against it, and she goes with me, until we hit the tiled floor together and Melody straddles my lap, her knees caging me in. My right hand is still knotted in her hair, while the other curves around her back, and even though I can't see shit, I know we're face-to-face by the way her warm breath skims my lips with each exhale.

I want to blame the raging storm—I want to say it's the threat outside that feels greater than the threat of *her*, therefore justifying the way I'm letting her cling to me.

Justifying the way I'm clinging right back.

Only…there was no threat yesterday when I let her touch me—when I let her take my hand between her palms and drag a lazy finger across the creases, like she was carving herself into me somehow. Branding me with sunshine.

There was no danger earlier today when some sort of fucked-up possessive feeling shot through me like a drug, and I felt the need to stake some sort of *claim* over her.

It's maddening.

It's confusing, nonsensical, and fucking *maddening* how I hate everything she stands for, everything she represents, and yet…I don't hate her at all.

"You're not shaking anymore." Melody's voice infiltrates my dark musings as she continues to invade me. She continues to trespass. "My father used to tell me that the dark is the very best secret-keeper. The things we say in the dark never have to leave it."

Her cheek dips back to my chest, her words muffled by my shirt, and the fine hairs on her head tickle my nose as I inhale a shuddering breath. Thoroughly entwined and swallowed by darkness, reckless thoughts spill out of me. "When I was a kid…some real bad shit happened to me. I spent a lot of time in the dark, and it fucked with my head. Played tricks on me."

I feel her head lift slowly from my chest, her eyes searching for me through the thick shroud of darkness, trying to see me.

She's always trying to see me.

"Parker," she whispers delicately, her face close, *too* close. Her hands start moving again in a skyward journey from my chest to my neck, trailing up to my face until both palms are cradling my jaw.

My body tenses at the contact, wanting to reject the tenderness of her touch—like it's some kind of foreign entity that doesn't belong. I snatch her wrists up. "Don't. I don't want your pity."

"It's not pity." Melody wriggles her arms free of my grip and returns them to my face, her fingertips featherlight against my rough jaw. "It's *empathy*."

"I don't want that either."

The whooshing sound from outside, almost like a runaway train, seems to die down, and I wonder if the threat has passed. I wonder if this will all be over soon, so I can get the hell out of here and never look back. The lights flicker for a brief moment, just enough for me to catch the glaze over her eyes and the pink stain in her cheeks.

And then it's dark again. Our secrets are still safe.

The soft pads of her fingers graze the bristles along my chin, and she inhales slowly. "Tell me more."

I try to swipe her arms away, but she actually fights back, maintaining her grip, cupping my face between her palms.

"Keep going, Parker."

A growl escapes me, and I fist her hair again as a wave of anger surges through me. "Fucking intrusive," I spit out, our foreheads knocking together when she arches into me.

Melody makes that sound again, a squeaky mewl, as I tighten my hold on her hair, and her sharp nails dig into my cheeks.

And *fuck*, this is the damn wrong time to be getting turned on.

"Keep going," she says raggedly, echoing my own words from that night in the rain. "Get mad. Let it out."

Her body bows against me, our groins pressing together and a hiss expelling between gritted teeth. "You don't want to know what I'm feeling right now."

135

"Yes, I do," she insists, her knees clamping around my hips. "You can talk to me. We're just two people taking cover from the storm."

"Is that what this is?"

"Yes."

I tug on her hair, my opposite hand grazing down her spine and curling around her hip until I'm grinding my erection into the apex of her thighs, and she knows *exactly* what I'm feeling. "Feels like something else to me," I reply in a low voice.

Melody's hands drop to my shoulders with a whimper, squeezing tight, her nails surely leaving little half-moons in my skin. She sucks in a sharp breath, her whole body tensing as her forehead falls against mine and rests there. She whispers my name as if she can't seem to muster anything more. "Parker…"

Jesus, this is fucked.

I haven't had sex in *ages*. I haven't even thought about it—not until her. Not until that night beneath the rain clouds when I watched her dance atop the hood of her car, weightless and free, her wet clothes stuck to ivory skin that I suddenly wanted to feel beneath my fingertips.

But that was just a fluke.

And this…

This is just the dark playing tricks on me. Playing tricks on both of us.

I can hardly make out her outline through the black veil between us, but I can picture her flushed cheeks, wild hair, and wide green eyes, like two emerald arrows to my chest.

All I want to do is pull them out, but they're embedded, lodged too deep, and it'll only make it worse. I'll bleed out.

Instead, I strengthen my hold on Melody's hip as her nose grazes mine. Our breaths intermingle, and my head falls back against the wall, her breasts flush with my torso. I feel her inching in, getting closer, her lips almost touching mine.

It's the dark. This isn't real.

I'm choking on her scent, dizzy and light-headed.

Melody's palms slide up to my neck, her thumbs dusting gently, and she breathes against my mouth, "You're shaking again."

Fuck.

It's not the dark this time, and it's not the storm—it's all *her*. She's twisting me up inside, smelling like lemons and grapefruit, feeling warm and supple in my hands, and making these little squeaky sounds that shoot straight to my groin. And I know I should pull away because her lips are far too fucking close to mine, but it feels like she's breathing life into me, and I don't know how to pull away from something like that.

Melody leans in, just a centimeter more, and our lips brush together. So soft, so light, hardly anything at all, but it feels electric.

Catastrophic.

I don't move. I'm barely breathing.

I just hold on to her so tight, I'm afraid I might break her.

But I'm more afraid she'll break me first.

She doesn't press any harder, though—she just lingers there, memorizing the shape of my mouth with her own. Melody grazes her lips gently across mine, inhaling a deep, trembling breath, and applies the most delicate kiss to my bottom lip.

But before we can cross any more lines, before she crashes through any more of my steel walls, the lights flicker back to life.

Melody jolts back with a sharp gasp, her hand lifting as she presses her fingertips to her lips, like she's in shock. She blinks against the harsh fluorescents with bright red cheeks, her straw-blond hair a knotted mess, and her expression...wide-eyed and mortified.

My chest tightens with lightning rage, and I ground out through clenched teeth, "Get off me."

Her eyebrows dip, hesitation seizing her.

"Fucking get off me, Melody."

Her own features grow taut and hard as she scrambles off my lap, pulling herself to trembling legs. "You don't have to be such a jerk," she bites out with a husky rasp.

"I don't kiss. I've never kissed." I move to find my own footing, internally scolding my dick to calm the fuck down.

"What?"

"I don't fucking kiss, okay? I never have. Not once."

Melody blinks at me through a mask of incredulity. "How is that possible?"

Smoothing out my T-shirt and ruffling my hair, I spare her a scathing glance. "I don't particularly care for women, that's how."

Her eyes pop, and she repeats, "What?"

Jesus Christ.

What a fucking mess.

I don't bother replying to her and storm out the door, practically kicking it open, kind of hoping the tornado is still lurking around somewhere so I can dive in headfirst.

"Parker."

Melody calls after me as I stomp up the staircase, but I quicken my gait and move to collect my tools so I can get the fuck out of here. A brief glance out her front window pauses my feet. "Shit…"

There are downed trees everywhere, one taking out a roof. Window shutters, glass, gutters, all lay strewn across the dusty street.

Debris, destruction, ruin.

I pace toward the window, my eyes taking in the wreckage as I scan her neighborhood, an eerie chill coasting across my skin. There's an elderly woman wandering her front yard in a floral nightgown, looking completely lost, in a daze.

I feel Melody come up behind me, so I turn to her, noting the tears welling as she stares out in silent horror at the scene before us—a scene that looks like it came straight out of an apocalyptic movie set. When she lifts her eyes to me, misted and gutted, my heart stutters.

Her anguish blindsides me because I feel it too, and I've never given a shit about anything before. Not *really*. I do care about Bree, and I care enough about my dog to have had the decency to drop him off with her on my way over here, so he wouldn't be alone during the storm.

But my sister's pain has never been *my* pain. Her heartbreaks and setbacks have never kept me up at night. I'm desensitized to other people's misery because I've always been too wrapped up in my own.

Not now, though. Not right now while she gazes up at me with those wounded, green eyes, like her whole world is nothing but shambles and faded embers.

I feel it too.

And it's kind of a sickly feeling—a kick to my gut, a searing lump in the back of my throat. I want to cut it out of me. Reject it.

Reject *her*, just like I've been trying to do since the day she stumbled into that meeting like my own personal tornado, determined to wreak havoc on me with her endless smiles and happy little sunbeams.

We hold our stare for another beat before Melody turns her attention back to the front window and zeros in on the elderly woman. She inhales sharply. "Mrs. Porter…"

I watch as Melody doesn't think twice, doesn't even fucking hesitate, before slipping into her shoes and running out the front door and across the street, dodging scattered debris and fallen tree branches along the way. My own feet carry me to the open doorway, my eyes following her petite figure as she meets Mrs. Porter on her front lawn and envelops the frail woman in a tight hug. No faltering, no indecision, no thought to herself or her own burdens.

Just empathy.

As I linger in the entryway, my fingers tapping restlessly against the frame and my insides humming with feelings I don't recognize, I do something I've never done before.

I make my way into Melody's kitchen, and instead of packing up my shit and bolting, I sift through her cabinets until I find a box of garbage bags.

Then I step out her front door and get to work.

17

PARKER

Bree barrels through my foyer later that week with a box of doughnuts, interrupting my afternoon nap on the couch with Walden, who is curled up in a ball near my feet. I'm pretty sure it's the first time he's ever actually made the effort to hop up here with me.

The backside of my arm is draped over my forehead as I grumble a hello to my sister, peering over at her with only one eye open. This is the first day off I've had in months, so I kind of just want to go back to sleep.

"Oh my God…look at your dog, Parker."

Bree's chipper voice has me blinking both eyes open as I pull myself halfway up by the arms. I glance at the black-and-white furball at the end of the couch, all withered and bony, with dark moles and skin tags casing his skin. "He looks old as fuck," I mumble, then scrub a palm down my face.

"His hair is growing in." Bree beams. "I thought he looked different when you dropped him off the other day."

She dashes—legitimately *dashes*—over to us, her brown curls bouncing with each step. My eyebrow arches with skepticism. "Doubtful."

"I'm serious. Look at these fresh patches of hair. Did you change his diet?"

"No. He eats the kibble you bought an absurd amount of, and sometimes that nasty shit in a can that looks like gelatinous slug guts."

"Seems to be working. Keep it up."

"Slug guts noted."

Bree leans over the back of the couch, giving Walden a scratch between his ears that causes the poor animal to startle awake because he's deaf as bricks. "Sorry, pup. Didn't mean to scare you," she coos, her smile wide.

Walden lets out a heavy sigh and goes back to sleep. *Lucky bastard.*

Heaving my legs over the side of the couch, I scratch at my overgrown stubble and throw my sister a quick glance. I do a double take when I discover her studying me with that knowing smirk, her chestnut eyes glittering. "What?"

"You're finally getting laid, aren't you?"

"What the fuck?"

Bree puckers her lips, staring at me, all squinty and scrutinizing. "You are."

"You're clearly under the influence of something."

"So are you," she quips. "What's her name?"

"Bye."

"Parker, come on. Your house is the cleanest it's probably *ever* been, your dog is suddenly sprouting fur like a Chia Pet, and..." She paces over to my side of the couch and twirls a manicured finger in front of my face. "This."

"My perpetual scowl?"

"You look...different."

An aggravated groan escapes me as I push myself up from the couch cushions and storm away, already knowing she's going to follow. *Relentless.* "Wishful thinking, Bree. I'm still the same old joyless curmudgeon you've come to know and, for some unknown reason, love."

Bree trails me into the kitchen, her never-ending optimism trailing with her. She coils her fingers around my wrist to stop my intentional avoidance. "Hey. Stop for a second."

Closing my eyes, my jaw tight, I slowly spin to face her.

"Parker."

"Bree," I drawl.

"Will you look at me, please?"

Fucking hell. I appease her request but make sure I do it as miserably as possible—eyebrows pinched, lips pressed together, glare indignant. Bree's gaze slides over me like she's studying for a final exam, soaking up each line and crease, memorizing every detail. She's in research mode. Her little nose scrunches up, making it look like the freckles peppering her high cheekbones scatter and spread. Her thick, dark eyebrows wrinkle with curiosity. I let out something that falls between a sigh and a huff, laced with exasperation, and fold my arms over my chest. "Are you done?"

Bree's taupe-tinged lips curl up. "Who is she?"

"I'm not sleeping with anyone."

"That's not what I asked."

I open my mouth to speak, then clamp it shut. My teeth grind and grate, the muscles in my arms twitching. I'm not planning on indulging Bree because it means nothing—*she* means nothing—but it slips out anyway. "She's just someone I met at those dumb fucking meetings you forced me into."

"Oh my God…"

I'm appalled when she starts to cry. "What are you doing? Don't fucking do that. Why are you doing that?"

Bree throws herself at me with a strained whimper, wrapping me up in a bone-crushing hug and weeping into the front of my shirt. Her hair smells like it did when we were kids, something like baby powder and wild orchids, and I can't help but deflate a little as the crimpy curls tickle my nose. "It's nothing… and it's not going anywhere."

"It's not nothing, Parker. It's *not*." She pulls her cheek from my chest, wiping away tearstains with the back of her wrist, then she presses her palm up against my heart. "One year ago, I thought I was going to lose you, but you were given a second chance. A chance I never thought you'd ever learn to appreciate."

I stiffen, glancing away and blowing out a hard breath. "You're making this a bigger deal than it is."

"Your happiness *is* a big deal, little brother. It's a huge freakin' deal." Bree gifts me with a watery smile, sniffling as she takes a step back. "I won't hound you for details. I don't think you're ready for that yet."

"Good. There are no details, and also, I'd rather jump into a pit of ravenous beavers than have that conversation with you."

She knocks me on the shoulder with a playful fist. "I'll break you down eventually," she says, traipsing toward the box of assorted doughnuts and plucking a glazed blueberry from the mix. Bree takes a big bite and mumbles through the crumbs, "Just stay away from beaver pits until then."

Evening falls, and I make my way over to my rolling chair when my cell phone pings with a message notification: *Magnolia.*

It's been a few days since the tornado touched down in Delavan—when Melody and I cleaned up the debris littering her neighborhood street, mostly in silence, not sure what to say to one another after what transpired between us in that darkened den. But I caught her staring at me from time to time, lost in her thoughts with a somewhat dreamy look in her eyes. Pensive yet whimsical. It was unnerving. That whole goddamn day was unnerving, so I haven't spoken to her since, and I'm dreading our next meeting.

I've talked to Magnolia, though.

She's my outlet. She's an anonymous stranger I can vent to, joke with, and even get vulnerable with—all things I can't do in my day-to-day life.

I can be myself with her. I can be the person I would likely be right now if life hadn't completely fucked me over.

Pulling up my account, I click on her little message box.

Magnolia: Tell me a confession.
Me: The pink Starburst is by far the worst flavor.
Magnolia: We're no longer friends.

Friends. Is that what we are?

I'm pretty sure I have no friends—except maybe Owen, but I don't think an eight-year-old boy I just met really counts.

Is this widowed stranger in my computer screen that I've never even seen considered a...*friend?* The notion seems ludicrous, but I don't correct her because I don't fucking know.

143

Me: Your turn.

A few moments pass before she responds.

Magnolia: I do have a confession...and it's probably TMI, but I can't talk to anyone else about it. You're kind of like my secret diary, only you talk back to me and give oddly good advice sometimes.

Hmm. Interesting.

Me: Sometimes? I'm offended.
Magnolia: You don't get offended.
Me: Touché. Okay, hit me.
Magnolia: You won't judge?
Me: Never.

Another long pause, and then:

Magnolia: Okay...I miss sex.

My fingertips stall on the keyboard, barely grazing the keys. I wasn't exactly expecting that, and I'm fairly certain I'm the worst possible person to give advice on the subject.

I've had sex twice. Fucking *twice* in my entire thirty-two years of life. I lost my virginity to some awkward classmate when I was sixteen because I thought it was something I had to do. It was weird and terrible, and I ignored her for the next two years of high school.

Then it happened again on my twenty-first birthday. One of Bree's tipsy friends dragged me up to her bedroom, hopped on my dick, and five minutes later I decided I had no desire to ever do that again.

While I'm inherently attracted to women in the physical sense, my emotional connection to them has always been nonexistent, if not bordering on toxic.

Whenever I look at a woman, I see my mother. They all morph into *her*, with her sneering laugh, her beady, yellowing eyes, her blanched skin. Her long, brittle talons that would scratch at me, leaving bloody nail marks in their wake, and her dark, wiry hair, always hanging loose and greasy around her sunken-in face.

They're all girls like Gwen and the rest of my foster sisters—all except for Bree. Sniveling, mocking, cruel. They're like my foster mother, with her sharp, pointy features and a thin mouth that never smiled.

They're all the girls in swim class who would laugh at me because I refused to take my shirt off in the pool, too horrified to put my grisly scars on display.

One of the girls ripped it off me once, then humiliated me in front of the entire class, pointing and laughing at the evidence of my abuse.

I *still* never take my shirt off in public, even when I'm working outside in the ninety-degree heat, and it's probably just another reason why I've had no interest in sex.

I'm too...exposed.

Swallowing, I shoot her the only feasible advice that comes to mind.

Me: So, have sex.
Magnolia: It's not that simple. I haven't been with anyone since...him. I haven't been with anyone before him. It's always been him. Only him.

My mind wanders, and I can't help but wonder if Melody has slept with anyone since her husband died. Maybe she rotates men in and out of her bed like a goddamn Ferris wheel.

Or maybe not.

Maybe she's lonely and celibate. Maybe the moment we shared together in her basement was as alarming and out of character for her as it was for me.

I send my reply.

Me: And now it's only you. What are you going to do about it?
Magnolia: Stew in my loneliness and complain to you, apparently.
Me: Cop-out. The Magnolia I know stopped wilting a long time ago.
Magnolia: Maybe.

Falling against the chairback with a heavy breath, I chew on my lip as I ponder a response.

And then that response comes spewing out of me like vomit.

Me: Advice time. Here it comes...

Magnolia: Oh boy.

Me: I think you need to go have sex. Raw, dirty, messy sex. The hair-pulling, biting, scratching kind. The kind that turns you inside out and reinvents you. You need to come so hard, you forget about everything else and you shatter into a million pieces, blinded by stars and galaxies, until you're fucking free-falling, levitating, weightless. Screaming and begging. And the only thing you can think about is doing it all over again.

I click send before thinking it through, and then I have instant regret. Especially after three solid minutes tick by and nothing.

Fuck.

What the hell was that? Where did it come from?

I've never experienced that shit before. Is that what...*I* want?

Wondering if I scared her the fuck away, I attempt to fill the silence.

Me: I lose you? Too much?

She finally responds.

Magnolia: No. I'm just sitting here trying to figure out if that was supposed to be a suggestion or an offer.

Wait...*what?*

I blink at the screen, scanning over her words at least a dozen times.

Double fuck.

I'm not sure what the hell to say to that, as it was entirely unexpected, so naturally, I continue to spew more absurdity.

Me: What do you want it to be?

Magnolia: I'm trying to figure that out too.

I rub both palms up and down my face with a strained exhale.

Triple fuck.

This conversation has taken multiple wrong turns into Too-Many-Fucks-To-Count-Ville, and I'm not sure how to get back on track. The truth is, I don't want to screw up what we have right now because I genuinely *like* what we have. I don't have to carry around my heavy armor and backbreaking baggage. I can be...*free.*

Taking our relationship in a sexual direction will only mess it all up, and I'll lose that.

I've lost enough.

Me: You know we can't do that.

Her disappointment radiates through the laptop before her words even appear.

Magnolia: I suppose you're right. I'm sorry.

Me: My fault. I shouldn't have said all that shit.

Magnolia: No, I'm glad you did.

Me: Are you going to take my advice?

Magnolia: I don't know. There IS someone who makes me feel...something. But he's emotionally unavailable. And possibly gay.

Me: Emotions are overrated. Can't help you with the gay part, though.

Magnolia: Me and my complicated life. Thank you for listening.

I'm mid-response when another message pops up.

Magnolia: Zephyr?

Me: Yeah?

Magnolia: Did you see the sunrise this morning?

My thumb flicks along my bottom lip as I stare at the screen.

Her and the damn sunrise. She asks me this question all the time, but my answer is always the same. It won't change.

Me: I did. But I don't think I saw what you saw.

We say our goodbyes a few minutes later, and I shuffle off to bed with Walden at my heels, plugging my phone into the charging port as I climb beneath the slate gray bedsheets. I'm surprised when it bursts to life with a new text message, and even more surprised when I glance at the sender and discover Melody's name. I swipe it open.

Melody: This is a long shot, and I understand if you don't want to...but I'm going to the lake tomorrow after the group meeting. I've spent over a year of my life being scared. Scared to heal, scared to move forward, scared to be alone. I'm done being scared, so I'm going to dance instead. There's nothing scary about dancing. I'm going to dance until I can swim.

One more message follows, and I almost choke on my breath.

Melody: I thought maybe you would want to dance with me.

18

MELODY

Peanut butter and banana sandwiches."

Ms. Katherine's lips stretch into the sweetest smile, the rouge of her cheeks blossoming like pink peonies, and I consider adding it to my growing list of starting points. She's a portly woman with a slightly crooked bob, dappled in brindle and silver streaks. A floral-print blouse adorns her ample frame, the fuchsia petals matching the nail polish on her fingers that are curled around a leather-bound journal.

"Did you know those were Elvis Presley's favorite?"

A chuckle clears my lips as I duck my head. "My mom would always tell me that when she'd make them for me."

"You should try them with bacon sometime. It's such an interesting flavor dynamic," she encourages, shifting her weight on the folding chair.

Amelia pipes in. "That sounds nasty."

"You're a vegan, aren't you, Amelia?" Ms. Katherine prompts tenderly.

"Yep, for almost a year now. Anytime I look at meat, I just see Nutmeg's little face."

I quirk a smile, braving a glance to my left. Amelia scratches the back of her knuckles with short black nails, causing a cluster of blood dots to speckle her skin. "How is Nutmeg?" I ask her when the starting points shift down the circle.

"She's good. I just knitted her little booties, but she doesn't really like them."

The mental image of a hamster in hand-knit booties sends a tickle to my heart. "Maybe she just needs to get used to them."

"Or maybe she's a hamster." Parker adds his commentary with his arms folded across a well-worn T-shirt as he leans back, his body language oozing casual indifference. But his features look softer somehow, his eyes shimmering when they slide over to me, then back to Amelia. "That could be it."

"She's very domesticated and highly intelligent," Amelia counters, lifting her chin. "I'll bring her to a meeting some time. You'll see."

Parker offers a shoulder shrug, his disposition more playful than hostile. "I'm exploding with anticipation."

"I can tell. You look like you might do something extreme—like smile."

"I might."

His eyes float back to me as he replies, and I look away, worrying my lip between my teeth. That evening in my basement stomps through my mind with angry steps and steel-toed boots, inciting me to cross my legs and fidget with the fringe along my jean shorts.

I don't understand it. I don't understand *him*.

He claims to not like women, yet he held me on his lap like a lover, fisting my hair and digging contradictory evidence to his claim into my thigh.

He's never kissed anyone before, yet he allowed our lips to brush together through the cloak of darkness, his body trembling beneath my weight, his chaotic heart vibrating straight to my core.

He acts like he doesn't care about anything, yet he stuck around to help me clean up the neighborhood, silent and stoic for the most part, looking wildly uncomfortable, but he *stayed*.

And then he ignored my text last night—he left me on *read*.

It's not as if I expected him to accept the offer, but he ghosted me when I took a leap of faith and offered him a raw, unguarded piece of myself…and I hate admitting how much that hurt.

Parker's eyes continue to dig into me from a few feet away, and my lungs feel tight, my skin warming beneath the heat of his gaze. I wonder what he's thinking. I wonder what he sees when he watches me like this, so bold and unabashed.

My cheeks grow hot, but I refuse to turn my head toward him, instead focusing on a little string dangling from the hemline of my shorts, longer than all the others. I pretend it's the most fascinating thing I've ever seen as I coil it around my pinky.

When the meeting wraps up, fellow members linger for chitchat, strengthening the bonds they've established with kindred survivors. Amelia fills me in on an anime series she's been watching, and as her words trickle into my ears, my focus wanes, shifting over to Parker. He taps his foot against the shiny flooring, appearing twitchy and restless, hesitating for a few beats before rising from the chair.

Then he paces to the double doors and pushes through, disappearing from my sight.

I straighten, compelled to follow.

"Go ahead, you're fine. We can talk another day."

Amelia's voice steals my attention, and I falter. "What?"

"You looked like you wanted to go after Parker. You can if you want. I don't mind."

"Oh, I…" Swallowing, I pick at the emblem on my handbag and clear my throat. "No, I'm sorry. I'm listening."

"Were you?" she teases, nudging me with her bony shoulder.

"Definitely. The show with the nuts."

"The nuts?"

"Macadamias."

"It's actually…*My Hero Academia*."

I blink. "Oh."

Amelia nearly doubles over with laughter, cupping a hand around her violet-lined lips. "Go, will you?" she orders, her giggles diffusing. "He's probably waiting for you."

"I highly doubt that."

"Why? It's obvious he likes you."

A shudder ripples through me. "No, it's not."

"Haven't you seen the way he looks at you?"

It feels like something gets stuck in my throat as I squeeze my purse between two clammy hands.

Amelia sends me a knowing smile, her pierced eyebrow arching. "He looks at you like he's never seen anything like you before. Almost as if you're one of those sacred relics perched behind tempered glass at a museum or a gallery, far too precious to touch. People stare in wonder, awestruck and tongue-tied, trying to unravel its mysteries, trying to imagine the rich history and compelling stories that hide behind the pretty exterior." She sighs, her umber eyes glazing over with a sense of magic. "It must feel really good to have someone look at you like that—like they're seeing you for the first time every time, and they're amazed all over again."

My tongue slicks over my lips, and I inhale an uneven breath, her words bursting inside of me and dispersing like little sparklers, crackling and fizzing. "You should write poetry. That was really beautiful."

Likely not accurate, but beautiful.

"I do, but it's kind of morbid." Amelia ducks her head, pushing a ribbon of inky hair behind her ear. "Pretty words for dark hearts."

We share a smile before I rise from the chair, giving her arm a light squeeze as I say my goodbyes. When I move toward the exit, I waver, my feet stalling, and I twist back around to address Amelia. "You look better, by the way. Like you're healing."

"Healing?"

I nod.

Amelia crumples the fabric of her baggy T-shirt between her fingers, the ghost of a smile pulling at her lips. "I'm accepting. I suppose there's healing in acceptance."

I'm uncertain of her meaning, but I don't pry. I simply offer her a final smile, bob my head, and make my way out the doors, down the hall, then escape into the setting sun.

My heart jackknifes when I spot Parker leaning against the trunk of my car, hands tucked into dark denim pockets.

What?

He straightens when he notices me approach. "Fuck, that took forever. Thought maybe Emo Chick put a spell on you."

The breeze steals my hair, while he steals my breath. That playful edge is still in full swing, his demeanor more carefree than I've ever seen him. I swallow. "You were waiting for me?"

"Yeah. I thought we had plans."

"Plans?"

Parker frowns, squinting at me through the hazy sunset. "The lake. There's no way in hell I'm getting in the water, or dancing for that matter, but I'll tag along if you want me to."

My sandals clap against the pavement as I close in on him, the long, flowy sleeves of my ivory blouse catching a draft when I sweep shaky fingers through my hair. If he weren't such a magnet, I'd probably still be frozen to the cement. "You're coming?"

"I don't have fuck else to do." Parker's eyes slide over my bare legs when I reach him. His whole stance tautens, the muscles in his arms contracting as he pulls his focus back up to my face. "You asked me to, didn't you?"

"You never replied."

"Was I supposed to?"

Despite the heavy energy swirling between us, I can't help but let out a quick laugh. "That's generally the idea. Standard protocol."

He sniffs, glancing down at his dirt-smudged sneakers. "I'm a bit atypical."

"Yeah." I smile. "I think that's why I like you."

Parker's gaze shoots back up. His eyes flame, flickering like emerald torches. "You like me?"

"Oh, um…" His question isn't flirty or cocky—it's genuine, almost as if he's shocked to hear such a thing. I feel my face burn at the admission, and I hope the modest sunburn shading my cheekbones hides the evidence. "I figured the cupcakes gave me away."

He studies me, wordless, a little frown appearing between his brows. The one he wears so well, so prominently. Parker looks as if he might respond in some way, run with my confession, but he doesn't. He just glances to his left, clearing a hitch in his throat, and says, "Ready?"

"Okay."

A buzz of anticipation shoots through me while I rummage around my purse for my car keys, then pace over to the driver's side door. Parker follows suit, climbing in and throwing me a brief glance as he secures his seat belt. His woodsy scent permeates the small space, smelling of hot springs, cedarwood, and freshly fallen leaves. It's masculine and intoxicating, and it makes my skin flush to a feverish level.

God, this is so strange. This feeling—familiar yet foreign. I'm desperately trying to move forward, I *want* to move forward, but every time my belly clenches and my heart gallops, it feels like a slap in the face to Charlie. A disloyalty.

Spit on his grave.

My hands curl around the steering wheel, gripping tightly, my teeth burrowing into my bottom lip. This trip to the lake is about letting go. It's about progressing, forging ahead—*healing.*

Accepting, as Amelia said.

Accepting that Charlie is never coming back, and I can stay committed to his ghost, weighed down by the heavy anchors of what could have been, or I can push through the high tide.

I can swim.

Parker settles into his seat, propping his ankle up on the opposite knee. He flicks his gaze over me, studying my idleness. "You good?"

Not yet.

But I will be.

I send him a reassuring smile and start the engine. "I'm good."

The sun is barely peeking over the horizon when we arrive at the lake, coloring the rippled water in shades of apricot and blush. It was a relatively quiet car ride as my playlist serenaded us with a mix of Silversun Pickups and Cigarettes After Sex. Mood music, bordering on sensual. Probably not the smartest choice, considering my body already feels like it's being firebombed every time Parker glances my way.

Heaving out a breath of personal encouragement, I exit the parked vehicle, relishing in the way the summer breeze skims my face and sends my hair into a tizzy. It's a tepid wind, the kind that reeks of nostalgia and hidden promises. It's the perfect evening to give my fears a worthy send-off and dive headfirst into the future I deserve.

With Charlie…

And without him.

It's all about finding the balance—cherishing his memory and carrying those precious moments with me, while not allowing them to sink me and swallow me whole.

The water calls to me with quiet enchantment, compelling me to rush forward and kick off my sandals as sand and pebbles dig into my feet. My blood is spiked with giddiness, so I turn around, pacing backward while I wave my arms at Parker. He's perched idle at the front of my car, watching me with hooded curiosity. "Come with me."

I know he said he wouldn't, he'd only tag along, but I'm certain he's riddled with his own fears, his own personal demons. We can wash them away together.

Parker shakes his head. "I'll watch."

"Are you sure?" I send him a glowing smile, my heart thumping as my feet continue their backward trek.

"Yeah."

I try not to let my disappointment hinder this feeling. This *release*. My smile holds strong as I nod my head and twist back around to face the water.

As I approach the water's edge, I'm flooded with a memory of Charlie. The recollection burns me as I inch closer to the shoreline, the sand turning wet beneath my soles. We came to this very lake a week before my entire world turned to ashes and soot. He held me fiercely, his arms encircling my waist from behind while the stars reflected off the surface of the water.

"It's almost our anniversary," he said, tightening his grip on me.

"I can't believe it. It feels like our story is only just beginning."

He kissed the top of my head, just a delicate whisper. "Remember what I told you on our wedding day?"

"Hmm, I'm pretty sure it was something along the lines of I love this dress, but I can't wait to get you out of it. *"*

155

Charlie's chuckle rumbled through me, vibrating my skin. "Accurate, but not what I had in mind."

I smiled knowingly. "I can't wait to love you forever, Mrs. March."

"That's right." He lowered his head to the crook of my shoulder, pressing his lips to the exposed crest. "Forever doesn't seem long enough, does it?"

My chest ignites with a blaze of potent remorse, crawling upward and singeing the back of my throat. A small cry slips out—the sort of cry that just hangs there, wretched and painful, contaminating everything within reach.

I feel him then, coasting up beside me.

Parker.

It's a distorted comfort, one I want to soak up, like the way the water swallows the colors of the sun. But I want to repel it at the same time.

This is another man.

This is a man who isn't my husband, isn't my best friend, isn't the love of my life.

This is a stranger, essentially, a stranger who is the opposite of Charlie in every way.

And yet, I need him right now. I need him to be my anchor.

Parker stares out at the darkening lake, stiff and rigid, his eyes dancing over to me when I peer up at him. He cases me, from my windswept hair to my parted lips, landing on my arm that is draped across my midsection, fingers latched onto my opposite elbow. His gaze glints beneath the dimming sky. "What did it feel like?"

His voice is low, throaty and almost tremulous. I blink up at him, processing his question, not understanding. Then I hold my arm out as I follow his stare. My jagged scar is on full display, bathed in dusk. "The knife?" I murmur, croaking out the words.

Parker's eyebrows dip, but his gaze slides back up to mine. "To love someone that much."

My heart seizes, my eyes stinging with fresh tears. I'm forced to look away as I pull my lips between my teeth, holding back another mournful cry.

"Sorry. You should go dance now."

Swallowing, I glance back up at Parker, who has returned his attention to the lake. He teeters on the balls of his feet, his jaw clenching. I'm startled by his words as the chilly water laps at my toes—he's never apologized for anything before, but he apologizes for this. For his brush with vulnerability, his tender curiosity. That's nothing to be sorry for.

"It felt like completion," I tell him, explaining it the only way that makes sense. "It felt like a pinnacle. Like everything in your life has come full circle, and this person is the culmination of every dream, every plea, every dandelion wish.

"And when your dreams dissolve, and the wishes scatter, it's hard to find joy in anything else. How can you ever obtain completion again when you're missing the biggest piece?" A ragged sigh escapes me, and I watch the emotions play across his face, a melancholy reflection pulling at his features. "I have to believe there's still joy in the journey—this *new* journey—and that life isn't all about the finished puzzle. There's just as much fulfillment in putting it together."

Parker's eye twitches, his gaze lowering to the soggy sand, and when he finally looks back up at me, I smile.

I smile wide, I smile proud, I smile through the tears—because that's what it's all about.

"It's time to dance," I declare.

A squeal breaks free when I skip into the lake, my legs blasted with the ice-cold water, my fears washing away with every step.

I spin to look at Parker. He stands at the shoreline, watching me dip deeper into the water until it skims my waist. I splash my arms up, the frosty droplets dappling my hair, tearing another squeal out of me, and I twirl in unsteady circles, my toes sinking into the murky floor.

More laughter, more releasing, more dancing.

I jump and hop and move and spin. My blouse sticks to me as the ends of my hair skate along the lake, spraying and misting with every inelegant rotation. I'm purging my sickness, exorcising my demons, with eyes closed tight and my heart thundering its cleansing beats…I'm flying free.

I'm swimming.

I'm about to dive in, to fully immerse myself in the dark water, when I make a final spin and…

He's there.

My body collides with his hard frame, my palms planting against his chest as a startled gasp slips out.

Parker grips my upper arms to steady me, his eyes gleaming with something new. Something undiscovered—something reserved for only me.

"You came," I whisper, wide-eyed and spellbound.

His hands slide down my arms, resting at my elbows. "I'm regretting it already. Wet jeans are a bitch."

My smile blooms brighter, and I can't help the delirious laughter from spilling free.

He's here. He's in the water with me.

For me.

There is something magically inconceivable about that.

"Dance with me." I fumble for his wet hands and hold them in mine, swinging his arms side to side, shimmying us in a ridiculous series of movements that don't at all resemble dancing. But it's joyful and fulfilling and *fun*, and for a startling moment, I feel complete again.

Parker doesn't make any effort to move with me, but he doesn't resist my attempts either. He just stands there, shaking his head, staring off over my shoulder and allowing me to turn him into my impervious dance partner.

And then I start to sing.

"Don't Stop Believing."

Because terrible lake dancing obviously calls for a hideous karaoke rendition of Journey's greatest hit.

I belt the off-key lyrics, out of breath, still swinging Parker's arms around with zero coordination and a lot of accidental splashes to his face.

He stares at me like I've gone mad, and maybe I have, maybe I really have, but when I force myself into the most awkward twirl ever, dipping underneath his arm that I'm holding high above my head, the unthinkable happens.

I complete my spin, nearly losing my balance, and face Parker just as he starts to smile.

He *smiles*.

An amused burst of laughter accompanies his grin, and I go still, clinging to his hand. "Oh my God."

"My thoughts exactly," he mutters teasingly, looking down at me with eyes made of mint and mayhem.

Or magic. Maybe it's magic.

Lunging myself at him, I almost topple us both into the water as I slink my arms around his neck and pull him down, murmuring into the crook of his shoulder. "You smiled…you smiled, Parker."

His body stiffens in my hold, his own arms hanging rigid at his sides. The water tickles my waistline as I try to inch up on my tiptoes and hug him tighter to me, my lips lightly grazing the little water droplets that roll down the arch of his neck. I inhale a shuddering breath, my fingers curling around his nape, playing with the damp scruff of hair.

His words in my bathroom skip across my memory:

"Smiles should be saved for things that bring us real joy."

I brought him real joy. *Me.*

Acting like a fool in a murky lake, singing off-key, and dancing like no one was watching.

But *he* was watching. And it made him smile.

My grip on him strengthens, and I can't help but press a tiny kiss to the side of his neck, nuzzling my nose into the glistening skin above his collar.

Parker's breathing shifts from slow and steady to uneven. "What are you doing," he mutters, and I think it's supposed to be a question, a blatant demand, but it comes across more like a whispered breath—something unwittingly vulnerable.

I lower my arms, skimming my fingers down his torso, feeling him shiver, then I reach for his hands. Hands wound so tight, his limbs must ache.

Cradling his fists in my palms, I lift them to my hips, dragging them underneath my wet blouse until his fingers uncurl and grip my waist. Hard at first, his tension palpable, causing me to bow against him with a little whimper. Then his grasp softens, so I sweep his hands up farther, over my ribs, until his fingertips brush the underwire of my bra. The water ripples around us as he inhales sharply. "Tell me what you feel," I say, my voice quaking, knees quivering.

Parker's hands slide back down over my slick skin, trailing the shape of my curves, then he latches on to my hipbones and tugs me closer. "You say that as if you think I know how."

My gasp meets the front of his chest. "You do."

"I'll never feel things like you feel, Melody. I'm not wired that way."

"You smiled," I remind him. "You laughed."

His fingers dig into my hips, forehead dropping to the top of my head. The air around us crackles and shimmers with possibility as he drags his hands back up my body with a subdued groan. I teeter and sway, my balance stolen by the muck beneath my feet and the man touching me in a way no other man aside from Charlie has ever touched me before.

Parker lets out a hard breath into my hair. "This won't end well."

He lifts his hands higher until he's palming my breasts through the lace of my bra, and a surge of white-hot heat sweeps through me, arousal pulsing in my core. I'm waist deep in ice-cold water, but I might as well be standing in an incinerator. "Parker…"

"Fuck," he grits out, his thumbs dusting over my lace-sheathed nipples, taut and pebbled. "You're fucking me all up inside."

I arch back, squeezing his sodden shirt between my fists for leverage. "Parker," I repeat through an achy moan, his thigh angling right between my legs. "Kiss me."

19

PARKER

ALL THIS TIME, I'VE BEEN WRONG ABOUT HER.

She's not sunshine.

She's glittering nightfall, pale moonlight, silver stars in midnight skies.

She's that beacon of light when darkness threatens and consumes.

No, she's not the sun...

Melody is the moon.

"Kiss me."

She grinds herself against the front of my thigh with brazen disregard for anything else. Her skin is slick and wet beneath my fingertips as I palm her tits through gritted teeth, my cock rock-hard despite the cold water. I'm trying not to lose control because I know the moment this begins, there's no stopping it. I'm in too fucking deep, and the only way out will hurt like hell.

But *goddamn*, all I want to do is wrap her legs around me and fuck her senseless in the middle of this dirty-ass lake.

Melody moans again, pressing herself fully into me. "Please."

Kiss her?

Jesus...no. I can't do that.

I won't.

She grips the back of my head and lifts her chin until we're eye to eye, noses touching.

…But *fuck,* I kind of want to.

I want to know if that smile that has haunted me for the last few months tastes as sweet as it looks.

A growl erupts in my chest, and I tug her hair back, just as a crack of thunder pierces the silent night. Melody stares up at me, chest heaving, eyes glazed with lust. Her perfectly pink lips part, beckoning me to sample them, and her bottom lip quivers as I inch closer until I'm a hair's breadth away from her begging mouth.

I think I'm going to—I think I'm going to kiss her right here beneath lightly falling drizzle, my shoes sinking into sludge while my body sinks into *her.*

But the moment shatters…*just like that.*

Melody's hands dip beneath my wet T-shirt, her fingertips grazing along my hidden scars, and I don't think she even notices because she's too preoccupied waiting for my mouth to claim hers…but I fucking notice.

And I freeze, going ramrod still and pushing her away, like she's my foe crossing over enemy lines.

Melody stumbles, hardly keeping her balance in the water, her eyes wide and wounded when she steadies herself and stares up at me. "Parker?"

"This is a fucking mistake," I ground out, moving backward, my shoes and soaked denim weighing me down. "Just…stay away."

"What?"

She looks like she might burst into tears, and I'd be fucking lying if I said it didn't do something to me. Shoving the unfamiliar feelings aside, I shake my head, throwing daggers at her with my eyes. "Stay the fuck away, all right?"

Melody wraps her arms around herself like a protective shield, trying to reject my venom. "What did I do?"

"What *haven't* you done? You just keep poking me—you keep invading, *intruding,* trying to find a way in. You're a goddamn nuisance."

I sling my barbed-wire words at her, and I think they cut us both.

But goddammit, this is for the best. It can end now, or it can end later, and it's going to cut a hell of a lot deeper later.

Melody's gasp of surprise mingles with the light rainfall, and she jerks her head away from my hard gaze, biting into her lip. "I don't understand," she says in a broken whisper.

"That's the point. You don't understand *me*. You never will, so it's better if you just stay the fuck away."

She shakes her head with disbelief, still avoiding my stare. "You're an asshole."

"Yeah," I bite out, continuing my backward trek to shore. "Looks like you dodged a bullet."

I don't wait for her response, and I can't stomach any more of her tears, so I spin around and stomp my way through the lake until I breach the shoreline.

Then I remember I left my goddamn truck at the support meeting.

Fuck me.

Growling my frustration, I make a mental note to avoid dramatic exits in the future when I have no means of exit, especially while drenched in piss water and seaweed, fishing undiscovered lake species out of my boxers.

It's a miserable four-mile walk to my truck, and I'd like to say it's for all of the abovementioned reasons.

But it's mostly because I can't get that damn look in her eyes out of my head.

Two hours later, I'm finally home, showered, pissed off, and pent-up. Walden lies at my feet, his chin resting between two hairy paws as he gazes up at me slumped on the couch.

I'm just kind of staring off into space, replaying the night in my head, wondering how I got myself into this absolute shit show.

I decide to break it down by facts.

Fact number one: I'm attracted to Melody.

As much as I want to live in my fantasy world of denial and pretend that it's all just a giant fluke, the truth is pathetically obvious. I'm fucking attracted to her.

My dick likes what it sees, and it wants to see more.

Fact.

Fact number two: I don't like women.

Except…I like Bree and always have, and I sure seem to like Melody, and hell, even Amelia is growing on me. And fine—Ms. Katherine isn't so bad either, especially today when she brought in little deli trays of assorted submarine sandwiches and a fruit platter.

So maybe that's not a fact. I'm going to skip that one for now.

Fact number three: I like people who feed me.

Fact number four: Emotions are garbage, and I'm incapable of genuine connection. Therefore, pursuing my attraction to Melody is a catastrophic mistake.

The woman has been through enough grief and heartache to last a lifetime, and if tonight was any indication of how a possible tryst would unfold, it would be in her best interest to stay the fuck away from me. I'm only going to drag her down and drown her in my own ocean of misery.

What kind of sexual relationship could we even have, anyway? How would she feel screwing a guy who detests intimacy and refuses to take his shirt off?

It's pointless, a dead end.

Breakdown: I want to fuck Melody, but I won't. Some women are okay. I like food.

Final thoughts: This exercise sucked, and I'm no closer to feeling any better.

My mind continues to stew, the black cloud hovering over me growing more aggressive than the rain clouds outside my window. It's raining—*again*. It's been the summer of rain, and I can't help but wonder if Melody is still out there, maybe perched on the sandy beach, doused in rainwater and remorse.

Fuck…she was so happy in that lake tonight, dancing and weightless, free as a bird.

And then I ruined everything.

My scars and old ghosts prevailed, snuffing out her spark and sending her right back into the darkness.

I made her cry.

I made her doubt.

I made her stop dancing.

And I hate that those thoughts are crawling beneath my skin and eating me alive. I'm not accustomed to regret or guilt. I don't *feel*.

But I'm feeling right now, and it feels like shit.

Walden nudges my sock-covered foot, making a little grumpy sound as I grumble right back. We're two peas in a pod, this old mutt and me.

When I lean forward to scratch the scruff between his ears, my phone pings to life beside me on the sofa. My skin tingles, and my stomach lurches, thinking it might be Melody—wondering if she's telling me to fuck off or maybe she's sending me a sweet, sympathetic message, which would be a billion times worse.

I snatch the phone up, seeing Magnolia's name instead. I open the message.

Magnolia: I know I promised that things wouldn't get personal. I'm sorry…I lied. I want to see you. I want to do a video call. I need to know that you're real, that I'm real, and that you see me. Will you do this for me?

What the fuck?

My cheeks fill with air before I blow out a hard breath, scratching at my still-damp mess of hair. She wants to do a video call? Shit… *no*. That sounds terrible.

I like our arrangement as is. No strings attached. Magnolia is my anonymous outlet, the only one I have, and one that I've grown to genuinely crave.

Magnolia lets me hide.

Chewing on the inside of my cheek, I shoot her a response.

Me: Where is this coming from? I like what we have. I'd prefer to keep it the way it is.
Magnolia: I understand—I do. I like what we have, too, but I'm yearning for more.
Me: Why? Because of your husband's heart? Is that the basis of this connection?

Maybe I'm being an ass, but I'm already on edge.

I've lost Melody—I don't want to lose Magnolia too.

And when her response doesn't come through right away, I'm pretty sure I get my answer.

Me: Thanks. Got it.

Magnolia: Please don't be that way. I thought you didn't get offended?

I grit my teeth.

Me: Not offended. Just disappointed.

Magnolia: If you're disappointed, maybe that means you're yearning for more too. You feel the same connection I do.

Me: The connection is rooted in what we have right now. I don't want to shake that up.

Magnolia: Are you afraid you won't like what you see?

Me: No. I'm afraid I will.

Her silence spans a few minutes, and I curse myself for saying that shit. Maybe it's true, though. Maybe I'm worried she'll be everything I never knew I wanted. And then I'll be letting down two women I've come to care for.

Magnolia's response finally pops up.

Magnolia: How about this: I don't want to infringe on your privacy. I understand your hesitation, and I respect it. So...what if you only saw me? You can keep your camera off. Your identity will still remain a secret.

Me: I can see you, but you can't see me?

Magnolia: Yes.

The temptation seizes me.

The curiosity.

Leaning back in my rolling chair, I fold my arms across my chest and pivot side to side, my heart thumping with indecision. This would change everything. This would upset our dynamic, and nothing would ever be the same.

But hell, *why not?*

Why the fuck not?

Hoping I don't regret this, I send my reply.

Me: Okay.

Magnolia: Really?

Me: Yeah. Set it up.

A few moments later, a link pops up in the message box, causing my insides to spiral. It's a Google Meet link. I'm pretty fucking terrible with technology, so there's a chance I might screw this up, but I take the risk and click the link.

Moving out of frame, I tinker with the settings to make damn sure my camera's off, then I slide back up to the keyboard and inhale a giant breath of courage.

Fuck, I'm nervous.

I don't know why, but I guess that means I kind of care.

My foot taps against the carpeted floor as I wait for something to happen.

Something happens.

Her camera flickers on, pointing toward a rust-colored wall.

I frown, prickled with a sense of familiarity. It's an ugly fucking color that I don't see too often—and I've been in a lot of houses.

No. Impossible.

"Can you hear me?"

The sound of her voice sends more tingles of déjà vu down my spine, but there's static, so I can't be sure. I fiddle with the settings again, unsure if my microphone is on. It seems to be muted, so I use the chat feature to send my reply.

Me: I hear you.

My reply pops up on the screen, and Magnolia speaks again.

"Okay…great. Are you ready?"

Definitely not.

Me: I'm ready.

There's a dramatic pause, and my pulse revs with anticipation as I wait for her to reveal her identity. I feel it in my ears, my temples, my throat. My hands are folded in my lap, fisted tightly, and my jaw aches as my teeth clench together.

Th-thump. Th-thump. Th-thump.

The camera jiggles, and a piece of white-blond hair floats into the frame.

My stomach sinks. My heart snares on a jagged beat.

That wall.

That voice.

Widowed and wilting.

Another beat passes, and Melody situates herself in front of the camera, timid and demure, rosy cheeked and practically shaking.

I blink. I blink again.

No, no, no.

Fuck. No.

"Hi."

She says it in the sweetest, softest voice, her smile as bright as the sun, while everything else crumbles around me, an avalanche of wreckage and astoundment.

Magnolia is Melody.

Melody is Magnolia.

And I should have known.

I should have *fucking* known.

This is supposed to be the point where I send her a *hello*, tell her she's fucking beautiful, let her know she's everything I never knew I wanted.

But I don't do that. I don't do that at all.

Instead, I slam my laptop shut, pick it up, and hurl it across the room with a violent growl, watching as it breaks into a million fractured pieces against my living room wall. Even my dog jumps up and shuffles over to his dog bed, rattled by my wrath.

My chest heaves, my body tremors, my mind reels with impossibility.

What are the odds? What are the goddamn odds?

Another wave of raging disbelief ripples inside me, and I manifest it into a typhoon of self-destruction. I trash my whole house, pulling things off walls, slinging dishes, clearing countertops, shouting obscenities, and then I collapse into a heap on the floor, my back flush with the kitchen wall.

Magnolia is Melody.

It makes fucking sense. There's no way I would develop a connection with *two* separate women at the same time, after living my entire life despising them all.

It could only be her.

Fuck.

Not allowing my anger to abate because it's comforting somehow, I jump back to my feet and hunt down my shoes and the keys to my truck. I'm not sure what I'm doing, I'm not sure how I'm going to handle this, I'm not sure how I'm going to look Melody in the eyes anymore—but right now her eyes are the only thing I want to see.

She needs to know.

She needs to know the truth.

20

MELODY

"Z EPHYR79 HAS LEFT THE MEETING."

A burning ball of shame funnels through me, a cruel, wicked windstorm, stealing the breath from my lungs. My fingers curl into tight fists as I stay rooted to the couch cushion, desperately trying to hold the tears back before they burst through like a broken dam.

Maybe he lost connection.

Maybe his phone died.

It could be the storm.

I suck in a breath so hard, my chest aches. Standing from the sofa, I pace over to my propped-up cell phone and close out the video call, then send him a message to see what happened before I jump to conclusions and join a nunnery.

Me: I'm going to choose to believe that your phone died, and that you didn't voluntarily leave after seeing me.

He doesn't appear to be online, so I try to stay hopeful that it was a fluke and had nothing to do with my face.

Shaking away the jitters and anxiety, I distract myself by scrubbing down my countertops twelve times like a psycho. I try not to think about Zephyr.

I try not to think about Parker.

I try really hard not to think about the way his hands felt on me or the way his words sliced me down just as I was about to leap into something new and frighteningly intoxicating.

Pushing through the weighty pit of dread in my stomach, I snatch my phone back up fifteen minutes later and check for a response.

Nothing.

But…it *does* say that Zephyr was active two minutes ago.

Oh my God.

He saw my message.

He saw my message, and he ignored it.

He *did* voluntarily leave that chat after seeing me for the first time.

Tears prickle my eyes like little rose thorns, and I feel sliced down all over again.

That's *twice.* Twice in one night I've been rejected and stomped on by two men I've grown to care about. Two men I've developed feelings for. Two men I've opened up to and become vulnerable with, despite the coil of guilt I've felt at betraying Charlie in some twisted way.

I toss my phone onto the kitchen counter, then storm out my patio door in bare feet as the rain pours down, pelting the earth and masking the wretched meltdown that is brewing in the back of my throat. After spending an hour wilting in the shower when I returned home, washing away Parker and the stains he left behind, it seems I need another cleanse.

My feet carry me out to the center of my spongy lawn, naked toes sinking into the grass. My loungewear is instantly soaked, the white tank top and cotton shorts sticking to my skin as I shiver beneath the cathartic rainfall.

So much rain lately.

So much to disinfect.

The storm clouds release a mighty downpour as I tilt my chin up and face the sky, closing my eyes and whispering a desperate plea. "I'm lost, Charlie. Tell me what to do."

Thunder rumbles in the distance, vibrating right through me, and that's when I hear it.

The sound of a familiar engine rolls up to the front of my house as tires screech to a halt and a car door slams shut.

No way.

Frowning, I swiftly pace over to the side of the house, drawing to a stop when I see him stalking through my lawn toward the front door, his face masked with harsh intensity—like he's on a mission.

Parker nearly stumbles to a halt when he spots me standing in the backyard, staring at him with a healthy mix of confusion and hostility.

Why is he here?

I don't want him here. He told *me* to stay away from *him*.

I cross my arms over my chest with an air of defensiveness—and also to hide the fact that rain doesn't mesh very well with thin, white cotton.

Parker's expression darkens, his features tightening as he shifts direction and charges toward me. "You're fuckin' soaked and half-naked," he grits out through the heavy rain, slicking his hair back as he approaches.

My face twists with disdain, and I turn my back to him, stomping away like a petulant child.

"Melody."

"Go home, Parker." I throw him a glare over my shoulder. "You're not welcome here."

He catches my wrist to spin me around, and I almost slip on the wet grass. My arm pulls free like he just scalded me. "Don't! Don't touch me."

"Goddammit, will you stop?"

"Why are you here?" I demand, chest heaving, outrage escalating. "You were pretty loud and clear at the lake tonight. I'm just a nuisance to you. A thorn in your side, a gnat in your ear. A fly in your fucking soup."

Parker opens his mouth to respond, to make his intentions known, but his tongue freezes and he hesitates. He just kind of stares at me for a moment, his brows pinching together like he's trying to work through something, or maybe he's just angry and agitated like he always is.

I try again, forcing myself to soften. "Why are you here?"

He swallows. "I…" Parker trails off, seemingly unable to get the words out. His whole body tenses, the muscles in his jaw ticking when his eyes dip down, raking over me and lingering on my partially exposed breasts plastered against the now see-through tank top. He flicks his attention back to my face, his gaze hot and stormy. "You drive me fucking mad."

My arms shoot up to block his view of my chest, my defenses flaring back to life. "If you came over to insult me, I'm not interested. I've had a really shitty day that you'll be pleased to know you contributed to."

"You think that pleases me?"

"Yes, I do."

Parker swipes dark, wet hair from his forehead, letting out a grunt of exasperation. "That doesn't please me, Melody. You want to know what pleases me?" He advances on me like a hungry predator. "Not giving a shit. Not *caring*. Being alone, keeping to myself, and not giving a flying fuck about whether or not you're still out in that lake, brokenhearted, or at home crying yourself to sleep, thinking you're not good enough for an asshole like me."

I refuse to let his words chip away my armor. "You're flattering yourself. I'm *fine*."

"You don't get it." He shakes his head. "I'm supposed to hate you. I'm supposed to hate everything you stand for. Now, all I want to do is fuck you." Parker yanks my arms apart, putting my breasts back on display for his eyes to drink me in. His voice lowers, the words cracking. "What the hell are you doing to me?"

My body heats, my pulse throbbing as his fingers tighten their grip on my wrists. My angry breaths of indignation turn shaky and uneven. "I'm just being me."

"Yeah," he mutters, hardly a whisper. "That's what I'm afraid of."

Parker inches closer to me, and I squeeze my eyes shut, my heart rate quickening.

No.

No, he doesn't get to do this. He doesn't get to rip me open, then think he can be the one to stitch me back together again. That's *my* job.

Reining in my growing arousal, I tug my wrists free and move away, watching as his eyebrows dip once more. "Go home, Parker." I hate the way my voice sways. "If you're looking to scratch an itch, I'm sure you have plenty of options."

"Is that what you think?" His frown deepens, lips pursing together as he studies me. "You think I'm out there chasing tail, and you just happen to be next on my long list of *options*?"

I shrug, faking my way through indifference. "Maybe. Probably."

Parker slowly nods, stepping forward and closing the gap between us. His proximity is alarmingly potent as his eyes skim across my face, a green blaze of wildfire. "How about this: I haven't had sex in eleven years—haven't thought about it, haven't wanted it. Haven't even cared." He leans down closer, until his lips graze my ear like a whispered kiss, and he breathes out, "Or how about this: I've jerked off more times in the last week thinking about *you*, than I have all goddamn year."

An electric jolt shoots through me, and my hands lift involuntarily, gripping the hard muscles of his arms to keep myself from teetering.

Parker's head raises slightly, pivoting until our eyes lock. "So, believe me when I say you're more than just an itch. You're a fucking revolution."

My fingernails claw into his tensing biceps, a little gasp escaping my throat. As my eyelids flutter right along with the colony of butterflies in my stomach, I lean into him, drawn to his words, his scent, his aura.

But just as I'm about to give in to him—*again*—he pulls away.

He steps back, leaving a chilly emptiness in his absence. My eyes pop open, spitting fire as he keeps trekking backward through my yard. Leaving. "Good," I seethe, sick of his mixed signals. Sick of the crumbs he throws me right before he steals them all away. *"Go."*

Parker holds my gaze for another moment before spinning on his heels and storming through my backyard.

His dismissal infuriates me.

What was the point of that?

What the hell was the point?

Fists clenched at my sides, I shout at his retreating back, "I hate you. You're *nothing* like Charlie. You're the opposite of him in every way, and it makes me sick that I…" Parker comes to an abrupt stop, his shoulders tautening as his head bows. I swallow. "It makes me sick that I…"

"That you what?" Parker faces me then, twisting in place. "Say it."

My bottom lip quivers with the words I can't seem to expel.

"Fucking say it, Melody." He traipses back over to me with fury on his face. "What makes you sick? That you want me?"

I shake my head as he advances.

"Admit it. You want me."

"No."

"No?" Parker comes to a halt when we're toe-to-toe, his chest swelling with labored breaths, something savage glinting in his eyes. "You're lying. You'd let me take you right here, right now, in the pouring fucking rain, like a wild animal."

Shudders rip through me, stopping my breath. His gaze slips to my heaving breasts, my nipples tight, nearly cutting through the thin fabric, and when he glances back up…there's a shift. Something palpable, visceral. I feel it, he feels it, and I think the sky feels it too, because just then, lightning cracks above us, an aggressive flash of heat that mimics the look in his eyes.

We pounce on each other.

I go for his mouth, but he dodges me, biting my jaw instead, then trailing his tongue along my neck as he shoves the straps of my tank top off my shoulders and pushes the fabric down past my breasts. Parker groans when my breasts spill free, dipping his head lower until he's sucking a nipple into his mouth and I'm arching into him, my body crumbling. My moan mingles with his as my hands frantically fumble with his belt buckle, unlatching it and searching for the zipper.

Parker bends further and grasps me right beneath the thighs, lifting me into the air and hooking my legs around his waist. I squeak in surprise, but it dissolves into a needy whimper when his erection presses between my legs and he carries me off somewhere, who knows where—I don't really care as long as he keeps sucking my nipple like that, his teeth nicking the sensitive flesh and inciting my pelvis to grind against the hard bulge in his jeans.

My back slams into the wooden planks of the backyard shed, and I yelp when Parker starts tugging my shorts down my legs, his mouth all over me, my hands scratching at his scalp and fisting his wet hair.

The storm rages on around us, or maybe we *are* the storm. We're the flashes of lightning, the thunder booming, the dark clouds of destruction hiding the bright moon. The rain pours down and drenches us, a welcoming contrast to the searing heat threatening to detonate.

My spine bows back when Parker's finger slips inside me, and I grasp at his shoulders, clawing and digging. "Oh God…"

"Goddamn," he rasps against the shell of my ear, biting at the lobe.

I hear his zipper unfasten as I thrust against his pumping finger, needing him deeper, needing *more*. Parker lifts his head from the crook of my shoulder, finding my eyes for one blinding, potent second, before he pulls his finger out of me and flips me around until my front is pressed up against the shed wall.

A gasp escapes me as the splinters dig into my skin, but I hardly notice because Parker snakes his arm around my midsection, palming my breast with one hand, while the other spreads my thighs apart. Instinctively, I arch my back, searching for him—*begging* for him.

His mouth is devouring my neck again, his tongue hot and demanding as he tastes me, sweat and rainwater, his hand leaving my breast to fist my hair and tug it back. Parker situates himself between my legs from behind, the tip of his cock seeking entry. The feel of him there, teasing me, has my body tremoring and aching as I grind against him. "Please."

"Fuck, Melody…"

As the thunder rolls overhead, Parker spreads me wider as his opposite hand curves around my throat, and he pushes inside.

Hard. Abrupt. Unforgiving.

Holy shit.

My cry is muffled when his hand clamps my jaw, two fingers slipping into my mouth, and I bite down. Parker's forehead drops to my shoulder, his prolonged groan making my skin hum as I slink one arm behind his neck to hold him to me.

He starts to move, his hips rocking against me, slowly at first, stretching me and making me squirm. His tongue drags along the crest of my shoulder, up to my neck, and he pulls the flesh between his teeth, grunting, while his cock hits deeper, his thrusts quickening.

I plant both hands against the shed for leverage while his fingers tug my jaw open, and I yelp again, unsure of what hurts, what stings, what's right or wrong, and what feels so good, the line between pain and pleasure becomes a glorious, permanent blur.

Parker's fingers leave my mouth and sweep down my body until he finds the juncture between my legs, and I press into his palm, a silent plea. With one hand gripping my hipbone, keeping me steady while he slams into me, the other rubs my clit into a delicious frenzy, pulling mewls and whimpers and unabashed moans from my throat.

His lips dip to my ear, his breathing ragged. "You're driving me fucking wild…you feel so goddamn good."

"Uhh…" It's all I can manage, his words and hands twisting me inside out, stealing my coherency and common sense.

Reinventing me.

I feel myself peaking, climbing, singing, and buzzing, while Parker fucks me against the shed in my backyard beneath black clouds and faded moonlight.

Like animals.

As his fingers work me to orgasm and his thrusts become more feral, my body tenses and thrums, and I break apart into a thousand tiny particles, atoms, and stars.

My climax nearly cripples me.

Knees buckling, I crumple forward, while Parker squeezes my breast, tweaking my nipple as a cry of pleasure tears through my throat. He rams into me with violent, frenzied strokes, grunting his release, burying his face into the slick curve of my neck.

"*Fuck,*" he grits out, shuddering against me, his palm still cupping my breast while his opposite hand clings to my hip, fingertips biting into the delicate skin.

And then it's over.

His movements temper, and he just holds me for a moment as we both come down from the heady high. It's nothing but raindrops and heartbeats and heavy breaths as Parker's grip on me loosens, his head lifting from my shoulder. I feel his heart vibrating into my back, his erection still firm and pulsing inside me, his fingers trailing lightly down my torso, almost a tickle, as he lets out a deep, equivocal sigh near my ear.

Then he slides out of me, letting me go, and I remain still, partially collapsed against the shed with my shorts dropped to my ankles and a sodden tank top bunched around my middle.

Rainwater mixes with Parker's release and spills down my thighs, reminding me that Charlie is no longer the last man to have been inside me. I gave that title to a man who claims to not even like women—who was cruel to me—*who didn't deserve it.*

I gave a precious gift to an unworthy man.

The realization rips a sob from my chest before I have time to even recover. I slump farther against the wet wood planks of Charlie's beloved shed—the shed that has now been defiled by a painful act of betrayal.

A betrayal to him. A betrayal to me.

With limbs quivering with regret, I simply stand there, hardly able to hold my weight and the weight of so much more.

My eyes squeeze shut, my face hidden behind my hands, when I feel a gentle touch graze the small of my back. Light as a feather at first, barely there at all, until he applies more pressure and rubs his palm up and down my spine, as if he's trying to comfort me somehow.

It's a tiny token of solace.

A gift in exchange for mine.

And then he's tugging my shorts up my legs until they're secured around my hips, the soaked cotton sticking to my skin like adhesive. I pull my forehead up from the shed, pivoting slowly, facing him. His pants are pulled up, but the belt hangs loose, and there's an angry nail mark etched into his neck from where I must have scratched him.

Parker stares at me with a faint wrinkle furrowed between his brows, and I swear there is concern etched into that crease—maybe even a semblance of empathy.

But it's all he gives me before pacing backward, gaze dipping down, jaw hard and tight like his fists that ball up at his sides.

And just like that, he's gone.

Parker leaves me there against the shed, tainted and torn, reeking of guilt and self-loathing and *him.*

And when I awake the following morning to chirping birds and ribbons of sunlight, I'm curled up inside the little wooden shed, body aching, skin filthy, dignity shattered.

Heartbroken.

21

PARKER

WHEN I WAKE UP THE NEXT MORNING, I HAVE NO IDEA WHAT THE FUCK is going on. I shoot up in bed, momentarily caught between some sort of dreamland fantasy and preposterous reality.

What time is it?

Do I work today?

Did I fuck Melody against a shed last night?

My dick twitches in my boxers, as if to reply, *hell fucking yeah, you did.*

Jesus. Christ.

I went there with every intention of unveiling my Zephyr alter ego, but I couldn't do it. I choked, and I couldn't spit the goddamn words out. *Why?*

Don't know.

Maybe because I'm a coward.

Maybe because everything would change.

Maybe because Melody wants *me* right now, and the moment she finds out who I really am…it won't be about me anymore.

It will be about *him.*

Him and his goddamn heart.

I have no clue why that even matters—why something so drippy and sentimental would actually *matter* to me—but I can't help but feel smothered by the realization that I don't want to lose her.

And I would…I'd lose her.

So apparently, the logical next step was to fuck her silly in her backyard to ensure that I'll never dig my way out of this giant, endless hole of mind-numbing madness and fuckery.

Solid plan.

Utterly masterful.

Scrubbing a palm down my face, I heave out a sigh of frustration, blindly reaching for my phone to check the time and gauge damage control.

Shit.

It's already after ten a.m., and I have more house projects given to me by Owen's thirsty mother, so I need to get the fuck going. But a text from Melody sent an hour ago steals my motivation. I swallow down a hard lump as I swipe it open.

Melody: You just left me there.

My heart stutters.

Fucking hell.

Was I not supposed to?

Were we supposed to cuddle and spoon? Talk about shit? I don't fucking know.

I scratch at the bristles on my chin, entirely overwhelmed by not knowing what the hell I'm doing. This is new territory for me—*all* of it. The sex, the false pretenses, the *feelings*. It's new for her too, because now that I know Melody is Magnolia, I have more insight into her life.

She's never been with anyone else before.

Only her husband.

And now me.

Her stain, her shameful mistake, her mark of Cain.

Now that I think about it, I suppose leaving her alone, half-naked in the rain after screwing her brains out was probably a dick move. But I thought that's what she wanted—for me to get the fuck away from her. She was literally sobbing with regret.

My thumb taps with agitation against the side of my phone while I consider a response, but nothing comes to mind. I'm not equipped to handle this shit. I've never had to *fix* anything before. What does she even want from me?

An apology?

An explanation?

To meet for coffee and chat about our feelings?

I'm not exactly sure what she's looking for, but I know what she deserves. *The truth.*

The truth about Zephyr.

But I'm too much of a pussy to give it to her.

So I turn off my phone, hop in the shower, and start my day.

———————

"Why don't you fight back? Too chickenshit, or did you eat too many Twinkies and it's too much effort to move?"

When I pull into the Jamesons' driveway and jump out of my truck, Owen is getting pushed around by some piece-of-shit kid in his front yard. Cruel laughter spills out of the tall, gangly bully, sporting a buzz cut, too-baggy jeans, and a smirk that I'd love to punt right off the prick's face. But I don't because I'd probably accidentally kill him, and prison time isn't on my bucket list. Not that I have a bucket list—bucket lists are for hopeful optimists, and I'm more of a cynical killjoy—but if I did, orange jumpsuits and horny inmates would not be on that list.

Owen stumbles back when the asswipe gives him a forceful shoulder shove, not making any attempt to defend himself. He just stands there with his head bowed, cheeks as red as his bloodshot eyes.

I abandon my tools and approach the scene, flooded with an odd urge to intervene. "Hey. Asshole."

The smirky kid loses said smirk when his head flicks over to me, and he steps back. "We were just messin' around. It's all good."

"Looks to me like you were being a Douchewaffle." They both stare at me, blinking, so I turn to Owen. "You all right?"

He lies with a timid nod.

"We were just playing," Douchewaffle insists, scuffing his sneaker against the grass.

Pursing my lips together, I nod, giving a flippant shoulder shrug. "Can I play?"

Douchewaffle noticeably gulps, fidgeting. Owen watches with interest.

I don't wait for a response and saunter over to my truck, snatching up a tire iron from the bed and heading back over to the two boys. Then I stand there.

I just…stand there.

Silent and menacing, my eyes locked on Douchewaffle.

Smoldering, as Melody would say.

He glances at Owen, as if asking for help, but Owen only quirks an amused grin as he keeps his attention on me. Douchewaffle glances at the tire iron. "Um, what's that for?"

I don't reply. I don't blink. I don't flinch.

I just stand.

And stare.

Basically, I intimidate the fuck out of this kid until he almost shits his pants, then bolts.

Slapping the tool against my opposite palm when the bully is out of sight, I shift my focus to Owen, who looks totally impressed, like I just taught a llama how to play the harp. "Don't let that punk mess with you. You're too cool for that shit."

"You think I'm cool?" Owen asks, appearing wide-eyed and awestruck as he smacks his bangs out of his face.

"Definitely. You're cooler than me."

"No way. That was the coolest thing I've ever seen."

"Making model cars is a lot cooler. I think you've got me beat."

His face lights up with a big grin, cheeks stretching wide. "I guess the Kamikaze is kind of cool. Want to see the new one I made?"

"Sure."

Stopping at my truck to gather tools for the day's projects, I follow Owen inside the house, trying to ignore the little pang of contentment that hums inside my chest. I've been feeling it more than I care to admit—something like happiness.

It's been brewing on and off for a little while now, pumping through my blood and defrosting my icy veins, seeping into untapped parts of me. Parts that have been dark and hollow for a long ass time. I'll notice it when Walden curls up beside me on the couch, or when Owen looks genuinely happy to see me, or when Bree stops by with random gifts and tells me about her day.

I'll notice it when Melody smiles at me. When she laughs. When she surprises me with cupcakes. When she shares her starting points.

When she looks at me like I fucking matter.

Yeah, I've been feeling it a lot lately. I've been feeling it since I met *her*.

As I set down my toolbox and make a pit stop in Owen's room, he brings out the new model car and tells me all about it, eager and enthusiastic, filled with pride. His whole demeanor shifts from insecure and beaten down to...*seen*.

For a moment, I'm transported back in time to that foster house after years of feeling lost and transparent—broken apart so expertly, I had withered away to dust. All it took was for one person to notice me. To stick up for me. *To care.* Bree's kinship was the one link I had to humanity, my only sense of purpose, and while she's probably the solitary reason I'm still alive today, so much damage had already been done. I was irrevocably branded with these scars and ironclad weights, molding my future into the desolate, dark hole I've come to embrace.

So maybe I see a little of myself in this kid.

Maybe I want him to have a fighting chance—a chance to rebuild before there is nothing left of value to extract from the rubble.

A starting point.

"Parker?"

I'm moving toward the doorway to start my work when I pause, giving him my full attention. "Yeah?"

Owen tilts his head to the side, deep in thought. His little tongue pokes out to wet his lips, brown eyes as wide as saucers. Then he wonders innocently, "What's a douchewaffle?"

22

MELODY

ONE WEEK.
One week of radio silence from Parker *and* Zephyr, and Parker has the *nerve* to show up to this meeting as if nothing were amiss. As if we didn't have raw, passionate sex in my backyard seven days ago. As if he didn't just leave me there alone in the rain, ignore my text, and refuse to make any follow-up contact.

Anger surges through me like a wave, tingeing my cheeks pink. He's just sitting there, one seat over, his legs sprawled out in front of him like usual, arms crossed. I don't think he's looked my way all meeting, which is unusual. Even when I gave my starting point, my throat catching, my tone trembling, he stared straight ahead, his expression unreadable.

Good.

I'm glad he can't bear to look at me.

Unfortunately, I don't seem to have the same kind of willpower. My shameful eyes can't stop peeking his way, drinking him in, from his scuffed, tan work boots to his tousled mess of dark hair. His eyes look tired. Ambivalent. The muscles in his arms flex and strain every so often, reminding me of how they felt wrapped around my body, holding me close, clutching me tight—making me feel things so unfettered, I'm still in disarray.

My body buzzes with potent memories. I can still feel his breath in my ear and his tongue along my neck. The fading bruise he left behind pulses with its own recollection. My core hums, my heart revs, and my thighs clench as I roll my gaze over his slack posture. Parker's right leg bounces restlessly, and I try to hide my perusal with the palm of my hand, hoping I'm shrouded by Amelia and her veil of black hair.

But as I unwittingly memorize the number of holes in his belt, replaying the sound of it unlatching in my hands, I feel his focus shift.

He's looking at me. He knows I'm watching him.

It's in my best interest to keep my eyes off his, to ignore the weight of his attention prickling me with a thousand tiny daggers, but it's impossible. I'm pulled into his spell in the same way the crest of a mighty wave would yank me down into the deep, dark sea.

Inevitable.

Our eyes meet for the first time since that night—since he walked away from me with that troubled, woeful expression etched across his face. The one that portrayed more emotion in a single moment than I think I've ever seen from him.

The one I can't stop thinking about.

The instant we find each other, everything else seems to disappear. The lights dim, and the voices fade. It's just *us*. And I think that's how it's always felt between us—that swirling energy, that magnetism. I was hoping we had gotten it out of our systems, but the magic in the air tells a different tale.

Fire rips through me, leaving kindling in its wake. I can feel every bite, scratch, thrust, and moan, and my body reacts the same way it did that night, all hungry and needy. Hopelessly bewitched. I cross my legs and squeeze tight to offset the pool of warmth pulsing between my thighs, silently cursing my physical reaction to him.

Parker's eyes flick over my face, his eyebrows creased together in that same worried way, and then he pulls his gaze from me, focusing straight ahead while his throat bobs with a drawn-out swallow.

My neck flames, radiating up to my ears. I jerk my head forward. *God*, I'm ridiculous—getting turned on by a single glance after Parker ghosted me the whole week, all while Stacy with a *Y* ugly-cries about her ailing grandmother in hospice.

Pathetic.

Ms. Katherine wraps the meeting up, and I'm grateful for the coming reprieve. The air is too thick and stifling with him so close. She clutches her journal to her chest as she says a few final words, her sweet smile almost enough to overpower the confusion funneling through me as I anxiously bob my knees up and down. The brown leather journal is worn and jaded, well-loved, and I can't help but wonder what's inside. She never talks about it. She never opens it up or decorates the pages with scribbles and notes.

"Did you guys...*do it?*"

Amelia's voice drags me away from my musings, and I spare another glance to my left, avoiding Parker on the opposite side of her. When her question sinks in, I flush, my heart fluttering. "What?"

"You and Parker," she says, low and hushed. "I'm feeling some interesting energy in the room today."

Lord, am I wearing some kind of badge of sexual infamy?

Fidgeting with the super interesting edging of my romper, I duck my head. "That's kind of personal, Amelia."

Her grin is wide. "I knew it!"

Parker raises his head but doesn't look my way, and Amelia continues with a weary sigh. "I'm never having sex. I'll die a virgin."

"Oh...well, that's not necessarily true. You're still so young," I tell her, eyes dipping.

Why are we talking about sex in earshot of Parker? There are so many alternative topics to choose from: astrobiology, the evolution of sloths, bagpiping, underrated serial killers, the best Beatles albums.

"I'm good," she continues. "There are a lot of off-putting fluids and weird smells, you know?"

I purse my lips through a blink.

"Besides, sex leads to babies, and what if I don't want the baby just like my parents didn't want me?"

Oh.

My heart seizes with a jolt of grief. "Amelia..."

She smiles, shaking her head with a dismissive chuckle. "Sorry, that was really dramatic. Never mind." Amelia hops up from her chair before I can say anything else, giving me a little wave. "See you next week."

And then she's gone, leaving me reeling with equal parts heartbreak for her and palpable realization that there is nothing left as a barrier between Parker and me. I can't help my eyes from floating to him briefly, noting the way he ducks his head back down, staring at the floor, the tendons in his neck straining as he rolls his jaw.

I release an exasperated breath, deciding to bolt. He clearly doesn't want to talk to me, and sitting here is awkward and emotionally daunting.

Throwing my purse strap over my shoulder, I jump to my feet and breeze right by him, eyes straight ahead, chin raised with an illusion of detachment. I keep moving forward, my pace quick and desperate, until the early evening air skims my face, and I can breathe.

"Melody."

I stop breathing.

My gait slows, unlike my newly galloping heartbeat.

Parker's hand clasps around my elbow, catching me just as I reach my car. "Hey, wait up."

Turning to face him, we both glance down at his hold on my elbow—the way his fingers curl around me with a strange mix of gentle urgency and the way his thumb dusts over my skin for a striking moment before he drops my arm and clears his throat.

Tingles dance along the expanse of skin he's no longer touching, and I resist the urge to scratch it. "Did you want something?"

"I, uh…" Parker shoves his hands into his pockets, dancing on the balls of his feet. "Fuck, I don't know."

A new wave of indignation burns my chest. "Great chat. See you next week."

He catches me by the arm again, hindering my departure. His eyes slowly close as he exhales, like he's thinking—like he's trying to find the words and piece them together in a way that makes sense. His grip on me tightens. "I tried to text you back. I wanted to."

I inhale sharply. "But you didn't."

"No, I didn't." Parker's eyes open as he takes another step forward, until we're nearly chest to chest. "Because I don't know what the hell I'm doing. I don't know what this is, what *that* was, or where I'm supposed to go from here."

"You think I do?" I counter, my voice wavering as the feelings running rampant through me threaten to take me down. "I've never done anything like that before."

His arm falls from mine again as he runs his fingers through his hair. Then he says in a soft, ragged voice, "I thought you wanted me to go."

All I can manage is a head shake as the emotions start to climb.

"You wanted me to stay?"

A nod.

"Fuck…" Parker spins around, linking his hands behind his head and regrouping before facing me again. "I told you this wouldn't end well."

"Why do you think that?"

"Because," he grits out, leaning in a little closer. "You're so fucking…*breakable*. And I'm stone."

Breakable.

Tears sting my eyes, and I clench my jaw, arms folding tightly across my chest. "Gee, thanks, Parker. That's what every girl longs to hear."

"Jesus, that's not what I—"

Spinning away and marching to the driver's side of my car, I hold a sob in the back of my throat like a burning ball of scorn. Parker reaches for me again, but this time I find the strength to yank my arm free, and I whip back around, hair flying with me. "Don't. Just *don't*."

He lets out a hard breath. "I'm no good at this shit, Melody."

"Clearly."

"What do you want from me?"

"Nothing," I force out, even though I kind of want to scream, *everything*. Reining in my anger and confliction, I heave in a shaky breath and glance down at my sandals. "I'm going out tonight. With Shane."

Silence permeates the turbulent wall between us, forcing my head up.

Parker just stares at me, that crease reappearing between his brows, his eyes flickering with wounded confusion. "What?"

My stomach sours.

Why is he looking at me like that?

Shane stopped by three days ago to check my pipes. He said it was standard procedure to make sure everything was still running smoothly, but I got the impression he was looking for an opportunity to see me again. It felt like he had checked *me* out more than the pipes.

Then when he asked me out for drinks, I faltered. My gut immediately declined his offer because I don't *feel* anything for Shane—no tingles, no flutters, no heart palpitations. I don't envision the way his lips would feel pressed to mine or daydream about his hands sliding over my curves, slick with rainwater, hungry and eager.

My body seems to want Parker and *only* Parker.

But Parker is unattainable.

And, well…Shane is interested. He's emotionally available. He appears to be reliable and stable. I've known him for a long time, and my brother vouches for him. Shane follows-up, and he says nice things, and he *smiles*.

I think I need that. I need to feel like there is hope after Charlie.

While I wasn't prepared to rush into anything intimate, I did agree to go out with him—as long as West and Leah could tag along.

A double date of sorts. A group outing.

Something fun and carefree with no expectations.

Only…now I'm doubting my decision because Parker is staring at me like I just ripped the rug out from under him.

My bottom lip quivers slightly as I reply, "I'm going on a date."

"Why?"

"Because he invited me out to Breaker's tonight, and I said yes." His frown deepens, so I continue. "You called me a nuisance. You said I drive you mad. You didn't text me back after we…" I trail off, swallowing hard. "You told me to stay away from you, so that's what I'm trying to do."

Parker deflates a little, his eyes dancing to the right as he processes my words. A few moments pass before he responds with a quick nod, taking a step back. "Yeah," he mutters quietly. "Okay."

He doesn't look at me again. He keeps his focus elsewhere as he continues to pace backward, fingers tightening into fists at his sides. I open my mouth to speak, but nothing comes out. Mostly because I don't know what to say. I'm not sure how to react to *his* reaction.

Parker doesn't deny my claims or attempt to take them back.

He just walks away, allowing me to believe all the things I hoped he'd retract.

I didn't mean that, Melody.

I take it all back.

Don't go on that date.

Fairy tales.

Shane is an obtainable reality, and Parker is a fantasy.

I watch him storm over to his truck, climb inside, and careen out of the parking lot without a single glance in my direction.

Gathering my wits, I slide into my own vehicle, and when the door is closed tight and my hands are gripping the steering wheel, a single word flashes in my mind...

Breakable.

Maybe he's right.

Maybe Parker's right, because all I want to do is shatter.

———————

Breaker's is loud and crowded, bustling with laughter, pool balls clinking, and clattering glasses as bartenders race to keep up with patrons. Leah's squeal ruptures through the chaos when West sneaks up behind her and hoists her in the air, his arms snaking around her slim waist.

"You ass!" she cries, but her teeth flash white, and a giddy laugh follows.

I smooth my hands over my red maxi dress, a smile lifting, as Shane gets into position beside me with his cue stick. I'm pretty terrible at playing pool, but it's a great distraction, considering the circumstances. There's no one-on-one pressure for deep conversation or intimacy.

"Five ball in the corner pocket," Shane murmurs, leaning down to aim his shot.

We've been here for an hour now, and I've been nursing my old-fashioned the whole time. I haven't been a big drinker since college—the incident with Charlie's mother was a one-time offense and a giant stain on my memory. I'll have a glass of wine every now and then, but I've never needed alcohol to have fun.

And then…I just stopped having fun altogether.

Shane succeeds in hitting the five ball in the corner pocket, and West boos, draping his arm around Leah's shoulders.

"What do you think, Mel?" Shane remarks, studying the table.

Pulling my lips between my teeth, I stiffen. Only Charlie and West call me *Mel*. "Hmm, how about the six?"

"That's a solid. We're stripe."

"Oh, right." The ice cubes clank against glass as I twirl the drink in my hands. "Nine?"

"That's what I was thinking," he says with a wink.

He misses the shot, and West assesses his next play after downing his beer.

As I'm gearing up for my turn, I feel two warm palms clasp my waist from behind, and I freeze. Shane's cologne wafts around me, something aromatic and crisp. Sage and mint. It's a pleasant aroma, but it causes my stomach to pitch instead of flutter.

I miss the smell of woods and rainfall.

"You look really sexy tonight," Shane whispers against my ear, leaning down over my shoulder and giving my waist a squeeze.

I inch my way out of his grip, throwing him a small smile. "Thank you."

"I mean, you're always sexy. Even that night at the brewery in your oversized hoodie and messy hair…I couldn't take my eyes off you."

I remember that night.

It was the night I almost killed myself.

Swallowing, I bob my head. A wave of guilt infiltrates me, knowing I feel nothing for this man, despite the fact that he's kind, attentive, good-looking, and smart. On paper, he fits. Shane could easily be a compatible partner.

But his eyes aren't green like the Everglades. His build is too broad, and he smells like a department store instead of the great outdoors. His hands don't look like they've ever really built anything before, his hair is coarse, not soft like silk, and his voice…his voice doesn't shoot tingles up my spine and goose bumps across my skin.

I'm ruined.

Leah strolls up to me with two shot glasses, an unidentifiable liquid splashing over the rims. I immediately scrunch my nose up. "Absolutely not."

"Aw shucks, fine. Worth a *shot*," she teases, handing the extra glass to Shane, who takes it eagerly.

I'm shaking my head at her awful joke when I notice her eyes skip over my shoulder and widen as she sets her sights on something. "What? What is it?"

"Holy hell, babe…" Leah steps closer to me, eyes still fixed on an unknown subject. "Don't look now, but your contractor is sitting at the bar, and he looks really, *really* good."

What?

My heart nearly detonates. "Parker?"

"I think so. Mr. Silent and Tortured?"

I nod mutely.

"That's him. Shit, he's looking over here." Leah jerks her head until she's fully facing me, eyebrows wiggling with mischief. "He's hot, Mellie. Poor Shane doesn't stand a chance."

Biting into my lip, I blurt, "I slept with him."

Leah's eyes bug out, gleaming gold and gobsmacked. Her lips shape into a glossy O, and she instantly snatches my wrist to drag me toward the bathrooms.

"I choked. You're up, Mel," West intervenes, trying to call us over before we disappear.

"Be right back!" Leah shouts. When we're out of earshot of the two men, Leah pulls me toward the far wall across from the restrooms, cupping my cheeks with her hands. Her long, talon-like nails are bloodred, matching the lip stain on her mouth—her mouth that quickly curls into a Cheshire grin. "Oh my *God*. Shut the fucking front door."

"It was a mistake," I croak out.

"It most certainly was not. That man is not a freakin' mistake, baby girl."

Amusement forces its way through the swelling anxiety, and I crack a smile before choking it back down. "It's a mess, Leah. He has the emotional capacity of a spatula."

She frowns, dropping her hands. "Not ideal."

"He said he doesn't even like women."

"Possibly concerning…"

"He won't kiss me. He said he's never kissed anyone before."

Leah slides her lower lip between her teeth, her gaze flickering across my face with quiet assessment. "But you like him," she concludes, tender but firm.

I blink, letting her words soak through all the doubts and misgivings. Through the dark clouds and bleak thoughts. If I chip away long enough, maybe I'll wind up at the meaty center of it all, which basically comes down to: "Yeah…I like him."

Her smile embraces me like a warm hug. It's the last thing I see before Shane wanders up to us, his beer dangling in his hand, tapping his thigh as he clears his throat.

"I was wondering where you ran off to," he says, his blueish gaze raking over me. "It's your turn."

Leah gives my arm a comforting pinch, almost like she's reminding me of my unhindered confession. I gift her with a soft grin, then share it with Shane. "Sounds good."

We follow him back over to the pool table, and I instantly scour the room for Parker. He's easy to spot, sitting alone at the bar with no beverage and only a familiar scowl to keep him company. His knee bobs up and down, his one foot propped along the rung of the barstool as his hand scratches at the back of his head while he fidgets in place. He looks nervous, uncomfortable. Totally out of his element.

Why is he here?

Did he come because of…*me?*

As I approach the table, Parker glances my way.

Our eyes lock, my heart skips, and my breath stalls in the back of my throat, causing my feet to halt midstep. My blood pumps hot, my insides singing.

And that's when Shane wraps his arm around my waist, tugging me against him and swallowing me up—as if he's staking a claim and asserting what's his. I watch the muscles in Parker's neck distend, veins dilating. His lax posture turns rigid as his eyes dip to the arm curled around my middle. When they lift back to me, they are violent and virescent.

Suffocating.

"Is that the guy who fixed your ceiling?"

Shane's voice kisses my ear, and I flinch, his proximity invasive. His hold on me tightens. "Yes."

"Want me to tell him to get lost?"

"No."

My response is quick, leaving no room for interpretation. Shane guides me back to the pool table, his hand sliding to the small of my back, and I finally pull my attention from Parker. I'm tempted to approach him, to find out why he's here, but West steals my courage before I can flee, handing me a cue.

"It's all you, little sis. Let's see what you've got."

I inhale a calming breath, trying to shake the weight of his gaze as my fingers curl around the cue. "I've definitely got this…three ball, side pocket."

"Risky."

My eyes skip to my brother. "Really?"

West chuckles as he swallows down the rest of his beer, abandoning the empty bottle on a high-top table. "Just go, will you?"

"Okay, okay…" Gnawing the inside of my cheek, I try to concentrate on the shot as I near the table, refusing the pull from the opposite side of the room.

Deep breath.

Leaning forward, I move into position, eyeing the number three on the red ball and sliding the stick between two fingers. I should have realized something was amiss when Leah's giggles fade and West's words cut off, but I continue with the shot, my backside jutted out and my focus fixed.

That's when I feel him.

A potent heat closing in on me, prompting the little hairs on my arms to dance to life while my skin warms with want. Parker angles himself over me, arms encompassing me from either side, his hands sliding down my own arms until he reaches my wrists.

His face lowers to the crook of my neck, lips grazing my ear, and he whispers, "Hey."

Hey?

A surge of heat spirals south at a single word. I realize all eyes are on us right now—my brother, Leah, my freakin' *date*—but I can't seem to move. I can't seem to withdraw from the lure of his spell.

I find an ounce of bravery and tilt my chin up, canting my head to the left. He's *right there*—our noses almost brush as our eyes meet. I swallow. "I didn't know you played pool."

My voice is shockingly steady, my grip tightening on the cue.

Parker inhales a hard breath, licking his lips as his gaze skims my face. "I don't. I just wanted an excuse to touch you."

I feel my insides pitch with arousal, and my eyelids flutter closed. "Oh."

"Take the shot," he mutters softly, his tone subdued, so only I can hear him.

Nodding toward the three ball, Parker pretends to position me, his groin pressing into my hip as his fingers coil around my wrists and his breath beats against the shell of my ear.

I pull the stick back…

And scratch hard.

Damn it.

"You missed," Parker says.

"Can I help you, man?"

Shane's aggravated baritone rumbles over to us, and I rise up from the table, noting how Parker takes his time backing away, his hand lazily gliding down my spine. It feels like he doesn't want to let me go. I come to my senses and pull myself together. "Shane, this is P—"

"We've met," Shane bites back.

Oh, right.

The smoldering.

Sensing how incredibly awkward this is, Leah attempts to come to my rescue with an overdramatic hair flip and an invitation to accompany her to the bar, but Shane stands there with stoic firmness, his wrists crossed and draped over the chalky end of the pool cue.

I glance back at Parker, who is aiming his own death glare at Shane.

This is not going to end well.

Shane cuts in again, his words pointed at Parker. "Is there any good reason why you decided to put your hands all over my girl?"

Parker doesn't reply. He just stands there, glowering.

I take the lead, spinning around and planting my palms against Parker's chest as if to prevent him from doing something regrettable, even though he seems to be content with the silent intimidation act. Maybe I just want an excuse to touch him too. "Let's go talk?"

It takes a moment for his eyes to flick back to me, but when they do, they flare with heat, and a fever stirs within me. He nods slowly. "Yeah…okay."

I turn back to my group, throwing a knowing look at Leah, a promise of future explanation at my brother, and an apology at Shane. Clearing my throat and pacing forward, I murmur, "Be right back."

23

PARKER

I'M NOT A VIOLENT PERSON.

And that's mainly because I've never given a shit about anything enough to have an emotional reaction that strong. But when that motherfucker put his hands on her, wrapped her up in his arms in some kind of macho, possessive move—like she *belonged* to him…

I saw red.

Jealousy crawled through my veins like a new kind of poison. Something sinister and unfamiliar. All I wanted to do was knock his teeth out, drag her the fuck out of that place, then scrub her clean of that asshole.

Every muscle in my body aches. Every cord in my neck strains. Every heartbeat feels like a ticking time bomb as I follow Melody out of the bar and into the damp humidity, almost ramming into her when she comes to an abrupt stop and whirls around to face me.

Her chest heaves with quick, hard breaths. "What are you doing here?"

I'm not answering that. She fucking knows what I'm doing here.

Instead, my hands clasp her hips, backing her up until she's pressed against the distressed brick building. A little whimper escapes her when her shoulder blades hit the wall, and the sound thunders through me. "He called you his girl."

"Does that bother you?"

My eyes dip to her lips as my fingers curl around her waist. Pink and parted, demanding to be kissed. Tensing my jaw, I admit, "Yeah, it does."

"Why?" she probes gently.

Fuck. She wants to talk about my feelings, while all I want to do is claw them out of me. I drop my forehead to hers, closing my eyes through a ragged exhale. "Because…I remember every noise you made that night, every breath you took, the way your body trembled and swayed, molding into mine like it was designed to," I confess, the words spilling out of me like a pathetic purge. "I remember every goddamn inch of you, Melody, and you sure as hell didn't feel like his girl."

You felt like mine.

I don't say that last part because I'm not prepared to deal with the implication of it, nor the inevitable fallout.

Melody's eyes drift closed as she swallows my words down, her fingers gliding up the front of my abdomen and then my chest. When I tug her arms away, her lids pop open, a glare surfacing. "I can't touch you. I can't kiss you…" A huff of disappointment hits the summer air, and she slithers from my hold. "This is pointless."

I watch her saunter away, but she doesn't head back inside the bar—she traipses down the back alleyway, her heels clicking with each deliberate step. I call after her, following. "Where are you going?"

"Away from you."

"In a sketch-ass alley to get yourself kidnapped?" My pace quickens until I catch up, moving in front of her to hinder her escape. "That Matchmaker killer was nabbing people not far from here."

She sighs weakly. "I'll be fine."

"Where are you even going?"

Trying to wind around me, she lets out another defeated sigh when I block her. "I'm going to my car. I had to park on the street. Can I please leave?"

"That dickwad didn't even pick you up? Jesus…I've never even been in a relationship, and I have enough sense to know that much."

"You…" Melody pauses, confusion settling into her features. "You've never been in a relationship? Ever?"

"No. I told you, I—"

"Don't like women," she finishes, glancing away. "That's kind of a huge red flag, Parker."

I take in the way a light blush shades her cheeks, and I wonder if I put it there. My feet move in closer. "There's a lot you don't know about me…a lot you don't want to know."

She nibbles her lip, raising her eyes to me. "You can tell me."

Goddammit.

She's looking for a way in. She's throwing me all these chances, all these bones, all these golden fucking opportunities to spill my guts to her, so she can *understand.*

But I've never let anyone in before.

And she'll never understand.

So my response is pulled from the only shred of certainty I have: *I want her.*

I fucking want her just as much as I wanted her that night in the rain. Savage, raw, and unrestrained. My gaze dips to her cleavage, recalling the taste. Salty skin and earthy raindrops. Her dress is red, seductive and curve clinging, and I recognize it from the night she invited me out with her friends while I was remodeling her bathroom. I glance back up. "You're wearing the 'fuck-me' dress," I state, my voice hoarse, giving away my growing arousal. Melody's irises flash, dancing with green and gold flecks. Tiny embers. Inching closer, I lower my chin until my lips are a hair's breadth from her ear. "Did you wear it for him? Or did you name-drop the bar earlier in hopes I'd show up and tear this dress off you?"

Melody's breath hitches as she raises her chin, our eyes meeting, faces only centimeters apart. She swallows, her gaze drinking me in while she considers her response. "Him," she finally whispers.

My whole body stiffens, my brows furrowing into a scowl.

"I wore it for him because I didn't expect you to show up tonight. I've learned to expect nothing from you—it only leads to disappointment."

She holds my stare for another moment before stepping away, then moving around me and heading back toward the bar, purse swinging beside her as her hips sashay with conviction.

Fucking hell.

"Where are you going now?" I call to her.

"Back to my date." Melody pauses her trek to add, "I want to see if Shane likes my dress."

I'm not sure why I submit to her goading, why I let the jealousy flow through my veins again like a toxic drug, or why I allow this uncharacteristic surge of possessiveness to provoke my feet into chasing after her.

But I do.

And then I'm in front of her, bending down and scooping her off her feet until she's draped over my shoulder, squeaking in surprise.

"Parker! What the hell?" Melody protests, squirming in my grip. "Put me down!"

Marching through the alley to the front parking lot, I veer toward my truck, my one arm holding her tight just underneath her backside. She hardly weighs anything at all.

"I swear to God—"

"You're not very threatening when you're upside down."

Melody growls in frustration, smacking her purse against the back of my thigh. "You're such an asshole."

"More than I can say for your date. He has more nose than personality."

Her belly bounces atop my shoulder with each hurried step, her hands pushing against me, nails digging into my lower back in an attempt to work herself free. Her efforts are fruitless. "Parker!"

As we approach my pickup truck, I slide Melody down my torso until her heels touch the pavement, maintaining my hold around her waist. She gives me a light shove, smoothing out her hair that has now landed in a hundred different directions and inching her dress down her thighs with a sulk.

A small smile betrays me as I regard her cheeks flushed from indignation.

Melody does a double take when she glances up at me, hesitating. Then an angry index finger lifts into the air and points right at my mouth. "That's what gets a smile out of you? Manhandling me?"

My smile grows wider despite myself, and I open up the passenger's side door to my truck, hinges shrieking. "Get in."

"So *you're* the one who's going to kidnap me?" Her arms fold across her chest as she spares a look of curious interest to the open door, then pulls her gaze to my face. Melody bites her lip, resolve dwindling.

She has every intention of getting in the truck.

"I don't know, am I? Kidnapping would require an unwilling victim." My eyes case her from head to toe, landing on her firmly planted feet. "You don't look unwilling."

Her teeth continue to glide along her bottom lip as her mind races, her knees bobbing up and down. "Where are we going?"

"My place."

The mood shifts with implication. Melody swallows, her gaze flicking across my face, glittering with temptation.

Honestly, I have no clue what in the goddamn fuck I'm doing. I didn't have a plan tonight. I didn't come here with the intention of literally sweeping Melody off her feet and whisking her away to my house for round two of mind-blowing sex.

In fact, I'm not even sure I'm ready for that. It sounds so…*intimate*. She'll be getting a glimpse into my lonely life. She'll meet my old-ass dog, she'll touch my things, she'll…sleep in my bed.

Fuck.

I've never had any woman aside from Bree inside my house before, and I sure as hell haven't had anyone in my bed.

We stare at each other with heady contemplation. I am reevaluating, and she is giving in. My fingers curl around the frame of the truck door, my mind spinning, screaming at me to back out, demanding I push her away indefinitely.

But Melody makes the first move, shattering my indecision and breaking our standoff.

She climbs inside the truck.

With her hands folded tensely in her lap, eyes pinned straight ahead, she leans back into the seat and lets out a nervous breath.

I close the door, and a new one opens.

FOURTEEN YEARS OLD

I'm sitting beneath the old willow tree in the backyard, drowning out the noise and chatter of my foster siblings, when Gwen rushes over to me. Frizzy copper hair catches the draft, covering her face and cloaking the sniveling sneer I know she's wearing well.

She pushes the bangs off her forehead when she reaches me, assessing my perch against the tree. My school bag hangs open, textbooks and notepads scattered around me. "Are you studying how to be cool?" Gwen asks, antagonizing me with eyes of blue steel.

I glance down, crossing my legs and ignoring her attempts to instigate. My hold tightens on the book I'm reading.

"We're going to go to the pool. Want to join us?"

Swallowing, I pretend to be fully engaged in the book, my gaze scanning over the blur of inky letters.

"It'll be fun," Gwen continues, stepping closer. Invading my peace. "Landon has an extra pair of swim trunks you can borrow. Lord only knows you could use a little sun…you look like a chicken with its feathers plucked out. Like you've never seen a day of sunlight."

My teeth gnash together.

I prefer the shade. The shadows.

They let me hide.

I tried to hide from my teachers and classmates when my first year of high school began—holing up in the bathroom stalls, even skipping classes. But when the principal contacted my foster mother, it only brought more attention to me. To my flaws and deficiencies. My shortfalls.

"All you need to do is take your shirt off, Parker," Gwen sneers. "What do you say?"

I feel my cheeks heat up, my stomach swirling with anxiety. "No thanks."

Gwen yanks the book from my hands, then drops to her knees in front of me, a toothy grin blossoming when my eyes meet hers. "How come? Gargoyles deserve to have fun too."

"Just leave me alone," I bite out, pulling myself to shaky legs, then leaning down to collect my school supplies. I'm startled when I feel a tug on the back of my T-shirt, causing my reflexes to spike and my agitation to spiral. Whipping around, I shove her arm away. "Don't touch me, Gwen. Please, go away."

"Just because *you* don't want to have fun, doesn't mean *I* can't have fun."

Gwen sprints toward me again, reaching for my shirt. She wants to humiliate me. She wants access to my scars so she can carve her own cruelty into them and leave her mark on me. "No! Stop." I dodge her, but she keeps coiling around me, slithering like a snake, all hiss and venom. Her hands grip the front of my shirt, tugging it upward until my burn scars reach her eyes.

She snorts at the evidence. "I feel sorry for you. You're never going to get a girlfriend looking like this."

The barb cuts deep, adding to my collection. I've been noticing girls in school lately, even though they don't notice me back. Part of me is angry at all of them because they remind me of my mother. And Gwen. Sometimes I hear my mother's laughter when feminine giggles catch my ears during lunch period, or sometimes I'll see Gwen's icy blue eyes when a girl rakes her stare over me in gym class.

But my body doesn't seem to agree. It doesn't seem to hate them like the rest of me does. My body is curious about girls, which only adds to my confusion and insecurity.

As Gwen continues to try and lift my shirt higher, a familiar voice breaks through my heightening shame.

"Hey! Witch Face," calls the voice. "You better go fly off on your broomstick before I shove it up your bony butt."

Bree storms over to the willow tree, dropping her own backpack to the grass and rolling up the sleeves to her blouse.

Gwen steps away from me, cowering slightly. "Oh, look, Parker's bodyguard to the rescue."

"Hardly," Bree snips. "Parker can easily knock your lights out. I just like to intervene before it gets to that point."

"Are you trying to be my bodyguard now too?" Gwen goads.

"No. I want the honor of doing it myself."

Bree holds up her fist as she wiggles her eyebrows with menace.

Gwen looks between us, deciding if she wants to keep tormenting me or busy herself with other forms of enjoyment. Sighing, she spears me with a cool glare before folding her arms and stomping off to the other side of the yard. "Whatever."

I let out a mouthful of air and smooth my T-shirt back down, waiting for my heartbeat to slow as Gwen skips out of sight.

"She's vile," Bree says, her chestnut curls bouncing as she shuffles over to me. "Do you think she's actually a witch?"

My sense of humor has faded over the years, so I just shrug at the jest, while Bree stops beside the tree and props her shoulder against it. She's eighteen now, finishing her last week of high school, and she's still the only person in this house who treats me like a human being instead of a monster.

A gargoyle.

I'm not sure what I'll do when she moves out and starts a new life.

"You know that's all bullshit, right?"

I lift my eyes to my foster sister, noting the warmth shimmering in her amber irises. "What?"

"The stuff she says about you. About your scars."

"She's not wrong." I scuff my sneaker against the freshly mowed grass, kicking at the loose blades. "They're hideous."

"No, they're not. Scars mean you survived something terrible. There's nothing ugly about that."

I gulp back the tight lump in my throat. "I'll never have a girlfriend one day. I'll always be alone."

Bree's thick eyebrows crease, almost like she's absorbing my pain and it hurts her too. She straightens from the tree. "That's ridiculous."

"It's the truth."

"It's not the truth, Parker. You are so much more than your scars—you're smart, you're funny, you're creative. And look at those dazzling green eyes and that dreamy bone structure." She leans in to ruffle my mop of dark hair, shooting me a wink. "You'll have no problem getting a girlfriend one day."

A smile slips out when I duck my head, but it fades as the dark cloud rolls back in. It does that a lot lately. Bree's presence and kindness will always be a welcome reprieve from the storm, but she's only one person. My ghosts and devils seem to be multiplying, and she's far too outnumbered.

Fidgeting with the hem of my shirt, I reply, "Once she sees my scars, she'll leave."

A weighty silence settles between us as a light breeze blows through and the willow branches dance to life.

A zephyr.

Bree reaches out and takes my hand, pulling it away from the fabric of my T-shirt, the only thing that hides the truth, and dusting her thumb along my knuckles. When I look up, she is smiling. "No, Parker. Once she sees your scars, she'll love you even more."

24

MELODY

I'M NOT SURE WHAT TO EXPECT WHEN WE PULL INTO THE LONG, GRAVEL driveway after the silent trip over from the bar, but a charming, ranch-style house with ruddy bricks, dark gray shutters, and simple yet effective landscaping is a pleasant surprise. Even though the sun has set, a light shines ambience onto the quaint front porch as my eyes roll over the large property.

There's a carport to the right, housing what looks to be pieces of furniture in progress, as well as a separate one-car garage. The yard is well maintained despite a scattering of tools, and the home is quiet and secluded, settled far back beyond the main stretch of road. A little oasis.

My feet crunch atop the gravel as I hop out of Parker's truck and meet him around the front of the hood, hardly able to make out his expression against the shadowy night. The silence stretches from inside the vehicle to the space between us, and while the air is dense and muggy, the tension between us is thicker.

Jitters coast through me, dancing along my skin and tickling my insides. A subtle glow from the moon and stars above illuminate two dithering green eyes boring into me.

I swallow. "Your house looks nice."

Parker slides his hands into his pockets, glancing toward the house, then back to me. "I built it."

I feel my breath catch as his words register. "You did?"

His nod is barely visible as his eyes skim my face.

"That's..." The humidity almost chokes me, or maybe that's my heart in my throat. I can't help a smile from breaking through my nerves when the thought of Parker building his home from the ground up assaults me like a bear hug. "That's really remarkable."

"It was something to do at the time, I guess." He dismisses the exceptionality of such a feat with a sniff and shuffles past me toward the front of the house. When I continue to stand there, a little bit slack-jawed, he pauses to inquire, "You coming?"

Am I?

My head turns to face him, lip caught between my teeth. He's nothing but a tall shadow beckoning me further into the unknown.

He brought me here for sex. I knew that when I got into his truck, ditching my date for the evening like a total jerk and frantically sending Leah a text of apology, begging her to tell Shane and my brother that I wasn't feeling well and decided to head home early.

Yeah right. There's no way they're going to believe that after I walked out of the bar with Parker, who left no mystery as to what his intentions were.

Leah texted me back almost instantly:

Leah: GET IT GIRL! I got your back.

A sigh escapes me, another smile lifting, and I nod my acquiescence, trailing behind him as he resumes his trek to the front door. Following him inside the darkened house, Parker flips a light on when we enter, and I notice movement out of the corner of my eye.

My head shifts to the right.

A dog.

Blinking, I stare at the animal just standing there a few feet away on wobbly legs. "You have a dog?"

"Yeah. That's Walden." Parker tosses his keys and wallet on the side table, then scratches at the base of his neck, stepping forward and following my gaze. "He kind of just sulks around all day and keeps to himself."

"Like you."

Glancing at Parker, I don't miss the twitch of his mouth as he tries to hold back a smile. He ducks his head to hide it, shrugging his shoulders. "I suppose there's a likeness."

My grin is bright as I look back over to the black-and-white dog with patchy fur and cloudy, bugged-out eyes. He watches us with interest, although his tail doesn't wag and he doesn't bark. He just observes. "He's really cute."

"He's fucking ancient."

"But cute." I chuckle, approaching the mutt that looks to be some kind of border collie mix. The dog's attention follows me as I close in, crouching down and gliding my fingers between his ears. "You look like a good boy."

Charlie and I had been thinking about getting a dog. We both worked long hours at the time, so it didn't seem fair to adopt a pet when we wouldn't be home very often, but the companionship had always been something I craved. I considered it again after Charlie passed, but then my grief became my companion—and that wasn't fair either.

There was too much competition.

But now…now might be a good time to consider it again.

Walden doesn't do much but sniff my outstretched fingers, but I can tell he's a sweet soul. A loyal friend.

As I rise to my feet, I notice Parker staring at me from the entryway, taking in the scene. I smile at him. "You didn't strike me as a dog person," I admit, sweeping a hand through my hair and moving toward him.

"Because I'm such a people person?"

His response pulls another laugh from my lips as I inch my way closer. Parker's stance seems to stiffen when I'm only a foot away, and I wonder why that is. I wonder why he's so closed-off and resistant to physical contact, to true intimacy.

Stretching my smile, I reach out to take his hand, brushing my thumb over his knuckles. He glances down at the gesture, frowning, and I feel him try to pull back, so I strengthen my hold. "Can I get a tour?"

"What?" he wonders distractedly, still staring at our joined hands.

"Of your house."

Parker finally lifts his gaze to mine, eyebrows pulled together like he's conflicted or in pain, and then he clears his throat. "Uh, yeah…I guess. Not much to see."

I release his hand, watching as he tenses his fingers, splaying them apart, then making a fist. "Lead the way."

Hesitation grips him as he glances around the room, avoiding my eyes. A sigh of resignation follows, and he points behind me. "Living room." His thumb flicks over his shoulder. "Kitchen." A beat passes, and he gestures to his right. "Small-ass hallway that leads to a bathroom and two bedrooms. There's a linen closet somewhere along the way."

"Wow." My grin broadens as I crinkle my nose. "Very descriptive."

That little ghost of a half smile reappears, spiking my heart rate. I would do anything to freeze the moment, so it never ever faded.

Pulling my focus off Parker, I wring my hands together and dip around him, sauntering into the kitchen. Curiosity claims me as my eyes peruse the modest space, clean but cluttered. My fingertips dance along the laminate top of the island while my feet wind around it, taking it all in.

This is Parker's life. His space. His *home*.

I'm realizing that I know absolutely nothing about this man—this man I gave something of value to. This man who I'm inherently drawn to for reasons I can't even begin to understand.

There's not much personality or charm given to the space. No knickknacks lining the counters, no birthday cards or photographs stuck to the white refrigerator, no color pops or decorations. There's nothing on his walls either. No canvas prints or family pictures.

It's sterile. Lonely, even.

Does he have any friends? Close family members?

Is he truly all alone?

The idea grips my heart in a tight fist as I continue to scan over the assortment of cereal boxes, a wooden spice rack, stacks of mail…

And a little pink Post-it Note stuck to the side of the fridge, wrinkled and creased. Familiar handwriting stares back at me, sending a tremor through me.

I think you saved my life that night.

It's the only personal sentiment sprinkled into his otherwise very basic living space.

When my eyes find Parker watching me from the same place I left him, a burst of emotion climbs up my chest and causes my eyes to water. "You saved my note," I murmur in a low, broken voice. I had attached this note to his cupcakes after that night in the rain when I had my breakthrough.

I'm not okay, but I'm not ready to give up that one day I will be.

He'd told me he hadn't even read the note.

Parker's expression is tinted with vulnerability as he stares at me, a little uncomfortable, like he hadn't expected me to see that. His jaw ticks while his eyes skim over me, then his gaze drops to the floor. Everything about him is rigid and hard.

Everything except that look on his face.

I approach him with slow steps and a swiftly beating heart, closing the gap between us and reaching for his hand again. It's clenched tight, only loosening slightly when I give it a gentle squeeze. When Parker glances back up at me, I don't say anything. I simply give his hand a tug and guide him toward the hallway, my insides buzzing when he doesn't pull away. He follows my lead.

I'm not sure where I'm going, but as I inspect the limited selection of rooms and note that only one of them has a bed adorning it, I push through the cracked door and step inside, drawing Parker with me.

Nerves seize me when my eyes land on the queen-size bed, shrouded in the shadows of the dimly lit room. A night-light on the wall provides a minimal glow, enough to drink in the sparse and uncolored space. White walls, gray bedcovers, a little wooden nightstand with a lamp. A dresser on the opposite wall. A laundry basket partially filled with T-shirts and jeans.

And that's everything. That's the extent of his bedroom.

Turning to face him, I let go of his hand and pace a few steps backward, until I reach the foot of the bed. Parker lingers just in front of the doorway, still stiff. Still strained. His gaze flickers with conflict as his Adam's apple bobs in his throat, eyes spearing me from a few feet away.

Gathering my courage, shaky fingers lift from my side and carefully slip the straps off each shoulder. He watches me, drinking me in from the shadows with guarded interest, his eyes dipping when the dress slides down, revealing my black lace bra. I tug it farther, exposing my ribs, my abdomen, my matching underwear, and then it glides down my legs into a halo of red at my feet. Parker follows its descent, then drags his sight back up my nerve-racked body, settling on my wide, terrified eyes.

I hold out my hand, encouraging him toward me.

I need him closer. I need to *feel* him.

His fingers tap along the side of his thigh as his head jerks away from me, a hard sigh escaping. "Fuck, Melody…I told you I'm no good at this."

A frown furrows as I lower my hand. "I'm not either. You're the only one I've done this with aside from…" I swallow, pursing my lips. "You're the only one."

Parker's attention stays fixed on the other side of the room, his stance restless, prepared to bolt at the slightest threat. Pacing toward him, my movements are cautious and controlled—as if *I'm* that threat.

"Hey, it's okay," I whisper when I approach, taking his tense hands in mine and guiding them to my hips. His fingers unravel and cling to me, digging into my hipbones with something akin to desperation. He's fighting something I don't understand. "Parker, look at me."

It takes a moment before his neck cranes toward me, green eyes glinting from the subtle glow of the night-light. He heaves in a rattled breath, holding me tighter. "This won't work, Melody. It can't."

No, don't do this. Not now.

I grind my teeth together and duck my head. Pushing aside the sting, I collect my wits and try to read him instead. I try to wind my way through this endless maze that is Parker Denison and locate the source of his block. His deep-seated resistance. "Tell me why it won't work," I prompt softly. Gently. "Please, talk to me."

"Because…" Parker's fingers uncurl from my waist, then skim down my body until his arms fall loose on either side of him. "Because I'll never be him… and you'll always be her."

My brows pull together, my heart stuttering.

Him is Charlie.

But who is...*her*?

I refuse to give in to the frustration of his push and pull, his indecision. I choke back the anger that bubbles to the surface. I won't allow the prickle of rejection to consume me and drive another wedge between us.

I *know* he wants this. I *know* he has feelings for me.

So I run with that.

I run with what I know because it's the only way to understand the things I don't.

"You want to know what's on the other side of grief and pain?"

My question causes a trace of curiosity to flicker across his face. Parker sighs, shifting his weight from one foot to the other. "Fuckin' rainbows and butterflies, right? All that shit therapists shove down your throat to keep your head above water."

I pin my eyes on his, punctuating each word like shrapnel to his skin. "What you *put* there."

A heavy silence fills the space between us, and I watch carefully as a frown draws across his brow line, pensive and wistful. He blinks, processing my response and swallowing down the remnants of it.

I don't wait for his reply because I'm not looking for one—instead, I step backward and slowly spin around to collect my discarded dress, stepping into it and pulling the straps back up over my shoulders. Straightening where I stand, I face him once more, noting that his thoughtful expression still stares back at me. I smile. "Let's go watch a movie."

As it turns out, Parker doesn't have cable.

Or Netflix. Or Hulu. Or Amazon.

I'm actually not even sure why he has a television. It's cased in a thick layer of dust, a telltale sign that he never uses it.

Settling beside him on the couch with a bowl of popcorn, I maintain a small distance between us, allowing him time to return from the dark place he entered in his bedroom. The room is dim, with only two working bulbs on his ceiling fan illuminating us in tungsten.

Parker glances at me, hands gripping his spread knees. "Popcorn doesn't go well with invisible movies."

I pop a kernel into my mouth with a grin. "We can talk instead."

"I don't go well with talking."

My smile widens as I pull my legs up to the sofa cushion, my knees grazing the side of his thigh. "You have a sense of humor behind all that grouch. You kind of remind me of…" I trail off, realizing he reminds me of…*Zephyr*.

Sort of. Sometimes.

The dry sense of humor and occasional quick wit.

But Zephyr doesn't exist to me anymore. He took one look at me and disappeared, leaving me questioning everything we had, everything we shared. Every joke, every pun, every sage word of advice.

I know I'm not completely monstrous to look at, so I have no idea what transpired that night. Part of me regrets taking it to video—he was right in the sense that everything was perfect the way it was. I must've ruined the illusion for him.

Still, it doesn't justify him ghosting me like that.

It was hurtful.

"Who do I remind you of?"

I blink at Parker's words, returning from my dreary musings and setting the bowl of popcorn on the side table. "Just…someone I used to talk to. It's nobody."

"Nobody?"

"He was…" Swallowing, I debate how much I should confess to him, but I suppose it doesn't matter anymore. "He was kind of a pen pal. He, um…he was the recipient of my husband's heart. I reached out during a particularly rough time in the grieving process, and he replied to me. We had a connection."

Parker studies me, expressionless. "Is that important to you?"

"What? The connection?"

"The heart."

I hesitate, my eyes dancing away from his.

Is it?

I mean, it was. For a while, it was everything. Zephyr and his heart were my final tie to Charlie—the last tangible piece of the man I loved with *my* whole heart.

I suppose it still is.

Important, anyway.

But it's not *everything*.

"Yes," I answer honestly, drawing my eyes back to Parker. The lines in his forehead crease, and his jaw stiffens. "He's gone now, though. We don't talk anymore."

"Why not?"

I spit the words out quickly because, if I don't, I'll choke on them. "He saw what I looked like and never spoke to me again. I must not have been what he was hoping for."

A flash of pain crosses Parker's face, a wince, almost as if my admission were a sharp slap across his cheek. He grits his teeth together. "Or maybe you were everything he was hoping for, and he wasn't ready for that."

My next breath lodges in the back of my throat, not expecting something so kind and reassuring to pass through Parker's lips. I inch closer to him on the couch, placing my palm against his thigh. "Thank you. That was really sweet."

"Sweet," he parrots, glancing at my hand. And then in one fell swoop, he snatches it up, pulling me by the wrist with his left hand and using the other to scoop me off the couch and position me on his lap. His fingers glide up my spine until he's gripping the back of my neck, our foreheads almost touching while I straddle him. "If you knew all the things I wanted to do to you right now, I don't think you'd be calling me sweet."

A surge of desire blazes through me as I press my groin into his, running my fingers through his soft hair. "I thought…I thought you didn't want to."

"Oh, I fucking want to. I want you so much it's killing me," he nearly hisses, grinding his erection into the heat between my thighs. "It's killing me because I can't…"

Parker's eyes close, and he goes silent.

"You can't what?" I brush a lock of loose hair from his forehead, then place a tender kiss to his hairline. "Tell me."

A heartbeat goes by, and then a growl rumbles through his chest, vibrating into mine. He yanks me off his lap and flips me over on the couch until I'm face-planted into the cushions. I squeak in surprise when he lifts me up by my midsection, my ass jutted out, ramming into his hard arousal. Parker's hands sweep up the back of my thighs as he drags my dress up over my hips, then palms my cheeks sheathed in lace. "Fuck, you're beautiful."

I hear his belt buckle unlatch, and something in me freezes.

God, I want him, there's no doubt about that...

But I don't want him like this. Something doesn't feel right. He's angry, and I don't want to be on the receiving end of his transferred aggression with my face buried in his sofa cushions. "Parker, wait."

He hoists me up until my back is flush against him, one hand cupping my breast. I lose myself for a moment, yielding to his touch, relishing in the way my skin dances to life when his lips dip to my ear, and he whispers, "You on that pill? I want to come in you."

His words shoot tingles straight to the throbbing juncture between my legs. I arch against him, nodding. "I am now."

A little late to be inquiring about that, considering I had to race to the pharmacy and purchase the morning-after pill following our foolish, unprotected sex romp in my backyard. Then I panic called my ob-gyn to order in a prescription for birth control since I've been on and off it for over a year now.

Parker rasps a quick "good" into my ear, and then his zipper unfastens as he tugs my panties down my hips. He gathers my mane of hair in his fist and moves it aside while he holds me up with his opposite arm. His mouth finds the back of my neck, his tongue teasing me into submission. When his fingers drift from my hair and snake around my midsection, delving between my thighs, I instinctively bow my back, seeking his touch.

A groan reaches my ear as he thrusts two fingers inside me, causing my legs to shake. I drop my head back against his shoulder, feeling his hot breath kiss my temple.

But when I twist around to make eye contact, he removes his fingers and pushes me back down onto the couch until I'm on all fours, and he's grasping my hips between both palms, aligning me with his pelvis.

Damn it.

"Parker, stop," I murmur, low and hushed—because part of me doesn't *want* to stop—but loud enough that he can hear me. Because we should. "Not like this."

He stills, his fingertips digging into my waist. "You want to stop?"

"I think so."

"Did I do something?"

Pushing up on my arms, I lift to my knees and situate my clothing, tugging up my underwear and pulling my dress back down. I face him, noting he's staring at me with a wounded expression, wrought with confusion, propped up on his knees like me. "I just…I want more than that," I admit, swallowing down a wave of emotion.

I feel a little silly.

This was supposed to be a sexy hookup, and I'm ruining it with feelings and a desperate need for intimacy.

"You want more than sex?" Parker's eyes narrow, like he's trying to figure me out. Read between the lines. "A relationship?"

"No, I just…" Collapsing into a sitting position, Parker does the same, inching down slowly and yanking his zipper back up. Our eyes meet, and I continue. "You don't want to look at me, or kiss me, or maintain any genuine connection. It just makes me feel…cheap. In a way."

He shakes his head through a frown. "That's not…fuck, I'm not trying to. I don't fucking know how to do any of this."

"Don't overthink it, Parker," I urge, scooting closer to him and clasping his hand between my two palms. "Just feel. Follow your instincts."

"My instincts? My instincts are telling me to bend you over and fuck the shit out of you right here on the couch. That didn't work out so well."

I can't help the amusement from seeping in, and I slip him a smile, placing one of my hands to his heart. "These instincts."

Parker flinches when I make contact with his chest, instinctually moving back.

"I know you want more too," I tell him. "I see your struggle. I *feel* it. I hear it in your voice, and I want you to know that I'm listening. When you're ready."

He ducks his chin to his chest, his eyes floating away from me. His heart thumps against the pads of my fingertips, hurried and turbulent, trying to tell me all the things he can't seem to say.

And then an idea comes to mind. I pull my hand from his chest and rise from the couch, my eyes inspecting the walls.

"Where are you going?" Parker wonders, watching me with stoic curiosity.

I find what I'm looking for and move to the far wall.

Then, I flip off the light switch.

"Melody?"

The room darkens to nearly pitch-black, the only light source being the moon radiating in through the front window. Parker doesn't have much furniture, so my trek back to the couch is fairly graceful, and his shadowy outline comes into view as I near him.

Instead of taking a seat beside him, I'm feeling bold, so I move into the same position I was in earlier. The same position I was in when the tornado hit—when the lights went out and all we had was each other to cling to.

I climb into his lap.

Parker stiffens below me, his breath shuddering as his hands reach out to gently grip my waist. "What are you doing?"

Leaning forward, I press a light kiss to his forehead, my hands lifting to cup his jaw. I whisper back, "The dark is the very best secret-keeper. The things we say in the dark never have to leave it."

25

PARKER

THE LIGHTS FLICKER OFF, AND MY BLOOD RUNS COLD.

"Melody?" I can just make out her shadowy silhouette as she finds her way back to the couch, slinking through the cloak of darkness that has filled the space. The moon from the open window behind her provides a sheer backlight while she inches her way closer. Melody hesitates for a moment when she reaches my parted legs, my belt still loose around my waist, button unfastened. For a moment I think she's going to settle in beside me, but she straddles me instead. Her knees climb up on either side of me, caging in my thighs, her dress riding up her hips and inviting my hands to grip her waist, pulling her farther into my lap. "What are you doing?"

Melody leans in, brushing a delicate kiss to my forehead. Her fingers graze up along my jawline until she's cradling my face in her palms like I fucking mean something to her. "The dark is the very best secret-keeper. The things we say in the dark never have to leave it."

I feel myself melting, liquefying in her hands, my brittle outer layers flaking and splintering. Her touch is calming, and the feel of her pressed into me, her breath coasting along my upper lip, causes me to wrap my arms around her middle and release an expulsive sigh.

She told me to follow my instincts, but my instincts have always urged me to lurk in the shadows and build shatterproof walls. Vulnerability is poison. Emotions are toxic. Becoming soft is a solicitation for pain and disappointment.

My instincts have never once demanded reckoning for the demons I've kept buried for so long. They've never encouraged me to exorcise them, to find solace and healing in another human being.

But Melody found a way in. She's breached me somehow, and all I want to do is eradicate every little thing that has soiled my veins for nearly three decades. Every cruel word and beating. Every cigarette burn. Every insult, every slap, every beesting and papercut.

Every second spent in that fucking closet wishing for death.

Melody dusts both thumbs over my cheekbones, her face only inches from mine. Her thighs grip me, her hair splaying over both shoulders like an added curtain. "I won't force you, Parker…it's okay if you're not ready," she breathes out gently, her words only adding to my desire to spill my guts. "But if you are, I'm listening."

"I want to. I just…" I swallow, my eyes closing. "Fuck, I wouldn't even know where to start."

She slides her hands down my face until they're resting on my shoulders. "Tell me who she is."

"What?"

"In your bedroom…you said that you'll never be him, and I'll always be *her*."

My mother's face flashes through my mind, a mask of evil. Yellow eyes, like the Devil himself. I thought maybe she was once—the Devil—until I learned that alcoholism discolors the sclera of one's eyes. I realized she was only a vile, selfish human who threw her only child away like he was trash, who whittled him down to almost nothing. Heaving in a ragged breath, I croak out, "My mother."

Melody tightens her hold on my shoulders, a little gasp breaking through. "She was abusive?"

"Yeah. My father passed away when I was five years old—he was a structural worker, iron and steel. He built tall ass buildings and shit." Chewing my inner cheek, I force myself to continue. "He fell on the job one day. Died on impact, from what I was told."

"Oh my God…" Melody presses another kiss to my forehead, sighing deeply. "That's awful."

"Yeah, it fucking sucked. We were close. It was just me and him and our mutt, Roscoe. I still remember the cops showing up that afternoon. The babysitter made this horrible screeching sound that I can still hear, clear as day. She took in our dog, and I begged for her to take me too. Unfortunately, that didn't happen."

Her head shakes back and forth in disbelief, her hair tickling my face. "Did you go to live with your mother then?"

I nod. "She ran off with some asshole right after I was born, leaving me with my father. She gained full custody when he died, and that was when my life completely fucking changed."

Memories pour over me, from those first few days of loss and confusion, to worry and anxiety, to constant bone-chilling fear.

"Her name was Roxanne," I continue, dropping my head to the back of the couch, my fingers grazing up and down Melody's spine. "She was an alcoholic— the real mean and nasty kind. She'd smack me around just for fun, pinch me, pull my hair, and make me cry. I think she got off on that shit."

"God, Parker…"

My jaw clenches, my body stiffening, yearning to throw my walls back up. "Her favorite thing to do was burn me with the butts of her cigarettes. I'd scream and beg for her to stop, but it only made her laugh. Sometimes I can still smell it…acrid and metallic. Smelled like death."

Melody sniffles, and I think I see a soft reflection of tearstains tracking down her cheeks. She glides her hands to my neck.

"She would go on these benders, locking me in my bedroom closet for days with a sandwich and a glass of water. No flashlight, no toys or games, nothing. It was pitch-fucking-black in there, to the point where my mind would play all these tricks on me. I'd see things. I'd create things. I had this imaginary friend…" I falter with an unsteady breath, regrouping. "I'd have full-blown conversations with fucking shadows. And then I actually thought I was dying—it had been days since I'd seen her or even heard anything outside the door. Sometimes I would hear yelling or laughter or things falling, breaking…

you know? I was certain she'd forgotten about me and disappeared, just like she disappeared on my father.

"Turns out she was dead. Drank her sorry self to death. A neighbor came by to check on us when she hadn't seen us for a while and found her in the kitchen. I heard the neighbor scream, so I started pounding on the closet door with all the strength I had left. I tried to scream myself, but I couldn't…I could hardly even breathe or keep myself upright."

I feel Melody's knees tremor against my outer thighs, her fingers quivering along the nape of my neck. Her forehead presses into mine as she inhales slowly. "I don't know what to say," she admits quietly.

"There's nothing to say. I've never told anyone about this before—not willingly, anyway. Just the cops. And my sister, Bree, a long time ago."

She sniffs. "You have a sister?"

"Foster sister. She's honestly been the only good thing in my life."

Until you came along.

"This is why you've never been in a relationship? Why you don't like women?" Melody wonders, somehow inching closer to me.

Swallowing, my hands fall down her back, landing at her hips. My silence fills the space between us, my answer evident. I don't want her pity or her tears. I'm not used to shit like that, and I have no idea what to do with any of it.

Truthfully, I'm not sure what I want or what I'm looking for, but the way she's holding me right now, wrapping me up in her warm limbs with the kind of affection I used to crave all those years ago…it's enough. It's a calm I haven't felt since I was just a little boy on my father's front porch as a gentle breeze rolled in, causing the daylily petals to dance to life.

Fleeting beauty. The most precious kind.

Melody nuzzles her nose into the crook of my shoulder, her tears dampening my skin. "You like me, though," she concludes in a raspy breath.

I let out a choppy sigh, instinctively holding her closer, losing myself in her warmth, in her citrus scent. She's the only beam of light in this dark room—my only escape.

She's my moon.

"I'm not her, Parker," Melody murmurs near my ear, making me shudder. "I would never hurt you."

Fuck, I know she's not her. She's *nothing* like her.

Melody March is a fucking revolution, and she's come to overthrow everything I've ever trained myself to believe about women, about intimacy, about... *hope*.

Maybe hope isn't toxic.

Maybe *she* is hope, with hair made of cotton, eyes like the sea, and a mouth I haven't stopped thinking about since she gifted me with that very first smile.

Sliding one hand up her back, I twist my fingers through her hair, tugging her head back until our faces are aligned. I blink through the layer of darkness between us, eyes adjusting, making out the faint glistening of tears staring back at me. Her lips part, welcoming me, tempting me, as her fingers curl around the base of my neck. I dip in closer until our noses touch. "I'm falling for you," I breathe against her lips, almost grazing them. "But I don't know how to fall without crashing and burning."

Melody makes a sound, a little gasp, her hands rising up to clasp my face again. She arches her body into me, whispering, "I'll catch you."

Those three words seduce me, and I move in, our lips lightly brushing together, just like they did in her dark basement. The only other time someone tried to kiss me was when I was fifteen years old—one of Gwen's friends, who was dared to. Set up to humiliate me. The moment our lips touched, the girl yanked my shirt up, displaying my scars to her gaggle of girlfriends.

A cruel prank, designed to tear me down, strip me of any remaining trust, and force me into the shadows where I eventually learned to thrive.

Until *she* found me.

Starlight and moonshine.

The perfect complement to the dark.

Melody shivers as I hold her, one hand cupping the back of her head, the other gripping her waist. Our lips touch so delicately, so curiously, a prelude to something profound. Unsteady breaths mingle together, heartbeats hurried, bodies buzzing. She makes this sexy little humming noise when I taste her bottom lip, gently pulling it between my teeth. Our pelvises grind together, our grip on each other tightening.

My hands find their way to her face, cradling her jaw, and I pull back to trace my thumbs along both lips, memorizing the shape as my gaze follows. "This mouth has captivated me since the first day you smiled in my direction, all sweetness and sunbeams. It fucking pissed me off."

She shivers. "You think about my mouth?"

"More than I care to admit." Her body buzzes with anticipation, waiting for me to take that kiss she's been dying to give me. I dodge her lips to trail my tongue along her jawline, nicking her skin with my teeth. "I've thought about how your mouth would feel against mine, and if your lips were as soft as that look I'd always see in your eyes when you'd watch me." Gliding my tongue back down, she arches her neck with a moan. "I've thought about it wrapped around me." I nip at her jaw again. "I've jerked off a hell of a lot of times picturing that pretty mouth sucking me off."

Melody turns to putty in my hands, and I feel her wetness seeping through my denim jeans.

I drag my fingers up to her silky mane of hair, scratching her scalp. "I want to kiss you now."

Before she can respond, I lean forward, nibbling her bottom lip, my tongue poking out for a quick taste. I kiss her gently—once, twice. And then my mouth claims her in a desperate, needy kiss, pulling a deep groan from my chest when I push my tongue between her teeth and taste her for the first time. She whimpers in return, her nails digging into my cheeks as she coasts her tongue along mine. I'm reckless and wild, the feel of her so intimately woven with me igniting something I've never experienced before. Something alarmingly addicting.

We tangle and dance, her warmth invading me, her light healing me from the inside out, and I feel like I'm drowning, sinking deep and endless, but it's okay...

I know she's there to catch me.

Pulling back for a breath, I clutch her in a fierce, possessive hold, rasping out, "You taste exactly like your smile."

Melody's chest heaves as she drags her nails down my jaw, then my neck. "What does it taste like?"

"Mine."

Another whimper hits my ears as we collide. I angle her face against my mouth, devouring her while my hips arch up, seeking the hot friction between her thighs. I'm rock-hard, my dick throbbing in my jeans, aching to feel her sheathed around me once again, tight and wet. My fingers wind behind her head to lace through her hair, forcing our lips to stay locked together as I use my opposite hand to reach down and unzip my pants.

Melody squirms on top of me, inching her dress up over her waist, then helps tug my jeans down. My hips lift automatically until I'm pulling my cock from my boxers and she's positioning herself over me, reaching between my legs.

Her fingers curl around me, stroking my length in her small, tight fist. My head falls back, a hiss escaping, when she rolls her thumb over the tip, wet with arousal. "Fuck, Melody. Don't make me come in your fucking hand."

She kisses me, sweeping her tongue along the roof of my mouth, then pulls back and asks huskily, "Has anyone ever touched you like this before?"

Fuck, no.

Melody is my first.

My first kiss, my first hand job, my first goddamn brush with humanity.

"Just you," I ground out, barely able to make out her hand pumping me slow and steady through the veil of darkness. But I see her eyes flash by way of ethereal moonlight, dancing with prowess, alight with desire. "Only you."

Her lips find mine, her hand still jerking me, and our moans blend as one. "God, I love kissing you," she says with a sigh.

"So kiss me," I say back, hardly coherent, biting at her lip. "Then ride me."

Melody makes this mewling sound that causes my dick to twitch in her hand. She lets go of me to yank her underwear aside, then situates the tip of my cock at her entrance, hot and slick. It takes all of my effort not to lose it and come undone like a total fucking tool as I slip inside only an inch. She hesitates, her fingers drifting to the hem of my T-shirt, an attempt to tug it off me.

I grab her wrists. "No."

Her expression wilts for just a moment, a shadowy frown staring back at me through the dark…but she nods.

An understanding.

Instead, she reaches for her own dress, pulling it up over her head until it's discarded, and her hair falls down in champagne waves. I weave my hands behind her back to fumble with her bra clasp while she continues to tease my dick, and I swear I stiffen even more the second the lace fabric slips free and her breasts are exposed, bathed in a hint of milky moonlight.

Fuck, she's pretty.

Melody grips the back of my head and thrusts her tits in my face as she sinks down onto my cock. I bite her nipple with a sharp grunt, causing her nails to pierce the base of my skull. "Parker…"

She grits out my name in a way no one ever has before. So defenseless. Unarmed. Melody gave me something that night in the rain when I fucked her against her shed like a goddamn animal, and I understood the value in it. It was raw and dirty, but it was precious too. She gave me something she had only shared with one other man—her husband.

It scared the shit out of me.

But right now she's giving me something else, and it's more than just her body. It's more than flesh and moans, or the way she's taking my cock like it was fucking made for her.

She's giving me real, genuine intimacy, a piece of her heart, and I don't know what to do with it. It's in the way her forehead rests against mine, her eyes pinned on me while she rises and falls in my lap with each frayed breath. It's in the way she clings to me, her fingers curled around the nape of my neck, thumbs dusting over the skin beneath my ears.

It's in the way she just said my name.

Normally, I'd resist vulnerability like it were poison, reacting with my own anger and venom. But I'm not angry; I'm just unfit and out of my goddamn element, so I funnel those feelings into passion instead, snaking my arms around her back, fisting her hair hard, and fucking her until she cries out.

"Ohhh my God," Melody moans, squeezing me tighter.

I angle my hips, thrusting upward and holding her in place, hitting a spot that makes her damn near untether. I'm not small—hell, pretty sure I'm a lot bigger than average—and she's so fucking petite and breakable, I'm afraid I might hurt her. Tugging her head down, I grit out into her ear, "You okay?"

Her hair tickles my nose when she nods. "Feels so good," she mutters hoarsely. "You feel so good."

Melody grips my shoulders and straightens, throwing her head back and gyrating up and down, twirling her hips. I latch on to those hipbones, my fingertips digging in hard enough to leave little bruises behind, and I pull her to me, sucking a taut nipple into my mouth. She bounces in my lap, moans and whimpers escaping her every time she slams down, hitting that sweet spot.

Jesus Christ, I could get used to this.

"Keep making those sounds and I'm going to go fucking feral on you," I hiss, my fingers scratching down the light layer of sweat casing her spine while hers grab fistfuls of my hair.

It feels like I'm tearing her apart, and she's piecing me back together.

"Do it," she says, still riding me, still taking me to the hilt. "Don't hold back."

A growl rattles my chest, and I pull out of her, scooping her up in my arms and throwing her backward onto the couch. Climbing over her, I'm tempted to flip her over, make this less personal, less intimate somehow…but I don't. My jeans and boxers hit the floor as I kick them off, her underwear following, and then we're face-to-face, our expressions shrouded in silhouette as I situate myself between her spread thighs and push back in.

Our groans are mutual, my palms trailing up to her cheeks, cupping her more gently than I'd intended, while my thumb drags down her bottom lip.

I move in for a kiss.

Melody's arms link around my neck, her legs crossing behind my lower back, and our mouths lock, every single piece of us hopelessly entwined. I think this is where I'm supposed to unleash—go savage on her, leave her bruised and quivering, begging for more through her fucking tears. But my hips move with deep, deliberate strokes, my tongue exploring her, more lazy than desperate, and my hands continue to cradle her face with tenderness instead of crazed urgency. There's a power in the air, some kind of palpable charge, and when I pull back from her lips to meet her eyes, I know she feels it too. The exact same sentiment twinkles back at me like a sky full of stars.

Our eyes continue to hold as my pace increases, thrusting into her while she holds me so fucking close, I feel like I'm suffocating and purging at the same time. Our noses knock, our lips hovering together, barely touching, breaths hot and needy. Her body tenses beneath me as I grip her face in a possessive, clingy clutch, unable to tear my gaze from hers.

Little squeaks and gasps permeate the air as her orgasm builds, her fingers lifting to my hair and tugging at the strands. When I angle my pelvis to grind into her clit and push into her, slow and deep, Melody begins to buckle, her limbs racked in tremors.

"Fuck…" I breathe against her lips, drunk on this feeling—this unfamiliar fucking feeling. "You're so goddamn sexy when you're about to come."

"God, don't stop…"

I don't want to stop. I don't *ever* want to stop, and the notion is equally thrilling and terrifying.

With my own release climbing, I lean down to kiss her hard, our tongues instantly battling, seeking, and craving. I feel her clench around my cock, her whole body tautening, bracing for climax, and I lose myself in it all—in her pleasure, in mine, in the chemicals threatening to incinerate me, in her fucking kiss that I can't seem to get enough of.

One more jerk of my hips, and she cries out into my mouth, gripping my hair so hard it would hurt if I weren't completely consumed by the feel of her pussy contracting around my dick, causing me to fucking unravel.

"*Fuck*, Melody," I groan, pulling back from her mouth to bury my face into the curve of her neck, holding her tight as I come inside her, pulsing and breaking.

The waves hit hard, taking me under. Melody squeezes me as I collapse on top of her, riding out the feeling until I'm nothing but shudders and shock waves, crushing her with my weight. Her palms slide up and down my back, over the fabric of my shirt, the only barrier between us. It's a comforting sweep of her fingers, and I lose myself in her touch for one blinding moment as I shift my weight beside her on the couch.

What was that?

What the fuck was that?

It was just supposed to be sex—simple biology. A physical reaction.

But it felt like a goddamn resurrection.

We lie there in silence for a few long heartbeats, my head tucked into her shoulder, and my arm draped around her middle. The smell of sex and sweat hovers in the air, mingling with traces of her lemony shampoo.

Melody's chest heaves with a labored breath. Shaky fingers dance along the expanse of my forearm as she whispers, "Are you okay?"

She echoes my words from earlier, but they are not the same.

I don't have an answer for her because I don't fucking know. I'm not okay, not at all. I feel dismantled and picked apart. Lost. Drowning in confusion and uncertainties.

And yet, I feel the most okay I've ever felt.

The only words I can muster as I stew in my inner turmoil are "Sorry I held back."

She asked me not to hold back, and instead of going apeshit on her, I took it to a weird-ass vulnerable place. Fucking dumb.

But Melody only gives my arm a gentle squeeze, sighing as her breathing steadies. "You didn't."

Swallowing, I try not to dissect the meaning of her words. I just lie idle beside her, my frazzled thoughts dying out and pacifying when she twists in my embrace and nuzzles into me, a sweet kiss meeting the side of my neck.

Once upon a time, the dark was my enemy—the place where I had never felt more alone.

But not tonight.

Tonight it's where I've never felt more alive.

26

PARKER

I REALLY COULD GET USED TO THIS.

We take the liberty of using our fifteen-minute meeting break to sneak out to the parking lot and fuck in the back of Melody's Camry, like two horny teenagers.

It's been a week since our intimacy-laced rendezvous on my living room couch, where she fell asleep on my chest like a satiated lover, and I stared up at my ceiling fan trying to count the amount of times it spun around in unsteady circles. Melody's languid breaths were a muted soundtrack to my racing mind, mingling only with Walden's wheezy snores from across the room and my kitchen faucet leak. The morning after came quickly, with Melody stirring awake just before five a.m., and I drove her to her car, still parked at Breaker's.

We didn't say much, but it was a comfortable sort of silence, brimming with quiet musings, heated glances, and the occasional smile from her. Melody even reached for my hand during the drive over to the bar, squeezing it in her warm palm, transmitting a flurry of feelings that shot straight to my heart. Before she hopped out of my truck, she leaned in and pressed a kiss to my lips, something sweet and wistful, murmuring softly, "Thank you."

I was too fucking tired to decipher the meaning.

Thanks for the good dicking?

Thanks for the really uncomfortable few hours of sleep on my small-ass couch, my elbow jabbing into her ribs, when there was a bed right down the hallway?

Maybe she was thankful for my impeccable hosting abilities. I didn't offer her anything to drink or eat—I basically just fucked her senseless, then sent her on her merry way.

I'm not exactly sure what she was thankful for, but I know what *I'm* thankful for right now—the feel of her crumbling in my lap, coming so hard, her nails almost pierce through my cotton T-shirt as her teeth bite into my shoulder to stifle a sharp moan.

A prideful smile lifts on my mouth when she pulls herself up in my lap, eyes drunk with postorgasmic bliss, cheeks flushed bright pink. Her hair is chaos, matching the energy swimming in the air. "That was quick," I tease, gliding my hands down her spine.

"I've been waiting all week for that."

Fuck.

Me too.

I'm pretty terrible at the whole communication thing, but I'm really fucking trying.

I texted her.

The night following our hookup, I texted her because I was thinking about her. I was thinking about a particular sound she made, kind of a raspy mewl, wondering the exact thing I'd done in that moment to procure such a sound, so I could do it again, a million times over.

So goddamn sexy.

I was also thinking about the texture of her hair, cashmere and cotton, clearly not from this world.

Witchcraft.

Then I was thinking about those glistening tears in her eyes when I'd confided in her about my shitty past, why they were there, what prompted such an emotional reaction from her because emotion means she cares—and I don't fucking understand *why* she cares.

About me.

I've kind of been a dick to her, an asshole, really, and yet she continues to hurl her empathy at me. She continues to invade and intrude, reaching deeper every single time.

Why? Why *me?*

So I decided to text her and get the plethora of burning questions off my chest, but all I ended up sending was: Hi

Melody responded with her own Hi, but hers was followed by one of those little happy face emojis because she has a vagina.

And that was it.

Luckily, Melody didn't seem too pissed when I sauntered into the meeting today with a strange flickering of nerves erupting inside me. She sat in her usual seat, one leg crossed over the other, looking prim and innocent despite the blazing, come-hither fuck-me eyes she kept spearing me with throughout the meeting. The moment we were released for break, she swept past me with a saucy smile, smelling like orange peels, a blatant invitation to follow.

One minute later, we were climbing into her back seat until I was balls deep inside her, and now she's sprawled against my chest, a mess of satisfied limbs and erratic heartbeats.

Weaving my fingers through her wild mane of hair, I pull her in closer until our lips touch. I'm still rock-hard inside of her, aching for release. "You were waiting to get fucked again?"

Melody clenches some kind of magical muscles that cause me to jerk with a groan. "Yes. I was also waiting for something else."

Here we go...

"Better communication, I get it. I really fucking suck—"

"Not that." Her smile alludes to the fact that she isn't pissed or resentful. "I actually appreciate that you tried. I know this isn't easy for you."

My dick wants to know why she stopped moving, but I muster a nod.

"That's not what I meant, though." Melody climbs off my lap until I'm slipping out of her, her small fist replacing her pussy. She tucks her sundress down with her opposite hand and leans over me, green eyes lifting to sink me with implication. "You said you fantasized about my mouth on you..."

A response doesn't even make its way to my lips before hers are wrapped around my hard cock.

Oh, Jesus, *fuck*.

I must've said that out loud because she smiles around me, using her palm to fist and stroke the base in time with her fevered sucks and eager tongue. My head drops against the headrest, a tapered groan expelling from my chest as my fingers sift through her hair, gathering those silky strands and guiding her head up and down. The image of her bobbing on my dick, taking me deep into her throat, is almost enough to send me spiraling. "Mother of fuck, Melody. I'm not going to last long."

Embarrassing but true.

She moans as she pumps me with a tight hand, slow at first, lapping at the precum that coats her tongue. Her movements steadily grow quicker as she jerks me, and I watch in utter fucking bliss as she sucks me off and brings me to my goddamn knees.

My grip tightens on her hair, my hips instinctually arching up as my climax builds. "You're going to make me come down your fucking throat," I hiss, my body damn near trembling as she hollows out her cheeks and sucks hard.

Fucking hell.

I lose all control, my body surrendering when an orgasm seizes me, and I spill into her mouth with a groan, watching as she fucking takes it, swallowing me down while she makes that sexy little mewling sound.

"Jesus…" I grit out, both hands tangled in her hair as she finishes me off.

When I come down, I'm dazed and out of breath, a little slap-happy, but mostly thankful.

I'm thankful for Melody March and her perfect fucking mouth.

And I'm really thankful for tinted windows.

We're only two minutes late when we wander back inside together with flushed skin and wrinkled clothes, our hair in utter disarray.

Amelia snorts, causing Ms. Katherine to pause midsentence, her own cheeks staining rosy red as she looks our way.

Because she knows we fucked. Everyone in this room knows we fucked.

A drowsy smile stretches across my face as we make our way over to our respective chairs, Melody trying desperately to hide behind her curtain of blond locks. Amelia spares me a humored, knowing glance as I settle into my seat with a hard exhale. I meet her eyes. They almost look violet, just like the streaks in her hair. "What?"

I'm expecting teasing or ridicule, maybe even some sage wisdom that borders on creepy. But Amelia just smiles back at me, and there's a softness there, something almost whimsical. "I'm really happy for you, Parker."

A frown creases my brow, but not my usual menacing scowl. I guess I'm a little surprised by the sentiment. "Why?"

"Because you found a way out."

"A way out?"

"Of the hole."

I blink. Our voices are hushed, so only we can hear each other. Ms. Katherine presses on about one of her favorite quotes, something about having two lives, but it sounds dumb, so I drown her out and keep my attention on Amelia. A fresh cut peeks out through the hem of her dark sleeve, and for the very first time, I'm not filled with derisiveness. A pang of empathy shoots through me instead, and I wonder why that is.

Swallowing, I nod at the new carving. "Adding to your story collection?"

A smile beams to life. "You remembered."

"About you calling yourself a storyteller because you like to give yourself morbid tattoos? Yeah. Kind of hard to forget."

"It's nice when your words stick with people. It feels good to be heard," she says quietly. "To be seen."

My frown deepens. "Is that why you do that shit? To be seen?"

Amelia tucks her limp, black hair behind one ear, showcasing her stretched earlobe and multiple piercings. "I guess so. But once you're really seen, you can never been *un*seen…you know?"

"Not really."

"Once you leave your mark on people, that's it. You're carved into them, permanently engraved. You become a part of *their* story. And that's a little intimidating."

Melody catches my eye beside Amelia, our gazes locking for a striking moment. Her warm, sunny smile elicits my own, and I realize we're just sitting there, smiling stupidly at each other from a few feet away.

When I bring my eyes back to Amelia, her own smile greets me, and she says, "I'm glad you got your happy ending."

A deep-rooted part of me wants to say something scathing, to repel her kind words with barbs and steel. But I don't because a bigger part of me doesn't want to do that at all. A bigger part of me feels like a total jackass for adding to her heavy weights and despair with my snide remarks and apathy. My teeth gnash together as I duck my chin to my chest. "I, uh…I'm sorry for being a dick to you. I know that doesn't mean much, and I'm not really good at this nice-guy shit, but for what it's worth…" I lift my eyes, straining my jaw. "For what it's worth, you're actually kind of cool, and I know you'll have a lot of stories to tell someday. Good stories—not the bloody kind."

"I like the bloody kind." Her grin broadens, a metal retainer and silver lip ring gleaming back at me. "But thank you for that. I won't forget it."

I send her a curt nod, feeling mildly uncomfortable with my foray into sensitivity. But it also feels sort of…*good*.

Ms. Katherine interrupts our weird bonding moment, turning her attention to Amelia while she clings to her leather-bound journal. A soft expression decorates her made-up face, and she bobs her head with encouragement. "Why don't you finish off the starting points for today, Amelia?"

Amelia twists the hem of her dark lace dress, sending me a final smile of gratitude before facing Ms. Katherine. She breathes out a contented sigh. "My hamster, Nutmeg."

27

MELODY

"M Y HAMSTER, NUTMEG."

The room fills with Amelia's willowy voice, her familiar response causing a smile to tip my mouth. She really loves that hamster.

Parker's vulnerable words to the troubled teen gallop through my mind as I straighten in the plastic chair, my head shifting left to peek a glance at him. His expression mirrors his stance, a little rigid and contemplative, lost in thought. Pensive. He apologized to Amelia only moments ago, releasing his burden of casual disregard to the girl with a beautiful old soul and ugly stories on her skin. My heart warmed.

Parker is changing, evolving before my eyes, and the hardened man I'd been drawn to for reasons unexplained is slowly cracking, his shell disintegrating little by little. I spent a lot of time studying him, trying to learn him, taking notes—he carried his pain so well, and I was desperate to know his secrets.

But his pain was never tempered.

It was buried.

He was a master at hiding, camouflaging in the dark, and if I've learned anything over the past year, it's that there is no healing in the shadows. Parker's graveyard of broken bones is breaching the surface, coming up for air, while golden shafts of sunlight rupture through the soil.

He called me a revolution that night in my rain-soaked backyard beneath angry clouds and black skies, and I'd been offended at the time. It sounded like an insult—anarchy, riots, disorder.

But maybe he didn't mean it like that at all.

Maybe I'm...*reform.*

Maybe I'm those glimmering sunbeams, eager to reach beyond the dirt and warm the cold, hollow remains underneath.

His confession slices through me as I study him. His past. His horrible, horrible past. Parker gave me a gift on his couch one week ago, and it was more than just his first kiss. It was more than his body molding into me, moving with me in perfect time, as his palms cradled my face like I was truly special to him.

He gave me his trust.

And as I watch him from my perch in the red chair with Ms. Katherine's voice posing as a comforting score to my musings, I know that I'm falling for him too.

Parker finally feels the heat of my stare, lifting his chin and meeting my thoughtful gaze from around Amelia. They blaze into mine, flickering green, and visions of my back seat grip me in a hot hold.

My thighs clench.

I wonder if he knows what I'm thinking about because his lips turn up, another smile surfacing. It's a smile that evaded me for months, one I craved to witness, to experience for myself, and now it's mine. It's just another offering of trust he's given to me.

I promise to keep that smile safe.

Smiling back, I duck my head, trying not to be ambushed by images of working Parker to oblivion with my mouth while I'm sitting in the middle of a suicide prevention meeting.

The class ends a short while later with Ms. Katherine issuing us her parting words. I'm not exactly sure where to go from here, considering the only time Parker and I really see each other is at these meetings. His communication leaves a little to be desired, and I understand why now, but there is already a part of me that's yearning for more—a part that's desperate to run with the connection we've been building, to keep it blooming and growing.

I want to water it, so it never wilts.

Knowing that will likely take initiative on my end, I rise from my chair, only to be hindered by Amelia.

She stands with me, tucking an inky tress of hair behind her ear. "What do you think is in there?" Amelia nods over to Ms. Katherine, who is flipping through her journal pages. "Do you think it's a secret diary?"

The curiosity grips me. "I'm not sure. I figured it was probably class notes. Ideas for the meetings. Projects or homework assignments."

"Maybe." Her dark eyes narrow thoughtfully before she blinks back over to me. "I'm going to make a coffee for the road. Come on."

My eyes move over her shoulder to Parker. He still remains seated, watching our interaction with his legs outstretched. He nods his head, just slightly, a fleeting gesture to reassure me that he'll wait.

I follow Amelia over to the table with coffee and snacks, clearing my throat. "I like your dress," I tell her, making conversation. I do like it. It's long and lacy, black as per usual. Kind of witchy. "Where did you get it?"

"I made it." She perks up. Amelia's obsidian eyes glide over to me when we reach the table, glowing with a purple hue beneath the recessed lighting. "I like your dress too. It matches your personality."

"How so?"

"It's sunny and warm. Inviting. Beautiful."

A smile blooms with gratitude.

Amelia flicks her finger at my mouth, her nose crinkling. "Just like your smile. I used to think it was too cold for you here…in this sterile space with all these ghosts." She returns her attention to the coffee selections, fiddling with the flavors. "I was afraid we'd haunt you. Scare you away. But you stayed, and you're exactly what we needed."

I watch as she twists around in place, her gaze darting to Parker before landing back on me. Swallowing, I wonder, "And what's that?"

"Sunshine, of course. You make these eternal winters so much more bearable."

My heart soars with affection. Amelia sends a crooked smile my way, then pops her vanilla coffee into the Keurig and turns on the machine. I observe her thin frame, collarbones protruding through the sheer fabric, while a smattering of jagged scars poke out beneath her three-quarter length sleeves. She wears her pain with pride, and it's a peculiar thing. This young woman is far too young to be so riddled with trauma and terrible stains. I swallow. "You have a beautiful heart, you know."

A chuckle greets me, almost self-deprecating. "That's sweet of you to say, but my heart is all wrong."

"What?" My brows pinch together with alarm. "Why do you think that?"

"My mother told me. She said she wished for a princess daughter with fairy wings and a heart made of sugar and spice, but she got me instead. A shadow. A funeral." Amelia lifts dark-tipped fingers to her breastbone, inching down the low-hanging collar of her dress. "I got this tattoo when I turned eighteen."

Eyes glistening with unshed tears, I dip my gaze to her skeletal chest. A broken heart tattoo stares back at me, placed right above her own perfect heart. My head sways side to side with disbelief. "No…your mother didn't mean that, and if she did, she's sick. She's unworthy of a daughter like you."

"You're sweet, Melody. It's okay."

"It's not okay," I insist, fingers curling at my sides. "Nobody's heart is wrong. We're given the heart that is meant for us, and if someone else doesn't see the beauty in it, it's not meant for them."

Something flashes in her eyes, something brief yet poignant. It's like she's drinking in my words and soaking them up, absorbing their truth. But then it flickers, fades away, replaced by something else. Defeat, maybe.

I'm angry in that moment. Violently angry. I'm furious at every unfit woman in the world who claims the title of "mother" when they are anything but. They are not a guidance or warmth or nurturing hug. They're a disease. They infect vulnerable, innocent children, poisoning them with untruths and cruel delusions, branding them with scars they will carry forever.

Parker's mother.

Amelia's mother.

Even Charlie's mother, with her wicked words and sharp tongue, after she had once told me that *I* was like a daughter to her.

I'm angry in that moment, I'm so angry at mothers like that, but I'm also *grateful.*

I'm immensely grateful for mine.

Amelia reaches out her hand, giving my upper arm a gentle squeeze as her coffee cup fills. "I'm really glad to know you, Melody."

A tear slips out just as Parker saunters up to our twosome, his attention shared between the both of us. "You okay?"

I'm not sure which one of us he's asking, but I respond with a tight nod.

"I'll leave you two alone now." Amelia secures the plastic lid on her Styrofoam cup, her violet gaze assessing us, a slim trace of joy sparkling through the sadness. "Have a nice evening."

Parker clears a hitch in his throat, scuffing his shoe along the linoleum. "See you next week, Amelia."

His words seem to halt her retreat, and she falters, neck craning to spare him a final glance. "You said my name," she responds through a grin. "Instead of Emo Chick."

"Oh, uh…" Parker stuffs his hands into his pockets, shuffling in place. "Yeah, I guess."

"Thank you."

Amelia shares her smile with me, and then she's gone, pushing through the double doors with her veil of midnight hair trailing behind her.

Turning to Parker, I nibble my lip, swiping away the fallen tear. He's glowering at the doors that fall shut, but his expression is wrinkled with confusion as opposed to hostility. I take his hand in mine, and he flinches at the contact, his instinct to pull back—but he doesn't. He allows me to interlace our fingers together as his gaze trails back to me. I smile up at him, then lead him out those same doors Amelia just disappeared through.

We traipse through the parking lot, hand in hand, and it's such a simple thing, holding the hand of someone you care about. But with Parker, it feels like a big thing. I catch him glancing down at our interlocked palms every now and then as the hot summer air coasts along our faces, and when we reach my car, I'm reluctant to let go.

Turning to face him, I maintain our hold. "Do you want to go do something? Maybe grab dinner?"

"Dinner?"

"Yes…you know, so we can talk. Spend time together."

Parker blinks at me, the glow of the burgundy horizon reflecting in his green irises. "Like a date?"

My smile is instant, just like the colony of butterflies that awaken in my belly, their wings dancing and dizzy. I nod up at him. "Sure. A date."

"Oh…" His unoccupied hand snakes back to scratch at the nape of his neck, his eyes darting around the parking lot, as if he might find his answer there. When they float back to me, it appears he did. "Yeah, okay."

"Really?"

"I don't see why not. I worked up a bit of an appetite earlier."

His subsequent wink might as well be an arrow to my heart. My balance teeters. "Is that so?"

"Yeah."

Parker releases my hand, raising both palms to cup my face, gently pushing me back against the trunk of my car. Jade eyes swallow me up, leaving just enough for his lips to taste. Our mouths lock beneath a painted sky, my heart thundering in my chest, stunned by his unexpected kiss. And when his tongue dips out to flick along my bottom lip, a request for entry, I oblige with my own starved tongue, and we lose ourselves for a few blissful seconds.

Pulling back with a low groan, Parker grazes his thumb along my cheek. "Maybe after dinner we can go back to your place. I seem to be insatiable lately."

My insides clench with anticipation. I drift away for a moment, fantasizing about a future that feels within reach. A fresh start.

A new man.

The concept is both compelling and…difficult.

I never truly believed there was any hope left after Charlie. The prospect of a new relationship, a different man in my bed, was harrowing, and it drenched me in guilt. Even now, a touch of doubt pinches at me, trying to sneak inside my healing heart.

But this feels *right*.

I don't know why—I don't know why I'm so drawn to this mysterious man with towers of baggage and high walls, but I'm determined to break through each and every barrier.

One smile at a time.

A grin pulls at my cheeks, and I lift up on my tiptoes, breathing my reply against his parted lips before I lean in for another kiss. "Sounds perfect."

———————

We officially had our first date.

I feel giddy, like a schoolgirl with a crush. Parker trails behind me in his pickup truck as we make the drive over to my house from the Mexican restaurant, and the smile hasn't left my face since we shared an order of flan and a parting kiss.

Parker likes flan.

He also likes burritos.

And spicy salsa.

Honestly, I think he just likes food.

Memories of the last hour embrace me with warmth as I pull up to the red light right before my subdivision. We didn't do a lot of talking, but that didn't bother me, and our gaps of silence were more reflective than awkward. Parker felt notably out of place, unsure of how to act or what to say, but the fact that he *tried*—that he agreed to the date, to spend time with me—was enough.

I asked him about his sister. Her name is Bree, and apparently, she's a robot. She works long hours in the medical field, yet she still finds time to help Parker with his construction business. She's always going out of her way to help people, especially him, and it tickles my heart to know that he's had someone in his corner throughout his life.

I can't wait to meet her.

The light turns green, and I glance at his headlights behind me, reflected in my rearview mirror. I'm swept up in a swarm of flighty nerves as my mind wanders to the future events of the evening. Should I take him into my bed or use the guest room? I'm not sure how I feel about bringing Parker into the bed I shared with Charlie.

Maybe I should get a new bed.

I'm in autopilot mode as I make my way down the familiar street that leads to my house, approaching the driveway. Parker follows a car length behind, pulling in and parking beside me when we reach our destination.

Heaving in a calming breath, I yank the keys from the ignition, swipe my purse, then exit the vehicle as the dusky evening air wafts around me, sending a tingle of excitement up my spine.

I hear Parker's truck door slam behind me as I turn to face my house, and that's when I freeze. The humidity manifests into a bone-chilling draft, casing my skin in goose bumps and causing my legs to tremble.

His body heat is hardly enough to warm me as he moves in beside me on the front lawn. "What is that?"

My eyes are wide and rooted to my front porch.

It's a hamster cage.

A squeak of disbelief passes through my lips, and my feet take over, carrying me across the yard until I'm standing above a black-wire cage housing a chunky hamster, brindle and cream. My heart lurches when I spot the note attached with a piece of tape, billowing in the breeze.

No.

Please, no.

Parker comes up behind me as I pluck the note off the cage with shaky fingers. "What the fuck? Is that…?"

His words scatter as my eyes scan the small paper square.

> We're storytellers, you and me.
> My story has come to an end, but yours is just beginning.
> I know you'll take good care of Nutmeg.
> She doesn't like her booties, but she loves the sun.
>
> Amelia

A sob rips through me.

Parker catches me when my knees buckle, and I fall against his chest, stunned and sucker punched. This can't be. *This can't be.*

"Jesus Christ," he murmurs, his arms wrapping me up in a tight hold. One arm releases me to fish through his pockets, and then his voice mingles with my grief, my wails of incredulity. "I need to report a possible suicide. I don't fucking know…"

His words trail off as I sink into a dark hole, my face and tears buried in his chest, and Parker's fierce grip around my waist is the only thing that keeps me from drowning in the abyss. I weep and wilt while he strokes my hair, his nails gently dragging along my scalp, trying to melt the ice that is settling into my bones.

We're storytellers, you and me.

Oh, Amelia.

If only she knew…she has so many stories left to tell.

28

MELODY

FINALITY HAS A PARTICULAR WAY OF MAKING YOU SEE EVERY SMALL, PRECIOUS thing. It opens your eyes with a newfound appreciation for everything that is present and tangible.

Even my heartbeat sounds louder, more *alive*.

Pressing my fingertips to my breastbone, I revel in the thrumming vibrations.

"You look like you haven't slept."

West eyes me on our parents' sofa, his fingers linked around his drawn-up knee as he faces me. My palms curl around the hot mug of tea I've been nursing since dinner ended. I turn to him, perched cross-legged on my favorite ugly couch. "I had a nightmare last night and couldn't fall back to sleep."

It's been forty-eight hours since Claudia Marks found her daughter, Amelia, swinging lifeless in the greenhouse, tethered to the rafters, hanging dead amongst the lively, cheerful crops and geraniums. By the time the police showed up to my house for questioning, the discovery had already been made.

I'm glad *she* found her.

Apparently, Claudia Marks is a well-known fashion designer with a sprawling waterfront mansion in Lake Geneva, so Amelia's death has been headline news, while making the rounds on social media. I had no idea.

I'm realizing there was so much I never knew about the young girl who spoke in riddles and rhymes, who had a troubled mind but a good heart. The fact that I didn't take the time to get to know her better haunts me.

Sipping the tea, I spare my brother a glance. His ice-blue eyes are narrowed at me in consideration. "What?"

"Are you seeing that guy?"

My grip on the mug tightens. West came by that night after I texted him about Amelia, and Parker was still there. There was a bit of uncomfortable tension between the two men, likely because of my brother's loyalty to Shane, and also because, well, Parker's people skills aren't entirely impressive.

Parker put some distance between us when West showed up, but I understood. And even though there wasn't any obvious PDA, the fact that Parker was alone at my house *not* doing work or projects painted a fairly clear picture of implication.

Shifting on the couch, I look away from his probing, brotherly stare. "I'm not sure, West. It's still new."

I suppose that's true enough. Maybe I'm downplaying it because it doesn't feel new—it feels raw, intense, *visceral*. It feels like it was always meant to be, like it's always been.

But we haven't discussed titles or exclusivity, so I have no idea what Parker is thinking or feeling. All I know is what he's shown me, and that's his smile, his secrets, his first kiss, his effort, his trust. It's the way he held me on my front lawn beneath sad stars and jaded moonlight, providing a quiet comfort I desperately needed in that moment. He stroked my hair, rubbed my back, silent, and yet his solace reverberated through me in remedying waves.

He spoke with the police officer who showed up for questioning, he helped me carry Nutmeg into the house, filling her little water bottle attached to the grates, and then he sat with me on the couch, my head on his shoulder, tracing invisible designs on my bare shoulder with his index finger until my brother stopped by.

So, yes, I suppose I'm seeing him.

I'm finally, truly *seeing* him.

West makes a sighing sound that reeks of disapproval. "Just be careful, Mel."

"I'm always careful." I expected this reaction from him but I'm irritated nonetheless. "You know I wouldn't jump into anything lightly."

"I'm just not sure I trust the guy. He's kind of a dick, and he's so different from…" His words are eclipsed by silence as he shifts his gaze over my shoulder. "Never mind."

"From whom? Charlie?"

More silence.

"You can say his name, West. The only thing worse than being reminded that he's gone is pretending that he never existed."

West's crystal eyes flicker blue and melancholy as they find their way back to mine. "Yes. He's different from Charlie. A *lot* different."

"Different means different—it doesn't mean worse. And honestly, you should be happy for me. I'm trying here. I'm trying to move on and start over," I explain, my tone gentle but firm. "You don't even know him."

"Do you?"

I clip my words before they leave my mouth when Mom and Dad saunter into the living room with two pieces of homemade cheesecake. I stretch my legs and straighten, placing the ceramic mug etched with elves and snowflakes onto the side table beside me. Mom loves her Christmas mugs, even in July.

"Mellie, my little Jelly Belly," Dad singsongs as he approaches with the dessert plate, grinning widely.

I simultaneously cringe and smile at the childish nickname, reaching for the plate. Mom hands the other piece to West. "Thanks, Daddy."

"There's nothin' that Ma's cheesecake can't fix."

Oh, how I wish that were true.

The tines of my fork dig into the confection while our parents sit on the opposite love seat, Dad's broad arm draping around our mother with that same affection he's always shown her.

Shamefully, that affection was the primary reason I stayed away for so many long, lonely months after Charlie passed—I couldn't handle witnessing everything I'd lost.

"How is it?" Mom inquires, adjusting a jeweled barrette clipped into her bob.

West responds through a giant mouthful. "Divine."

We fall into easy conversation, and I watch my parents kiss and cuddle with eyes of appreciation, instead of envy. I drink in my mother's permanent smile and my father's baritone laugh that always rumbles straight to my core. My heart flutters with joy, with gratitude, with *life*, as I swallow down the love in the room and let it warm me up.

My parents have never once allowed me to believe that my heart was wrong. Even on the bad days. Even when it was broken, weeping and bruised, they loved it anyway. They saw the beauty in it, flaws and all.

And for that, I know I am truly blessed.

Before I leave that night, I'm overcome with the need to do something. After I say my goodbyes to West and help my mother tidy the kitchen, I pull out my cell phone and open up my Hangouts app. My last message to Zephyr stares back at me, sent a few days after my disastrous video debut.

> Me: Zephyr, oh wise one, you're so good at giving advice. I was won-
> dering if you had any insight into rejection.

He never responded.

Sucking in a breath, I let my thumbs dance across the keypad with one final message to the anonymous man with Charlie's heart.

> Me: I just wanted you to know that I'm doing okay. I realize you don't
> care, because if you did, you would have checked in by now. You
> wouldn't have left me doubting everything we shared—doubting
> myself and my worth. I'll never know what happened or why you aban-
> doned me, but I respect what we had enough to let you know that I'm
> okay. You were right when you said I stopped wilting a long time ago...
> but I think I'm finally blooming.

I don't expect him to reply, just as I don't expect a new text message from Parker to light up my phone after I return home that evening and climb into bed. Swiping open the screen, my eyes scan over his message.

> Parker: Hi

Oh, jeez.

An amused grin stretches my cheeks.

Me: Hi :)

I'm about to hook my phone up to the charger and go to sleep, not antic-ipating another reply, but a follow-up text buzzes through, causing my heart to stutter.

Parker: Just wanted to say that you're the best thing that's ever hap-pened to me. Good night.

A breath sticks in my lungs, my eyes welling with stunned tears. The seconds tick by in slow motion as I reread his words over and over.
And over.
Trembling fingers manage to put letters together to form something coher-ent, but nothing I say could possibly transmit the intensity of emotion swim-ming through my veins, shooting little shocks of happiness to my heart.

Me: That means more to me than you'll ever know. Thank you.

Flipping off the bedside lamp and blinking away my tears, I fall into a peaceful sleep, nightmare free, with my cell phone clutched against my chest.

When I pull into the support meeting parking lot the following week, he is stand-ing outside, leaning back against the brick siding with his hands in his pockets.
Waiting for me?
The image steals my breath as I cross over to him from my car, greeting him with a small smile, my side braid bouncing along my shoulder in time with my steps.

Parker pulls up from the brick, tousling his hair with one hand as the other taps at the paint-smeared denim tapered along his legs. "Hey."

"Were you waiting for me?" I stop just short of him, watching his eyes case me, from my strappy sandals to my messy braid.

He swallows. "Yeah…I thought maybe you didn't want to walk in alone. You know, after…" Parker heaves in a deep sigh, his attention shifting to the left, like he's reining in his thoughts.

My hand lifts to grasp his bicep, squeezing gently. "That was sweet. Thank you."

While I wouldn't say I'm angry, I'm a little disappointed that he never contacted me after that heartfelt text last week. I messaged him the following day to see if he wanted to get together and grab lunch, but all I got was radio silence.

Parker's jaw ticks as he stares at me, eyebrows knitted together. And then his tension releases with a long exhale, his eyes closing. "I shouldn't have sent you that text."

My heart sinks. "What? Why not?"

"Because it was sappy as shit, and now that it's out there, I don't know what to do about it."

"Parker, it wasn't sappy. It was beautiful and sweet."

"It was embarrassing. You're ruining me."

My knee-jerk reaction is to feel outrage, to unleash my claws and sink them into him. But I reel back my emotions and try to understand him instead. His eyes look tired, swimming with confliction, worn and flustered. There's no animosity there.

Parker genuinely has no idea what he's doing.

He's never been here before; he's never had a reason to care or *feel*.

He's never had a reason to say something like that, and I know that must be terrifying. Vulnerability is terrifying, especially if it's something he's not accustomed to.

"Listen to me…" My fingers trail down his arm until his palm is linked with mine, and I watch as his gaze follows. "You're not ruined. You're *evolving*."

"Into a fucking pussy, apparently."

"No, into a three-dimensional human being with complex feelings and empathy. There's no shame in that."

His head swings back and forth, as if he's rejecting my claims, but his hand clamps around mine in a desperate, possessive hold. "This wasn't supposed to be anything more than sex. I thought fucking you would get you out of my goddamn system, but all it did was bury you deeper. Bury *me* deeper. Now there's no way out."

My insides twist. "Are you looking for a way out?"

Parker's eyes dance back to me, clouded with confusion, like he's being pulled in two separate directions. It's me versus the safety net of his lifelong complacency. "No," he murmurs softly. Then a frown furrows his brow. "I don't know."

Inhaling a shuddering breath, I remove my hand from his hold and nod my head, soaking up his answer. His indecision. "I think maybe you should think about this before we take it any further," I tell him, glancing down at the pavement beneath my shell-pink toenails. "And I'm not saying that out of resentment, Parker, I'm really not. I'm saying it because I *have* to protect myself. I have to protect my heart. I'm not sure it will survive another loss."

When I look back up, his frown has deepened, his gaze tortured and searching. Parker's Adam's apple bobs in his throat while he considers my words. "I'll never intentionally hurt you, Melody."

"Intentional or not, it doesn't hurt any less."

He clenches his jaw, teeth grinding together. His chin falls to his chest, a hard exhale following, and when he pulls his head back up, he's closing the gap between us. Parker's hands reach out to clasp my cheeks, fingertips digging into the skin and causing a gasp to escape my lips. And then his forehead is pressed against mine, our noses touching, as he rasps out, "I'm so fucked."

He plants a hard kiss to my hairline, then bolts.

Parker leaves me there, just outside the entrance, and I watch in bafflement as he makes a hurried escape to his pickup truck and hops inside, careening out of the parking lot with screeching tires.

My eyes water. I needed him today—I needed him to get me through this first meeting without Amelia. I can hardly stand the thought of two empty chairs beside me.

Chest rattling and stomach spinning, I suck in a breath of courage and push through the main entrance, weaving down the hallway until I come across the familiar double doors.

I'm the last to arrive. Everyone is sitting, stoic and silent, while heads turn to face me as I quietly enter.

Alone.

Without him.

"Hello, Melody," Ms. Katherine greets, and even her dazzling smile has dimmed. Mascara streaks paint her cheekbones, evidence of her grief, while plump fingers tighten around the journal in her lap. "Have a seat."

Realizing my shoes have frozen to the squeaky floor, I find my footing and glide over to one of the three empty chairs, all in a row. Agony grips my heart.

"As most of you know, we lost a member of this community last week. A precious, valued member. A unique human being with a big heart and bright mind," Ms. Katherine begins. Sweat dots her dark eyebrows as her focus lands on every one of us. "The one thing that brings us all together each week is the same thing that can easily tear us apart. I'd be lying if I said I felt no responsibility for what happened to Amelia—I was entrusted to help guide her, to keep her safe and protected from the ugly burden that weighs us all down. My duty is to show you the light in the dark tunnel we walk through together. To show you the beauty of life when the allure of death consumes you. It's hard not to feel like I failed."

My timid voice interrupts, unsteady and unplanned. "I was her Lifeline."

A heavy plume of guilt hovers in the air, so thick I could cut it with a knife.

I wish I could. I wish I could slice it to shreds, cleave and carve it, sever it from my bones and bleeding heart.

But guilt is a stubborn invader, and it can't be forced out.

Ms. Katherine's expression is etched with tender compassion as her focus settles on me. "Lifelines are there for those who choose to use them, Melody. These meetings are a choice; this outlet of support is a choice. This weight is not yours to carry," she says gently. Ducking her head with a sigh, she finishes, "Just as it's not mine. It's hard to see these things objectively when emotions overpower."

My eyes sting with fresh tears.

"We are not responsible for the choices that others make. It's part of the human condition to latch on to the whys and what-ifs because that gives us power when we feel like we have none. But we're looking for power in the wrong place," she explains. "The power is not in the past—it's in the present. It's in how we choose to move forward and how we can mold our grief into something useful. Something beautiful."

I drink her words in like sustenance. I never thought to look for beauty in grief. How can there be any trace of goodness in something so ugly?

At the end of the meeting, I stay rooted to my plastic chair as fellow members file out the double doors. I remain seated and still until the room is empty, save for only me and Ms. Katherine. She studies me fondly, almost as if she anticipated this engagement, this one-on-one interaction.

Swallowing a biting breath, I whisper, "How did you mold your grief into something beautiful?"

Ms. Katherine's smile stretches her round, flushed cheeks, and she pats the leather-swathed journal that rests atop her thighs. "Can I tell you a story?"

My nod is instant. Eager.

"I used to be a fourth-grade teacher," she begins, dusting a patch of dark bangs from her eyes. "My students were my entire world. My saving grace. My friends and family called me Katy, but nothing sounded sweeter than *Ms. Katherine*." Her eyes glint, turning wistful. "It's against the rules to have a favorite student…but there was one. A boy. His name was Daniel Augustine, and he was a quiet little boy. He kept to himself most of the time, stoic and introverted. Invisible to most…but to me, his spirit shined bright."

Goose bumps prickle my skin, my instincts already telling me where this story is going. My lungs burn, stinging my chest.

"Daniel came to me on the last day of class with a gift. He told me I was important to him, that my lessons were valuable, and my classroom was an escape."

"What was the gift?"

She holds up the journal. "This."

My eyes case the worn leather, a somber smile lifting on my mouth. "How thoughtful."

"Yes," she says, her gaze drifting to the floor, posture stiffening. "When I returned to the classroom that fall, I was given terrible news. Daniel had passed away over the summer. He'd found his father's handgun and had taken his own life."

A gasp breaks through, and tears slide down my cheeks. "He was so young…"

"He was. It was a horrible blow that threatened to take me down. I hardly slept for months, wondering how I missed the signs, wondering what I could have done to help him…to change his fate." Ms. Katherine's eyes glisten beneath the recessed lighting, her voice wavering. "I finished out the year, and then I quit teaching altogether. I didn't see the point."

I swipe away the gathering tears with my wrist as I await the rest of her story.

"Eventually, I began to see things differently. I knew I could stew in my guilt, my regret, my *grief*, knowing the outcome would never change…or I could manifest those feelings into something good. Something commendable."

"Something beautiful," I finish with a sniffle.

She nods. "I created this group so I could reach other troubled souls. So I could make a difference. Even if I only touched one person, if I could only change one person's fate and help them see the good in life, the beauty in living and *surviving*—then it would all be worth it. Daniel's death would not be in vain."

Hot tears continue to fall, and I feel her words as much as I hear them. Glancing at the journal still clutched between her fingers, I lick my lips. "Can I ask what's inside your journal? You bring it to every meeting, but I've never seen you open it."

Ms. Katherine's smile breaches her sadness. "It's my starting points."

"Your starting points?"

"Yes." She rises from her chair, hesitating for a moment before she hobbles over to me. Taking her place beside me, where Amelia used to sit, she hands me the journal. "Here. Have a look."

Faltering at first, I blink at the offering, eyeing her outstretched palms holding the beloved journal. It feels invasive somehow, like I'd be intruding on her privacy. On her secrets. But Ms. Katherine doesn't appear apprehensive, and she continues to hold it out with assurance. With a hard swallow, I take the heavy booklet made of leather and paper and bring it to my lap. Tracing curious fingers down the spine and over the front cover, I inhale sharply.

Then, I open it.

I'm startled at first, taking in the names at the top of each crinkled page. Familiar names. Robert, Jane, Nancy, Kevin, Stacy…Amelia.

My eyes widen, a breath lodging in the back of my throat. I glance to my left.

Ms. Katherine sends me a knowing smile. "My starting points are *your* starting points."

More tears rush to my eyes, and I can hardly see the pages. The ink and pencil sketches become a blur as I frantically wipe my eyes with trembling fingers, not wanting to stain the entries. Collecting myself, I sift through, eyeing the scrapbook of our sessions—of our lives. Each member has pages dedicated to them, riddled with quotes and hand-drawn pictures of our starting points.

Robert pushing his young daughter on the swings.

Stacy picking strawberries with her grandmother.

Kevin playing the piano.

A small cry breaks free when I discover Amelia's page subtitled "The Storyteller." A lifelike drawing of Nutmeg is shaded in pencil as a beautiful girl with ribbons of dark hair clutches the animal between her hands.

I feel Ms. Katherine's warm palm glide up my spine, an offering of solace. It's enough to keep me turning the pages until I find my own dedication.

Melody.

I'm dancing in the lake beneath a picturesque sunset, my hair flying free, my arms spread wide. I'm smiling. I'm living.

I'm not ready.

My emotions twist into dread when I continue to flip the pages, unprepared to see Parker's sad, blank pages. He never gave his starting points—not once.

Anxiety grips me, and I close my eyes, my heart thrumming with mournful beats. My chest aches. My skin turns clammy.

I don't want to see…I don't want to see his empty pages.

But I force myself to continue until I land upon his entry.

Parker.

It's one page, and it's not blank.

My stomach pitches when my eyes land on the drawing. It's a sketch. Carved in pencil, shaded with color, brimming with detail.

Looking back at me is a woman with straw-blond hair, irises spun green, and a smile as bright as the summer sun.

It's me.

Quiet tears manifest into a heartrending sob as I break down, falling sideways into Ms. Katherine's welcoming arms.

Parker's starting point is me.

29

PARKER

THE VIOLIN IN THE DOWNTOWN STORE WINDOW CATCHES MY EYE.
Faltering, I can't help but slow my feet, coming to a complete stop as my sister rams into me from behind, her nose in her cell phone.

"Shit, Parker." Bree follows my thoughtful stare, her acorn eyes narrowing. Long, thick eyelashes flutter, fanning freckled cheekbones. "It's a music store. You don't like music."

She's right, in a way. I never really cared for music because its purpose didn't align with my own. Evocative, emotion laced, riddled with feeling and lyrical prose.

I'm a deadened ice block. A glacier.

Well…I was.

Now there's music filtering through my blood, pumping anthems and lullabies straight to my heart, causing the calloused organ to dance and sing.

Melodies.

Pursing my lips, I blink at the instrument, an idea unraveling as Bree slurps a berry-infused smoothie through a wide straw. I shrug. "Violins are kind of fucking cool, right?"

"Cool?"

"Yeah. The music they make…I mean, I get the appeal. Like vibrating ocean waves." Braving a glance in her direction, I clear my throat and add, "Or some shit."

She gawks at me, rising to her tiptoes and placing the underside of her palm against my forehead. "Do you have a fever?"

Fuck yes, I have a fever.

I'm sweating, burning up, possibly hallucinating. I have been for a while.

I swat her hand away and turn from the glass window display. "Never mind."

"No, Parker. Not *never mind*." Bree races to catch up to my long strides when I storm down the sidewalk. "What's gotten into you?"

Her. She's all over me, infecting my blood.

And I'm addicted.

My gait quickens, a feeble attempt to outrun her questions and probing. It's been years since my sister has gotten me out of the house to do aimless sibling shit, like take an afternoon walk and drink pretentious smoothies together.

My smoothie tastes like asparagus, so I toss the plastic cup of green sludge into an approaching garbage can as Bree strolls up beside me. Stuffing my hands into my worn-out jeans, I arch an eyebrow, pretending to have no idea what she's talking about. "I'm fine."

"That's my point. Is this about the woman you're not sleeping with?"

I waver. "Things may have changed since we last spoke about it."

"What?" Her eyes bug out as she snatches my wrist, dragging me over to a bench we've conveniently stumbled across.

"It's not…" My words evaporate into the midday August haze, and the ensuing draft steals the lie from my tongue.

It's not a big deal.

Yeah fucking right.

Bree pulls me down to the bench, her knees twisting toward me as she lassos my attention with her wide, light-brown eyes. "Parker."

"Bree."

Her gaze shimmers beneath the sunless sky, a hand clasping my knee with a tender squeeze. "Are you in love, little brother?"

What the fuck?

Her question sends my insides into a spiral, and my heart pinwheels out of control. "That escalated."

"Are you?"

"No." My fingers curl into tight fists atop my lap. "I have no fucking clue what love is. We both know that."

My sister strengthens her grip on my knee, dark chocolate curls swinging along with the shake of her head. Her lips toy with a smile as she tries to connect the dots somehow. But she doesn't know the dots. The dots hold no context.

Fuck the dots. The only thing they lead to is annihilation.

Regrouping, I shift back against the bench and scrub a palm down my jaw. "I'm just fucking her, okay? Jesus. You make it sound like a damn historical event."

Bree's smile turns watery as wetness springs to her eyes.

I lurch back, horrified. "Don't you dare fucking cry. I'm serious, Bree."

"I'm just so happy."

About my dick finally getting action. Awkward.

But I know that's not the real reason because Bree has always had a way of seeing right through me. Seeing straight down to my deep, dark center—materializing every little brush with emotion, every taste of humanity, hoping she could drag those crumbs to the surface and build a new home for me.

She's always held out hope. She's always wished the very best for me, and for the longest time, my best was simply surviving. My heart would beat with sleet and snow, with icy disdain for life itself, but it was *still beating.*

Because she wanted it to. She needed it to.

And shit…maybe *that's* love right there. Maybe that's the way I've loved for all these years without even realizing it. I've prided myself on my unwavering indifference. I've relished my apathy. I liked to tell myself that I didn't give a flying fuck about anything, that death would be a welcome reprieve to this meat suit, this *coffin*—but if that were the case, I'd be dead.

Bree has kept me alive.

And now, Melody is showing me what it's like to truly *live.*

My eyes glaze, drifting beside me on the bench and watching as streams of tears slip down my sister's cheeks while she processes this revelation with me. She feels it in the same way I feel it. She's always been in tune.

Bree uncoils my fingers until our palms are latched and squeezing tight.

"Fight for her, Parker." She inhales a frayed breath. "Whoever she is, fight for her in the same way I've never stopped fighting for you."

I close my eyes just as the sun peeks out behind a sky of white clouds.

This war might end in bloodshed, but for the very first time, I'm inclined to draw my sword.

Melody March is my true starting point. My reason for finally wanting… *more*.

And that's something worth fucking fighting for.

———————

I'm hard at work that night, sweating beneath my covered carport—my makeshift workstation during the milder months. I'm not exactly sure what I'm doing or how long it's going to take, but I'm compelled to do it anyway.

My carving is interrupted by two blaring headlights, accompanied by the sound of crunching gravel. Using the back of my wrist to swipe the line of sweat off my brow, I squint into the intense beams. When they flicker off, I instantly recognize Melody's car.

Shit.

I toss a stray tarp over my work in progress just as she slips from the vehicle and closes the door, her sneakers kicking up pebbles and rocks as she approaches me through the dimly lit drive. My legs are pulled in her direction, meeting her halfway. "What are you doing here?"

Melody bites her lip, the endearing habit illuminated by my work lamps. Nervous fingers slip into the pockets of her denim shorts when we're face-to-face. "I wanted to see you."

I repeat her words, as if I didn't hear them loud and clear. "You wanted to see me."

What a simple, straightforward concept. Melody wanted to see me, so she came over to see me. At nine o'clock on a muggy Saturday night after six days of no contact.

After I left her all alone at that meeting, even though I'd told her we could walk inside together. The image of her in my rearview mirror, standing in front of the building entrance, still haunts me, her eyes wide and wounded, her long braid dancing with the breeze.

I wanted to wrap it around my neck like a noose and let myself choke.

My heart twists with guilt. I was a fucking coward, a real asshole, deciding that running from my problems was a better solution than fighting for the possibility that this might not end with the both of us defeated, gutted, and bleeding out.

"Yes," she says softly.

She's not pissed off. She's not even a little bit mad.

I swallow. "Why?"

Why isn't she going off on me? Clawing at me with sharp nails or cursing me out with even sharper words?

Why isn't she...*done*?

Melody continues to fight for something I've given her little reason to fight for. *So damn intrusive.*

And fuck if it's not exactly what I need.

Taking another tentative step forward, Melody's emerald eyes blaze with purpose as she keeps them locked on mine. The swell of her milky breasts heaves with every breath, stealing my attention before I slowly rake my gaze back up, stalling at her mouth.

Those full, parted lips stare back at me, teasing me with memories of them wrapped around my cock, sucking me off until I saw stars.

Fuck, now I'm hard.

Fighting the urge to strip her stark naked in my front yard, I pull my focus off her pink lips, and ask again, "Why are you here, Melody?"

My voice cracks with weakness.

Or...maybe not. Maybe it's strength.

Strength to keep standing here, facing her, because I know I'm not fucking running this time.

"I wanted to know if you've thought about it," Melody murmurs, her tone braided with emotion and a touch of lust. She's feeling everything I'm feeling. "About taking this further."

I told her this wouldn't end well, but the one-fucking-percent chance that it *could* compels me to dive right in headfirst.

Lifting my hand to her jaw, I dust a rough thumb along her cheekbone, my gaze skimming the perfect curve of her face, drinking in her doe-eyed expression. "Yeah, I've thought about it."

"Y-You have?" Her voice shakes with a yearning for more. "What have you decided?"

My thumb slides to her mouth, tugging down her bottom lip as my entire body warms and thrums with need. With *potential.* Melody surprises me by poking her tongue out and tasting the pad of my thumb, laving it gently around the tip and making me shiver. My reply is temporarily seized by her fucking mouth as I'm blasted with more images of her between my legs.

A low growl rattles my chest, and I press forward until our torsos touch. Her breasts tease the front of my shirt, her nipples pebbling beneath her braless halter top. Both of my hands reach out to grasp her cheeks in the same way I did last week in the parking lot, only this time, I'm not letting her go. I'm going to fire my burning truths at her, and if they cremate me in the process, torch me into cinders and soot, then so fucking be it. "You're mine," I grit out, my heart thundering and soul alight. "You're what I've been waiting for. You're what I've been searching for my whole life, and I didn't even know it." Her gasp only makes me hold her tighter, and I swear I see tears glinting back at me, ready to fall. "Melody…you're my starting point. You're my turning point." Pulling her forehead against mine, a strangled sound escapes her, and I finish with conviction, "You're the whole damn point."

Our mouths crash together, a collision of surrender, and Melody grips my shirt in her fists for support as I walk her backward to the hood of her car. Our lips don't part. Our hearts don't waver. Tongues hungry, souls hungrier, I reach under her thighs and hoist her up until she's seated on the hood. Her arms snake around my neck to hold me closer, and I moan into her mouth when our groins meld together. My erection throbs between my thighs, aching to be inside her again.

"I'm taking you right here," I rasp, kissing down the side of her neck as my fingers weave through her hair. "Just like I wanted to that night in the rain when you danced on the hood of your car, soaked to the bone and fucking gorgeous."

My fingers find the button to her shorts, and I unfasten them in record time, yanking down the zipper and discarding the denim from her hips.

Melody kicks them free with a needy whimper. "Yes. Please."

"Please what?" A flimsy piece of red lace she calls underwear keeps me from the heat between her legs. "Tell me what you want."

"You."

"Be specific, Melody. Tell me how you want me."

Jesus…for a guy who never gave much of a fuck about sex *or* talking, I seem to have progressed into dirty talk pretty effortlessly.

It's her.

She brings out a side of me I never knew existed—possessive, dominant, savagely protective. I want to own every inch of her. Brand her with my scent, my *essence*.

Melody drags her fingertips to my hair, tugging at the strands. Then she shoves my face between her thighs until my nose collides with the damp fabric of her panties. "I want you there. Taste me."

My heart skips, and I freeze. I've never done that before—I've never eaten a woman out. I've never had any desire to.

But then, I've never had a desire to do any of this until she came along.

Swallowing down a pathetic surge of apprehension, I breathe in her scent, heady and feminine, emanating potent desire. It spurs me. My cock thickens with need, with an intrinsic yearning to taste her. Another growl erupts, something absolutely virile, and I crook my fingers under the strip of lace, sweeping it down her legs until she's bare and exposed.

Melody spreads her knees as she leans back against the car hood, a lusty gasp escaping her. She sifts her hands through my hair, urging me close. Demanding I feast. "Please, Parker…"

Fuck.

It's all I need.

My tongue flicks out, teasing and tasting. Once, twice. Again. She squirms atop the vehicle, a mess of desperation. "More," she begs.

She's soaking wet, pulsing and achy. Her hips arch up from the hood, seeking my mouth. A smile curves, a feeling of masculine pride washing over me, of *power*, and I hook her legs over my shoulders and lift her hips until my face is buried between her thighs.

"Ohh…" She moans, writhing beneath me, digging her nails into my scalp.

My own groan mingles with hers as my mouth devours her, my tongue licking and sucking, thrusting inside, then working her clit until she shudders with fierce vibrations.

I fucking love it. I love the way she tastes, the way she reacts to me.

One hand clings to her outer thigh to hold her in place, while the other goes rogue, coasting up her body as her back bows and slipping beneath her halter to palm her breasts.

"Parker, God…"

The way she says my name nearly wrecks me. Lifting my head from her wetness, I grit out, "Fuck, you taste like…"

"What?" she pants, raising up for more contact.

My hand releases her thigh to fumble with my belt buckle, unfastening my jeans until they're pooled around my ankles with my boxers. I grab my cock and start to stroke before I dive back in. "Like the fucking end of me."

She arches up when my tongue licks her, bottom to top, and I jerk myself while I work her to orgasm with my mouth.

Moans, squeals, whimpers, gasps.

It's not long before her thighs are quivering over my shoulders, and her hands are desperately tugging at my hair as her body breaks and crumbles.

Melody comes hard on my tongue, crying out beneath the starry sky, and before she even takes a breath of recovery, I'm yanking her down the hood until I'm situated at her entrance, inching inside. "I need to fill you. *Feel* you." I kiss her, hard and punishing. Claiming. "Tell me you want me."

She doesn't hesitate. "I want you. So much."

Pushing inside with a rough groan, I collapse over her, finding her mouth again and thrusting deep. My hand slides up to the back of her head, protecting her from the windshield as I drive into her, my hips jerking clumsily, already feeling myself becoming unhinged. She's ruining me and putting me back together at the same time.

Melody squeaks and mewls as I fuck her on the hood of her Camry, both of us still half-clothed but stripped down in every other way. I raise my head to find her eyes sparkling with starlight, and our noses kiss, our foreheads knocking as I cup the base of her skull in my palm with tenderness yet rail her with punishing strokes.

"I…" My voice fades away, and I'm not even sure what the fuck I was going to say. Probably something mushy and pussy whipped. Her eyes are pulling these feelings out of me, these deep-seated, complicated emotions, and my mouth is itching to purge them with words.

"What?" Melody clasps my face between her hands, a gentle coaxing. "Tell me."

My hips thrust harder to override the sentimental waves coursing through me. "I love the way you feel around my cock."

That was absolutely not what I was going to say, but it works.

She melts, closing her eyes and wrapping her arms around my neck, linking her wrists at the nape. I bury my face into the curve of her shoulder and lose myself in her warmth, her softness, her irresistible delicacy, and when I come, it's shattering.

I'm shattered.

My walls, my barriers, the remnants of my armor.

I'm hers.

As I come down from the high, I hold her, scooping her up and cradling her like a lost lover beneath the dusky moonlight.

In this moment, nothing else matters.

In this moment, everything matters.

I feel *everything.*

A blessing and a curse and, inevitably, my undoing.

As our ragged breaths steady and our heartbeats settle, I pull up from her embrace to smooth back her hair and find her eyes. A lump forms in my throat when I note the vulnerability swimming in her depths of bright green.

This is new for me, but it's new for her too.

We are both two broken souls, fractured in opposite ways.

She loved and lost…

And I was lost before I could ever love at all.

But here we are, pulled together by forces unseen and unexplained, clutching each other underneath an August sky, soaked in sweat and heady truths.

Releasing a shuddering breath, I lean in to press a kiss against her welcoming mouth. "Thank you," I whisper, my hands curling around her waist.

Melody flicks her nose with mine. "For what?"

"For not giving up on me."

The pads of her fingertips slide down my jaw, skimming the coarse bristles, and the look in her eyes is full of affection and warmth.

It makes me feel wanted.

It makes me feel alive.

It makes me feel...*petrified.*

Because I know, deep down, one day...she will.

30

MELODY

I T'S MY BIRTHDAY.

I'm twenty-nine years old today, and I almost didn't make it to this day. The thought alone is an extra reason to celebrate. Tendrils of morning sunlight permeate the glass, a golden reminder of everything I'm fortunate enough to wake up to today and every day. Even the birds in flight outside the window seize my attention, causing my heart to flutter in time with their vibrant wings. Little starting points.

Bringing the triple-shot iced coffee to my lips, my cell phone vibrates on the café table while Leah sits across from me, scarfing down a breakfast sandwich.

Parker.

My smile is immediate when his name meets my highly caffeinated eyes.

Parker: Happy Birthday.

Leah addresses me with a mouthful of food, her crumbs dispersing all over the high-top. She's one of those flawless beauties who can get away with eating like a total savage and still look cute. "Is it him?"

"Yes," I reply through a widening grin.

It's been two weeks since I showed up at Parker's house unannounced, and we had hot sex on the hood of my car in the middle of his driveway, officially consummating this…well, whatever this is. Parker doesn't really do titles.

Whatever it is, it seems to have swallowed me whole, and I'm just kind of floating through life right now with a goofy grin and fumbling heart.

I send him a reply.

Me: Thank you :)
Parker: You busy tonight? I have your present.

My chest warms. I wasn't expecting much from Parker, and not because I don't think he cares or is incapable—I just figured he was so new at this, he wouldn't know what to do. Besides, the truth is, we still don't even know each other all that well. He doesn't know my favorite color, my favorite coffee flavor or television show, my shoe size, my taste in literature, or my quirky fascination with house plants.

He doesn't know that I haven't been able to eat or even look at peaches since last April.

Gnawing at my lip, I shoot back:

Me: I'm having dinner with my family at 5, but I can probably skip out around 7 :)
Parker: Okay. Meet me at the lake at 7:30.

The lake?

My curiosity piques, sending a tingle of anticipation up my spine.

Leah licks the grease from her fingers as she swallows down a bite. "Are sexy birthday plans commencing?" she wonders with an eyebrow waggle.

I close my phone and return my fidgety hands to the plastic coffee cup. "Possibly. He said to meet him at the lake tonight."

"Ooh. Skinny dipping."

"Definitely not."

"Fishing?" Her thumb plummets in a downward motion.

"Also no."

"Maybe a romantic, beachside dinner?"

That doesn't sound like Parker either, but my shoulders shrug at the suggestion. "Whatever it is, I'm excited. Just the idea that he has something planned for me is sweet and thoughtful."

Smiling reflectively, Leah softens, propping her elbows to the tabletop and spearing me with her shimmering, copper eyes. She flicks a loose strand of blue-black hair from her face. "This guy is pretty special, huh?"

My cheeks stain with blush.

God yes.

I'm not sure what it is, but there's been a draw from the very start. A tether. His frosty disposition and crass words weren't enough to deviate me from the crackle in the air every time he'd glance my way with his penetrative green eyes.

Every time our skin would brush, I'd feel it. Every time he'd say my name, I'd feel it.

Some things can't be explained. Some things just *are.*

We straddle the line between magic and mayhem with every look, every touch, every white-hot kiss.

Tightening my grip on the latte, I reply with a nod. "I *really* like him, Leah, and that scares me. My heart has never felt more vulnerable."

"I think that's the key to happiness, though, don't you think?" Her tongue slicks along her upper lip with consideration. "If we never let our guard down, no one would ever be able to reach us."

My thoughts drift to Parker with his steel walls and heavy armor. He never let anyone in, and his heart had become a hardened shell. He thrived on loneliness, on misery.

Maybe Leah's right. Vulnerability is a risk, but the reward is so much greater.

I inhale a prolonged breath, soaking up her words as I sip my beverage. "He's different...he's different from Charlie," I admit. "West doesn't like him."

Leah's eyes roll up. "Forget West. He's just butthurt that you didn't go for Shane, so you could all go out for beer-infused, sports-centered group dates. His opinion is irrelevant."

A snicker escapes me. "So you're Team Parker?"

"Girl, I'm Team Melody. Always have been, always will be."

Love churns between us as we share a smile—the kind of love that's rare and infinite. We've had each other's backs from day one, and her unwavering support of me has never waned or teetered. She's the most unselfish person I know. "You know I love you, right? I don't tell you that enough," I murmur, my words spilling from the purest place.

Leah crinkles her button nose at me, taking a sip of her espresso before replying. "You don't need to tell me, baby girl." Her unnaturally long eyelashes flutter with warmth. "The loudest love is wordless."

––––––––––

It's been the perfect day.

Coffee and chitchat with my best friend, a mini-spa day in which I indulged in a facial and hot stone massage, some bonding time with Nutmeg as I let the curious hamster explore the guest bedroom, and then dinner with West and my parents, featuring my favorite meal: Mexican lasagna, Spanish rice, a southwest salad, and spicy cornbread rolls. Mom makes everything from scratch, including the rich sheaths of pasta, and it's a meal I look forward to every single year.

Normally, I'd be dying on the couch from a carb coma at this point, playing Yahtzee with my family, and trying to keep my overly competitive brother from throwing the dice across the room, but tonight the celebration is cut short when the clock strikes seven.

I have another celebration waiting for me.

Saying my heartfelt goodbyes, I practically race out the door, shooting Parker a quick text as I hop into my car.

Me: On the way :)

He responds instantly.

Parker: I'm here.

My heart thunders beneath my ribs, firing its curious beats. His blasé messages leave me with little indication of what he has planned, but that doesn't stop my mind from hashing out every potential scenario as I make the fifteen-minute drive over to the lake.

I think back over the last two weeks, wondering if he left me any clues. Any breadcrumbs. We've only seen each other a handful of times due to his chaotic work schedule, but when we did…

Oof.

Tingles spark to life as flickering flames, igniting low in my belly and spreading through me like a forest fire. Parker brings such *passion* to our sexual encounters, such heat. I never expected that side of him—the raw hunger and need. The desire to claim me in any way he can, to devour me, to possess me, body and soul.

The words he says, the way he holds me.

It's intoxicating.

That, combined with our undeniable chemistry, is a lethal elixir that has me equally frightened and thirsty for more.

When I pull into the familiar parking lot, I spot his truck first, sitting in the otherwise empty lot. My heart rate picks up speed, nearly choking me as I slide into the spot beside him and rein in a steadying breath.

Then I slip from the driver's side and pace around his truck, which was hindering my view, and my limbs go still, my flip-flops sticking to the cement like putty.

Parker is perched in the sand a few feet away, sitting atop a checkered blanket. Walden rests beside him with his chin tucked between two bony paws, his furry head only poking up when he spots me across the beach.

Swallowing, I move in closer. Parker is leaning back on his palms, legs outstretched with something resting between them. I squint my eyes through the hazy setting sun.

A…*violin?*

My mouth goes as dry as the sand beneath my feet when I inch toward them. "Parker?"

A small smile lifts his lips, and Parker straightens on the blanket, reaching for the instrument between his knees. "Hey."

"Hi," I croak out, stopping my feet at the edge of the checkered spread. My eyes meet his, swimming with glimmering nerves. Green, jittery flecks. "You… you play the violin?"

Parker clears his throat, palming the neck of the instrument, glazed with a cherrywood varnish. He fingers the adjacent bow with his opposite hand. "I half-ass learned one song, but it's not good. Fair warning." His eyes close for a moment, chest puffing with a heavy breath. "I didn't know what to get you for your birthday. I've never had to think about shit like this before, so my mind was racing with what you might like…books, clothes, girly house stuff. No fucking clue. I thought maybe I didn't know you well enough to get you something worthwhile. Something you'd actually enjoy and appreciate.

"Then I realized: I do fucking know you, Melody. I know the deep, important shit, like the way your eyes light up when you're dancing in the freezing lake singing god-awful eighties songs, and that you cry when you hear violins play, and that your mom would make you peanut butter and banana sandwiches whenever you were sad, and all the little things that keep you waking up each morning, living and breathing. I know your starting points."

Tears trickle down my cheeks, pooling at my jaw, and I stare at him, dumbfounded.

Awestruck and bewitched.

Parker continues. "So I built you this violin. It's a little shoddy—not my best work because violins are kind of a bitch to hand carve, but…it plays." Pausing, he reaches for his cell phone lying beside his right knee and scrolls his finger over the screen until a music app opens. His gaze connects with mine before he taps the song. "Dancing in the lake. The song 'Unchained Melody.' The sound of violins. Peanut butter and banana sandwiches. August…" He waves his arm out, as if gesturing to the current month. "Sandwiches are in my bag."

I don't even remember moving, but suddenly, I'm kneeling in front of him in the sand, holding a heartrending sob in the back of my throat. Walden perks up to sniff me, and I trail my fingers through his soft fur before returning my attention to the man who is stealing my heart.

Although…he can't steal what was already his.

I'm blurry-eyed and sniffling as I watch him in wonderment, realizing how much he truly heard in those meetings. Even on the days I thought he was sleeping, he was silently listening. He was listening to me, noticing me. Absorbing.

Parker etched my words and purest memories inside of him, carrying them around until they outweighed his darkness. I've been a part of him for all this time.

My voice quakes as I lick the tears from my lips. "This is the most amazing gift. Parker, I…I'm speechless."

"You're about to be deaf in a minute. I'm telling you, this won't be good. It took hours of YouTube videos to figure out what these damn strings even do."

Laughter sneaks into the cry that escapes me. "I can't believe you did all this…"

He taps his phone screen back on, then hovers his index finger over the song selection. A smile of apprehension greets me as he swallows hard. "Fuck, okay…ready?"

I nod eagerly.

Parker presses play, and my favorite song floats through the speaker: "Unchained Melody." My heart feels like it's weeping from only the first note, and then it falls apart, a quivering mess, the moment Parker places the bow along the four strings.

The instrument sings to life, so entirely out of tune and off-key, my tears fall harder. Parker chuckles through his blunders, shaking his head as he misses almost every note, but that only makes it sweeter.

More *perfect*.

Zephyr's words flash through my mind as the strings assault me with preciously flawed melodies: *Perfection is an illusion.*

He couldn't have been more wrong.

Perfection is right now, this very moment, sitting on my favorite beach with Parker Denison as he siphons every last drop of remorse and fear, every lingering shadow, from my wildly beating heart.

The sun rises inside me again.

He only lasts another thirty seconds before a final self-deprecating laugh spills from his lips, and he grits out, "Fuck it."

In a flash, Parker sets the violin aside and pulls me up by the wrist while the song still echoes from the speaker. Walden watches with a cocked head as I squeak in surprise, finding my footing and skipping through the sand toward the water, Parker leading the way. "What are you doing?" I question through a stretched grin.

Parker kicks his shoes off, then yanks a white sock from each foot. "Your starting point was dancing in the lake, not sitting in the sand. Come on."

"You...you're going in the water?"

"Why do you think I wore shorts?"

Our smiles match as we face each other for a fleeting, poignant moment, causing my lungs to burn with adoration. A new wave of tears flood me. The sun hovers low in the sky, casting an ambient orange glow along the surface of the water, bathing us in half-light, and I'm not sure if I've ever felt more ablaze.

With my toes in the sand, our hands entwined, my favorite song serenading us, and a sweet, old dog as our witness, Parker tugs me toward the water's edge. I let out an onslaught of delirious giggles when my bare feet hit the icy lake with a splash.

"Fuck, it's cold," Parker bites outs, dragging me through the sludge until I'm flush against his chest. His arms snake around me, holding tight. "But you're not."

My nose kisses the front of his T-shirt. "Because I'm the sun, right?"

There's a lengthy pause, a considerable silence, as Parker digests my question while the water licks our thighs. He breathes a tapered sigh into my hair. "You're the moon."

The moon?

I pivot my face until my cheek is pressed up against his heart. The beats are loud and songful, a worthy harmony to the melodies drifting over to us from the beach. My eyes close with contentment. "Why am I the moon?"

"You're the guiding light in a dark sky," Parker murmurs, his breath tickling the top of my head. "You shine strong when the rest of the world is asleep... when no one is even looking."

A strained gasp of impossible emotion is swallowed by his shirt. Muffled by his heartbeats. I almost choke on my own voice as I repeat raggedly, "I'm the moon."

I'm Charlie's sun, and I'm Parker's moon.

I can be both.

I'm an eclipse.

We sway lightly beneath the horizon as "Unchained Melody" plays on loop across the shore. Parker's arms wrap tighter around me, holding me like a lover, while we dance quietly in the stillness of the water. I'm transported back to my living room as a little girl, my tiny feet perched atop my father's shoes as we danced to this song, and it's a moment that has always stayed with me. I felt so loved in that moment, utterly adored, and those same feelings sweep through me right now as I cling to Parker beneath a sky of orange and gold.

Is this…*love?*

It feels so profound—so fundamental.

Does Parker love me? Is he capable?

Am I?

His arms unlink from behind my back, then he grazes his fingers up my biceps until he's pulling me free of the embrace. I'm startled at first, confused, but his touch is gentle and careful. Parker takes one of my hands in his, and I note how much mine is trembling—either from the cold water or from the flurry of questions funneling through me.

Our eyes lock as he guides my hand to the hem of his T-shirt and inches my fingers underneath the fabric. My breath catches.

His scars.

He's letting me feel his scars.

Parker goes rigid, his body rejecting the intrusion, but his eyes remain soft and steadfast. His palm curls around my wrist as he maintains control of my exploration, and I hold that same breath when the pads of my fingertips touch the cemetery of old wounds, of grisly trauma, he's kept hidden from me all this time.

The tissue feels puckered and worn as my fingers dance from one scar to the next. Parker keeps my reach low, level with his abdomen, and I watch his face twist with quandary as his innate need to push me away battles with these new feelings of vulnerability. He's letting me in. He *wants* to let me in.

I graze a finger along the edges of a larger scar, soft yet jagged, and Parker inhales a sharp breath. His grip on my wrist is deathlike, his eyes closing tight.

He's fighting. He's fighting so hard to keep this connection—to break through this final wall, the one that's most resilient.

It's painful to watch.

My heart falls faster than my tears, my hands tremoring even harder as I splay my fingers along his beautifully marred skin. "You're perfect."

"No…" Parker hisses through his teeth. "You don't need to lie to me."

Another cry breaks loose, broken and mournful. My lungs feel strangled. "I'm not lying, Parker. The cruel things you tell yourself, your toxic beliefs—*those* are the lies. They're ugly and poisonous, not *you*."

His muscles clench, resisting my truths. "Seventy-nine scars, Melody. I'm a fucking monster."

"*No*. You're a man," I bite back. "You're the man I've fallen head over heels for, scars and all."

Parker lets go of my wrist, then curves his hand behind my head until he's palming my skull, fingertips digging into my scalp. He crashes his mouth against mine, his tongue tearing through my lips until I cry out with a moan.

I grip his shirt in my fists, my back arcing as he devours me with his kiss. It's laced with fire and embers, everything we are, everything we'll always be.

But as our tongues duel and fight for dominance, my mind rewinds, pausing on his words. Shivers race down my spine, curling my toes into the murky lake floor.

Déjà vu. An alarming sense of familiarity.

With my favorite song in my ears, his lips on mine, and an insatiable fullness in my heart, everything is perfect.

Everything is perfect, except for the pulsing in my temple and the goose bumps on my skin.

Seventy-nine…

…*Zephyr79?*

31

PARKER

WALDEN AND I STROLL IN THROUGH MY FRONT DOOR WELL PAST TEN P.M., and the goofy fucking smile on my face hasn't faded since I drove out of that parking lot.

Is this happiness?

Am I *happy*?

It's almost an impossible notion. Goddamn preposterous, honestly. But this floaty feeling coursing through me, making my legs feel weightless, keeping this stupid-ass grin on my face, feels like it might be happiness.

I swear my damn dog even feels it.

Walden follows me to the couch as I collapse onto the cushions, sighing deeply. The animal paces over to me with slow, cautious steps, wavering once or twice before bridging the gap between us. His eyes are wide and curious, his head tilting to the side as if he's trying to read me somehow. Like he's trying to process this brand-new version of his caretaker.

As I close my own eyes, I feel a warm presence hop up beside me, a furry little face sniffing my jaw and giving me a quick lick. Walden curls into my thigh, resting his chin atop my knee, and I link my arm around his bony body. His sigh is long and content, matching mine, and we sit there together amidst the comfortable silence.

I realize then that this is the very first time he's ever licked me. Ever laid upon me in this way. Ever showed affection.

I'm not sure why he's coming around now, after all these years.

Glancing down at the ball of black-and-white nuzzled against me, a contemplative frown furrows between my eyes. Bree had mentioned she thought his hair was growing in, but...*holy shit*. It really is. Thick, shiny tufts of healthy fur have filled in the mottled patches of his skin. He looks like an entirely new dog, thriving and restored.

He looks cared for.

Happy.

Loved.

A burning swallow claims my throat, my chest tightening with revelation. I'm thrown back in time, reminded of a dreary day in the foster house with Bree, when she snuck into my bedroom with a potted plant. The leaves were vibrant and green, fragrant with earthy musk. The soil was damp from a fresh watering, and my sister cupped the terra-cotta pot between her palms like it was a precious thing.

Setting it beside me on my nightstand, which was nothing but one of those individual folding tables, Bree said to me, "Living things thrive on other living things. The energy you give off will be the energy received. Give this little plant the very best version of you, and you can grow together."

I recall thinking it was silly at the time, but I was only ten or eleven, so fantasies still appealed to me then. I spent the following week forcing myself to smile, trying to conjure up the tiniest pocket of happiness, so the plant would bloom and grow. So it would want to be my friend.

I watered it. I talked to it.

I even named it "Leafy."

But the fucking thing died anyway. It wilted before my eyes, withering away to brown leaves and sad soil. It was a little pot of death.

A mirror image to myself.

I knew then that I couldn't fake happiness. I couldn't fight for joy that didn't exist. Even the goddamn plant knew I was a hopeless case.

But Walden...he's changing right before my eyes, a striking parallel to my own metamorphosis. And it's real this time, it's not an act or a ruse.

It's *real.*

I'm happy.

Riding out the emotional waves, I pull Walden closer to me and stroke his soft, newly grown-in mane of fur. He makes a wispy sighing sound, something peaceful, and snuggles in farther to the crook of my hip. He knows the truth.

He knows it, and I know it.

I'm fucking in love.

I don't hear from Melody at all the next day, which throws me a little. It's already late, dusk fading into dark. After the night we shared together—the gift I gave her, and the gift she gave *me*—I expected a message. A phone call, even. Maybe a surprise visit. It felt like we had bridged a final gap somehow, and all the scattered pieces were falling into place.

We'd ended the evening in my truck, with her in my lap, riding me as the sun set beyond the horizon, and I clung to her tighter than ever before. I'd invited her back to my place, thinking I'd finally bring her into my bed and make love to her until dawn, but Melody had declined, telling me she had an order of cupcakes she needed to fulfill.

After climbing out of the shower an hour ago, I finally gave in and texted her. Maybe that's what she's been waiting for—effort on my end. Better communication.

And hell, that's fair.

Palming the cell phone in my hand, I realize I keep checking it every few minutes or so, anxious to see her name light up my screen.

I'm not used to this feeling of expectancy, this antsy *yearning*.

I toss the phone to the other side of the couch, internally glowering at myself for acting like a lovesick fool. But just as I pull up from the cushions to go search for a distraction, I hear the telltale ping.

Pathetically, I dive back to the sofa at record speed and dig my hand between the cracks where my phone slipped through. Snapping my arm up, I swipe at the screen, unlocking her response.

Only…it's from *Magnolia*.

Magnolia: I wasn't going to contact you again, but here I am.
Something is nagging at me, and I can't let it go.

What the fuck?

Pinching the bridge of my nose, I settle back down onto the couch, my insides twisting. I was so fucking close to deleting this entire goddamn account after she messaged me the last time, telling me that I left her doubting her own worth.

Fuck, that hurt. That hurt like hell.

But I thought it was over. I thought Zephyr would finally disappear, become a distant memory, and Melody would never have to know we were one and the same.

Or more importantly, that *I've* known that fact since the night in her backyard, when I fucked her against her shed instead of telling her the truth—the whole reason I went over there in the first place.

Coward.

But I knew she would see me differently once she knew, everything would change, and I couldn't lose that.

Holding my breath, I wince when another message comes through.

Goddammit, Melody…message me. *Respond to* me.

Magnolia: What does the number stand for in your screen name?

My mind stutters.

Why is she asking me this *now*?

After all these months. After all this silence.

Magnolia: Is it your birth year? Your address? Maybe it's your favorite number?

I clench my jaw as her messages continue to ambush me.

Magnolia: Your jersey number in high school? The amount of coins in your change jar? Your ideal temperature outside?

My grip tightens on the phone case as one more question pops up.
I blanch.

Magnolia: Is it the number of scars on your body?

What. The. Fuck.

My brain starts spinning, going into overdrive, but it doesn't take long for me to remember. To realize my slipup.

"Seventy-nine scars, Melody. I'm a fucking monster."

Shit, shit, *shit.*

It's over.

She knows I've deceived her.

Only a minute passes by before she messages me again, only this time, there are no words.

It's a Google Meet link.

A fucking video chat.

Blowing out a hard breath, I drop my head against the back of the couch, my heart nearly detonating inside my chest. My skin hums with dissolution. My insides churn with loss.

But I'm done playing this game, so I click the damn link, then fiddle with the settings, trying to figure out the camera feature. Melody's camera remains off. I stare at a black screen, wanting nothing more than to get this over with. She already knows; she just wants to see it for herself.

My camera flickers on.

Fuck.

I sit idle on my couch, holding my phone out while my guilty expression stares back at me from the phone screen. I don't say anything. There's nothing to say.

All I do is wait.

I wait for her inevitable scorn, her furious disbelief.

Her anger. Her betrayal.

But all I get is a knock on my front door.

What?

I spare a final, knowing look to the camera before standing from the sofa and making the short trek to the door.

Melody stands on my front stoop, clutching her own phone in a trembling fist, her eyes pooled with tears, her mouth parted, lips quivering along with her hands. She sucks in a sharp breath, like she's seeing me for the very first time.

But she's not.

She's seeing *him*. Her husband.

I swallow, staring at her through gritted teeth and balled-up fists. Closing out the video on my phone, I shove it into my pocket and step backward, allowing her entry. Melody moves in with slow, purposeful steps, her eyes locked on mine, circling around me. It's almost as if we're predator and prey, but I'm not sure who the predator is, who will pounce and who will flee.

Melody paces toward me until we're toe-to-toe, misty-eyed and flushed.

I can't read her—I can't fucking read her.

Is she pissed? She should be.

Is she hurt? Probably.

But her eyes shimmer with something akin to wonder, *enchantment*, and that feels so much fucking worse. My limbs go taut as anxiety grips me. "Jesus, Melody, say something."

She opens her mouth to speak, and a little gasp breaks through. She's tongue-tied.

Fuck.

"Damn it, listen to me—"

Melody's mouth silences my words, cutting them off with her eager tongue. Her kiss is punishing, desperate, merciless, one hand fisted in my hair, while the other...

The other goes straight to my chest. My heart.

She pulls back for a breath, her tears spilling out, glistening her cheekbones, and she whispers two words before crashing her lips into mine once more. "My Zephyr."

32

MELODY

I<small>T'S HIM.</small>

I know I should be outraged, indignant, *boiling mad*—and I was.

I *was*.

Until I saw him.

Parker discovered who I was during that fateful video call, and instead of unveiling his true identity, he came to my house and had sex with me. He allowed me to believe that his alter ego had found me unappealing when he could have tempered my insecurities with the truth.

I had every intention of battering him with my bruised heart, assaulting him with the tears of my betrayal, but then his eyes locked on mine, and all I felt was…

Relief.

It's him.

Parker is Zephyr.

Parker has Charlie's beating heart inside his chest, functioning and strong.

Alive.

And the moment he opened his front door, I understood—I knew why he couldn't tell me. He said to me once that he didn't feel worthy, that his heart was a burden.

He was ashamed.

He felt like his scars and dark past made him an unfit candidate for such a precious thing.

"My Zephyr," I breathe against his lips before stealing another violent kiss. I'm starved and achy. I *need* him. "I should have known it was you."

Parker envelops me in a fierce embrace, dragging his lips from my mouth to my neck, then whispering in my ear, "I'm sorry. Let me expl—"

"No…I understand." Clasping his face between my palms, I redirect him to my mouth, melting when our tongues collide. My right hand lowers back to his chest, relishing in the sweet vibrations of his heartbeats. Of *their* heartbeats. "Make love to me."

He groans. "Melody…"

"Please, Parker. I need you," I shamelessly beg.

It all makes sense now.

God, it makes sense.

This draw. This tether. This unexplained connection.

Parker hesitates, resting his forehead to mine and inhaling a deep, shaky breath. His eyes close tight, his brows pinching together with conflict. He wants to talk, explain. He wants to fix this first.

Except…nothing is broken.

All of the pieces finally fit.

I step back, biting my lip as I reach down for the hem of my sundress, lifting my arms and pulling it up over my head. The sunny fabric falls from my fingertips, landing in a delicate pile beside my feet. Slipping out of my sandals, I take one more pace backward, then raise my chin, finding Parker's eyes.

His green gaze rakes over me in a slow pull, drinking in my curves and lace. There's a look of anguish etched into his expression, fighting with the lust, and I know he feels guilty, I know we should probably talk first…but my body is singing for him, and my heart is hungry.

My hand extends, palm outstretched, much like the time I beckoned for him in his bedroom. The night he froze.

Don't freeze, Parker…melt with me.

He glances at my hand, blinking slowly, then meets my heavy stare from a few feet away. There's another silent moment of hesitation before surrender washes over him, claiming him in a mighty grip, and his eyes flash with potent resignation.

A delicious chill sweeps through me.

Parker moves in with two long strides, then bends down to scoop me up, hoisting me up by the thighs until my legs wrap around his waist, my hands clinging to his shoulders. Our gazes hold for a striking beat before he starts walking, and I'm certain he's bringing me to the couch, but Parker surprises me—he carries me down the short hallway to his bedroom instead.

We've never done this in a bed before.

There's never been cool, silky sheets entangled with sweaty limbs, or a squeaky box spring, or spooning and cuddling atop a pillowy mattress. We've never woken up together with shafts of golden daylight dappling us in warmth.

The prospect sends a new wave of tingles to my core.

Parker deposits me on his bedsheets, unmade and smelling entirely of him. Heady and masculine. Earthy and clean. My legs are still clinging loosely to his hips as he leans over me, a darkened shadow in the unlit room. His hands trail up my body, from my thighs to my stomach, to my breasts cased in ivory lace.

"You're so fucking gorgeous." He palms my breasts before gliding his hands to my neck. There's no pressure, only tender possession. "Goddamn perfect."

My thighs clench his waist as I arch my back, causing him to moan. I lift up, reaching for his belt, and his hands tangle in my hair as I unlatch him. Shoving down his pants and boxers, I waste no time in slipping off the bed to my knees, curling my fingers around his cock, and bringing him into my mouth.

He hisses, fisting my hair tight. "Fuck…"

I stroke him in a firm grip, suckling the tip, my own moans mingling with his.

Parker releases me, pulling back from my mouth and stepping out of his bottoms that are pooled around his ankles. Watching him through the wall of darkness, I reach behind me to unclasp my bra, then shimmy out of my underwear, scooting farther back on the bed—an implied invitation.

I'm fully expecting him to pounce on me, but a long moment passes where

Parker just stands there, silent. I can't make out his expression through the dark, only his shadowy silhouette, but as soon as I'm about to inquire, ask him what's wrong, my heart seizes.

Parker reaches behind his back, gathering his T-shirt in his hand, and pulls it up over his head, tossing it to the floor.

Oh my God.

A whimper of disbelief escapes my lips as I inch forward on the bed, wishing I could see him better. He falters before moving toward me, his heat closing in, and my arms outstretch, desperate to feel him. To touch him. To know every hidden inch of him.

Parker settles between my parted knees, his body stiff as a board, his breathing heavy and ragged. I pull him closer by the hips, instantly pressing my lips to his abdomen—his collection of scars. My tongue pokes out, laving the marred flesh, as I rain a scattering of delicate kisses to his skin. He shivers, nearly shaking, cupping the back of my head in his palms as he stands before me, fully exposed for the very first time.

I pull back for a quick moment, my hand searching for the bedside lamp. I want to see him. I need to see everything he's offering me.

But Parker snags my wrist before I can find it. "No, please...not yet." His voice sounds pained and uneven. It cracks as he finishes, "Just give me this night."

My throat swells with emotion, hating that he thinks I'll judge him or think any less of him once I see his scars.

Despite my desire for more, for *all* of him, I nod through the veil of darkness, conceding to his request.

Parker releases a sigh, part relief, part something else, and then he's climbing onto the bed with me, his knees on either side as we shift into a comfortable position. He leans over me until I'm blanketed with his warm skin, our bare bodies finally touching, my breasts flush against the hard plank of his chest. The contact does something to me—almost more than I can bear—and I arc upwards, my spine bowing, trying to get even closer. Trying to crawl inside his skin and build a home.

He trembles against me with a soft groan, his hands moving to cup my face as my legs instinctively loop around his middle. His erection lies heavy between us, causing me to throb with a kind of need I've never felt before. Inching my hips up, a demand more than a query, Parker reaches between us and situates himself at my wet opening.

"Please…" I'm nothing but a begging, quivering mess, my fingers sifting through his thick hair while he cradles my jaw.

His thumbs brush over my cheekbones as he leans in to kiss me, and when our mouths lock together, his tongue and cock thrust inside, filling me completely. Making me whole. Our moans are instant, unbridled, only hindered by our desperate, tangling tongues.

Parker's hips rock against me, slow and deep, and I feel him everywhere—in my heart, my throat, my womb, in every yearning, buzzing cell.

His forehead presses to mine when he pulls back from my mouth, his fingertips digging into my cheeks as he holds me steady, his hot breath hitting my lips with every longing groan. Our eyes are fixed together, and even through the cloud of darkness, I can see the intense emotion staring back at me. The toe-curling connection.

God, it's too much.

My body is too sensitive, my soul too bare.

The intimacy is so thick, it hovers between us like a third party. A witness. The emotional avalanche to my senses is so brutal, so violent, a cry breaks through my lips, and I'm not sure whether I should tighten my hold to stay afloat or push him away and swim to shore.

I cling.

My hands sweep across his bare shoulder blades, my thighs cinching us in a lethal clutch. Parker moves harder, deeper, our hearts galloping beneath our ribs, hands gripping and latching on to every reachable inch.

"My Melody," he whispers against my mouth, moaning softly when my core clenches around him. "My Magnolia. My moon."

Every aching piece of me weeps with adoration.

With joy.

With…*love.*

I arch my neck, sighing when his lips graze along my jaw until he finds my throat. He bathes me in hot kisses, his tongue sweeping over the crest. Finding my voice, I croak out, "Did you see the sunrise this morning?"

Parker doesn't waver as he nicks my neck with his teeth, then lifts his head until we're face-to-face, still moving inside me. "I did." He finds my eyes in the dark. "But I don't think I saw what you saw."

Inhaling a sharp breath, I lift up to kiss him, soft and brief. "What did you see?"

We both groan at the same time when Parker angles his hips, hitting me just right, in that sensitive, tingly place. I feel myself unraveling.

Swallowing, he continues to thrust, pushing my hair back from my forehead and holding me anchored. "I saw you," he says, quiet but firm. "I see you in every sunrise. Beauty...promise." He thrusts hard, and I shake and shiver. "A fresh start. A new beginning."

I whimper, hardly hanging on. "Parker..."

"I love you, Melody."

My gasp triggers a hot wave of tears, his face blurring above me as my eyes water.

Parker's voice is strained, almost desperate. "I fucking love you," he says ardently. "Just...know that."

"I—"

"No." He presses his lips to mine and murmurs, "You don't have to say it back."

But I want to.

His tongue slips between my lips, stealing my words away, and his pace quickens, his strokes becoming more hurried. Parker dips to my ear and whispers with command, "Now, I want you to come all over my cock."

Oh God.

His words alone have me buckling with bliss, quaking beneath him as my one hand grips the back of his neck, while the other tugs his hair. Skin on skin, bodies slick with sweat, grunts and pants and moans severing the silence of the dark room. It's undiluted passion—pure intimacy.

And it's my undoing.

Parker slams into me, hitting so, so deep, growling with need, and I feel myself peaking, the tingles swelling into the ultimate crescendo.

And when the mighty waves of ecstasy claim me, I cry out, loud and unhinged, holding him tighter and closer than ever before. My nails dig into the nape of his neck as stars burst behind my eyes and my body detonates in his arms.

Parker clutches me to his chest, gathering me in a fierce embrace as he follows behind me, groaning into my ear as his body tremors with the ripples of his release.

As the shocks flicker and fade, he collapses on top of me, shifting his weight to the side and pulling me close in a protective hold. His erratic breaths beat against my temple, and I dance my fingers along his upper arm, feeling satiated, fulfilled, and adored.

Loved.

Parker slips out of me, but he doesn't move away—he only pulls me closer to him until I'm curled against his chest, drifting away.

Before my dreams steal me from the moment, I hear him whisper into my hair, "I love you."

I fall asleep with a smile, knowing that for the first time in sixteen months, I'm finally and fully at *peace.*

———————

Daybreak spills in through dark curtains, tickling my sleepy eyelids.

Stretching out my legs, my toes graze against his toned calves, and memories from the night before assault my senses with currents of euphoria.

A smile draws my mouth up as I blink awake, opening my eyes to the sunlit bedroom. Craning my neck, I glance beside me, finding Parker lying on his back with the bedsheet pulled up to his trim hips.

My heart lurches.

He's fast asleep, only partially covered, his scars on full display.

Swallowing, I inch in closer, feeling like an intruder.

Did he mean for me to see him?

He would have put his shirt back on if he didn't want me to... *right?*

It's not difficult to talk myself into raking my gaze over him, soaking up his beautiful, tarnished skin, and moving in until my fingers lift and graze along the evidence of his terrible abuse. Tears sting my eyes, my throat closing up.

He's covered in scars, most of them the size of a cigarette cherry but some larger, more jagged and cruel. My stomach twists with anguish, with blinding empathy, and all I want to do is hold him tight and never let him go.

I heave in a shaky breath, dragging my index finger up the length of his stomach until I reach his muscled chest. More little scars. More horror stories. More—

Wait.

Something in me goes still, my eyes scanning over him with confusion. Trying to make sense of something that doesn't make any sense at all.

My insides pitch with anxiety. The warm tingles swimming through me turn to ice, freezing my veins. With a shaky hand, I sweep my fingers over the plane of his chest, as if I'm trying to uncover something that isn't there.

No.

This…can't be right.

Parker stirs beneath my frantic, roaming hand, his lashes fluttering as he stretches out his limbs. He inhales a slow breath, lazily coming back to reality, when all of a sudden, his whole body tenses and his eyes pop open, registering my presence. Processing my discovery.

We lock eyes.

Mine spear him with stunned panic, while his…shimmer with apology.

He stares at me, his gaze like a warzone—but less like he's running into combat and more like he's crawling his way off the battlefield, beaten down and bloody.

This doesn't make sense.

He's Zephyr. I *know* he's Zephyr—I saw him on the camera. He told me things only Zephyr would know.

This doesn't make any sense.

Parker sits up straight, and I jump back, away from him, almost as if he just burned me. Disbelief surges through me as my eyes dart back to his chest, still searching for something that doesn't exist.

A cry breaks loose, and I cup my hand around my mouth, realization sucker punching me right in the gut.

He lied.

Parker has been lying to me this whole time.

Seventy-nine scars…and not a single one of them is mine.

> *Three things cannot be long hidden: the*
> *sun, the moon, and the truth.*
>
> —BUDDHA

33

PARKER

I NEVER MEANT FOR THIS TO HAPPEN.

This wasn't deception by design or a ploy to break her heart. If I could relive every cigarette burn, cruel word, sharp slap, and dark, hungry night alone in that closet, I would—I would relive it a million times over just to erase this fucking godforsaken look in her eyes.

Her betrayal feels tangible; I can taste it on my tongue.

And it tastes so much worse, more bitter, than I ever could have imagined.

Melody scurries away from me as I sit up and try to reel in my chaotic thoughts. I meant for her to see me this morning. I knew it would all be over come sunrise. I should have told her the truth last night, the moment I saw her standing on my front porch, but the coward in me won out. The *man*. The man who somehow broke through the rubble and ruin all because of her.

The man who fell in love.

And I know how goddamn selfish it was to ask for one more night when I should have told her the truth the moment I found out who she was. But I needed to feel her one last time. I needed to be inside her, soaking up her warmth and storing it away, so I could keep her with me long after she'd left.

Her two hands fist at the bedcovers, drawing them up over her nude body. Shielding herself from my guilty eyes. "Is this a trick?" she whispers in a trembling breath, still inching backward on the mattress, putting more and more distance between us.

My jaw clenches tight, my teeth rattling. "Melody…let me explain."

"Please do."

I scrub a palm down my jaw, my eyes closing as I try to locate words. I should be more prepared, but my thoughts are scattered and my throat feels tight. It's impossible to prepare for loss—especially when you finally have something worth losing. "I had no idea it would ever go this far," I say softly, but desperation is laced into every word. "You were just supposed to be an outlet. An anonymous, faceless email address."

Her voice quivers. "You lied to me."

"I didn't…" My head drops back against the headboard as I try to regroup. "I never came out and said I had your husband's heart. Not once. You assumed, and I…I just went with it."

Melody's face twists with scorn, her grip tightening on the bedsheet. "You *deceived* me."

"Fuck, I didn't know you were *you*," I proclaim. "When I finally figured it out, I was in too goddamn deep. I had feelings for you. You have no idea what it's like to finally fucking *feel* something for another human being after three decades of just existing—of just wanting life to end so I could escape this burden, this emotionless prison." Catching my breath, I toss my legs over the side of the bed and storm over to her in my boxers, throwing my arms in the air. "Jesus, Melody, look at me. I'm a fucking joke. I finally had something good in my life, something that made me want to do better, *be* better… I couldn't throw that away."

Tears spill from bloodshot eyes, her entire body trembling beneath the covers. Her gaze rakes over me, softening when she lands on my scars.

I tent my hands in a hopeless plea. "Please, try to understand."

"Understand that you posed as the recipient of my husband's heart during the most vulnerable time in my life?"

Fuck.

Every syllable slices me to the bone. My guilt eats away at me like acid. "I never, in a million fucking years, thought our paths would ever cross outside of the emails."

Her head sways side to side, incredulous. "How did this even happen?" She swallows, shifting her eyes away from me. "I got your email address from a confidential source."

That day from over a year ago spirals back to me, a day that didn't mean much at the time because nothing meant much—I had no idea it would change the entire course of my life. Pulling my lips between my teeth, I look down at the floor. "My sister."

"Your sister? What do you mean?"

"My sister, Bree. Bree Whitley. She was the doctor who tried to save your husband that night. She was the one who gave you my email."

Melody blanches before me, her cheeks turning pallid. "W-What?"

"She couldn't give you the real recipient's information, Melody. She could have been fired." I try to explain, tousling my hair with my fingers. "But you begged her, and she felt for you because that's who she is, so she asked me for a favor. She asked me to reply when you reached out, just one anonymous email, and that would be the end of it. I didn't fucking want to, but as the months went by, your message followed me around, whispering in my god-damn ear."

Her eyes glimmer green and wary.

I lean forward, my heart contracting painfully when she inches back on reflex.

I'm losing her. Every solemn second that passes by with the evidence of my deceit on display before her eyes, only thickens the barrier between us. I rub a hand over my face, cupping my jaw as I try not to lose myself right along with her. "Melody…please, try to see this from my side. Try to see *me*."

"That's just it." She gathers the bedsheet, pulling it with her as she rises to her feet and steps toward me. Her tearstained cheeks are illuminated by the sunshine pooling in from the cracked curtains, a jarring contrast to the dark cloud hovering over us. "I've always seen you, Parker. *You*. You should have trusted me with the truth."

My muscles stiffen when her fingertips reach out to graze along my scarred abdomen, her hand quivering when she presses it to my skin.

"You trusted me with this," she murmurs, her voice raw. Her index finger traces along a small scar, then skims up the expanse of my torso, her palm landing on my chest—my swiftly beating heart. "But not this."

My eyelids flutter closed, my veins pulsing with wayward emotion. I soak up the feel of her warm touch, knowing another long winter is about to roll in. "I thought it was the wrong heart."

"No." She sniffles, pulling away and inhaling a breath. "It wasn't."

Melody drags the sheet with her as she spins away, exiting the bedroom and leaving me to stew in my impossible grief and shitty, selfish decisions.

It wasn't.

Past tense.

She's fucking leaving me.

Panic boils my blood, strangling my lungs, and I chase after her, catching her as she pulls up the straps to her sundress and slips into her sandals. "Melody, wait. Fuck…please."

Hesitation claims her for a breathtaking second before she continues her task and fetches her purse.

I swoop in to block her escape, a desperate, final appeal. My hands stretch out, cradling her jaw, my thumbs brushing away the remnants of her tears. Kissing her forehead, I linger there, then breathe out, "I'm so fucking sorry. Don't go." I pepper her face in fervent kisses until I reach her mouth. Melody doesn't move away, but she doesn't kiss me back either. She remains still, frigid. "Let me fix this. Tell me what I have to do."

"It's out of your hands now. Please, let me go."

Fucking hell.

My forehead drops to hers, my grip tightening. Devastation infects me like a disease, a disease far more lethal, more venomous than apathy. It weakens me. My legs shake, and my heart shrivels up, like a flower trying to bloom during the frost-killing hour. "I've never fought for anything before," I grit out, my grief palpable. "Don't tell me this is over. Give me a reason to keep fighting."

She blinks slowly, lifting her chin. Her gaze lingers on my mouth before she brings her eyes to mine, releasing a shuddering sigh. "You have a reason, Parker." Melody places her palm to my chest once more, absorbing every penitent beat that seeps through her fingertips. "It's not me."

My hold on her slackens, and Melody slips free of my embrace, moving around me to the front door. She doesn't waver. She doesn't say another word or spare me one last glance before she disappears, evaporating like she was never here at all.

Another ghost to haunt me.

Melody told me that night in the rain, the night she hopped onto the hood of her car, drenched in new purpose, her soul cleansing and purging before my eyes—she told me that all broken things can be fixed. The hard part is deciding that they're worth fixing.

As the thick silence settles over me, an old friend turned enemy, the truth is evident with every minute that ticks by in her absence.

We're not worth fixing.

Numbly moving into the living room, I collapse onto the couch, feeling more alone than I've ever felt before. And in that moment, I miss my apathy. I miss my cold, dead heart. I spent years of my life feeling envious of those who felt grief, who were crushed by the heavy boulder of loss. It meant they had something to love.

But maybe I had it right all along.

This sickness feels so much worse.

Resigning myself to my misery, I heave out a deep breath, my eyes only lifting when I feel a little wet nose tickle my bare knee.

Walden.

He stands there, staring at me with his cloudy, wide eyes, his head tilted to one side. Trying to read me. Or maybe he's trying to tell me something.

I get my answer when he hobbles back, bending his neck down and pushing at something with his snout. Frowning, I sit up, my gaze shifting to the floor.

My heart skips.

There, sitting at my feet, is the red ball.

34

MELODY

INCENSED FEET CARRY ME THROUGH THE CAROUSEL DOORS, MARCHING ME straight to the check-in desk. I'm greeted with a quick glance before the receptionist continues tapping away at her keyboard. "How can I help you?"

My limbs are still twitching with adrenaline and disbelief. "I'm here to see Dr. Whitley."

"Do you have an appointment?"

"No."

"Oh…well, is she expecting you?"

An indignant lump climbs up my throat. "She should be."

The flaxen-haired woman's eyes flicker with dubiety as hospital noise clamors around us. After a long pause, she inquires, "Can I have your name, please?"

"Melody March," I say, my chin trembling as I watch the woman send a page over the intercom.

"It could be a while if she's with a patient. Have a seat in the waiting area."

My anger simmers to low-boiling anxiety while I make my way to one of the vacant chairs across the lobby. I fold my hands in my lap in an attempt to quell the incessant shaking.

It's only been thirty minutes since I pulled out of Parker's driveway, my ugly-cry meltdown instantaneous the moment I climbed into the driver's seat and closed the door. Sobs racked my body as my fingers coiled around the steering wheel, my forehead smashed against it, tears pouring out of me in angry, turbulent waves.

He wants me to understand, but how can I?

I've never felt more betrayed, more *deceived*. My heart feels like it's been put through a blender, shredded and pureed. The roller coaster of emotions over the last thirty-six hours has left me reeling and drained—from Parker's incredible, thoughtful gift at the lake to the slow build realization that Parker was Zephyr, to the actual discovery and subsequent elation that Parker had Charlie's heart… and to the magical, intimate night we shared together when I felt with utmost certainty that I was in love.

I was in love again.

Then, everything unraveled—crumbled at my feet, ashes and dust. The bitter residue clings to my skin.

Parker deceived me, regardless of intention. Trust is a fragile thing, and he tampered with it. I opened my heart to another man when I was at my most vulnerable, and he made a charade out of it.

I feel violated.

"Mrs. March?"

My breath catches when her voice carries over to me, and I straighten in the chair, turning my head to meet her wide acorn eyes.

Bree.

Dr. Whitley.

The Grim Reaper.

Flashbacks of that day claim me for a striking, painful moment, rendering me speechless. I'm flooded with memories of her words, her remorseful embrace, the way her curls tickled my temple as I collapsed into her arms, and even the smell of her sweet, powdery shampoo—a paradox to the pungency of death, hovering heavy in the air.

Garnering my strength, I raise from the seat, still shaking. Bree's dark eyebrows furrow into a perplexed frown as she studies me, while wearing hospital scrubs and a giant corkscrew bun.

"How could you?" My words are a jaded whisper laced with venom. I'm not prepared for this confrontation, not in the least. Nothing was planned. I simply started driving, somehow finding my way into the hospital parking lot. "How could you do this to me?"

Bree's frown deepens, her head swaying side to side. "I…I'm sorry, but I'm not following. What is this about?"

"It's about your brother. It's about the heart he doesn't have."

A charged beat passes, and then her brown eyes flash with awareness. She swallows. "Let's discuss this in my office. Please, come with me."

I follow blindly, wordlessly. Everything around me is a blur as we make our way to the opposite end of the hospital, and she ushers me inside a cheery, sunlit room. Bright and happy. The antithesis to the turmoil funneling through me.

When she closes the door, Bree pauses, fingers lingering on the doorknob as she collects her thoughts. Lips pursed and eyes glazed with apology, she spins around to face me. "It's…you? You're the one he's been falling for?"

I refuse to acknowledge the way my pulse revs at her words. "I'm the one he's been lying to, yes."

"Melody, please…have a seat." Bree gestures to a chair, but my arms cross with defiance. She nods through a sigh, pacing in front of me as she processes this development. "My God, I never thought…" Her words dissipate, and her shoulders sag. "You have to understand, this wasn't a setup or a wicked plot to hurt you. I had no idea it would go this far."

"You asked your brother to pose as the recipient of my dead husband's heart," I exclaim, my emotions climbing. "That is not okay. Why would you do that? I trusted you… I never once thought you'd mislead me."

Her eyes shimmer with unshed tears. "My heart ached for you," she replies softly. "I felt your pain. My compassion makes me a good doctor, but it's also a curse sometimes. The line between professionalism and humanity becomes blurred."

The month following Charlie's death filters through my memories, blindsiding me. My eyes squeeze shut as I recall the way I'd fallen at Dr. Whitley's feet, a weeping mess on my knees, and begged her for a phone number, an email address, *anything*.

I was desperate for a way back to Charlie, and I would take anything I could get.

"Please, please," *I pleaded, broken down and hysterical. "Give me something. I promise I'll respect his privacy and keep everything anonymous. I swear it. He's all I have left of him."*

Dr. Whitley refused at first. "The recipient has requested anonymity. That information is confidential. I could be stripped of my medical license, Mrs. March."

No, no, no.

I remained on my knees, rooted to the hospital floor, much like the night of his death when I'd collapsed in the hallway. Dr. Whitley had picked up the scattered remains of my purse, placing them back inside with gentle care, and then she'd held me while the horrified shudders spiraled through me, until I'd struggled for air and required an oxygen mask.

I felt the hyperventilative state closing in again.

"I want to help you," she said delicately. "If there was something I could do, I would. I'm so sorry."

But my pain eventually broke her. I rose to my feet with puffy eyes and red cheeks, utterly dismantled, and as our gazes locked and held for a few potent heartbeats, I saw her resolve weaken. I felt her acquiesce.

Glancing away, Dr. Whitley released a hard, conflicted breath. "I'll see what I can do."

It took me two more months to finally find the courage to email him.

Zephyr79@gmail.com

Parker Denison.

Bree's words puncture through my thick wall of resentment, causing me to soften. I know I put her in a difficult position, but I didn't care at the time—nothing mattered in that moment. Nothing mattered when the *one thing* that mattered most was ripped from my hands. "Why him?" I breathe out, tightening my arms around myself. "Why not you? If you had no intention of giving me the real recipient, why not pretend to be him yourself?"

Certainly, that would have made the most sense.

Why bring Parker into this?

She falters, biting her lip and tucking her chin to her chest. Bree mimics my stance by crossing her arms, wrapping herself in a hug while she considers her response. It feels like light-years pass us by before she replies. "I thought I could help him by helping you," she murmurs to the floor. "Give him something to care about. A connection. I thought maybe…" Her voice wavers as fresh tears fall free, tracking down her freckled cheeks. "I thought you both could find healing in one another and work through your pain together. I never intended to manipulate anyone's emotions… I didn't think it would go this far."

I stare at her through watery eyes, my heart being pulled in two directions.

I feel angry. Betrayed.

I feel compassion. Understanding.

Bree sees my struggle, so she moves in, clinging to it. Taking my hands in hers, she squeezes me gently, a silent plea registering through her touch. "Melody, listen to me. If you need someone to blame, blame *me*. Don't blame Parker. I take full responsibility."

The bitterness crawls back up my throat. "He's known the truth for months and didn't tell me," I bite out, pulling my hands away. "I could have gotten past it then, if he had just been honest with me, but now…"

Her sigh is deep, her eyes closing. "I didn't know. I didn't know you were the woman he'd developed feelings for," she explains. "I thought nothing ever came of it. I followed up a few times that month, but Parker told me you never got in touch."

"It took me months to finally reach out. I didn't know what to say."

"God…" Bree brings her fingertips to her temples, stepping back, her expression full of anguish. "I'm so sorry, Melody. I never meant to add to your pain. And for all of Parker's flaws, he's not a vicious person… I'm sure he was scared to tell you."

I shake my head. "It doesn't make it right."

"No, but it makes him *human*." She paces forward again, gripping my shoulders with taut fingers. "Parker has never had feelings like this before. There's never been anyone like you. And I'm not trying to justify it, I promise. I'm just trying to paint a picture, so maybe you can see things from a different perspective." Bree skims her thumb over my collarbone, her copper-tinged eyes glistening with remnants of her tears. "My brother has been through hell. He's suffered the worst out of life, truly, and I've done everything in my power to keep his head above water. And maybe I've kept him afloat all these years, but it's *you* who has finally taught him how to swim. I've seen the difference you've made. I've seen a light in his eyes that has never been there before."

My throat stings with sentiment, and I'm flooded with conflict. Parker's desperate, candid plea for forgiveness flashes to my mind, cutting deep, and I have no idea what I'm supposed to do. My soul feels conned, but my heart still beats with yearning and empathy.

I realize now why Parker didn't want me to announce my love to him last night.

He didn't want to take possession of such a cherished thing under false pretenses.

"I fucking love you. Just…know that."

Tears burn my eyes until I'm unable to hold them in any longer. They trail down my face, one after the other, adding to my rising pool of mixed emotions.

Bree brushes the tearstains from my cheekbones, a solemn smile pulling at her lips. She continues. "You're special, Melody. You're special to him. And maybe I'm a little biased, but Parker is special too, and maybe…maybe this all worked out exactly how it was meant to."

My eyes lift to hers, my insides spiking with a new surge of gall. I take her words to heart, perhaps more than I should, but my mind is spinning, and my feelings are all over the place. I latch on to what I can. "Meant to?" I repeat, pushing her hands off me, my tone dripping with quiet outrage. "My husband's death, this deceptive matchmaking ploy for your brother, toying with my emotions when I was at my most vulnerable was all…*meant to be*?"

Bree's head swings back and forth, her eyes widening, lashes fluttering. "No, God…that's not what I meant. I'm not trying to minimize any of this. I'm just trying to find the good in it all."

"There's no good in lies and broken trust."

She nods, soaking up my truth. "No, you're right. I'm so sorry for putting this all in motion."

I inhale a rickety breath, the tears still spilling. Everything is too fresh, and my emotions are raw and heightened. I need time, space. I need to calm down and look at this rationally. "I-I should go," I whisper, darting around her toward the door.

"Melody…please."

Hesitation seizes my steps, my hand curling around the doorknob.

Bree's voice cracks as she urges, "Please forgive him. He loves you."

Her final plea meets my back as a harrowing cry breaks loose, and I race out of the office.

He loves me.

Parker loves me.

And I think that's why this hurts so much.

35

PARKER

TEN DAYS.

Ten fucking days without her, and I'm going out of my mind. Bree has been breathing down my neck ever since Melody confronted her at the hospital, checking in on me, bringing me food, bringing me even more food, and making sure I don't go off the deep end.

But this isn't like last year, after my injury that sent me into a black, depressive hole, inciting my sister to enroll me in the suicide support group.

No, this is different… *I'm* different.

Melody fixed me, and I'm determined as hell to fix *us*.

My initial pathetic text message to her shortly after she'd left my house that day, broken down and hollowed out, went unanswered for forty-eight hours.

Me: I fix shit for a living…I can fix this too. Tell me what to do, Melody.

Then, she finally responded.

Melody: I need time and space to process everything. I'm sorry. I know that's not what you want to hear, but that's just what I need.

After a week of stewing in my miserable guilt, overworking myself just to keep my mind distracted, rereading her text, and missing the fuck out of her, I've reached a sickly point of desperation. Melody hasn't even been to the meetings.

She hasn't been to the damn meetings, all because of me.

She's avoiding me, and I get it—I fucking get it—but I've lived my entire life remaining idle and inactive. Maybe it's time to fucking fight.

I'm just not sure how to fight for something so goddamn important. I don't know what weapons to wield or how much armor to possess. Do I go at her all bare bones and bleeding heart? On my knees, pleading and shaking, defenseless, with the blade of a dagger to my chest?

Stick it in, Melody. Twist it deep. What's one more scar?

Or is fighting for her giving her the time and space she's requested?

But then again…*how* much time? Do I wait for her to reach out, putting more and more distance between us?

Time is the greatest measure for healing, after all.

It's the greatest measure for forgetting too.

Fuck, I'm all over the place. I'm clueless and unprepared for how to deal with the consequences of my selfish fucking choices, so I'm throwing myself into work as a distraction. At least I have that. It's more than I can say for this time last year.

And luckily, my job today is a final project at the Jameson residence, finishing up painting and adding crown molding to one of their fifty thousand extra rooms.

Owen.

I'm going to miss that kid when I'm officially done here.

"Parker!"

Owen comes barreling at me in the foyer, bright-eyed and bushy-tailed, a heartening contrast to the defeated little boy I discovered that first day. A smile lifts, despite my own inner turmoil, as Owen's mother follows behind him with a mug of coffee, her silk robe trailing her feet. I nod my greeting, setting down my tub of primer. "Morning."

Long, salmon-colored talons click the ceramic as Mrs. Jameson flashes me her teeth, her lips hardly stretching through the obvious Botox. "Good morning, Mr. Denison. It's a shame we'll be saying goodbye after today."

Because I was such a happy little ray of sunshine while I was here.

Palming the nape of my neck, I clear my throat, my mind calculating the number of times I told her to "fuck off" under my breath—pretty sure it was a lot. "Yeah, I appreciate the work. Hit me up if you need anything else."

"I'll do that."

Implication bleeds from her pretentious pores, and I cringe internally.

And outwardly.

Owen pipes up, rocking on the heels of his light-up Batman sneakers. "Maybe you can babysit me sometime, Parker. We could make model cars and watch movies."

"Wouldn't that be lovely?" Mrs. Jameson agrees.

Shit. It's a miracle I've kept my dog alive this long.

I nod through a tight-lipped smile, stuffing my hands into my pockets.

"Can I show you the new car I made? Before you start work?"

I glance at Owen's mother for approval, and she tips her head toward the winding staircase, causing Owen to squeal with elation, urging me to follow. When we reach his bedroom, he throws himself onto the bed where a new creation rests, the mattress bouncing with his weight. I linger in the doorway for a moment, a sentimental sort of feeling washing over me as I drink in his childlike glee and red, chubby cheeks.

"Do you like it?" Owen holds up the neon-orange car with little black wheels, zooming it through the air and making whooshing sounds. "I think it's my favorite."

"Yeah, bud. It's really good."

"I thought you'd like it. Friends usually like the same stuff."

My mouth twitches in reply.

Sunlight scatters along the bedspread, illuminating Owen's tangerine masterpiece like a spotlight, and I observe the time and care given to such a prized achievement. The meticulous paint lines. The perfectly placed wheels. The little tiger stripe design on the side, etched into the wood grain with precision. My skin prickles with warmth. "You worked hard on that. I can tell."

Owen bobs his chin in agreement, his tawny eyes shimmering with pride. He swipes his matching bangs off his forehead, then wheels the toy car across the bedcovers like it's a racetrack. "Yep, it took me all month. It broke three times before I got it just right."

I swallow. "Yeah?"

He nods, still focused on his task as he winds the car in circles, spinning around on his knobby knees. "I couldn't give up. I knew it would be worth it if I just tried really hard to put it back together," he tells me distractedly. "There were tons of little pieces, so it took a lot of work. I stayed up way past my bedtime some nights."

A surge of correlation unfurls beneath my ribs, causing me to fluster. I start to internalize the fuck out of his words, applying them to my own mess.

"Do you think it's worth it?"

Blinking out of my haze, I glance up at the car that Owen holds up, high and mighty. A beloved trophy. A treasure. It twinkles in the glimmering streaks of daylight leaking in through partially open blinds, and a sigh escapes me as I whisper back softly, "Yeah…it's definitely worth it."

A few hours later, I'm packing up the last of my supplies and slipping into my boots after saying a final farewell to Owen. Mrs. Jameson prances into the grand foyer that gleams with tinsel and jewels, stopping me before I reach the door.

"Mr. Denison," she calls out, her bare feet scuffing along the hardwood floors. A champagne flute dangles from her manicured hand. "I just wanted to thank you."

"Uh, yeah, it's not a problem."

Thanks for the huge-ass tip.

"No, I mean for the joy you've brought to my son during your time here."

My muscles cramp as I reach the front door, stalling my steps. I feel my heart clench at her words, but I'm not sure how to reply, so I just glance up, swallowing back the growing lump in my throat.

She softens before me, her bristly exterior peeling away to reveal a caring mother beneath all the glamour and gimmicks. Light-brown eyes dance golden beneath the glow of the chandelier, and she spears me with genuine gratitude. "Owen told me you helped stick up for him against the neighbor boy. I didn't even know…" Mrs. Jameson sighs wearily, flipping a swathe of auburn hair over one shoulder. "My husband is always away on business, and I'm…distracted a lot. It opened my eyes to all the things I've been missing, you know? Anyway, not to get all sappy on you, but Owen has always been a sensitive, introverted child. He keeps to himself. It's been difficult finding him friendships, and I thought Brody was a good influence… I didn't realize my son was being bullied."

I drink in her words, my teeth gnashing together as I choke back the waves of sentiment. My eyes skim her face, searching for fakery, for guile, but all I see is a woman who wants to do better. There's a noticeable hitch in my tone as I respond, "Sure. He's a good kid."

"He is, truly. Thank you for seeing that," she says. "Thank you for seeing him."

My tight, emotion-infused nod sees her off, but she stops me one more time before I can slip out.

"One more thing: if you will…I'd love to have a way for my son to keep in touch if that's not too much to ask. Letters or emails, perhaps? It would be a beneficial outlet for him, I think."

"Oh, uh…" Sifting through my pockets for a pen and paper that don't exist, I find myself agreeing to the suggestion. "Yeah, why not?"

Mrs. Jameson skips over to a decorative side table, snatching a pen and stationery pad from the drawer, then shuffles them over to me. "Wonderful. He'll be so excited to have a pen pal."

A pen pal.

I can't help the grin from tipping my lips at the notion.

Nothing could possibly go wrong there.

"Sounds good," I say, scribbling my information onto the floral notepad and handing it back. I glance down at my handwriting before Mrs. Jameson plucks it from my fingertips and folds it in half, smiling her thanks.

Zephyr79@gmail.com

When the sun hovers low in the cloudless sky later that day, I pull up to the front of her house and kill the engine. Hesitation and doubt keep me rooted to the seat for a solid twenty minutes before I work up the courage to climb her front steps, and then it takes me another five minutes to actually knock.

I'm goddamn clueless.

Should I have flowers? Chocolates or some shit?

An epic speech?

Shit. I need an epic speech.

But it's too late, because my knuckles rap twice against the yellow, steel door, a sunny contradiction to my thrumming anxiety, and her footsteps echo all around me.

Melody opens the door, the remnants of a smile kissing her perfect mouth, and when she sees me standing here, her lips thin. Her smile fades. Her eyes flash with surprise, glinting a stormy shade of green beneath her porch light. "Parker," she says in a startled breath.

I observe the way she peeks over her shoulder, like she's wary or nervous, then sneaks outside to join me on the porch. My eyes peer through the door crack with cautious curiosity. "You have company?"

Laughter filters outside, pulling my head to the left. It's only then I notice the extra car in the driveway.

Melody clears her throat, her arms crossing over a blush blouse. "My brother and Leah stopped by. I've been kind of a hermit this past week." She pulls her lip between her teeth, gaze darting everywhere but to me. "What are you doing here?"

"I wanted to see you."

I wanted to see you, so I came to see you. See, Melody? I'm fucking trying here.

But my eyes don't manage to get my point across because she's not fucking looking at me, and my voice evades me the longer we stand here on her stoop, inches apart, yet miles away from one another. My skin feels itchy, my lungs parched. My fingers yearn to reach out and touch her.

Melody's lips shape into a small O as she blows out a steadying breath. "Parker, I'm not sure why you came, but…I don't think I'm ready yet."

A prickling heat stabs at my chest like a hot poker. I swallow hard. "Look at me, Melody."

She shakes her head through watery eyes.

"Why? Why won't you look at me?"

"Please. I'm not ready."

Fuck.

A growl of desperation sweeps through me, and I reach out, cupping her face between my palms and forcing her attention on me. Bending down, I drop my forehead to hers as she squeaks out a strained gasp. "Look at me. Fucking *see* me," I rasp out, my fingers weaving through her soft hair. "I'm here, and I'm trying. I don't have lavish gifts or words that will magically erase the stupid shit I did, and fuck if I know how to grovel, but I do have one thing…and that's *me*. Right here, right now. Standing on your doorstep, asking you to give me another fucking chance. To look past my mistakes and see everything else. Look at the real *me*, Melody. The man you brought to life, who has no goddamn clue what he's doing but is doing it anyway because it fucking matters. *You matter.*"

Her tears fall instantly, tiny little waterfalls cascading down flushed cheeks, and a hoarse whimper escapes her parted lips.

My focus slips to her mouth, and my own lips tingle, aching to taste her. To reclaim all the things I know we had. The things we *still* have.

I lean in, ever so slowly, so gently, giving her a chance to push me away… but she doesn't move. Melody stands there on wobbly legs, clutching my wrists in two tight fists as I graze her mouth with mine. Our breaths beat hot and hurried, erratic, and I inch forward, pressing a featherlight kiss to her trembling lips. I can't even prevent the moan that crawls up my throat when her warmth invades me, nearly incinerating me where I stand.

Melody clings tighter, rising up on her tiptoes, kissing my bottom lip with a needy sigh. But her sigh manifests into a sob, and she pushes back, escaping my clutches. "No…" she whispers, tone cracking. "I'm not… I don't…"

She sways slightly, catching her balance on the adjacent pillar. My instincts flare, and I move in to scoop her up in my arms, smoothing her hair back and kissing her temple. "Are you okay?"

"I'm fine. I-I just feel lightheaded. Nauseous. The stress…"

Jesus Christ, am I making her physically ill?

Just then, the door pulls open, and Melody jumps back. Her brother glowers from the entryway, his icy stare pinning on me, his fists balling at his sides.

"You have a lot of fucking nerve showing up here, man," West snaps, shoving his way through the screen and beelining toward me. "Look at her—she's about to pass out from the grief you've caused her."

My stomach pitches with regret. But I don't have time to process his claims before his fingers are curled around my shirt collar, and he's moving me backward until I'm slammed up against the side of her house.

I don't move. I don't react. I just stare into his clear-blue eyes, my breathing heavy, my muscles locked up.

"West!" Melody shrieks. "Let him go. God, you're acting like a barbarian."

Leah meets Melody on the lawn, reaching for her hand and adding, "Ease up, you brute. You're just making this worse for your sister."

West slackens his hold on me, shaking his head through gritted teeth. His sigh of resignation carries over to me before he finally lets go and paces back. "Just go. Stay away from my sister." Frigid warning laces his words. "She's been through enough."

Swallowing, I peer over his shoulder at Melody, who still looks ashen, winded and wilting, and *Christ*...it's my fucking fault. I thought I could come here and sweep her off her feet with a poignant look or an apologetic word. I thought I could right my wrongs with a kiss. And I felt her crumbling, I *felt* it, but it's too soon.

She's not ready, and I can't force it.

I drop my chin to my chest, my eyes closing as I draw in a lowly breath, and before I make my exit, I move around West and head toward the woman I love.

Her eyes widen as I close in, reflecting the golden haze of the setting sun, and when I stall before her, drenched in defeat, Melody forces the smallest smile.

After everything, she's still smiling.

Fuck.

I kind of want to ask her why, and I really want to kiss her, but the only thing I do is reach for her hand, splaying her fingers until her palm is outstretched. Fishing through my pocket, I pull out a folded-up note and place it in her hand, curling her fingers around it. "Don't ask me how I got this."

She frowns. "What?" Melody blinks with bewilderment, glancing down at the hidden treasure, then back up to me.

With a hard swallow and a frazzled breath, I hold her hand in mine and lean in, my words tickling the shell of her ear. "Zachary Adler," I murmur, brushing a calloused thumb over her knuckles. "Thirty-six, recently divorced, works in finance. Father of two. More importantly…he has something you're looking for."

Lifting my head to meet her eyes, I see the realization flicker to life, her pupils dilating as we hold our stare for one long, powerful beat. And with a final kiss to the top of her head, I inhale her scent, sweetness and citrus, and I let her go.

I traipse through the front yard and hop into my truck, starting the engine and gripping the steering wheel in a firm clutch. Running shaky fingers through my hair, I spare a glance out the passenger window at Melody, who is hugging herself through spilling tears with the little piece of paper tucked inside her fist.

I speed away.

Then…I drive.

I drive in circles, around town, into different towns, backward, forward—for hours.

Hours.

I drive and drive and drive, aimlessly, with no destination in mind and with only my racing thoughts as a bleak passenger.

And that's how I wind up on that fucking bridge.

36

MELODY

MELLIE!"

A muffled familiarity finds its way to my ear, and I glance up through the dusky window, spotting my father standing on the front porch, his arm waving animatedly, encouraging me inside. When I glance at the time, I'm surprised to discover I've been sitting in my parents' driveway for over fifteen minutes, lost in idle thoughts and haunting unknowns.

My eyes scan the crinkled note lying atop my dashboard with the name and address of a complete stranger in every way—except for one.

Charlie's true heart recipient.

Shaking myself back to reality, I turn off the car and force myself inside the house. The scent of Italian herbs and spices assaults my senses as I join my father in the entryway, causing my belly to churn with a new wave of nausea.

So much stress.

"You fall asleep out there, kiddo?" He chuckles, giving my shoulder a squeeze after I discard my purse.

His salt-and-pepper scruff has grown out from the last time I visited, matching the silvery streaks in his recent crew cut. Tall and distinguished, my father has always had an intimidating look about him, but on the inside, he's nothing but softness and syrup—the sweetest man I know. I smile through my queasiness. "I was just thinking."

"Thinkin' about Ma's cheesecake, I hope. It's fresh out of the oven, blueberry and lemon."

My nose crinkles at the thought of ingesting anything, but I nod agreeably, giving a small wave to my mother when we pass through the kitchen.

Looking up from the stovetop, she beams at my presence. "Melody, I didn't know you were stopping by."

For whatever reason, my eyes mist. "I wanted to see you guys," I murmur back, my voice sounding thin and papery. "I've missed you."

Dad wraps a hulky arm around me, tugging me to him. He places a kiss to my hair, quick and light, but the gesture triggers a torrent of emotions to flood me, and I collapse against his chest, unplanned. I feel the worry in his embrace, the unconditional love, and it only makes me cry harder. The course of the last two weeks ripples through me in waves and shudders, and before I know it, the three of us are huddled on the couch as I inhale quieting breaths and wait for my breakdown to ebb.

"Oh, Mellie…my little Jelly Belly," Dad whispers along the top of my head, stroking a loving palm up and down my upper arm.

Mom laces her fingers with mine on my opposite side, and a semblance of peace finally settles into my bones.

Then, I purge the events of the last four and a half months—Zephyr, Parker, emails, scars, love, confusion, kismet, and deceit. It all spews out of me, and they sit silently, patiently, absorbing my messy tale that the universe has thrown at me, leaving me windblown and breathless. I'm not sure what they'll think of me or how they'll react, and I don't know what I'm even looking for—advice? Solace? Support?

My father squeezes me tighter. "My little girl fell in love again."

I stiffen at his words, my heart thundering. Out of everything I just confessed, that was the takeaway. That was the salient point. Swallowing, I nod against the crook of his shoulder, burrowing deeper. "And now I don't know what to do."

"There's only one thing you *can* do if you want to move forward," Dad mutters gently. "You're weighed down by self-made barriers. You're still drowning in the past. You need to set yourself free." He shifts on the couch, pulling me closer. "Mellie, you gotta dig deep. Locate what exactly is preventing you from getting past this. You say you feel deceived, lied to. But is it more than that? Is there a deep-seated part of you that is still clinging to... *guilt?* Guilt of finding love with someone else?"

Shivers track down my arms, and the notion steals my breath.

My mother's voice pipes up. "It wasn't the heart itself you were looking for, sweetheart...it was permission. Allowance to move forward and start anew. But that's something only *you* can give yourself."

I fall farther into my father's embrace as I clench my mother's hand, my lungs tightening with revelation. Is that the true source of my conflict?

An underlying sense of guilt for leaving Charlie behind for good?

If Parker truly had Charlie's heart, it would have felt like a tiny consent. An authorization from the universe—from *him*. In a way, I'd have both men with me: Parker in my arms, while still holding Charlie in a loose grip.

When I discovered the truth, I was stripped of that ideality. And yes, it hurt that Parker lied, that he chose to hide instead of trust me with the truth, but maybe the real struggle is buried within myself. I'm forced to make a choice.

Remain in the past or let go for good.

Dad sighs, his chest laboring beneath my tearstained cheek, and he whispers softly, "There's only one thing left to do."

"What's that?" I croak out.

A heavy beat of silence hovers in the air, shimmering with possibility. With something attainable. With *hope*.

"It's time to unchain Melody."

There's teasing in his tone, but his words trumpet through me, symphonies and stars. Fresh tears coat my eyes, but this time, it's a breakthrough...not a burden.

Parker thought he had the wrong heart.

He hid the truth from me because he was afraid I would reject him once I discovered that he wasn't carrying a piece of Charlie inside his chest.

He didn't do it out of spite or malice; he did it out of *fear*.

Fear of losing me. Fear of losing himself and everything he'd cultivated.

Fear is a very human thing—a *forgivable* thing.

And I know, without a shadow of a doubt, that I didn't fall in love with the wrong heart.

I fell in love with the right heart at the right time.

I fell in love with Parker Denison.

As my tears fade to strength, I'm filled with certitude—optimism. I can see the future dancing in front of my eyes, colors and songs, rebirth and bright lights.

Parker.

I also dance. While my mother hugs me tight and makes her way back into the kitchen, my father pulls out his old record player, dusting off a familiar sleeve and placing the disc over the spindle. When the needle touches vinyl and the record starts to spin, the song bursts to life, and I'm transported back in time to this same living room as a young girl, over twenty years ago.

Giggles break through my happy tears as I step onto my father's sock-covered feet with little grace, and he clasps my hand in his, holding me steady behind my back with his opposite arm. We laugh, we cry, and I heal as "Unchained Melody" filters through my ears and fills my soul.

I'm still not sure what I came here for.

All I know is that I leave with exactly what I need.

Tires bite at the gravel as I slow to a stop, rubber against rock. The dark sky twinkles with a sea of stars and milky moonlight, and I can't help but smile as I turn off the engine.

Reaching forward, I pluck the little piece of paper off my dashboard, dusting my thumb over Parker's handwriting, then I heave in a deep sigh and slide the note into my front pocket.

The air is humid when I step from the car, hitting me like a brick wall. It takes a moment to find my breath, but less because of the sticky late-August night and more because of what I'm about to do.

My feet carry me forward as jitters scatter along my skin and mosquitoes buzz into my ear, and when I come to a stop at my destination, I sift through my pocket for that note.

Parker thought I wanted this. He thought I wanted this faceless man with Charlie's heart, and he thought I wanted it more than I wanted *him*.

The thought alone causes my chest to ache.

Falling to my knees, my gaze dips down to the precious stone, a stone that has absorbed many of my tears and desperate pleas. My eyes blur as I reach out to trace the carving of his name with shaky fingertips.

CHARLES JAMES MARCH

1994–2023

For a moment, my thoughts drift back to that fateful day on a downtown street.

The day the sun died.

I can still smell the homemade pizza in the air. I can hear the sirens ringing in my ears. I can feel the frosty raindrops on my skin.

I'm lost. I'm so lost…

Thunder cracks above me.

I'm losing him.

"Charlie," I sob, watching in numb horror as he's fastened onto a stretcher. Everything happens fast, startlingly fast, and paramedics are talking, possibly in tongues, taking vitals, and I'm still clinging to the illusion that this is all a terrible dream.

Charlie's eyelids flutter as he flickers in and out of consciousness. "Mel…"

"I'm here. I'm right here."

I used to visit his grave daily, until it became too much to bear. I had to force myself to stop coming because I feared my own soul would somehow bleed out, seep into the soil and earth, right along with his.

I inhale a shuddering breath, memories trickling through me like melancholy drizzle.

"No, no, please…I can't do this alone," I cry out, nearly hysterical. "What happens to the sun when the sky falls?"

My question hangs between us while everything else keeps moving. Charlie is carried to the ambulance, and I'm on my feet, racing alongside the stretcher, still crying, still disintegrating.

"Charlie!" I reach for his cold hand, squeezing tight as the rain falls fast and mercilessly. "The sun falls with it, Charlie. Please…I'm nothing without you."

Tears blanket my eyes while my fingers continue to skim over the lettered engraving. Charlie's final words fill me with serenity.

Assurance.

Permission.

"But…it still shines, Mel," he murmurs hoarsely. Charlie swallows, his peach-spun eyes trying to find my face through the wreckage and rainfall. His fingers grip mine with the last of his strength, and for the tiniest second, I am warm. "It just shines in a new place."

A watery smile pulls at my lips as my heart releases the heavy weight of guilt.

"I miss you, Charlie," I say with gentle sadness, my voice catching on a muggy draft. "I miss you so much, and I always will. But I wanted you to know…I found a new place to shine." My chin lifts, my eyes settling on the full moon. "I thought you would be so disappointed in me. I thought that somehow, wherever you are, you'd be looking down on me with anger and shame, horrified that I moved on without you. That I found love again after everything we'd shared. After everything we'd built." I suck in a rickety breath, searching for all the things I want to say. "But that's not true, is it? You gave me your blessing with your final words, you gave me permission to move on and let go, and *God*, I didn't know what it meant then…I didn't understand your meaning because how could I? I thought the sun died that day, and I would never shine again."

Crickets and cicadas sing a soothing soundtrack to my final farewell as I bend down to place a kiss along the etchings of his name. "The sun never dies, though. It only sets," I finish, licking fallen tears from my lips. "Then it rises, and a new day begins."

With Parker's note in one hand, I reach behind my back to pull a second note from my rear pocket. It's a letter I've kept for the past two months, ever since I received it in the mail—a letter I had no idea what to do with.

Until now.

It's an apology message from Eleanor March, Charlie's mother, atoning for her cruel behavior the night I almost drove my car into a tree. She was drunk on wine and impossible grief, and she manifested that fury into misplaced blame. She blamed me for living. She blamed me for surviving and carrying on when everything she held most dear was lost.

Through the hurricane of suffering and bereavement, we look for outlets to blame, something that will alleviate even the slightest weight of the burden.

So I sympathize, I do, and I forgive.

I forgive her.

But I'm not looking to make amends or revisit old wounds. All I want is peace.

Fetching the lighter I snagged from my parents' house, I flick the little wheel with my thumb as I clutch the pieces of paper in my opposite hand.

Zachary Adler.

Eleanor March.

A flame bursts to life, illuminating the shadows around me, and I watch as the fire licks at the parchment, the corners crackling into kindling and climbing higher. Before it reaches my fingers, I toss the remains onto the gravestone, observing the way the embers flicker and burn, turning the paper into cinders.

Goodbye.

I blow away the ashy residue, then press my palm to the stone one last time. "It's time to rise," I whisper into the night. "It's time to eat peach pie again."

Pulling to my feet, I feel a weight lift, a new beginning waiting for me, and all I want to do is go to him. I want to wrap my arms around his neck, jump into his arms, and tell him that I see him.

I *see* him—the man he is, the man he's always been, and the man I love with my whole heart.

But I don't.

I don't do that because before I step out of the cemetery and reach my car, my phone rings.

Leah.

My fingers swipe to accept the call, and I place the cell phone to my ear. "Hey, what's up?"

"Girl, don't freak out. Where are you?"

"What?"

Static and poor reception crackle in my ear.

"Have you seen the news?"

There's panic laced into her tone, causing goose bumps to pimple my flesh. I swallow through a worried frown. "No, I… What is it? What's wrong?"

Leah falters before continuing. "It's Parker, babe. He's on TV," she says with careful urgency. "It's a breaking report…"

My blood runs cold.

I can't breathe.

"He's hanging off the Delavan Bay Bridge."

37

PARKER

I REALLY FUCKING HATE HEIGHTS.

There's no good reason for it. It's not like my fear of the dark, where it was conditioned into me as a child due to traumatic circumstances. This is just some random, shitty phobia I decided I had while working a high-rise job with coworkers a good five years back, before I broke off to do my own thing. I'd glanced down from the scaffolding and almost pissed myself.

So when I was contracted for a roofing job last April, my knee-jerk reaction was to turn it down. Bree said she'd get me out of it if that's what I really wanted, but shit, money was tight that year, and honestly, I kind of felt like a pussy… so I took the job.

And then I fell off that goddamn roof.

It was a two-story drop that nearly killed me, and if it weren't for a big-ass sycamore tree that partially cushioned my fall on the way down, I likely would have died on impact.

Instead, I landed myself in the hospital with a broken fucking back and a grade 3 concussion.

At the time, death would have been a welcome alternative. When they were wheeling me through the hospital on that stretcher, and I finally came to…I was pissed.

Why couldn't it just be over?

I craved peace, but all I got were six long, torturous months out of work, unbearable pain, and medical bills out the ass. A dark cloud of depression funneled through me, blackening my veins, poisoning my thoughts, and while I was stuck in my house, bedridden and crippled, all I wanted to do was die.

Work was my outlet. My saving grace. I needed to keep moving, remain in motion, stay busy—but that was stolen from me. I wasn't sure if I'd ever heal properly and be able to work again, and the prospect was dauntingly terrifying.

On a particularly grim night over the summer, delirious on painkillers and feeling little hope for the future, I told Bree to just fucking kill me. Smother me with a pillow. Lace my Fruity Pebbles with rat poison or some shit. Didn't matter. I just wanted out.

She lost her mind, of course, freaked the hell out and almost had me committed right then and there. From that point forward, my sister stopped by my house daily to make sure I didn't do anything stupid, and as soon as I was up walking around again, regaining some semblance of my only marginally better life, she enrolled me in those dumb meetings.

That's where I met her.

Melody.

My moon.

That's when everything changed for me, and I guess I have that roof to thank.

But as I'm standing on this goddamn bridge with a complete stranger, staring over the edge into an endless black abyss, I can say for damn certain, I still *really* fucking hate heights.

"Just let me do this, man. Get the hell out of here."

I'm not sure what kind of twisted shit the universe is up to, but out of all the motherfuckers in the world, I'm the one standing here trying to talk this guy out of jumping fifty feet into the bay.

Me.

I'm literally enrolled in a suicide support group.

And I'm kind of pissed at myself for not paying more attention to Ms. Katherine's pep talks.

"Go," the man says as he hangs off the outer side of the guardrail, facing the water, limbs shaking, his sweat glinting off the line of streetlamps. "Let me die."

Shit.

When I saw this guy about ready to launch himself into Delavan Bay, I stopped without really thinking anything through. I didn't have a plan—no earth-shattering advice or profound lectures. No magical words to knock some sense into him.

So I'm basically just standing here, clueless and thoroughly unqualified, inching my way closer, while my brain short-circuits trying to figure out an angle.

Swallowing, I close my eyes and try to envision the meetings, hoping to pull some sort of grandiose wisdom from the bits and pieces I actually paid attention to.

Why did I take so many fucking naps?

Those jarring fluorescent lights burst to life overhead, and I picture myself rooted to that red plastic chair as idle chitchat swirls around me, but their words are muffled, faces blurred, because Melody's hair is tied into a loose braid today, draped over her left shoulder. She's fiddling with a little blue hair band secured to the end that matches the color of her sundress. And when she glances my way, her eyes shimmer with tiny cerulean flecks sprinkled into those pools of bright green.

Damn it.

This isn't the right angle.

The stranger heaves in a deep breath of courage, dragging me back to the bridge. His body dangles carelessly over the water, his fingers loosening on the rail. "I appreciate the effort, but I need to do this," he says, chin to his chest.

Wait, no, *shit.*

Starting points!

"Hamsters," I blurt. "Do you like hamsters?"

This captures his attention, and the man snaps his head toward me, a confused frown settling into place between sweat-laden brows. "What the hell are you talking about?"

I pace forward with slow, careful steps, my heartbeat doing the exact opposite. It's jackknifing inside my chest as adrenaline pumps through my veins. "Okay, maybe not hamsters. Something else." *Fucking hell*, I'm terrible at this. "The smell of Grandma's gumbo simmering on the stove during Easter brunch."

He blinks.

"Flying your kite with Dad. Rainbow sherbet. The scent of wet grass after a summer thunderstorm." I add, as an afterthought, "We've had a lot of those this year. So great."

"Are you on drugs?"

My feet carry me right to the edge of the rail, and I extend my arm like a tentative plea. "Starting points. You know, shit that makes you happy. Little things that don't suck. Like…dancing in the lake."

I'm close enough that I can make out the color of his eyes—dark, dark brown, matching his shoulder-length hair and goatee. The man glances at the water, then back to me. "Sure, yeah. I'll go do that one right now."

Shit…poor selection.

"Fuck, I don't know. What do you like?"

Cars begin to park along the entry to the bridge, bystanders stepping from vehicles to gawk and wave their cell phones around. A curious audience trickles in, one by one, gathering a few yards away and causing my insides to spiral with nerves.

The man looks just as wrought with distress when he notices the crowd. His grip on the rail tightens, his body going rigid. When he turns back toward me, his umber eyes gleam with animosity. "Why couldn't you leave me alone? I'd be dead by now," he bites out through clenched teeth.

"But you're not." I spare a glance down below and shudder at the sight of the cavernous bay. "That's good, right? If you wanted to be dead, you would be."

"You're distracting me. I can't concentrate with you here, rambling about goddamn hamsters."

Deciding I need a new approach, I coil my fingers around the guardrail and take an unsteady step up onto the elevated cement block. The railing is level with my stomach as I cling tight, careful not to bend over too far. "You know, you probably wouldn't die from the fall."

Maybe I'm just trying to convince myself in case there's another roof incident, but the math seems to check out. I'm no expert on diving off of bridges, but a fifty-foot drop into deep, nonturbulent water sounds like it would fucking suck while still being survivable.

The man beside me shivers from only a foot away, his Adam's apple bobbing with conflict. "I can't swim."

Well, fuck.

My mind spins, trying to locate a plan C—except, I didn't even have a decent plan A or B when I got myself into this mess. The only question that springs to my lips is, "What's your name?"

There's always a chance I can build a rapport with this guy, and maybe he'll like me enough to stick around.

Then I recognize my faulty reasoning...

I'm really not all that likable.

A few beats of thickening silence lingers between us, the growing background noise muted by the intensity of this moment. The man finally licks his lips as his troubled eyes lift to me, and he replies in a ragged voice, "Milo."

"Milo." I repeat his name through a nod, hoping I look more confident than I feel right now. "Good name. I bet someone out there would really miss saying that name."

Well, shit, that wasn't awful. I mentally high-five myself.

Milo grumbles, his gaze dancing out across the murky waters. Streetlight and moonglow illuminate his haggard frame, chalky complexion, and the dark circles beneath his eyes that almost match the shade of his irises. In a swift breath, he confesses, "I killed someone."

My insides pitch, and I freeze.

Awesome.

I'm trying to uplift a goddamn murderer.

"It wasn't..." Milo's head swings back and forth, his inner turmoil palpitating off him in waves. He fists the rail with gritted teeth. "It wasn't on purpose. I didn't mean to."

My throat closes up, lost for words, and I simply nod my head as I process his admission.

Milo continues, his legs quaking beneath him. "I thought I could live with it, but I can't. I can't do it anymore."

I swallow. "What happened?"

"It was stupid. It was so…fuckin' stupid." His clammy palms squeeze the metal bar, while his chest puffs out with a tattered breath. "I lost my job last spring, and it was hell. I've got a kid, you know? So my brother, he's always getting himself into trouble, always coming up with these schemes. He said he'd help me get some cash, just a temporary thing, until I got back on my feet. I didn't know he wanted to rob people." Milo stops to regroup, closing his eyes tight. "But he convinced me it would be fine, easy, because he just has that way about him. Nothing is ever serious—it's all fun and fuckin' games.

"Until you ram your truck into some poor, innocent guy and find out the next day that you killed him. I *killed* him."

My eyebrows pinch together as I stare at Milo, an icy chill sweeping through me that even the hot August night can't touch. *Fuck.*

Ominous water ripples below us, and I acknowledge the real gravity of this situation. Choices need to be made. Milo needs to decide if he's going to hurl himself off this bridge, and I need to decide if I'm going to stop him.

This guy killed someone—accident or not, he killed a man as a consequence of doing bad, illegal shit. Maybe he deserves to meet a grisly end. Maybe the world would be a better place.

But…maybe that's not the point.

Letting out a frazzled sigh, I tap my thumbs along the rail, trying to figure out what I'm supposed to do with this knowledge, with this impasse.

What would Melody do?

Her porcelain face and emerald eyes seize me for a wistful moment—her goodness, her heart, her *empathy*. She sees life through a lens made of hope and decency. She smiles through adversity. She shines in the dark. She chooses compassion over…everything.

Melody talks people off of bridges.

I don't give myself any time to think before hoisting one leg up over the guardrail, my grip on the bar white-knuckled. My whole body tremors with fear, and I refuse to look down at the bleak chasm below as gasps and flashing lights from the group of spectators assault me. Police sirens sound in the distance, adding to my harrowing anxiety.

"What the fuck, man? What are you doing?"

My opposite leg follows suit, and I'm clutching the guardrail for dear life, the heels of my boots teetering off the edge of the cement ledge.

Holy fucking shit.

"Well," I mutter, my voice hitching. I'm facing the opposite direction, chin tucked to my chest as I try to collect my bearings. "You seem pretty upset over killing a guy, so I figured you wouldn't want another death on your hands."

I blow out a hard breath, finding the courage to glance up at Milo. His stunned expression stares back at me, slack-jawed and bewildered.

He gapes at me. "Are you insane?"

Am I?

I'm about to shrug my shoulders, but my balance staggers at the gesture, so I just force out a strained, "Maybe."

Since I'm facing the roadway, my eyes travel over to the large crowd of rubberneckers, likely live tweeting and making TikTok videos as we speak.

Police officers roll in, catching Milo's attention, and he hollers over his shoulder, "Stay the fuck back, or I'll jump!"

My insides churn with dread. "Please don't do that," I say in a low voice, finding the strength to pivot myself on the overhang until I'm facing the same direction as Milo, my torso dangling forward over the bay. "If you jump, then I'll have to jump in after you."

"Bullshit," he spits back. "Just leave me the hell alone. Get out of here."

"I can't do that. I mean, I'm already in this." I suck in a wavering breath. "And then, what if you survive, but I drown? You'll have to live with the responsibility of taking *two* lives. That would really suck."

"Dude, you're stressing me out. Just go."

"What do you love?"

Milo falters, sparing me the briefest look. His chin trembles, the fear evident despite his determination to drown himself. "My son," he croaks out. "And my brother."

"Aren't they enough to live for?"

"My brother's in prison. I was driving *his* truck when I hit that guy—someone got the plates, and Alfie was arrested. He refused to give me up, so now he's rotting in a jail cell all alone, even though *I'm* the one who killed a person."

I bite my lip with consideration. "You could always turn yourself in."

"I'm too chickenshit. I'd rather just end it all."

"What about your son?" I continue, keeping the conversation going. Keeping him distracted.

"He loses either way, but this way is better."

"How so?"

Milo lets out a growl of protest, shaking his head. "I see what you're doing, trying to get me to talk—to *think*. I've already made up my mind, and you can't change it."

Braving a glance to the depths below, I sway as a swell of queasiness claims me. I push through the fear and pull my head up to watch the stars instead. "My dad died when I was just a little kid, and it really fucked up my whole life. He didn't off himself like you, though, which I can only imagine will add an extra layer of trauma and heartbreak for your son."

Milo remains silent, bristling at my spiel.

My fingers tense, curling stiffer around the clammy metal as I continue to spout off a bunch of random shit, hoping something manages to stick. "You know, I actually wanted to die not too long ago. I wasn't actively suicidal, but I would've been really damn okay if I just stopped waking up in the morning. It's a shitty, black-hole type of feeling, and I'm not sure there's anything *anyone* can say to help you see through to the other side.

"I could stand here all night giving you reasons and sob stories, glimpses of hope. But only you can decide that your life is worth living. Only you can see the other side."

He's quiet for a long time, maybe an entire minute, and we both keep our gazes fixed straight ahead, lost in the sea of stars. Milo cranes his neck my way, his eyes reflecting a new set of emotions, something I haven't seen yet as I turn to face him.

There's a crack in his conviction.

"What's on the other side?" Milo asks in a low, weary tone, his voice hardly audible over the commotion behind us and the heavy draft that coasts through.

Melody steals my thoughts once again, her previous words to me lighting me up like a moonbeam. I reply with surety. "What you put there."

A palpability hovers between us, a striking sense of clarity, and I think this is it, I finally got through to this guy, and I can crawl off this fucking bridge and go home to wallow in my own personal misery—but then I hear it.

Her voice.

It's Melody.

"Parker!"

My body swivels along the ledge, turning to face her, to *see* her, to drink her in beneath the glimmering night sky. Our eyes lock from a few yards away, and she's hysterical, trying to run to me, but she's being held back by a beefy cop.

"Melody."

Her name is only a whisper on my tongue, a tender breath, and I know she can't hear me, but I say it anyway. It calms me.

I'm calm.

Milo follows my stare. "That your girl?"

"I really fucking hope so."

"Hell, man, you—"

The moment he spins back to face me, everything goes to shit.

The air leaves my lungs when Milo slips, losing his footing. He scrambles to keep his grip on the rail as my one arm instinctively reaches out for him, but I miss, and he fumbles, and then he's free-falling face-first into Delavan Bay as my heart sinks to the bottom of the water before he even hits the surface.

Motherfuck.

Everything happens in slow motion, or maybe it's a split second, I'm not really fucking sure, but all I know is that I'm left with another choice.

Melody shrieks, clawing her way through the wall of cops, who let her go in order to race down the bridge toward the other side of the bank.

"No! Parker, don't you dare!"

She's running to me, sobbing and desperate, and all I want to do is climb back over the railing, scoop her into my arms, and kiss away her trails of tears.

But I don't.

All I do is smile.

Then I let go of the guardrail and jump in after him, while Melody's horri-fied cry follows me all the way down to the dark, icy water.

Redemption is a bitch.

38

MELODY

I'M ON THAT DOWNTOWN STREET ALL OVER AGAIN, MY LUNGS PERFORATING, my limbs staggering, my heart skyrocketing with unbridled terror.

"No! Parker, don't you dare!"

It's more than a request, more than a plea. It's the ultimate demand.

My truest wish.

He holds my stare for a second, only a second, as I lessen our gap and sprint toward the guardrail, where the man I love is dangling fifty feet above the water. I see the battle on his face. The struggle. It's only a flash before his eyes spark green and gallant, and then…

He smiles.

I waited months to see that smile. There was a time when I would have done anything to watch it bloom across his handsome face, planting new, healthy roots inside of him.

But right now, it slices me straight to the marrow, a grisly blade between my ribs.

They say a picture says a thousand words, but I only see one.

Goodbye.

An ugly cry expels the moment Parker lets go, plummeting into the bay, only a blink before I reach him. "No! *No!*"

Devastating hysteria possesses me, something wretched, and my body moves on impulse, legs violently shaking as I start climbing over the railing with zero regard for anything but jumping in after him. Autopilot, tunnel vision, chaotic instinct—it infiltrates my blood, infecting me with a desperate sort of mania.

Before I can leap, two solid arms wrap around my midsection, pulling me back, up, and over, like I'm nothing more than a feather. Weightless.

Cobwebs.

My heart thunders in protest, legs flailing as I try to escape the stranger's grip, but he continues to drag me away from the rail. "No! Let go of me!"

"Whoa, whoa, calm down. I'm an officer. There's an embankment around this way—follow me."

I don't even spare him a glance.

I just start running.

My ballet flats pound the pavement with a furious gait, bruising my soles, and my lungs contract with burning, painful breaths. My throat stings, my muscles ache, and my heartbeats eradicate me from the inside out as I blindly rush down the verge toward the water's edge.

Groups of people hover, while medical personnel try to hold them back, and before I can even think about diving headfirst into the water, someone calls out, "We got 'em!"

Oh my God.

I case the bay with wild eyes, spotting two figures in the water a few yards down, just as EMTs meet them, assisting them back to land.

With a strangled cry, I race forward, pushing through bodies and arms and whispered chatter. "Parker!"

He's wading through the water, sluggish and unsteady, dragging the other man with him.

He's moving, he's walking, he's breathing.

He's alive!

A paramedic takes the man from his arms, carrying him to the grass, as a second one pulls Parker up over the edge, until he collapses, coughing and sputtering.

"Parker!" I shout, my knees aching with every swift, furious step. Rocks and pebbles dig into my feet through the thin soles, but I don't stop running until I reach him. "Parker, God…oh my God…"

He lifts up for a moment, then falls backward, spitting out mouthfuls of water. "Melody…" he chokes out.

My body launches itself against his, uncaring of anything but feeling his beating heart pressed into my chest. Sobs leak out of me when his arms snake around my back, clutching me tight. "I thought I lost you. I thought you were gone," I weep into the collar of his drenched T-shirt.

Parker wheezes, buckling onto his back as EMTs sweep in to check his vitals. He weaves his hand through my hair, trying to hold me as close as he can while rejecting the medical attention. "I'm fine," he grits out, still coughing. Still gasping. "I'll be fine."

He's soaked and shivering, the bay water seeping through my thin dress as I cling desperately. Tears continue to spill from my eyes, and I pepper him in frenzied kisses. Parker's chest expands and deflates with every deep, arduous breath, and my lips trail from his neck to his jaw, until they meet with his.

I kiss him.

I kiss him hard, my tongue tearing through his lips, hungry to taste his warmth for myself. It's evidence, it's fact, it's *proof*—he's alive.

Parker pulls back to catch his breath, another waterlogged cough rattling his lungs. "Fuck, that sucked."

His ribs hiss, his chest whistling. My terror mounts higher, drenching me in worry as a paramedic tries to shoo me away, ambushing Parker with blood pressure cuffs and oxygen. The other man lies motionless a few feet away, surrounded by medics, while stretchers are rushed through. It's a harrowing scene, causing a surge of nausea to roll through me.

Parker coughs and chokes, spitting more water into the grass, and I go pallid.

Is he okay?

Is he drowning before my eyes?

My vision twinkles with stars, tiny particles of light, and I feel myself teetering, a dizzy spell galloping through my brain and making my temples pulse and throb. "P-Parker…don't leave me…"

The air crackles with daunting energy, something forbidding, and I feel

Parker's fingertips dig into my waist as he lifts up on his haunches, his face blurring before me as the background noise turns to static.

"Melody?"

Alarm infuses his tone, his grip on me tightening. With fluttering eyelids, I begin to float away, tipping over from my knees as everything becomes jumbled chaos.

"Jesus…someone fucking help her!"

His panicked words fade out, turning to ringing in my ears, and Parker catches me before I hit the ground, but he can't save me from the darkness that swallows me whole…

These lights are familiar.

Sterile and unaesthetic.

Blinking through a sharp inhale, I reach for my wrist, thinking I'm back in that hospital bed after my suicide attempt—tangled in starched sheets, my vein and my heart bleeding out. I expect to see my parents' tearful faces hovering over me, wracked with disappointment.

Panic seizes me.

No…I'm not ready.

As reality works its way back through me, my fuzzy brain begins to temper, and when my eyes land on my arm, there is only a fading scar staring back at me.

I glance at my opposite arm and wince. A long needle and white tape are secured to the underside of my elbow.

And then…memories assault me, a rush of noise and colors and lights.

Parker!

I sit upright, my heartbeats ricocheting off my ribs as I fumble for the call button to summon a nurse. The last thing I remember is Parker gasping for breath in my arms as paramedics swarmed us, and then I was captured by queasiness and dizzying lights.

He jumped off a bridge.

He jumped off a bridge right in front of me, and now I don't know where he is.

Tears rush to my eyes while anxiety courses through me. My fingers fumble with the button, pressing it over and over until the mint-green curtain shimmies before me and a familiar face pokes through.

Dr. Whitley.

Bree.

"Melody," she says softly, her chestnut ringlets piled high on her head. "How are you feeling?"

I swallow. "Why am I here? Where's Parker?"

Her smile is easy, natural. Like mine. Bree paces forward with careful steps, coming up beside my cot. "You fainted. When you came to, you were overcome with panic, so we administered a sedative."

Warmth radiates from bronze-tinged eyes as she reaches out to place a tender palm along my arm. It's an intimate gesture, something beyond what a regular doctor would do.

But I suppose I'm not a regular patient.

Licking my chapped lips, I feel my bottom lip start to tremble. "Parker... is he okay?"

She nods quickly. "He's going to be fine. I'll monitor him for any long-term side effects and watch out for signs of lung infection, but he's acting like his usual stubborn self." Bree's smile blooms through watery eyes. "He hasn't stopped asking about you. He's so worried."

My heart rate quickens. "Can I see him?"

I need him. I need him in my arms, flesh to flesh, beating heart to beating heart.

"Soon," she tells me. "I'm about to go sign off on his discharge papers, and then I'll get you guys out of here. But first..." Bree pulls her lips between her teeth, the pressure of her touch increasing on my arm. She falters, inhaling a long, shaky breath. "I need to go over some results with you. We ran a blood test when you were brought in."

I freeze, my muscles locking. Nerves race through me, triggering more nausea.

Oh God...am I dying?

My mind is inundated with worst-case scenarios: brain tumors, cancer, cancerous brain tumors.

Bile climbs up my throat.

Bree takes a seat on my bedside, her eyes glinting with tears as she squeezes me, her unsaid words coiling around me like a serpent.

No, please.

I'm not ready!

I can almost envision a reverend pushing through the curtain, a barrage of mourning and last rites.

"You're pregnant, Melody."

No! A brain tumor!

Wait.

Her words penetrate my fog of fear, and I slowly begin to register what she actually said. Goose bumps scatter along my arms as my heart thunders with stunned, stupefied beats. A sharp breath hitches in the back of my throat. My mind spins. My limbs start to quiver.

I'm pregnant.

I'm pregnant.

Our respective tears fall at the same time, and Bree lets out a choked-up, weepy laugh. "Congratulations."

I lift a hand to cup my mouth. A sob, riddled with equal parts joy and disbelief, is muffled by my palm, and I close my eyes to process this unexpected bomb. "How…how far along am I?"

Bree swipes two fingers under her eye, streaking the tears away. "Judging by your hCG levels, you're about eight weeks along. We'll need to schedule an ultrasound to be sure."

Emotions torpedo through me, stealing the air from my lungs.

The morning-after pill must have failed.

I've been pregnant this whole time.

Holding back an incredulous cry, I wonder aloud, "Does Parker know?"

She shakes her head, her dark curls dancing in her topknot, and then she slides a loving hand up and down my arm. "That's for you to tell him, Melody. Although, I'd give anything to see his face when you give him the news." Bree reels in her own elated emotions, sighing deeply. "God, my little brother is going to be a father..."

Her own love for Parker radiates off of her, heady and potent. She drifts away for a moment, her eyes reflecting years of memories—pain, joy, kinship. I see her relief, her pride, and I wonder what hardships they went through together. I want to hear their stories, relive their friendship and bond. I'm yearning to know everything.

A swell of forgiveness and understanding fills me as I clasp the back of her hand with my palm. Bree is a good person. Her aura is pure and kind, and her heart bleeds with empathy. She would do anything for her brother.

And I realize then...if she craved to see Parker's smile just as much as I did, I can't really blame her for what she did.

We're not so different, she and I.

While my tears continue to track down my cheeks, I give her knuckles a gentle squeeze. "I'm sorry," I whisper in a ragged breath. "I understand why you did it."

Her eyes widen to copper saucers as her throat bobs with a swallow. She nods through her own tears. "I truly didn't mean to hurt you, Melody. Please know that. My intentions were noble, but I realize now that it wasn't right. It wasn't my place to meddle."

"I know," I assure her. "It's okay."

A grateful smile tugs at her lips. "Thank you." Her gaze dances away, settling on the bleached sheets, and she adds softly, "Thank you for everything...for what you've done for Parker. I feared my brother would never find happiness or joy or see life as anything other than a burden. An affliction."

Heartache stabs at me as I listen thoughtfully.

"His heart is strong, but it never had anything to fight for," Bree finishes, finding her way back to me and sealing her words with a glimmering smile. She lifts her hand, placing it atop the bedcover that's draped over my belly. "Now he has everything."

39

MELODY

HOME.

   This feels like home.

Not necessarily the four walls or the ruddy bricks or even the curtain of tall, lush trees that surround the property, giving it an air of peaceful seclusion.

It's *this*.

This man.

This new life fluttering in my belly.

After Bree discharged us from the hospital, she led Parker to my room. His eyes were tired and weary, but his arms felt safe and eager as he pulled me into an emotional embrace, kissing the top of my head and hushing away my tears as they fell hard against his chest. We held each other for a long time, while three precious heartbeats filled my soul with hope.

We shared an Uber ride over to our vehicles, still parked near the bridge, then drove separately to Parker's house, where I plan to share my news with him.

Stepping out of my car, I jog toward him down the gravel driveway, entwining our fingers together when we meet beside his truck. Parker inhales a weighty breath, leaning back against the hood with a sigh. His eyes don't find me right away. They are cast just beyond my shoulder, flickering with something I can't quite read. "Hey…look at me." My hand lifts, and I graze my fingertips along the bristles shadowing his jawline. "Are you okay?"

Parker tenses, wavering before meeting my searching stare. "Sorry, I just…" He blows out a hard puff of air, like he's trying to regroup. "I feel all fucked-up inside. Itchy. Off-kilter."

"You just went through a trauma, Parker. It's understandable."

His eyes close tight as a sticky breeze rolls through. "I feel like I fucking failed."

My stomach pitches at his words. "Don't say that."

"Why not? It's the truth. I failed you, and now I failed him," Parker bites out, looking away again. He withdraws before I've even had a chance to try and reach him. "He's dead. I knew it when I was dragging him out of that goddamn bay."

A heavy sorrow saturates the air around us. Bree gave us the grim news before we left the hospital—they'd done everything they could, but the man on the bridge didn't make it.

My eyes shifted to Parker in that moment, and I swore I could see a tiny light flicker out. A cloud rolled in, casting shadows all over him.

He dimmed.

"Parker…" I lower my hand from his cheek, grasping both of his palms in mine. "Don't do that to yourself. This is not your weight to carry. I just witnessed the most selfless, heroic thing I've ever seen in my life, and it only makes me want you a thousand times more."

Parker's eyes dip back to me, flaring as he registers my words. His grip on my hands tighten. "Don't say shit you don't mean, Melody."

"I mean it," I reply in a whispered, valiant breath. "You didn't fail me—you made a mistake. Mistakes make us human. Mistakes have the potential to mold us into better, stronger people." His eyes catch the pearly starlight as they dance across my face, brows creasing with reflection. "You did a good thing tonight, Parker…a really good thing. The outcome doesn't erase that."

His shoulders deflate, his forehead dropping to mine as he pulls me closer. We hold each other in silence for a few beats, wrapped up in the mere vitality of one another, serenaded by the song of the cicadas and our healing heartbeats. "I'm so fuckin' glad you're okay," he mutters, pressing a light kiss to my hairline. Then he says with a sigh, "Thanks for following me home. I'm probably going to hit the shower and head to bed."

I nuzzle into him with a nod. It's the middle of the night, nearing the early morning hours, and it's been an exhausting day. Maybe my big reveal should wait until tomorrow when we're both more clearheaded.

Parker gives me another kiss before straightening. "You're good to drive home?"

My heart skips.

I flinch as I take a step back, not expecting this. My skin prickles with dismissal as a brisk wave of queasiness causes my belly to swirl. "You don't want me to stay?"

He stiffens. A beat passes while he processes the mood, tousling his fingers through unruly hair. Parker studies me, his gaze taking in my startled expression through incandescent moonlight. "Shit, you want to?"

"Of course I want to," I say, an earnest plea. "You almost died, Parker. I-I watched you almost die…only a few hours ago. You dropped fifty feet right before my eyes." A surge of panic bubbles to the surface, snuffing out my words and stealing my breath. "Please, don't make me leave. I need to hold you, wake up with you beside me, breathing and warm…"

"Fuck, Melody, I'm sorry." Parker collects me in his arms, gliding his hands up to my face, cupping my cheeks. His green eyes shimmer with anguish. "Jesus…please stay. I want you to."

My breathing is unhinged, bordering on manic. All I can muster is a nod.

"I figured you were still pissed at me," he explains, worry laced into his words and his touch. He brushes his thumbs along my flushed cheekbones. "I wasn't sure if we were okay. I didn't want to assume all was forgiven just because I launched myself into the fuckin' bay."

"We're okay." I say it quickly, confidently, and then I repeat it. "We're okay, Parker. It's over. I forgive you."

Pulling our foreheads back together, he sucks in a hard breath through gritted teeth. A sound escapes him, one I've never heard before. Ragged, strained, almost painful.

Heartrending relief.

"Fuck…" Parker's fingers coil around to the base of my neck, clamping hard, his desperation sinking into me. I feel his need. "Are you still mine?"

My favorite song echoes in my mind, and I keep nodding, my tears spilling free. "Yes," I murmur, watching his eyes snap shut, like he's soaking up my assent and carving it into his bones. "I'm yours. I'm only yours."

"Goddamn, I don't deserve you."

Leaning up, I place a kiss to his bottom lip, lingering as I mutter, "You deserve more than you know."

Another kiss follows, just as light, but then the tip of my tongue flicks out for a quick taste along his lip. Salt and sweetness. Sensuality stirs between us, pulling our emotions in a new direction, and I melt into him with a sigh of longing.

Parker's hands vanish beneath the hem of my sundress until he's gripping my bare waist, his heated stare locked on my mouth. Our pelvises grind together as I lean in closer, and his fingers inch behind me, sneaking underneath the trim of my underwear. He groans when his palms slide inside, cupping my backside. "Christ, Melody, get in the fucking house. I need to be inside you."

A whimper escapes me. "Wait…wait, you should rest. Recover," I urge, despite the way my body buzzes with disagreement.

"I don't need rest." Parker squeezes my ass, tugging me flush against his erection. "I've been asleep for nearly thirty years. All I need is you."

Our lips crash together, tongues tangling instantly. My head falls back when he raises a hand to my head, tugging on my hair, angling my mouth to taste me deeper through a frenzied growl.

I pull back to breathe. Grazing my hands up his chest, I rest them on his shoulders as we collect our bearings, and I force myself to say, "Shower. Rest." His body hums and sways with both exhaustion and lust. "I'll still be here in the morning."

Parker's resolve wanes, his long sigh kissing the hairs on my head. A small nod of concession follows. "Okay."

We make our way inside, giving Walden a few minutes of attention before Parker slips into the shower and I retreat to his bedroom. Sifting through his drawer of T-shirts, unfolded and in disarray, I pluck one out and decide to use it as a nightshirt.

Butterflies scatter low in my belly as my bare feet traipse to his unmade bedside, and I slink beneath the cool sheets. I melt into the covers, inhaling his familiar scent.

Earthy woods and musky raindrops. Hints of cedar and pine. It's not cologne—Parker isn't the type—so it must be his soap or fabric softener.

A smile lifts with warmth.

Will our baby be a boy, smelling of a Colorado mountainside?

Or a girl? Citrus and sunshine?

Will he build and carve, or will she bake and smile?

Enchanting thoughts skip across my brain, dousing me in daydreams. *A baby.* I've wanted children since I was a child myself, from little toy dolls to babysitting the neighborhood kids. Charlie and I had a life plan, a plan that was cut short, cruelly severing my visions of ever becoming a mother. Months went by where I was plagued with vivid memories of that water running red in the shower, blood trickling down my thighs, my body purging all final remnants of hope.

Hope.

Parker said once that hope was for the weak.

It was my very first day at those meetings, and his words burned me. They rattled me straight to the core.

But maybe he was right—hope *is* for the weak. The frail and the struggling. The *breakable.*

Hope is the glue.

And there is no shame in that. There is no shame in weakness, in wanting more, in failure or defeat. Without those moments of weakness, we would never truly appreciate the beauty of our strength.

Hope is the stepping stone for grief and suffering, and then it's up to us to do the rest. To fill in our dark holes, stitch our wounds, and make our way to the other side.

A wistful smile still paints my face when Parker steps into the bedroom twenty minutes later, his hair damp and mussed, adorning a light gray T-shirt and boxer briefs. He lingers, his eyes skimming over me through the lamplit space, flickering with thoughtful emotion.

I sit up, gently patting the empty space beside me. "Hi."

His own smile twitches on his mouth. He wavers for a brief moment, like he's taking it all in, then paces forward. "I'm not sure I'll ever get used to this."

"Seeing me in your bed?" I grin.

"Seeing you in my bed, my space, my fucking clothes." Parker climbs onto the mattress, prowling toward me, his arm draping over my torso and pulling me close. He trails a rough hand up and down my midsection, drinking in the sight of me in his T-shirt, and settles it on my stomach. He finishes in a low breath, "Everywhere."

Inhaling sharply, I meet his gaze. "I feel you everywhere too," I whisper back, placing my hand atop his as he palms my belly. "You're inside me."

His eyes flare with heat. "Fuck, I really want to be."

"You are." When Parker tries to move his hand downward, I halt his efforts, keeping it low on my abdomen. "You're inside me right now."

A frown appears between his brows when he realizes I'm trying to tell him something. "Like, in your heart and shit? Is this a girly metaphor?"

My smile blossoms wide, a chuckle slipping out. "No. It's a fact. You're literally inside me."

"Shit, Melody, maybe I swallowed too much sewer water, but I'm not—" Parker cuts himself off, going still. He blinks once. Twice. His attention goes straight to our joined hands, resting on top of my stomach, and when his focus flicks back to my face, the revelation is clear. It's striking. "Are you telling me you're fucking pregnant?"

Tears shoot to my eyes, and all I can do is nod.

"Jesus Christ..." Parker scrubs a hand over his face, holding his jaw as he reins in a breath. A silent, heavy beat passes between us, the air charged and thick, his eyes closing tight. When his eyelids ping back open, jade irises are glistening with emotion and disbelief. "We're going to be parents?"

My head bobs with fervor, my chin trembling. "Yes," I reply, only a gasp. "Your sister told me at the hospital. They ran a blood test."

"Fuck. Holy fuck."

Parker launches at me, his one hand still clasped over my belly, while the other tangles in my hair, fisting the long strands as his face hovers above me. My core clenches at the indescribable expression on his face, the awe, the love.

He lets out something like a moan as he holds me tight, and I lift up to kiss his lips. "Parker, I love you."

Another desperate sound escapes him as he tenses on top of me. "Jesus, you're fucking killing me right now."

"I love you." I say it again, coiling my legs around his hips while my hands cradle his face. "I love you so much, Parker Denison. *You*. All of your scars, your shadows, and your perfect, perfect heart. I'm not giving up on you. Not now, not ever."

He smashes his lips to mine, starved and crazed, clutching me like I'm his most prized possession—his whole purpose. Lifting to his knees, he pulls me with him, then falls back to the headboard in a sitting position until I'm strad-dling his lap. "I can't believe you love me. I can't believe you're mine." His words spill out ragged, his hands climbing my back, fingers gripping me at the nape of my neck. "I can't believe I put a baby in you."

"Believe it," I whisper. "Believe me."

"God, I fucking love you."

Parker kisses me again with unbridled hunger, our tongues dueling to the beats of our hearts. He tears the shirt off my body, throwing it to the floor beside us, then dives forward, taking my breast in his mouth. My back arches with plea-sure, our intimacy spiraling into sheer desire. I grab fistfuls of his hair, a breathy moan mingling with his. Thick hardness presses into my inner thigh, and I grind into him, wetness pooling between my legs. "Are you sure you're not too sore?"

He sucks my nipple into his mouth, biting gently. "I'm sore as fuck, but there's no way in hell I'm ending this night without being inside you."

My head drops back when he nicks me again, then trails his tongue up my chest to my throat, pulling the skin between his teeth. On instinct, I reach over to the bedside lamp to switch it off, but Parker steals my wrist before I can.

He shakes his head. "No."

Inhaling a sharp breath, I watch as he gathers the fabric of his T-shirt, then pulls it up over his head, tossing it next to mine. His body sits bare before me, seventy-nine scars on display, and I fall in love with every single one. I trace my fingertips along the puckered marks, smooth and soft, feeling him stiffen as his fingertips bite into my hipbones.

Parker hisses when I lean down to pepper kisses along his torso, my tongue poking out to lave along the expanse of scars. He cradles the back of my skull in his hands, arching into my roaming mouth with a soft groan. "You ruin me, Melody," he murmurs, weaving his fingers through my wild hair. "You shatter my walls. You vaporize my darkness, overthrow my demons. You destroy every goddamn misaligned belief I've carried with me all my life."

My lips trail up his chest until we're mouth to mouth, breaths intermingled, and I say, "It's time to rebuild."

Words fade into needy kisses and frantic touches, and I'm devoured by his tongue, his hands, his palpable love for me. His hips lift up to tug his boxers down as I shimmy out of my underwear, and I position myself in his lap, his erection teasing me.

Our eyes lock for a powerful heartbeat, the last few hours swirling around us with electrifying energy.

Near death.

New life.

And then I slide down onto him with a husky cry, fingernails digging into his shoulders.

Parker's face falls between my breasts, stifling his moan of pleasure. Strong arms envelop me, wrapping around my back, anchoring me to him. We don't move right away.

We just *feel*.

When my hips begin to rock on instinct, taking him slow and deep, Parker grips me tighter, his hands skimming up my spine and tugging me closer until our mouths meet.

Skin on skin, my body buzzes with restoration. His tongue pushes past my lips as fire blazes through me, my heart quickening, my pulse dancing. I ride him faster, harder, both of us groaning with every collision.

He's alive.

I'm alive.

We are living, breathing, fucking, loving, evolving. Our blood pumps hot. Our veins thrum and throb. Our skin sweats, and our limbs cling.

My womb sings with life.

The thought alone ignites my core. I'm fevered and driven, rising and falling onto him at a desperate pace, attacking his mouth as I tug handfuls of his hair to steady myself.

Parker yanks my head back, nearly crumbling. "Jesus fuck, if you keep riding me like that I'm going to lose it."

I kiss him again without slowing down, nipping his lip with my teeth. "I want you to. Lose yourself in me."

Show me how alive you are.

"You want me to lose control? You want me to come in two fucking seconds?"

"Yes."

Our pelvises crash together, and I bite his lip again, grinding myself against his groin. My body sparks with the prelude to release.

"Fuck, Melody…" Parker palms the base of my skull in a punishing grip, our teeth knocking together as he hisses out, "You're coming with me."

His opposite hand snakes between us, fingering me until those sparks catch fire and I go up in flames. Parker slams into me with violent thrusts, unraveling the moment I'm shuddering in his arms, nothing but dynamite and shooting stars. His release flows through me, his life force, and he buries his deep groan into the crook of my neck, holding me tighter than ever as we ride the waves together.

I go limp in his arms, and we both collapse against the headboard with a hard sigh. Parker glides his hands up and down my back with tender strokes, his heart beating fast and furious into my own, our breaths uneven yet perfectly aligned.

A smile claims me, and I feel myself drifting away as I lay sprawled atop him, our bodies still joined. But as a soft, hazy glow permeates the curtains, the first hint of daybreak, I'm overcome with another inherent desire. My cheek lifts from his chest. "Parker?"

His exhaustion is evident, but he musters a soft, "Hmm?"

"I know you're tired, but I want to do one more thing before we go to sleep."

Long lashes flutter as his eyelids open, and then he reaches down to squeeze my backside. "Mmm, you're insatiable."

"Not that." I grin, pulling myself off him and reaching for his hand. "Come with me."

We take a moment to freshen up and find our clothes, and then I'm leading him through his house, Walden trailing behind us, until we're standing on the front porch, gazing up at the blossoming horizon.

It's a celebration.

A new day. A new beginning.

A new life.

We watch the sunrise together that morning, side by side, hand in hand, with Walden resting comfortably beside our feet. And as vibrant colors paint the sky, sheathing the treetops in magenta and gold, I think we finally see the same thing.

Hope.

40

PARKER

I FOUND A WAY TO GIVE HER A FOREVER AUGUST.

Our daughter, August Amelia, twirls the skirt of her birthday dress in ungraceful circles, two small palms cocooning her furry little friend.

I was never any good at life, and here I am now, *living*—while somehow managing to keep my kid alive as well as my dog, who is a thousand years past ancient at this point, Melody's aggressive infiltration of house plants, and this fucking hamster that clearly surpasses every law of hamster physics.

"Daddy, look!"

Oh, fuck, did it finally croak?

Bracing myself, I step closer to my daughter as the blades of grass tickle her bare toes. Her toothy grin has me letting out a breath of relief. "What is it, sunshine?"

Sunny blond pigtails dance with the breeze, while wide green eyes twinkle in the midday glow.

She's a spitting fucking image of her mother.

"Nutmeg wear birfday hat."

A smile twitches on my mouth as I glance inside August's cupped hands, taking in the tiny pink blossom that rests atop the hamster's head. It's a singular petal that blew free of the young peach tree flowering in our backyard.

It was one of the first things Melody did when she moved in with me three years ago. She planted a peach tree in honor of her late husband, and we're hoping it will finally bear some fruit this summer.

"Parker!"

Melody's panicked voice carries over to me from the back door, and I turn in place, casting worried eyes upon my very pregnant wife. She waves me over, looking frantic.

I race toward her. "Shit, what's wrong?"

"It's an emergency."

Double shit.

"Are you going into labor?"

Melody is thirty-nine weeks along with our son, so planning a big party for August's third birthday was risky. My mind has been consumed with harrowing images of the party being interrupted by Melody's water breaking during "Happy Birthday," painful contractions, and our son popping out on the kitchen floor next to the dog bowls.

"No, it's worse," she exclaims in a flustered breath, her braided pigtails swinging side to side as she shakes her head.

I pale.

Then I glance down at her swollen belly, just to make sure my kid didn't already fall out and I fucking missed it.

"I burned the cupcakes," she confesses, a horrified cry following. "Who am I? You should just take over."

What the fuck?

Melody's expression is riddled with regret.

In the years that I've known her, my wife has never once burned a cupcake. She's well-known around town, practically a local celebrity, having opened up a successful bake shop downtown late last year. It was a natural progression once her in-home bakery became too much to maintain, and the ratio of flour dust to oxygen inside our home was becoming concerning.

I purse my lips through a frown. "The last time I tried to bake cupcakes with you, I forgot three critical ingredients. It was a terrible fucking idea."

Her eyes flare, then shift to August, who is coming up behind me. "Language," she whisper-scolds.

Oh, right. I'm trying to be more careful now that our daughter repeats literally everything.

Clearing my throat, I amend, "It was a terrible *fudging* idea."

My eyebrows waggle. Melody blinks.

"Fudging," I repeat, then let out a drawn-out sigh. "You know, fudge. Cupcakes. C'mon, that pun was gold."

She stares at me for a moment before a smile stretches and her eyes shimmer with humor. "Oh my God." Melody bursts into a fit of giggles, flipping one braid over her shoulder. "I'm sorry, Parker. My mind turned to sludge an hour ago, and I'm living in a perpetual hot flash."

Her cheeks are rosy red, the flush spreading down her neck and chest. My palms reach out to pull her close, one pressing along her stomach, while the other reaches around her neck.

Fuck, she's beautiful.

Placing a lingering kiss to her forehead, I whisper, "Now you know what it's like for me being around you every day."

She shivers. "Yeah right…I'm a bowling ball within a bowling ball."

"You're fucking gorgeous." My lips travel down her cheek, landing on two full lips, and I murmur suggestively, "How much time do we have before people show up?"

Melody melts into me for a blissful moment, temptation seizing her. But she quickly collects her bearings and delves right back into panic mode. "Twenty minutes."

The doorbell rings.

She goes ashen.

August pushes past us both with a squeal of excitement, still holding on to Nutmeg, while Walden hobble-skips along with her to the front of the house.

I take Melody's face between my hands and bring her gaze to mine, smiling softly until she noticeably relaxes. "Melody March-Denison."

"Yes?" she squeaks.

"How many batches of cupcakes did you already make?"

"Twelve."

"Twelve batches, a dozen each? That's one hundred and forty-four cupcakes."

She nods.

"How many regular cakes did you make?"

"Two."

"Okay, well…if my math checks out, that equals approximately a lot of fucking cake. Everything will be okay, nobody will starve, and our grandchildren's grandchildren will still have leftovers to spare."

Melody heaves in a calming breath, curling her fingers around my wrists. Her eyes flicker with acceptance as she lifts her chin. "You're right."

"I know."

"But…" Her tongue pokes out to slick her lips, and she swallows hard. "I burned the lemon ones."

"With the meringue filling?"

She nods again.

"Fuck."

Our mutual disappointment is interrupted when our daughter comes bounding back through the house, beaming with enthusiasm, her lacy dress billowing behind her little legs. "Uncle West and Auntie Lee-Lee!"

West and Leah enter the house with massive gift bags, likely containing obnoxiously loud toys that I'll need to lose the batteries for. Melody tugs me inside through the back door and darts straight to Leah. The women do their girly hugging thing as West approaches, eyeing me warily in his khakis and lame polo.

"Hey, asshole."

My arms cross, my gaze assessing him with equal distaste. "Hey."

It's been an interesting few years getting to know Melody's brother. The truth is, we don't have much in common. He likes beer and sports, while I like things that aren't beer and sports. He enjoys going out to bars. The only thing I enjoy about bars is the leaving part. He has terrible taste in movies and even worse taste in music, and he was a huge pain in my ass during the wedding planning two years ago when Melody and I decided on an intimate backyard ceremony instead of a ballroom extravaganza.

But fucking West just had to take over and hire a shitty rock band to serenade us with god-awful Nickelback covers all night. He even got up on stage and sang that "Photograph" song as some kind of horrifying dedication, and Christ, that song was terrible enough to begin with—the memories still haunt me.

He also made a giant fucking spectacle of himself when he got trashed and drunkenly proposed to Leah in front of our seventy-five guests.

She slapped him. Then she kissed him. And then she slapped him again.

I'm pretty sure that sums up their entire relationship.

Last summer, they took a spontaneous trip to Las Vegas with another couple and "accidentally" got married by an Elvis impersonator who doubled as a male gigolo. Nobody is entirely sure what the fuck is going on between them, and honestly, I don't think they do either.

But for all of our animosity, bickering, and insults, I think the thing we hate most is that we really don't hate each other at all.

The asshole isn't half-bad. He loves the fuck out of Melody, and it's hard not to respect someone like that. Not to mention, he really came through when I got this nonsensical idea of building an entire second level onto my little ranch house. I figured we could use the extra space with our growing family, and apparently, I hate sleep and free time.

West helped me get Melody's house fixed up to put on the market, and then he dedicated a hell of a lot of time to helping me with the new addition. He's an electrician, so he actually knew his shit, and we semi-bonded over circuit breakers and ground conductors.

He narrows his eyes at me as we hold our stare, but West cracks first, a smirk lifting. "You get that dimmer switch all installed in the new nursery?" he wonders, shoving his hands into his pockets.

"Yeah. You figure out the HVAC problem for that one douchebag customer?"

He snickers. "After all that, it was an issue with the flame sensor."

"Shit."

A beat goes by, easy smiles passing between us.

We fist-bump.

August bounces up and down in front of us with a wide smile, her pigtails bouncing with her. She holds up her arms to Leah, stealing her raven-haired godmother's attention away from Melody. "Lee-Lee! Look at my fucky hamster. She has birfday hat."

Oops.

I try my best to dissolve into the hardwood flooring when all three heads jerk toward me.

Leah clears her throat in an attempt to cover up her laughter. "Your *fucky* hamster. Wow, Aug, I can't believe how cute she looks in that hat. And how...alive."

She mouths to me, *How is it still alive?*

The thing has got to be four or five. Pretty sure it's an alien hamster. Or a robot, like my sister.

I shrug.

Speaking of Bree, I step away from the crowd to pull out my phone. She was heading over to the party after her shift at the hospital, but it's typical for her to get roped into more work.

While there are no notifications from Bree, there *is* a new Hangouts message waiting for me.

A genuine smile creeps in when my eyes skim over the message from my favorite pen pal.

RacerDude: I made the baseball team!!!

Fuck. Yes.

Zephyr79: Atta boy. I knew you would.

RacerDude: Thank u for helping me pitch the other day. I know u don't really like sports.

Zephyr79: It was fun. You're a natural. You can pay me back with a joyride when you're a famous race car driver someday.

RacerDude: Yea right! Oh.. Mom told me to tell you that we have a b-day present for August. Sry we can't make the party today.

Zephyr79: That's okay. She drew you a picture. It's just a red scribble, but it's supposed to be a car. Act excited.

RacerDude: Cute!! :-) thx August.

Zephyr79: Gotta go, but let me know when you have your first game. We will be there. Proud of you, Owen.

RacerDude: Ur the best. TTYL

Slipping my phone into my back pocket, Melody is standing in front of me when I raise my head. Her knowing smile flashes bright.

"Owen?"

"Yeah. He made the team," I tell her, unable to hide my own proud grin.

"That's so wonderful. I knew he would." Melody moves in closer, wobbling a little like Walden does, which is charming as fuck, and leans up to kiss me. It's sweet and gentle at first, but I clasp her cheeks between my palms, deepening it instantly. She sucks in a sharp breath and lets it out as a squeaky sigh, our tongues touching and tasting, and we lose ourselves for a moment, uncaring of the guests only a few feet away.

A satisfied moan escapes when I pull back. "Mmm. You taste like lemon frosting."

"I got hungry," she whispers, caressing our noses together, her eyes glazed.

Another groan filters through my lips when she grinds up against me. "You're making *me* hungry."

I'm about two seconds away from begging Leah to keep an eye on August so I can borrow my wife for highly important *reasons* when the doorbell rings again, stealing our opportunity. Electricity still crackles between us, green embers dancing in Melody's eyes, and she lets me know with just a look that these flames will be stoked again later.

Can't fucking wait.

But first, it's time to watch my little girl annihilate a *Peppa Pig* piñata.

––––––––––––

The sun sets low in the sky, highlighting the horizon in a burnt-orange blush. It captures my attention for a striking moment, and I remember my father's words from all those years ago.

Fleeting beauty.

The most precious kind.

But as my eyes dip away from the setting sun and take in the blur of smiles, laughter, and joy all around me, I realize something pretty fucking powerful.

It's all fleeting.

Life itself is fleeting.

I watch from a lawn chair perched in the front yard as partygoers disperse, scooping my daughter into strong arms, giving her twirls and kisses, thanking Melody for a spectacular party. West snakes his arm around Leah, kissing her temple, and I see the love between them—despite the tumultuous tide of their relationship, there is affection, and there is *love*. I kind of want to shake them, tell them to get their shit together and appreciate what they have, because it's all so fucking fleeting, but I think that kind of awareness can only be learned, not taught.

Melody's parents wave their goodbyes to me from across the yard, and I smile my send-off. They've taken me in and treated me like their own damn kid over the past few years, and I couldn't be more grateful. I was robbed of that kind of relationship, that special brand of connection that only a mother or father can give. It broke me. It whittled me down to near nothingness, shaping me into someone I didn't even recognize.

Bree did, though. She saw me—the *real* me, that little boy buried deep down inside, with a cherry-stained chin, laughter in his eyes, and a strong, worthy heart.

"Eat up, little brother."

My sister pulls a chair up beside mine, handing me a container of miniature lemon loaves. I eye the offering with a half smile. "Because my wife didn't bake enough cake to have us all in permanent carb comas?"

Her acorn eyes glimmer with the glow of the red-yellow sundown. "Lemon cake is the happiest dessert," she says, her teeth flashing white. "Melody texted me to grab some on the way over because she knows it's your favorite and she burned them. I couldn't say no to her twenty-seven sad-face emojis."

"She always gets you with the emojis." Taking the plastic container from her hands, it crinkles in my grip as I rake my gaze over the treats. My heart swells. "Fuck, I don't know what I did to deserve that woman."

Bree shrugs, her coiled tendrils of hair bouncing over her shoulders. "It clearly wasn't your quality baking abilities."

I cringe. "Yeah, no. Maybe it was my warm and fuzzy disposition."

"It definitely wasn't that either."

"My endearing personality?"

"Highly doubtful."

We share a playful grin as the mid-March breeze blows by, fresh and cooling.

Bree reaches over to my chair and places her palm across my chest, patting gently. "It was this. She saw what I've always seen."

My heartbeat skips at the sentiment, and my gaze drifts over to where Melody is wrapped in a warm embrace with Ms. Katherine. The two women pull back with tears glinting in their eyes, a testament to their strong bond and compassionate hearts. August dances around them in a princess crown, waving two glow sticks in tiny fists, her face still sticky with bright pink frosting.

A sigh escapes me, something wistful and pure. "Goddamn, I'm lucky…"

Bree's fingers trail from my heart to my hand, and she gives it a light squeeze. "It's not luck, Parker. This was all you."

I swallow, drinking in the scene before me.

"You built this life, just like you built your home—from the ground up, with careful tools, hard work, and a lot of blood, sweat, and tears." Her arm stretches outward, showcasing the fruits of my labor. "You put this here."

My chest thunders with enlightenment. *I did this.* I chose this life for myself—*this* was what was on the other side for me. This was what was shrouded beyond the hurdles of hardship.

My heart.

My hope.

My real *home*.

The truth is, I never truly had a home until I had her. I had four walls and a place to lay my head, but no place to lay my heart. I planted roots here, but those roots had nowhere to grow. They were stagnant and shriveling.

Wilting.

My life could have gone in so many other directions. I had the power to make different choices, take alternate routes. It would have been so easy to coast along those dark waters until I gave up the fight and let myself drown.

But I chose to swim.

We hold the key to our own happiness, and what we put on the other side of that door is entirely up to us.

Our beginning doesn't have to be our end.

Bree lets me go and rises from the chair as the final guests depart and Melody saunters over to us with August in her arms and our baby boy in her belly.

"I'm going to take off," my sister says, meeting Melody halfway and enveloping both girls in a fond hug. "Enjoy the peace."

She lifts her hand in goodbye as I stand and wave back. When her car rolls out of the driveway, gravel crunching beneath the tires and music fading off as she disappears down the dirt road, I turn to face a smiling Melody.

Her eyes are tired, gleaming with exhaustion, her skin pink from either a hot flash or wind burn. A long, flowing dress tickles her ankles, smeared with fingerpaint and cake. Both braids came loose, leaving her straw-blond hair in a mess of waves and tangles as a crisp wind sends it dancing behind her like a veil.

She's burned out and overworked, but she's still smiling.

I return the smile, plucking our three-year-old from her weakening arms, taking some of her weight. "Story time?"

Both girls nod with bright grins, and we collectively move to the back of the house and perch ourselves in the grass near the slow-growing magnolia tree. Walden joins us, prancing through the cracked back door with his red ball in his mouth, his long, healthy tufts of hair shining beneath the ambient sun.

August scurries from my lap the moment we're situated, racing toward the house. "I get Nutmeg! She love stories."

Melody and I share a tender glance as Walden settles beside us. I stroke a palm through his fur, and his sigh of contentment filters through me, adding to my placidity.

"I back!"

My daughter runs forward with the hamster in her hands, crawling into my lap.

August loves story time. She's our little storyteller.

Every evening we gather together and talk about our favorite part of the day. We call it story time, but it's more a moment of reflection. Appreciation. We look for the good in each day, even if the entirety of it felt like shit.

There is always something.

However small or insignificant, there's always a glimmer of hope—of sweetness.

A starting point to build from.

I wrap an arm around my wife, pulling her against my chest until both of my favorite girls are entangled with me. We spend the next ten minutes talking, reminiscing, and watching the sun cast its final rays of golden orange along the skyline, bathing us in dusk.

Before we head back inside, a gentle breeze blows through, stealing our breath.

August stills in my lap and wonders aloud, "What that, Daddy? It tickle me."

My fingers weave through Melody's hair as a smile paints my lips. She snuggles in closer, already knowing the answer.

I asked my father that same question one sunny afternoon on his front porch as the daylilies danced to a funny sort of breeze. Swallowing, I reply, "A zephyr."

Giggles erupt from little pink lips. "That silly."

Holding them both tighter, I recall a hazy memory with my father as I sat beside him on the porch swing with a lapful of plump cherries and a mischievous pup at my feet. He told me that every time a breeze rolled through it was a zephyr—a gentle promise of new beginnings.

Zephyrus was the god of the west wind, the god of springtime, a representation of fresh starts and growth. A beacon of hope and new life.

For whatever reason, I carried that moment with me. As a scared child, locked in that closet, I'd feel him with me every time a gust of wind shimmied beneath the door, a calm presence amid the darkness.

My father. *Zephyr.*

He became my companion, my imaginary friend, whispering in my ear to hold on.

Winter doesn't last forever.

Spring is coming.

It took a long fucking time to find my new beginning—my starting point. My blooming magnolia in a field of wilting and decay. But I wouldn't change a goddamn thing…because everything led me to her. To *them*.

August leaps from my lap to dance around the yard, her hair and dress spinning as her feet whirl in clumsy circles. My eyes water at the vision. So precious, so beautiful, so *fleeting*.

A hard puff of air escapes me when Melody takes our daughter's place, hopping into my lap and leaning back against my chest.

I grin. "So intrusive."

She nuzzles in closer, her fine hairs tickling my chin as a chuckle breaks free. "Like the sun, right?"

My arms encase her body, pulling her as close as possible. I breathe in her citrusy musk, her flowery skin, and the warmth that bleeds from every inch of her. "Yeah…that's right."

Melody will always be the sun, shining bright, a beautiful new beginning.

But above all, she is my moon.

The perfect end.

"We go inside! Nutmeg sleepy," August calls over, her smile sparkling, just like her mother's. "We go home."

Home.

With the love of my life tucked inside my arms, I watch from the grass as my daughter skips to the back door with a hamster in her hands and an old, sweet dog trailing her ankles.

My heart soars. "I love you, Melody," I murmur softly, placing a kiss to the top of her head.

She sighs deeply before we rise to our feet, and then she twists in my embrace. Glancing up at me, the sweetest smile blooms to life, and her eyes twinkle jade and joyful, whispering the words before they even leave her lips. "I love you."

I smile back.

Home.

They say that home is where the heart is…

And I know I found them both when I found her.

Epilogue

MELODY

THE FUTURE
(THE DAY THE SUN SETS)

I'VE ALWAYS BEEN TETHERED TO THE RAIN SOMEHOW.

Drizzle beats against the glass window with gentle pitterpatters, filling the room with something peaceful. A nostalgic ambience. It's the perfect complement to my sedated heartbeats and the music drifting from a nearby speaker, serenading me with "Unchained Melody."

My mind reflects along with the quiet storm clouds, and I think back to all of life's pertinent moments that fused with rainfall. I lost something of great value on a rainy downtown street, but I also gained immensely over the years.

Breakthroughs, lovemaking, childbirth, and wedding vows.

Dancing, kisses, baseball games, and birthday parties.

Rain poured down on the day Ms. Katherine retired from Loving Lifelines, handing the reins over to me and giving me a deep layer of added purpose to my life. I can still recall the way her wet hair matted over her forehead as we stood in that familiar parking lot beneath a weeping sky.

"Shine bright, Melody. Your smile is a gift to even the saddest soul."

My pulse thrums with bittersweet memories.

Yes. It's fitting, I suppose—it's always been the rain and me.

Heaving in a rickety sigh, I blink back tears, my gaze settling on the ceiling fan above me. It's been an emotionally exhausting day of reminiscing and teary send-offs.

Final goodbyes.

Familiar faces have trickled in and out of the room with words of love and peace. All precious pieces of my heart. Our two beautiful children, our grand-children, our plethora of great-grandchildren. Our friends and family who are still living. Even our senior dog was brought in for a sweet farewell.

The goodbyes have been said.

All except for one.

It's just me and Parker now, wrapped up in each other, lying beneath the warm, quieting sheets of our king-size bed. We used to joke about trading the bed in for something smaller, a queen or a full, because the extra space always proved futile. Every single night, I would wind up on his side of the mattress, pressed up against his back or chest, lost in the comforting beats of his heart.

In all of our years together, we never slept apart. Not once. There were no business trips, no travel obligations, no arguments that separated us before nightfall settled in.

Every evening was spent together in this bed, beneath this roof he built him-self, side by side. Limbs tangled, hearts aligned. Through late-night newborn feedings, heated passion, summer thunderstorms, movie marathons, and pan-cake breakfasts, this bed became a focal point in our long and happy marriage. Home base. We'd play card games, read books, discuss our day. There were tickle fights, cuddles with the kids, and wet dog noses.

I love this bed.

I love that my final moments on this earth will be spent here—*with him.*

Parker trails his fingers up and down the expanse of my arm, weaving them through my thin, white hair. His breath skims my temple as he leans in for a kiss. "My Melody." His lips are warm and tender as they linger. "My Magnolia. My moon."

Tears rush to my tired eyes.

My favorite song plays faintly on the nightstand, intermingling with the sound of steady raindrops against the glass. He hasn't left my side for weeks—taking care of me, holding me, lifting my spirits as my health declined. He's my rock, my anchor, and my greatest gift. "I'm scared, Parker. I'm scared to leave you," I whisper, my voice cracking with grief.

He's trying to be strong for me. He's trying to be brave.

His arms tighten around me, frailer than they used to be, but the strength of his love has never waned. "What have we always done when we get scared?"

"We dance." My throat feels parched and rusty as tiny teardrops track down my cheeks. "There's nothing scary about dancing."

"That's right." Parker nods, his own tears spilling free and disappearing into the silky fabric of my nightgown. "We dance until we can swim."

I would give anything to dance with him, but my body is weak, and my heart is fading. Inhaling a shuddering breath, I reply, "I think I'm too tired to dance."

I wish we could dance our way through infinite lifetimes, but I'm grateful for the one we had. The one we created together.

It's been such a good life. A *great* life.

It's the life I chose, and it's the life I would choose a thousand times over.

And to think…I almost didn't make it this far. I would have missed out on so much.

"Close your eyes, Melody."

His words are a choked whisper against my temple, and I cling to him with delicate hands, my eyelids fluttering. I'm flooded with a wave of peace.

"We're in the lake," he says. "We're dancing in the water, holding each other tight, and nothing else matters. It's just you and me, carefree and young, swaying together beneath a vibrant sunrise. There's laughter. There's violins. There's *love*."

"I see it, Parker. I see it," I rasp as emotions sweep through me. "I'm with you."

He pulls me closer, peppering kisses along my neck. "I'll be right behind you, Melody. Wait for me."

"I'll wait." I nod, squeezing him as tight as my body will allow. My breaths are ragged and worn, my limbs fatigued, but our love is mighty. *Eternal.* Blinking away more tears, I turn to him, finding his beautiful green eyes fixed on mine. "What do you think is on the other side?"

Parker doesn't hesitate. He leans in, pressing a final kiss to my lips. "What you put there."

I smile.

I'll see you soon.

With his hand held tightly in mine and his heartbeat pressed up against my cheek, I inhale a deep, contented breath, and I close my eyes.

I'm ready now.

THE END

If you enjoyed **THE WRONG HEART**,
check out Jennifer Hartmann's
JUNE FIRST

1

FIRST BLOOD

BRANT, AGE 6

Y ou're such a fartknocker, Brant!"
Wendy and Wyatt speed away on their bicycles, the tires spitting up mud and grass blades as they cut through the neighbor's lawn.

A fartknocker.

What does that mean?

I watch them go from the edge of my driveway, while Theo kicks up one of the loose stones that rim our mailbox. Dad is going to blow a gasket if he sees a rock out of place. He loves weird stuff like mailbox rocks, perfectly edged sidewalks, and grass that looks greener than my babysitter's new hairdo.

I don't really get it.

I don't get fartknocker either.

"Wendy is a dweeb," Theo mutters under his breath.

"Sounds better than a fartknocker."

"It is."

The sun sets behind an extra fluffy cloud, making it look like a giant piece of cotton candy floating in the Midwestern sky. My stomach grumbles. "Want to stay for dinner?"

Theo tries to fix the stone with the toe of his sneaker, but it doesn't look the same. Dad will notice. Theo sighs, popping his chin up and gazing down at the end of the cul-de-sac where the dreadful Nippersink twins disappeared. "Is your mom making that chili?"

"No, it's fish." My mom loves to cook. Aside from giving me cheek kisses and tummy tickles, I think it's her favorite thing to do. I love the food she makes, even brussels sprouts.

Even fish.

"Yuck," Theo says. He glances at his property, the ranch-style house made of bricks, two down from mine, and shrugs. "Besides, I think my mom might have a baby tonight."

"Really?"

"Maybe. She said her belly felt like a hyena was chomping through her loo-der-us."

"That means the baby is coming?" I shove my hands into the pockets of my shorts, frowning at the image that pops into my head. That sounds really bad. It sounds worse than when I got bit by Aunt Kelly's cat because it looked sad and I wanted to feed it one of my apple slices. I caught a fever the next day. "I thought babies were a happy thing. What's a loo-der-us, anyway?"

"I dunno. I think it's the thing in my mom's belly that the baby lives in. Sounds gross to me."

A shudder ripples through me. That does sound pretty gross. I always wanted a brother or a sister to grow up with, but Dad works too much at the office or in the yard, and Mom says it's hard to take care of little babies that poop and cry all the time, so I guess it's just me.

At least I have Theo.

He's my neighbor and best friend, and maybe his new baby brother or sister will feel like mine, too. Maybe we can share.

"What do you think you'll name the baby, Theo?"

My eyes follow Theo as he hops onto the ring of stones around the mailbox, trying to balance himself. He slips and lands on his butt, right in the wet grass, and when he stands up, blotches of brown mud stain the back of his jeans. He rubs at his bottom, making a groaning sound. "How about Mudpie?"

We both laugh, picturing a cute little baby named Mudpie. I skate my gaze around the cul-de-sac, a new name flashing to mind when I fix on a fluttering insect with sunshine wings. "I like Butterfly."

"Yeah, okay. Mudpie if it's a boy, and Butterfly if it's a girl." Theo nods, still massaging his sore butt. He sweeps sandy-blond bangs away from his forehead, revealing eyes glinting with the same dark-blue color as his shirt. "Hey, Brant, maybe you can come over and meet her after she's out of Mom's belly?"

I'd love that!

I'm about to reply when I register what he just said. "Her?"

Theo shrugs again, scrunching up his nose. "I think it's a girl. I can just picture her wearing little pink dresses and giant bows. She'll be real pretty, don't you think?"

"Yeah, I bet she will be."

"I'm going to take good care of her. I'll be the best big brother ever," he says, bobbing his head with a prideful smile. It's the same smile Dad has when he stares at the lawn after a fresh mow. "I'll be like Mario, and you can be Luigi if you want. She'll be Princess Peach, and we'll protect her from all the bad guys in the world."

I picture it. I envision grand adventures and battles, sword fights and bravery. The images shoot a tickle straight to my heart.

I always wanted something worth defending, and Mom won't let me have a puppy.

Theo's new baby will have to do.

"I like that idea, Theo. We'll make a great team."

Our daydreams are interrupted when Theo's mother pokes her head out of their house, her belly so round and large, it holds the screen door open all by itself. There must be something as big as a watermelon inside—there *must*.

Maybe we should name her Watermelon.

"Theodore! We're heading to the hospital!"

Theo's dad rushes out, carrying at least seven bags, two dangling from around his neck. His face is beet red, the same color as the van he tosses the belongings into, and he looks like he might faint. He might even have a heart attack. He's sweating a whole lot.

"Now, Son! We're having a baby!" his father shouts, tripping on a divot in the driveway as he races back to the front of the house.

My friend's eyes pop. "She's coming, Brant! Did you hear that?"

"I heard it," I say eagerly, a little bit jealous of my friend. I want a baby sister. In fact, I'd trade anything in the world for a baby sister.

You hear that, sky? I'll trade anything for a baby sister!

I'm not sure why I tell my secret to the sky, but Mom always looks up at the ceiling when she says her prayers at night. Maybe she's talking to the sky.

Maybe it listens.

The cotton candy cloud doesn't answer back, and neither does the setting sun. The birds don't sing. The treetops sway and shimmy, but they are also silent.

My wish is stolen by the early summer breeze, never to be heard.

Theo mounts his bicycle, waving goodbye at me as he scoots along with his feet. He nearly topples over on the sidewalk, shouting with excitement, "See you later, Luigi!"

I grin at the name. *Luigi.* It means I'm a fighter. A protector.

A hero.

And it's a lot better than *fartknocker.*

"Bye, Mario," I yell back.

Theo almost tips over again when he tries to send me another wave, the bike swerving madly, but he catches his balance and darts home just as his father races his mother to the van. She's holding her plump belly, making awful, painful sounds. She sure doesn't look happy.

I don't get it.

"Brant, honey…it's almost dinner time."

I startle and glance over my shoulder. Mom is waving me inside from the doorway, her dark-honey hair whipping her in the face when a gust of wind rolls through. "Coming," I call to her, stealing a final peek at my friend hopping into the vehicle with his parents. One more excited wave from Theo sends them off as they pull out of the driveway with squeaky tires.

"Come inside, Brant. You can help me butter the garlic bread."

Pivoting, I let out a sigh and jog through the grass to my front stoop. Mom wraps a tender arm around my shoulders, then kisses the top of my head. I look up at her, twisting the hem of my shirt between my fingers. "Theo's mom is having a baby tonight."

She smiles, resting a palm atop her own belly. It's flat and slender—the opposite of Theo's mom's. There are certainly no watermelons hiding inside. "Oh my goodness. I knew it would be any day now." Mom glances up, watching the van disappear around the corner. "I'll have to make them some casseroles when they return. Is Theo excited?"

"He's really excited." I bob my head. "He said I can visit when they come home. Can I, Mom?"

Two brown eyes gaze down at me like warm melted chocolate, and she gives my shoulder a light squeeze. "Of course. The Baileys are like family," she murmurs. "And maybe I'll reconsider that puppy you keep asking me about."

"Really?" My own eyes ping open, wide as saucers I'm sure. "Can we name it Yoshi?"

"I don't see why not."

I hop up and down, anticipation coursing through me. "Thanks, Mom."

Another breeze sweeps by, causing Mom's long hair to take flight like a sparrow. She closes her eyes for a moment, tugging me close to her hip. "You're a good boy, Brant. Your heart is kind and brave. Maybe..." Her words vanish within the breeze, and I'm confused at first...a little worried that something is wrong. Then she finishes with "Maybe we can start over somewhere. Just you and me."

"What about Dad?"

I wait for her answer. My body sags against my mother, her scent a familiar comfort as her fingers trail through my mess of hair. She smells like something sweet. A dessert of some kind—honey and caramel. Maybe even taffy apples.

"Tomorrow, it will be June." Her voice is just a hush, and I hardly even hear her. My mother sweeps her palm down the nape of my neck, then my back, giving me a light pat before she pulls away. "June always feels like a new beginning."

I think about her words well into the evening. I think about them while sitting around the dinner table as Dad talks about how Collins at the office sabotaged his spreadsheets, then yells at Mom for overcooking the salmon fillets.

He even throws a fit over the stones around the mailbox, blaming the neighbor dog for getting off its leash and ruining all of his hard work. I keep my mouth shut as I smash my glazed carrots into tiny spheres of mush, not wanting Theo to get into trouble. I knew Dad would notice.

He loves those rocks.

As bedtime rolls around, I still can't stop thinking about Mom's words. I don't know why.

June always feels like a new beginning.

What did it mean? And why did Mom want to go somewhere without Dad?

Mom tucks me into bed that night, singing me a lullaby. She hasn't sung me a lullaby in a while—not since I was in preschool. Her voice is soft and glowing, almost like how I picture the moon. If the moon had a voice, it would sound like her. She singsongs the words, telling me that over the rainbow, bluebirds fly. I think about bluebirds, and I think about rainbows. The words make me feel happy, but she sings it so sad.

She reads me my favorite book about Dumbo the elephant, while my own stuffed toy, a floppy gray elephant named Bubbles, is tucked in my arms. Mom cries as she reads the story, just like she always does.

Then she places a gentle kiss to my hairline, whispering by the light of the stars from my window, "I'll always protect you."

I snuggle under my striped bedcover, a smile hinting on my lips, listening as her footfalls fade from the room.

Dreams try to find me, but my mind is restless.

I'm thinking about Wendy and what a dweeb she is. Wyatt too.

I think about the puppy we're going to get…Yoshi. I wonder if he'll make friends with the neighbor dog.

I wonder if Dad will like him more than the neighbor dog.

I think about my mother's voice made of moonglow, and I wonder why she said those things to me on our front stoop.

And finally, I think about Theo's baby.

Mudpie or Butterfly?

Is Theo's mom's belly still big and full? Did the baby come out of her looder-us yet?

Maybe it'll be two babies, just like Wendy and Wyatt. One for Theo, and one for me.

We can both be Mario.

As the minutes tick by, my thoughts begin to quiet, and I'm whisked away by a magical dream. I'm in the sky, sitting atop the crest of the banana moon.

It's loud up here.

I'm drowning in the chatter of a thousand wishes.

And somehow, somewhere, I think I hear my own…

I'll trade anything for a baby sister.

AUTHOR'S NOTE

Thank you so much for going on this journey with Melody and Parker. I connected with this book on a very deep, emotional level, and I truly hope my love for these imaginary people shined through the pages. Their story unfolded organically, went off course in a million different ways, but ended exactly the way it was always meant to.

The epilogue was the hardest thing I've ever had to write. It took me two full days to get those 974 words down…

But I believe in those 974 words so hard.

For a book that centers around suicide and giving up the fight prematurely, I wanted to depict the opposite of that. I wanted to showcase the beauty of living and what might be waiting for you on the other side of your struggles.

In my eyes, it's the perfect full-circle end for Melody and Parker, and the ultimate happily ever after.

Please take a moment to listen to this beautiful song. It popped up on my suggested playlist when I was nearing the end of this book, and I think it was fate. ♥ **See You on the Other Side by Brian Fallon**

If you or anyone you know suffers from suicidal thoughts, please seek help. You are wanted, and you are loved.

National Suicide Prevention Hotline:

1-800-273-8255

WALDEN'S STORY

Fun fact: *Walden was real!*

This sweet, old pup was our sanctuary foster—which means, when we fostered him, we knew we were going to be his forever home. His health was declining, and he needed a warm, loving place to lay his head during the final few months of his life.

When Walden first came to us, he was in bad shape. His hair was falling out and extremely patchy, he was malnourished and frightened, and he preferred to keep to himself, tucked away in his dog bed in the corner of the house. But as the days turned into weeks and we spent every waking moment loving on this sweet soul, trying to acclimate him, the most amazing transition occurred before our eyes.

His hair started to grow back in. His wobbly walks morphed into happy sprints in the backyard. He followed us around the house and snuggled with us on the couch.

This wilting dog bloomed before our eyes.

We had Walden for a little over one year. Saying goodbye was one of the hardest things we ever had to do, as this pup left a very profound impact on our family. We learned the true power of love, and the physical manifestations that come with it. In Walden's final hours, his fur was thick and healthy, his eyes were alight and vibrant, and his heart was very full.

When I began outlining this book, I knew that Walden was going to be the perfect companion for Parker.

I'm so happy I was able to immortalize this precious animal with words. His time with us was short-lived, but his spirit is long-lasting.

We miss you, Walden.

PLAYLIST

"Displaced"—Azure Ray

"Drown"—Seafret

"Get Hurt"—The Gaslight Anthem

"Afraid"—Sarah Fimm

"Colorblind"—Natalie Walker

"Letter Never Sent"—Young Summer

"Out of This World"—Bush

"Angel of Small Death & the Codeine Scene"—Seafret

"Here Comes the Rain Again"—Hypnogaja

"Not In Love"—Olin and the Moon

"My Skin"—Natalie Merchant

"Weightless"—Black Lab

"The Other Side"—David Gray

"Winter In My Heart"—Vast

"It Is What It Is"—King Henry (Megan Lick)

"Fade Into You"—The Moth & the Flame

"Make This Go On Forever"—Snow Patrol

"Sympathy"—Goo Goo Dolls

"Canción de la Noche"—Matthew Perryman Jones

"Quiet Lies"—Matthew Mayfield

"Speechless"—Morning Parade

"Boxes"—The Goo Goo Dolls

"Unchained Melody"—The Righteous Brothers

"See You on the Other Side"—Brian Fallon

ACKNOWLEDGMENTS

Acknowledgments are always the very last thing I write.

And that's not because they are the least important—it's because they are the *most* important, and I never feel like I'll be able to express my immense gratitude in only a few paragraphs.

But I'm sure as hell going to try.

First, thank you to my husband for giving me the time and space required to mentally retreat and bring this story to life. Writing is emotionally draining, it's isolating, and it depletes me just as much as it fills me up. The balance between reality and my imaginary world is a difficult one, and I'm very appreciative of the understanding and grace my family provides me. Thank you for the brainstorming, the brilliant ideas, and the unwavering belief that I am meant to do this.

Thank you to my ride-or-die, Chelley Schultz. Seriously, this book would probably be trashed, right along with my sanity, if it weren't for you and your wisdom, selfless support, and perfectly timed *Sesame Street* and cheerleading GIFs. I feel like this book was a mutual journey. You were there from the initial plotting, to the very first words, to the massive direction changes, to the final, teary-eyed end. Thank you for believing in my ability to bring these characters to life and stay true to their story. You have a way of turning my doubt into determination, and I'm so happy our paths have crossed. (Even though the Charlies of the world may disagree.)

Thank you to E. R. Whyte for being there every step of the way, for the little love notes and wonderful suggestions, and for being the best editor ever. You were my very first author friend, and I can't imagine this adventure without you. You inspire me.

Thank you, Vanessa Sheets, for your warmth, light, and positive spirit. You keep me going and smiling. And huge thanks to the rest of my awesome beta readers.

Big thanks to Megan Lick—this girl gets a big shout-out. You're my beta-reading bestie, and truly, you were the one to trigger my creative spark with this book and spin the story in a direction I never anticipated. Thank you for going on this adventure with me. Thank you for going on all of life's adventures with me.

Thank you to my incredible fans and friends in my readers' group and promo team for cheering me on with my writing journey, and with life in general. This community means everything to me. Thank you for the messages, the tags, the comments, and the sweet, encouraging words. Thank you to my early readers for showing your love for this book with shares and reviews. I don't feel worthy, but I feel ridiculously blessed.

Lastly, all the thanks in the world to my amazing children and family for always pushing me, believing in me, and keeping me inspired. You are my greatest gift.

This was a love story, but it was also a "love your life" story.

And I hope you do.

Every damn day.

ABOUT THE AUTHOR

Jennifer Hartmann resides in northern Illinois with her devoted husband and three hooligans. When she is not writing angsty love stories, she is likely thinking about writing them. She enjoys sunsets (because mornings are hard), bike riding, traveling, bingeing *Buffy the Vampire Slayer* reruns, and that time of day when coffee gets replaced by wine. Jennifer is a wedding photographer with her husband. She is also excellent at making puns and finding inappropriate humor in mundane situations. She loves tacos. She also really, really wants to pet your dog.

Follow her at:

Instagram: @author.jenniferhartmann
Facebook: @jenhartmannauthor
Twitter: @authorjhartmann
TikTok: @jenniferhartmannauthor